William A. Craigie

Scandinavian Folklore

Illustrations of the Traditional Beliefs of the Northern Peoples

William A. Craigie

Scandinavian Folklore
Illustrations of the Traditional Beliefs of the Northern Peoples

ISBN/EAN: 9783744768528

Printed in Europe, USA, Canada, Australia, Japan

Cover: Foto ©Andreas Hilbeck / pixelio.de

More available books at **www.hansebooks.com**

Scandinavian Folk-Lore

Illustrations of the Traditional Beliefs

of the

Northern Peoples

SELECTED AND TRANSLATED

BY

WILLIAM A. CRAIGIE, M.A.

B.A. Oxon., F.S.A. Scot.

ALEXANDER GARDNER

Publisher to Her Majesty the Queen

PAISLEY; AND PATERNOSTER SQUARE, LONDON

1896

PREFACE.

From the oldest times down to the present day the Scandinavian countries have been rich in tradition and folk-lore. The memories of the Northern peoples were long, and their beliefs inclined to the mysterious and the marvellous. When saga-writing began in Iceland in the 12th century, it rested upon a mass of traditional lore, which comprised not merely genealogy and history, but also an element of the supernatural. This had often permeated the original fact to such an extent as to render its historic basis doubtful, but at the same time it made the legend more impressive, more picturesque, and less easily forgotten. The same spirit is manifest throughout all the centuries. Scandinavian folk-lore covers a period of fully a thousand years, changing to some extent with the rise of a new faith and the growth of new ideas, yet remaining the same in its inmost nature. For this reason it is one that must always be of great interest and value to the student of popular beliefs.

When we consider that the science of folk-lore owes more to Great Britain than to any other country, it is remarkable that so little has yet been done to bring the traditional beliefs of Scandinavia before the professed student or the more general reader. Even the few works

that have appeared on the subject are now both scarce
and dear. It is in the hope of making a wider knowledge
possible, that I have gathered together the materials
contained in the following pages. The book is, in fact,
an attempt to repeat, with fuller resources, the design of
Thorpe in the second volume of his *Northern Mythology*. When Thorpe published his work in 1851, the
material at his disposal was very scanty. Modern
Icelandic folk-lore remained untouched, editions of the
sagas were less accessible than now, and several valuable
collections (especially in Danish) were then non-existent.
So much new matter has become accessible in this way
since then, that a new and fuller work on the same lines
is both possible and desirable. But while the intention is
the same, the plan of the present volume is slightly
different from Thorpe's. The pieces contained in it have
been selected with a view to cover the whole range of
Scandinavian folk-lore, both in point of time and of content. They are intended to supply concrete instances of
each separate conception in popular belief, as well as its
leading variations. Hence the tales are grouped according to their subjects, and not (as in Thorpe) according
to their place of origin. The details in the design, however, have been affected by considerations of space, and
its divisions are not all equally full and adequate.
Especially is this the case in the sections on Ghosts and
Witches, where the wealth of the material prevented full
justice from being done to it. Still, each section gives a

fair view of the kind of lore current on that head, and indicates the period over which the belief is known to extend. The passages from the sagas prove its existence in early times, the later anecdotes show the form in which it has been familiar down to the present day. The work is thus a constant alternation of the new and old, but the two are seldom greatly at variance, and both together bear witness to a unity of faith that underlies them.

Wherever possible, the belief has been brought out by a narrative embodying it, not by a mere statement of its existence. The story is the soul of folk-lore, by which the general concept is made living and interesting. There is naturally much in popular belief and practice which is not thus clothed in anecdote—all the thousand and one observances with regard to man and woman, beast and bird, weather and seasons—but this belongs to another branch of folk-lore than the one here illustrated. How the story in many cases preserved the belief we may see in our oldest sources, the sagas, and the same is true even now. These tales were part of the unwritten literature of a people which read little or not at all, and as such they were handed down from parent to child. They served both for instruction and amusement, often under circumstances where the interest they excited, and the imagination they called forth, were a salutary relief from the pressure of real life. The beliefs of folk-lore are not necessarily dark and degrading superstitions, as well-meaning persons have often hastily supposed. The good that might lie in them, the honest purposes for which they might be used, are well brought out in the following incident, told by a Danish collector of the present day. " Iver Skade's wife told me, in a most affecting manner, how she, when a child, stood till far on in the night, blowing the bellows for her father, who was known as an excellent scythe-maker. During the day he fished in the firth ; in the evening and by night he worked in his smithy. He seldom got more than four hours' sleep, as he had a large family and was very poor. As soon as the children were strong enough for the task, they took turns of blowing the bellows or working the hammer, while their father told them stories to keep their eyes open." Another woman learned them from her mother, who took her along with her while she went about and begged, and told the tales in order to make the long wanderings lighter for the child. Under these and similar conditions, of poverty or loneliness, has much of the Northern folk-lore been preserved, and it has had a value of its own as an educative force for minds cut off by circumstances from other mental interests.

This fact is often brought out by the tone of the modern tales, compared with their grander counterparts in the sagas, where the spirit of a great age still lingers in the thoughts, and an artist's power over language is manifest in the words. The newer forms are poorer in thought, and barer in language, but this, of course, is partly due to the fact that they are given as taken down from the mouths of the people, without any literary adornment. This difference in the character of the tales themselves has necessarily produced a difference in the style of the translations, although in both cases my aim has been to make the English as natural as was consistent with the form of the originals. To improve the narrative would often have meant rewriting the tale, and if the story does not always run smoothly, this is perhaps not entirely the fault of the translation. It is not always easy to avoid a childish simplicity in translating from Danish, or a stilted archaism in the rendering of a saga. In various instances, particularly in passages from the sagas, some condensation of the narrative was necessary to prevent the tale from being too long, but the abridged passages are always unessential for the folk-lore, and are faithfully recorded in the notes. In translating the few modern Icelandic verses which occur, I have been careful to retain both alliteration and rhyme, where these appear in the originals : only thus can one do full justice to the technique of Icelandic poetry.

In every instance the contents of this volume have been translated from the language of the country to which they belong—Icelandic, Færöese, Danish (Norwegian), and Swedish. The only exceptions to this rule are a few passages of Swedish origin, which were translated from Danish versions in *Nordiske Sagn*, a small collection published at Copenhagen in 1868. The present work was indeed begun as a translation of that volume, but has so far outgrown it, that the pieces taken exclusively from that source form a very small proportion of the whole (some 30 out of 311). In a few instances, where no better version presented itself, passages have been taken which were already included in Thorpe, or still earlier in Keightley's *Fairy Mythology*, but in all cases these have been translated afresh. For the most part the bearing of the stories is clear enough in itself, or may be gathered by comparison, but a few additional particulars are added to many of them in the notes. These, however, are mainly intended to give the sources for each passage, and make no pretensions to completeness in other respects. As the names of persons and places in the tales will be strange to the majority of readers, I have often simplified the forms of the latter by dividing them into their component parts. Some hints as to their pronunciation will also be found at the beginning of the notes.

I have to record my sincerest thanks to Herr E. T. Kristensen for his ready permission to make full use of his valuable collections of Danish folk-lore, as well as for several manuscript contributions; and to cand. phil. Olaf Davidsson for similar kindness with regard to his small volume of Icelandic tales. To Fröken Th. Rambusch in Copenhagen I am indebted for several researches after necessary books, a service always willingly and conscientiously rendered.

WILLIAM A. CRAIGIE.

St. Andrews,
Nov., 1896.

CONTENTS.

III.—BERG-FOLK AND DWARFS.

Contents. xiii.

Contents.

Contents.

Contents.

Contents.

IX.—WIZARDS AND WITCHES.

Contents.

X.—CHURCHES, TREASURES, PLAGUES.

I.—THE OLD GODS.

Thorgils and Thor.

WHEN Christianity came to Iceland, Thorgils in Flói was one of the first to adopt the new faith. One night he dreamed that Thor came to him, looking very ill-pleased, and accused him of breaking faith with him. "You have treated me badly," said he, "chosen for me the worst that you had, and cast the silver that was mine into a dirty pool, and I shall pay you back for that." "God will help me," said Thorgils, "and happy am I that our partnership is broken off." When he woke, he found that his best boar was dead, so he had it buried beside some tofts, and would allow no part of it to be used.

Again did Thor appear in a dream to Thorgils, and said that he would think no more of taking off his nose than killing his boar. Thorgils answered that God would rule in that. Thor threatened to destroy his property; Thorgils said he did not care. The next night an old ox belonging to him died, and on the following night Thorgils himself watched his cattle. When he came home in the morning he was all black and blue, and folks are convinced that he and Thor must have met on that occasion. After that his losses ceased.

Thorgils was invited to Greenland by Eirik the Red, whose acquaintance he had made at the court of Earl Hákon in Norway. Thorgils had made all preparations

A

to set out, and was waiting for a fair wind, when he dreamed that a big red-bearded man, very grim of look, came to him and said, " You have planned a voyage that will be very troublesome for yourself, and ill success will be yours unless you return to your faith in me; in that case I shall still take care of you." Thorgils answered that he would never accept his protection, and bade him depart at once, saying, " My voyage will succeed as God Almighty wills it."

Then he thought that Thor led him out on some cliffs, where the sea broke over the rocks. "Among such billows shall you be," said Thor, "and never get out of them, unless you turn to me." " Nay," said Thorgils; " depart from me, hateful fiend! He who redeemed all men with His blood will help me." Then he awoke, and told his dream to his wife. " I would stay behind," said she, " if I had dreamed the like of that, and I shall not tell this dream to the others."

Now came a fair wind, and they sailed out of the firth, but after they had lost sight of land the wind fell completely, and they tossed about for a long time, till both food and drink ran short. Thorgils dreamed that the same man came to him, and said, " Have things not gone as I told you they would? " and much more he said, but Thorgils drove him away with hard words. It drew on to Autumn now, and some of the men said that they ought to call on Thor, but Thorgils forbade this, and said they would get themselves into trouble, if any man sacrificed on board his ship. On this account no one ventured to call upon Thor. Again Thorgils dreamed that the same man came to him and said; "Again have you shown how faithless you were to me, when men wished to call upon me; yet I have looked after your men, who are now in extremities unless I help them, and you will now reach harbour in seven nights, if you earnestly return to me." "Though I never reach land," said Thorgils, " I will show no favour to you." Thor answered, " Though you never do me any good, yet give me my own property." Thorgils thought over what this might be, and remembered that it was an ox, which he had given to Thor when it was a calf. Then he awoke, and purposed to throw it overboard. On learning this, Thorgerd offered to buy it, as she was short of provisions, but Thorgils refused to sell it and had it thrown overboard, saying that it was no wonder though things went ill, when Thor's property was on board.

They reached Greenland not long after this, but the expedition was a failure.

King Olaf and Thor.

ONE time as King Olaf Tryggvason was sailing along the coast in his ship, the *Serpent*, he was hailed from the rocky shore by a man of middle stature and red-bearded. King Olaf put in close to land, and took him on board, where he attracted general attention. The crew made jest of him and he of them, and hurled abuse at each other till King Olaf noticed it, and had the man brought before him. To the King's many questions the stranger had always a ready answer, till finally the King asked, " What kind of folk used to live on shore here?" "Giants and big folk lived here for many a day," said the man, "until sickness came among their number, and only two big women were left alive, who did great mischief to men when they began to settle here. Then the men took counsel, and called on this red beard of mine, and that stood them in good stead, for I killed the women with my hammer ; " and as he said this he flew forward over the bows and into the sea. Then said King Olaf, " Bold was the Devil when he came so near us, but he went off quickly too."

Raud and Thor.

RöGNVALD, son of Lodinn in Ærvík, burned the hall of his step-father Thorolf, who had treated him ill, and all that were in it perished. Rögnvald had taken his own son Gunnar out of the place before he set fire to it, but the boy, on seeing the smoke, said, " far rather would I be there with my foster-father than here with you, for you will not deal well with me when you have dealt so ill with him." To prevent the child telling who had committed the deed, Rögnvald tied him in a boat and set him adrift. The boat drove with wind and tide northward along the shore, and finally stranded on an island, over which ruled a man greatly given to sacrificing to the gods ; he had there a great temple dedicated to Thor. This man found the child, who would not answer a single word to all his questions, and as nothing could be discovered about him, his finder took him as his own son, calling him Raud (Red) from the colour of his dress. He grew up to be a big and handsome man, and so well beloved by his new foster-father that at his death he left him all his possessions. Raud kept up the old sacrifices, and it is said that by means of these he put so much might into the image of Thor that was in the temple that the fiend spoke to him out of the idol, and moved it so that it seemed to walk about outside with him during the day, and Raud often led Thor about the island.

At length King Olaf Tryggvason came that way in his Christianizing of Norway. That morning Raud went to the temple, as was his custom, but Thor was very gloomy and gave him no answer when he spoke to him. Raud thought this very strange, and tried in many ways to get speech of him, and asked what was the reason of his silence. At last Thor answered with a deep sigh, and said that he was not acting so without cause. "I am greatly distressed at the coming of those men who are making their way to the island." Raud asked who they were, and Thor said it was Olaf Tryggvason and his men. " Blow through the bristles of your beard against them," said Raud, "and let us oppose them doughtily." Thor said it would be of little use, but they went out, and he blew hard through his beard. With that so hard a storm came against the King, that he could not bear up against it, and returned to the harbour he had set out from. This took place several times, but it only made the King more determined to reach the island, and in the end, with God's might, he was more powerful than the fiend that stood against him. Again Raud came to the temple and found Thor frowning and ill-pleased ; the King, he said, had landed on the island. " Then we shall stand against them with all our might," said Raud, "and not give in all at once." Thor said that would do no good.

The King then summoned Raud to come to his presence, but he refused ; "I will not go to meet him, for I like not his coming, and still less does my mighty god Thor like it." Olaf however came to him, and calling together all that were on the island preached the Christian faith to them. Raud still refused to give up the god who had helped him in all his troubles. The King threatened him unless he obeyed him, whereupon Raud answered that they would make trial of their gods. " I shall make a great fire, and you and Thor shall stand one on each side of it, and take each other by the hands. The one who pulls the other through the fire shall be victor, and I expect that Thor will be stronger than you." " Who ever heard the like?" said the King ; "no man ever dared before to set up devils to contend with me where I preached the holy faith. Yet I shall try this, on condition that no one shall help either Thor or myself." A great fire was then made, and Thor went up to it, but very unwillingly. Then they took each other's hands and struggled hard, till Thor lost his footing and fell forward into the fire, where in a little while he was consumed to ashes. At this Raud gave up all his faith in him, and some time afterwards became a Christian.

Thor and Ureböstone-field.

AT the upper end of the three-mile-long Totak Water, which goes right up under the high Houkli-Fell in Vinje Parish, in Upper Thelemark, is a very remarkable but terrible stone-field which, as seen from the lake, resembles a village, with house-gables and towers. Its name is Ureböstone-field, after the lonely farm of Urebö, which lies opposite. Of its origin, the peasants tell the following tale: "On the level ground, now covered by the stones, there lay by the side of Songa-elv two farms, some say

even a church, from which the largest stone, which sticks
up in the middle of the stone-field like a church roof, is
called to this day ' The Kirk Stone.' On these two farms
two weddings were once going on, where, in old Norse
fashion, the ale-horn passed quickly round the company.
Just then it occurred to the god Thor to drive down and
visit his old friends, the peasants of Thelemark. He went
first to one of the farms, was invited in, and entertained.
The bridegroom took the ale-barrel itself, drank to Thor
and handed it to him. The god was pleased both with
the drink and with the liberal way of giving it, and so
went off very well pleased to the other farm to taste the
wedding-ale there too. Here he was entertained with the
same, but they showed so much want of consideration as
to give him the drink in a common bowl. Thor, perhaps
spoiled at the first farm, and perhaps also hot in the head
with the deep draughts he had taken from the barrel, was
greatly incensed, threw the bowl on the floor, and went
his way swinging his hammer. He took the bridal-pair
who had given him the barrel to drink from, and their
guests, along with himself up to a mound where there
still lie some big stones called ' The Bride's Stones,' to let
them be witnesses of, and free them from, the destruction
which he had determined to bring on those who had in-
sulted him by their meanness. Then he went up on
Nuten, and struck the mountain so hard with his ' heavy
hammer,' that it rattled down and buried under it the
other pair, farm and all. But in his anger Thor did not
reckon his strength and balance properly, so that with
the blow the ' heavy hammer' slipped out of his hands,
and flew down with the pieces of rock, among which it
got lost. Thor had then to go down and look for it, and
in his anger and irritation began to throw the rocks hither

and thither, and threw and pulled them about until he found his hammer. With this there was formed a regular road up through the stone field, which to this day is called 'Thor's-way.' Being made in such a hurry, one may well believe that it is not particularly good, and it is a proof of what habit can do, that the little hill-ponies go with heavy loads along this path, which consists of huge steps of rock, and that in spring or autumn the cattle pass along it on their way to and from the hill pastures."

Thor's Hammer.

IF a man has anything stolen from him he may find out the thief, if only he is possessed of " Thor's hammer." The material of this is bell-metal, thrice stolen, and hardened in man's blood on Whitsunday, between the reading of the Epistle and the Gospel. A spike must also be made of the same material as the hammer ; and the man must then dab the point of this on the thick end of the hammer, saying at the same time, ' I drive into the eye of Vig-father (Odin), I drive into the eye of Val-father, I drive into the eye of Asa-Thor." The thief then gets a pain in his eyes. If he does not restore the stolen goods, the process is repeated and he loses one of his eyes, and if it has to be employed a third time, he loses the other eye as well.

Another method is for a man to steal bell-metal from a church between the Epistle and the Gospel, and make a hammer out of this. When he wishes to know who has stolen anything, he must take a piece of paper and draw on it either a man's eye at least, or better still, the whole head with both eyes, drawn with his own blood. He must then take a steel prick and put the end of it into one of the eyes, and then strike the other end with Thor's hammer, saying at the same time, "I cause him pain in the eye (or 'knock the eye out of him'), that stole from me." The thief then loses one of his eyes, or both, if he does not disclose himself before it comes to that.

Thor's Stone Weapons.

THORWIGGAR (Thor's wedges) is the name given to the smooth wedge-shaped stones which are sometimes found in the earth, and are believed to have been thrown by Thor at some troll or other. In many places, where the meadows come close up to high hills, stories were often told about the terror of the trolls, when there was thunder, and how they then in various shapes, but especially that of large balls or clews, came rolling down from the hills seeking protection among the mowers, who, well knowing the danger, always kept them back with their scythes, at which (they say) it often happened that the lightning struck and shivered the scythes, and upon this the trolls with pitiful wailings returned to the hill.

Lifting-stones (Lyfte-stenar) are found in many places, and are a memorial of Thor. Although not always particularly large, they contain such a weight, that scarcely any man now-a-days is strong enough to lift them. Thor is said to have used these as balls to play with. Of the lifting-stone at Linneryd in Kongahärad, Smaaland, there is a story that Thor, as he once wandered past here with his servant, met a giant, whom he asked where he was going.

"To Valhall," said the giant, "to fight with Thor because he has burned up my cattle-house with his lightning." "It is no use measuring your strength with him," said Thor. "I hardly believe you are man enough to lift this little stone up on this big one here." The giant grew angry and seized the stone with all his might, but was unable to lift it off the ground, Thor had so transformed it. Then Thor's man tried, and lifted the stone as lightly as his glove. The giant struck at Thor all he could, but the god with his hammer smote him dead at once, and he is said to have been buried in the large cairn near the spot.

Odin and King Olaf.

IT is said that the same evening that King Olaf Tryggvason came to spend Easter at Ogvaldsness, there came also a very old man, clever of speech, one-eyed and weaksighted, and wearing his hood down over his face. He got into talk with the King, who found great pleasure in his conversation, for he could tell tidings from all lands, old as well as new. The King asked him many questions, and he was able to answer them all. They sat together far into the evening, and at last the King asked who the Ogvald was that the farm and ness were named after. "Ogvald," said the stranger, "was a king and a great warrior; he mainly worshipped a cow, which he took with him wherever he went by land or sea, thinking it wholesome always to drink its milk; from that comes the proverb that many men use, 'carl and cow shall go together.' He fought with a king named Dixin, and fell in

the battle.   He was then laid in a mound on the ness not
far from the farm, and in another mound near it was laid
the cow, and the stones set up that still stand there."

During the night the stranger disappeared, and King
Olaf was persuaded that it was the fiend who had come
in the likeness of Odin, intending by his talk to keep
them awake so long that they might sleep past the time
for divine service.

The Keel of the "Long Serpent."

THE winter after King Olaf returned from Háloga-land
he had a ship built under Lad-hamren, far larger than
any other ship that had ever been built in Norway. Many
men were employed at it, some to fell trees for it, some to
dress them, some to make nails, some to bring timber and
other things required.   Everything intended for it was
carefully selected, but they could not get a tree suitable
for the keel, considering the length of the ship, and for
this they searched far and wide.   One morning the two
builders, Thorgeir and Thorberg, were early on foot before
all the others, and had gone down to the place where the
ship was to be built, still thinking over where they might
get a tree for the keel.   There they saw coming toward
them a man of great stature, swarthy complexion, frowning look, one-eyed and unprepossessing, who addressed
them and asked if the ship-building was going on much.
They said "No."   He asked the reason of this.   They
answered that they could not get a tree large enough and
good enough to form the keel.   "I have heard so," said
the stranger ; "and yet the King has had search made

far and wide. Now you may come and look at a little tree-stump that I have brought hither, and see whether it will do for the keel or not." They asked his name, and he said it was Forni, a peasant out of the Thrænda-lög, and an old acquaintance and friend of the King's. They went down to the sea with him, and saw there a little boat in the water, along with a huge tree that the man had apparently towed behind him. They rolled the tree up on the beach, a work in which they found the stranger a very handy man; then they looked at it closely, and were well pleased with it. They asked what he would take for it, but he said he would name no price to the King; they might have it if they wished, and he would get a suitable return for it. With that he got into his boat and rowed out into the fjord, while they went home again to the town. When the King came down later on, they told him they had got a keel-tree, and how it had come to them. The King said he had no recollection of this Forni, and bade them show him the tree, which they did. He looked at it, and stepped on to it at one spot, saying, "Hew it asunder here." This was done, and out of it there darted a venomous serpent. "Now I think I know who this Forni was," said the King; "it was the evil Odin, and we may see that he meant this serpent to bore out through the ship when we were out at sea, and so sink us all to the bottom." Then he had the bishop brought, and made him consecrate the tree, after which they laid it down for the keel and built the ship. Said the King, "The ship shall take its name from this serpent, and shall be called *The Serpent*, and on account of its size and length I think it may well be named 'The Long Serpent.'"

The Smith and Odin.

IT happened after Yule in the Year of Peace (1208), that one evening a man came riding up to the house of a smith who lived at Nesjar, and asked him to lodge him there that night and shoe his horse for him. The smith was willing, and long before daybreak they rose and set to work. "Where were you last night?" asked the smith. "In Medaldal," said the stranger; now that is in the north of Thelemark. "And where were you the night before?" "In Jardal," said the stranger, which is in the extreme north of Rygjar-fylki. "You must be a tremendous liar," said the smith, "for that cannot possibly be." Then he set to work on the shoes, but could not make them to please himself. "Never did it go this way with my work before," said he. "Just you work as the thing goes of itself," said the stranger, and in the end he turned out bigger horse-shoes than he had ever seen, but when they applied them, they were found to fit the horse, which they then shod. "You are an unlearned and wit-less man," said the stranger; "why do you ask no questions?" "Who are you?" said the smith; "or where have you come from, or where are you going?" He answered, "I have come from the north of the country, and have long been dwelling here in Norway, and now I mean to go east into Sweden. I have long been on ship-board, and must now accustom myself to horseback for a time." "Where are you going this evening?" said the smith. "East to Sparmörk," said he. "That cannot be true," said the smith, "for that can hardly be ridden in seven days." As the stranger mounted his horse, the smith again asked, "Who are you?" He answered, "Have you ever heard of Odin?" "I have heard his name," said the man. " Then you may see him here now," said the stranger, "and if you do not believe what I have told you, look how I leap my horse over the fence." With that he drove the spurs into his horse, and ran it at the fence of the courtyard, which it sprang right over and never touched, although it was seven ells high. The smith never saw him again, but four nights later the battle at Kungslena between the Kings Sörkvir and Eirik took place. The smith himself told this story to Earl Philip that same winter in Tunsberg, and one who then heard it told it to us. The smith's name was Thord Vettir, and his homestead is called "í Píslum."

Odin the Hunter.

IN old days there lived in Hjörring a king, who ruled over Vendsyssel, and was widely known for his wild delight in the chase and his contempt for Christianity. One Sunday, while the people were at church, and King Jon was hunting in its neighbourhood, his dogs started and followed a hare, which, to conceal itself, ran into the church, and up before the altar. Both the dogs followed at its heels, and of course greatly disturbed divine service, as the priest was just in the middle of his sermon, but the confusion was made still worse, when King Jon came riding into the church to get hold of his prey, which the hounds had already secured. The priest grew angry at this, and said that he thought it highly unbecoming thus to disturb the service, but the King did not trouble himself for that. " If I may only keep my hunting both here and after my death," said he, "other folk may well keep both divine service and heaven for me." Having by this time got hold of the hare, he turned his horse in front of the altar and trotted out of the church. He died some time after this, but can find rest nowhere, and on clear summer evenings he rides in the air followed by his hounds. The sound of this can often be heard, and it is bad to meet him when one is alone.

When three doors with locks stand open in a line with each other, Jon the hunter and his dogs have power to enter, if they are in the neighbourhood. In this way he entered a large farm on Hjorte-næs, and asked what they had to spare for Jon the hunter that day. The farmer went out and brought a big ferocious bull, every bit of which they ate up on the floor of the room, for they were thoroughly hungry. When this was done, the hunter told the farmer that in future he should have great luck with his cattle, and so it turned out: his cows often had two calves thereafter.

A woman in Svendstrup was up one morning before daybreak to brew the Christmas ale, and had let the two doors of the brew-house stand open. These were right opposite each other, and by and bye three hounds came running in and began to lap the ale out of a vessel. She guessed they were Un's hounds, and was afraid, but thought it best to make friends with them, so she went up and patted them, saying, "Poor things." They then ran away again, but it was not for nothing that she had been so friendly with them, for when she went outside after daybreak she found a gold horse-shoe lying outside one of the doors.

Odin Pursues the Elf-Women.

WOJENS the Hunter is said to have been a king at one time. I am not sure whether it was a berg-woman or an elf-woman that he once came across, and received from her a letter that he several times tried to bury, but could discover no means to get rid of it. Then he wished that from that time forth he might pursue the under-ground folk so long as the world should last, and so he has done ever since.

A man beside Lyng-aa had gone out early one morning to shift his horses; when he had done this and was about to return home, to his alarm he heard a loud rushing sound in the air. This drew nearer and nearer, and all at once a man on horseback stopped in front of him. " Hold my hounds," he shouted, and the man obeyed. There were three of them, fastened together with a silken leash, and the peasant examined them closely until the hunter returned after a few minutes' absence, having two elf-women, tied together by their long hair, hanging over his horse's back. " Give me my hounds," said he, " and hold out your hand here, till I give you some drink-money." The man did so, and the hunter stuck the points of his three fingers into the peasant's hand, where they left large burned spots behind them. Then he rode off with the same rushing noise, accompanied by the screams of the elf-women and the barking of the dogs.

A man was once walking from Ersted to Aarestrup, when he saw two elf-women come running towards him as fast as they could. They sat down there on the south side of the village, saying to each other, " He won't catch us yet, for he's not clean." The man continued on his way, until he was met by one on horseback, who was no

other than Jons the hunter. " Did no one meet you?"
he asked of the man. " Yes," said he, " there came two
little things running as hard as they could." " What did
they say to each other?" asked the horseman. " They
said, ' he won't catch us yet, for he's not clean.' " He
took water in his hand and washed himself, and then said
to the man, " If you will lie down now and put your
fingers in your ears, I shall pay you well for it when I
come back again in a little while." The man did so, but
began to think the time long, and wanted to take his
fingers out of his ears. First he took one finger out, and
heard some one fire a shot, though at a considerable distance ; he thought it might be as far as Hobro. At this
he lay down again for a little, but once more he grew
tired of lying like this, and so raised himself from the
ground and took the other finger from his ear. Again he
heard a shot, but this time as far away as the neighbourhood of Horsens. At this he made haste to put his fingers
into his ears again, and lay down in his old place. Soon
after that the horseman rode up with the two women,
tied together by the hair and hung over the horse's back,
one on each side, and said to the man, " You shall have
good payment, but it should have been better You have
taken your fingers out of your ears, and that did me so
much damage that I had to ride from Hobro to Horsens
to catch the last of them. My horse has lost a shoe on the
road there, which you can go and pick up, and that will
be payment enough for you." When the man reached
the spot and found it, it proved to be of gold.

Odin in Sweden.

IN Gothland, and especially in Smaaland, there still live in the mouths of the people many tales and traditions of the Old Odin. At Siituna in West Gothland (which is supposed to have been a town, as traces of paved streets and a market-place are found there), Odin's horses are said to have pastured on the beautiful meadows now called *Ons-ängar* (Odin's meadows). In Bleking a sheaf used to be left on the field for Odin's horses. Of the noise which is sometimes heard in the air by night, and resembles that of horsemen riding past, the people say, "Odin rides there." At the farm of Kraaktorp in Asa parish in Smaaland are the remains of a wall, where Odin's stable and manger are said to have stood. In this parish, more than a hundred years ago, there was excavated a grave mound, where Odin was said to be buried, and which, on that account, after the introduction of Christianity, was called Hell's-mound. There was then found a vault, on opening which a strange fire, like a flash of lightning, burst out, and a stone coffin and lamp were dug up there. Of a priest named Per Dagson, who lived at Trojenborg or Höns-hytte Skans, the story goes that he ploughed up a part of the rampart, by which a number of human bones were brought to light. When the rye sown there shot up, Odin came riding from the hills every night, so huge that he towered above all the farm-buildings, spear in hand, and kept watch outside the front entrance, preventing any one from going out or in the whole night. This happened every night until the rye was cut. The priest took indeed two crops off the field, but allowed it to fall back again, on account of the great trouble that Odin caused him. There is also a general tradition of a gold ship, which is said to be sunk in Rune-mad beside Nyckel-berg. On this ship Odin is said to have taken the slain from Braa-valla to Valhall. Kettils-aas in Als-heda is said to take its name from a man named Kettil Runske (Rune-master), who stole Odin's runic staves, and by means of these bound Odin's hounds and bull, and finally even the mermaid herself, who tried to come to Odin's aid.

Odin's Cave and Garden.

WHEN Christianity came to the North, Odin fled over to the island of Möen in Denmark, and hid himself in the Klint, where his place of abode is still pointed out. At that time the priests called him the Giant from Upsala, but he is now popularly known as Jön Upsal; from this name also is no doubt derived the exclamation one hears so often on Möen, "But Giant though!" whereas in other places they say, "But Jesus though!" A man who now lives in Copenhagen is said to have seen Jön throwing out his sweepings one time as he was sailing past the Klint, at anyrate there was a thick cloud of dust coming out of his door. Various persons still alive are said to have landed in Jön Upsal's garden when they had lost their way in the forest on the Klint; it is large and beautiful beyond all description, and stands in full flower in the midst of winter, but if any one afterwards tries to search for the garden again, of course it is never found.

Frey.

WHEN King Olaf Tryggvason heard that the men of Thrandheim still worshipped an image of Frey, he went thither and seized it. Then at a meeting of the people he hacked it to pieces before their eyes, and gave them the following account of its origin :—" This Frey that you have worshipped was no living man, but only a wooden one, made with men's hands, and now lies here hewn into small pieces and food for fire. You must also know that the man named Frey was a great King in Sweden, and when he was dead a very great mound was made for him and his body laid in it. After he was set there, it was spoken about that some men should go into the mound beside him to keep him company, for his death was greatly mourned by all, but though all had loved him while he lived, no one would stay with him now that he was dead. The Swedes then made a door in the mound, and three windows ; at one of these they poured in gold, at another silver, and copper at the third, and so still gave to Frey the tribute that they had formerly paid him for giving them peace and plenty. Yet they kept his death secret, and the people believed that he still lived, and this went on for three years, but even when they knew that he was dead they would not burn him as the custom was, for they thought that he still caused all kinds of good. They called him the god of the world, and worshipped him a long time. But, as I said before, no living man would stay in the mound beside Frey, so the Swedes made two wooden men, and set them in the mound beside him, thinking that it would be some amusement for him to play himself with them. After a long time it entered the minds of some Swedes to break into the mound, for by this time the doors and windows were closed up, and they knew that there was much treasure there. When they had torn it open, several were let down by ropes to the floor, and saw there much gold and many precious things, but when they thought of taking the treasure away, they became so much afraid that they did not dare to take anything but the two wooden men, who had been given to Frey to entertain him. With these they were drawn up to their comrades, and the mound was closed again, but the Swedes took the wooden men, and worshipped one themselves, the other they sent here to Thrandheim, and it has been worshipped here, and both of them have been called by the name of Frey."

Gunnar and Frey.

A NORSEMAN named Gunnar Helming, being suspected of having killed one of King Olaf Tryggvason's men, thought it best to make his escape to Sweden. At that time Frey was the god most worshipped by the Swedes, and such might was given by the fiend to the image of Frey that it talked to the worshippers. These believed that Frey was to some extent alive, and in this belief they had given him a beautiful young woman to wife, who also had main charge of the sanctuary and all that belonged to the temple. Gunnar Helming finally arrived there, and asked Frey's wife to help him and let him stay there, giving out that he was a freedman from abroad. "You cannot be a lucky man everywhere," said she, " for Frey looks on you with no friendly eyes. Stay here and rest yourself for three nights, and let us see then how Frey likes you." " Far better would I like," said Gunnar, "to have your help and favour than Frey's." Gunnar was a most entertaining man, and after he had been there three nights he asked Frey's wife whether he was to stay there or not. " I hardly know," said she, "you are a poor man, and yet it may be that you are of good kin, and in that case I should like the more to give you some assistance, but Frey does not care for you, and I am afraid that he will be angry. Stay here half a month and see what happens." " Things are as I would wish them to be," said Gunnar, " Frey hates me and you help me, and I have no desire to be with him."

The longer Gunnar stayed there, the better he was liked by all. Another time he spoke to Frey's wife, and asked what he was to do. She answered, "Folks here like you well, and I think it advisable for you to stay here this winter, and go with myself and Frey, when he is entertained in order that he may give them good seasons : but he is not pleased with you." The time came when they went from home, and Frey with his wife sat in a cart while their attendants went before them. As they went along a mountain road a severe storm came upon them, and the way became very heavy. In the end all the others left them, so that only Gunnar remained with the two in the cart. He began to get exhausted as he walked and led the horse, and after a time gave up the attempt, and took his seat in the cart. In a little the woman said to him, "Do your best yet, or Frey will rise against you." He walked again for a little, but soon became tired, and said, " I shall risk meeting Frey if he tries to attack me." At this Frey rose out of the cart, and began to wrestle with him. Gunnar soon saw that he had not strength enough against him, and vowed that if he overcame this fiend, and it were granted him to return to Norway, he would turn again to the true faith, and make peace with King Olaf if he would receive him. Immediately on his thinking this, Frey began to stumble, and then fell, whereupon the fiend who had lain hid in the image leapt out of it, and left the empty shell behind. Gunnar broke this in pieces, and gave the woman her choice, either that he should leave her there and look after himself, or that when they came to houses she should say that he was Frey. She chose the latter course, and Gunnar put on the idol's dress. The weather then began to clear, and they arrived at last at the feast to which they were invited, and there they found many of those who should have accompanied them. All thought it a great thing that Frey should thus have shown his power in coming there with his wife in such a storm, when all the others had run away from them, and no less that he now went about and ate and drank like other men. During the winter they went round and were entertained, but Frey spoke little to any but his wife, and would not allow any living thing to be killed to him as before, and would accept no offering but gold or silver, good clothes or other valuables. As time went on, it was noticed that Frey's wife was evidently with child, and all thought more than ever of their god Frey. The weather too was mild, and everything so flourishing that no one could remember the like. The news travelled far of how mighty the god of the Swedes was, and at last came to the ears of King Olaf, who suspected what lay under it. One day in Spring he called Sigurd the brother of Gunnar, and told him his suspicions. "I shall send you east there after him, for it is a piteous thing for a Christian man's soul to be so miserably lost." Sigurd

went to Sweden, and found that Frey was indeed his
brother Gunnar, who stole away with him, taking also his
wife and all the money he could. The Swedes, on finding
out what had happened, pursued them, but soon lost their
track and returned home. King Olaf made peace with
Gunnar, and had his wife baptised, and both of them kept
the true faith ever after.

Thorgerd Hördabrúd.

WHEN Sigmund Brestison had been for some time in
Norway with Earl Hakon, he asked the Earl to aid him
to return to the Færöes and avenge his father. The Earl
gave him two ships and men to accompany him, and in
the spring he was ready to set out. When he was at last
ready to go, Earl Hakon went out with him, saying,
"One should lead forth that man whom he wishes to see
back again." When they had gone outside, Hakon asked
him in whom he put his trust. "I trust to my own might
and strength," said Sigmund. "That must not be so,"
said the Earl, "you must look for help to that quarter in
which I put all my trust, and that is in Thorgerd Hörda-
brúd. We shall go and visit her just now, and seek
success for you from there." Sigmund bade him do as
he thought fit, and they went to the wood by a cart-road,
and then along a path in the wood itself. They finally
came to a clearing, in which stood a house with a wooden
fence round it. It was a beautiful building, the carved
work on it being ornamented with gold and silver. Hakon
and Sigmund with a few others went into this house,
where there were many gods; it had also many glass

windows so that there was no shadow in it. At the inner
end was a woman magnificently dressed. The Earl threw
himself down before her feet, and lay there a long time.
Then he rose up and told Sigmund that they should make
her some offering, laying the money on the seat in front
of her, " and we shall have this token," said he, " whether
she will accept it or not, that I have wished her to let go the
ring that she has on her hand. From that ring you will
obtain good luck." The Earl then laid hold of the ring,
and it seemed to Sigmund as if she closed her hand, so
that he could not get it off. The Earl lay down again
before her, and Sigmund noticed that he was in tears.
Again he stood up, and laid hold of the ring, and this
time it was loose. He gave Sigmund the ring, charging
him not to give it away, which he promised not to do.
With this they parted and Sigmund went to his ship.

In the midst of the battle with the Vikings of Jomsborg
at Hjörunga-vág (Lidvaag in Söndmöre), Earl Hakon left
his men and went up on the island of Primsigd. The
island was thickly wooded, and Hakon went to a clearing
in the forest, where he lay down, looking to the north,
and prayed in the way he thought best, calling upon her
in whom he put all his trust, Thorgerd Hördabrúd. When
she remained deaf to his words, he guessed that she must be
angry with him, and prayed her to accept of him various
things in sacrifice, but all of these she refused. Then
he offered her a human sacrifice, and, thinking that he
would be still worse off, if he could get no certainty of his
prospects, he began to increase his offers to her, until
finally he gave her her choice of any man she pleased for
sacrifice, except himself and his son Eirik, and Svein. At
long length Thorgerd accepted the sacrifice from him,

and chose a son of the earl's, named Erling, who was then seven years old and very promising. When the Earl thought his prayers and vow were heard, he grew more hopeful, and taking the boy he gave him into the hands of his thrall Skofti, who put him to death in the way that Hakon directed him.

After this the Earl went to his ships, and urged on his host anew. " I know for certain that victory will be granted us," said he, " and go ye forward better, for I have called upon Thorgerd Hördabrúd and her sister, and they will not fail us now, any more than in time past."

Now there had been a pause in the battle while Hakon had gone to sacrifice, and both sides had prepared for the struggle as they thought best. The Earl went on board, and they laid the ships at each other a second time ; Hakon was now over against Sigvaldi, and went forward most doughtily, trusting to Thorgerd and Irpa. Then it is said the weather began to thicken, and clouds rose rapidly from the north ; this was about three o'clock in the afternoon, and the clouds drove so fast that soon the whole sky was overcast, and on that followed a snow-storm, accompanied, as it seemed to them, by lightning and thunder. All the Joms-vikings had to fight facing the snow-shower, which was so severe, as well as the storm that went with it, that men could scarcely do more than stand. Many had thrown off part of their clothing during the day while they were hot, and now the air began to grow cold, yet they fought irreproachably. It is said that Havard the Hewer, Bui's companion, was the first man who now saw Thorgerd Hördabrúd in Hakon's host, and many others after him ; and they thought they saw too, when the snow grew a little less heavy, that an arrow flew from every one of the witch's fingers, and every one

of them was a man's death. Sigvaldi and his fellows saw
this now, and he said, as Bui and his men fought fiercely
when the storm came on, " It seems to me that we have
now to fight not merely with men, but rather with the
worst of trolls, and it may well seem worse and more
dangerous to go against these, and yet our only course is
to hold out against them as best we may."

As for Earl Hakon, when he saw that the snow grew
less heavy, he called again upon Thorgerd and her sister
Irpa, and with that the storm began anew, far greater
and more vehement than before, if that were possible. In
the early part of this second shower, Havard saw that
there were now two women on Hakon's ship, both of
whom were acting in the same way as he had seen before.
Then said Sigvaldi, " Now I shall flee, and let all my men
do the same, for now we have to fight with trolls and not
with men, and it is so much worse now that there are two
trolls, where there was only one before. We shall no
longer oppose them, and we have this comfort, that we
flee not for men, although we make our retreat, and we
never vowed to fight with·trolls here in Norway." With
this Sigvaldi turned away his ship, and called to Vagn
and Bui to flee as fast as they could.

Freyja and the Kings.

To the East of the River Vana in Asia, lay the land
called Asia-land or Asia-heim. The people who inhabited
it were called Æsir, and their chief city Asgard, a great
place of sacrifice. Odin was King over it, and appointed

Njord and Frey as priests. Njord's daughter was called
Freyja ; she followed Odin and was his mistress. There
were four men in Asia, named Alfrigg, Dvalin, Berling,
and Grer, who lived but a short way from the King's hall,
and were so dexterous that they were masters in all
handicraft. Men of this kind were called dwarfs ; they
lived in a stone, and mixed with mankind more than now.
Odin loved Freyja greatly, and indeed she was the most
beautiful of all women of that time. She had for herself
a bower that was both fair and strong, so that it is said
that if the door was shut and locked, no man could enter
it without Freyja's consent. One day Freyja went to the
stone, which then stood open, and the dwarfs were busy
making a gold neck-ring, which they had almost finished.
Freyja admired the ring, and the dwarfs admired her.
She offered to buy it from them both for gold and silver
and other valuables, but they said they had no need of
money. Each one said he was willing to sell his part of
the ring, and would have nothing else for it than that she
should lie one night with each of them. In the end they
made this bargain, and after the four nights had passed
Freyja received the ring.

Loki however told Odin of this, who ordered him to
get the ring from Freyja. In order to do so he had to
change himself into a fly, and creep in through a hole just
large enough for a needle to enter. Freyja demanded it
back from Odin, but he refused to restore it, unless she
could bring it about that two kings, each having twenty
kings under him, should fall out, and fight under such
spells that those who fell should immediately rise up and
fight as before, until some Christian man should be so
bold, and have so much good fortune from his liege-lord
as to venture to go into this battle and slay them. Then

only would their troubles end.   Freyja agreed and took the ring.

After this she sent Göndul the valkyrie to a sea-king named Hedinn, and instigated him to carry off Hild, the daughter of Högni, a king in Denmark.   He also took Högni's queen, and laid her before the keel of his dragonship as it was pushed into the sea, so that she died there. After meeting with Göndul again he saw how much ill he had done, and sailed away west over the sea.   Högni followed him and overtook him at the island of Hoy. There they began to fight the everlasting battle, and so strong were the spells laid upon them, that even those who were cleft down to the shoulders stood up again and fought as before, while Hild sat and looked on.   This went on until Olaf Tryggvason became king over Norway, and some reckoned that 143 years had passed, before one of his followers freed them from their troubles.

In the first year of King Olaf's reign it is said that he came to the island of Hoy, and lay there at anchor one evening.   It was a constant thing at this island, that the sentinels disappeared every night, and no one knew what became of them.   This night Ivar Ljómi had to keep watch, and after all the rest had fallen asleep, he took the sword which Ironshield had formerly owned, and which his son Thorstein had given him, and went up on the island in all his war-gear.   There he saw a man coming towards him, tall of stature, and all covered with blood, and with a very gloomy look.   Ivar asked his name ; he said he was Hedinn, son of Hjarrandi from Serkland, " and, to tell you the truth, I and Högni, son of Halfdan, are to blame for the sentinels that have disappeared here, for we have been laid under so great spells and bondage, that we and our men fight on both by night and day, and this has gone on for many generations, while Hild, Högni's daughter, sits and looks on. Odin has laid all this on us, and there is no release for us, unless some Christian man fight with us ; no one that he slays shall rise again, and so each one shall be freed from his troubles. Now I pray you to go to battle with us, for I know that you are a good Christian, and that the king you serve is of great good-fortune; my heart tells me too that we shall have some good from him and his men." Ivar consented to go with him, at which Hedinn became glad, and said, "You must beware not to encounter Högni in front, and not to kill me before him, for no mortal man may meet him face to face, or kill him, if I am dead first, for he has in his eyes a helm of awe, and spares no living wight. The only way is that I go in front of him and fight with him, while you come behind and slay him, for you will have little trouble in slaying me though I live longest of us all." Then they went to battle, and Ivar saw that all this was true that Hedinn had told him. He went behind Högni, and hewed at his head, and cleft it down to the shoulders. Then Högni fell dead and never rose again. After that he killed all the men who were at the battle, and Hedinn last of all. By this time it was daybreak, and he returned to the ships, and told this to the king. During the day they went ashore to where the battle had been, and could see no trace of what had taken place, but in proof of it there was the blood on Ivar's sword, and sentinels never disappeared there after that.

Loki.

IN Thelemark they tell of an evil being, Lokje, who is sometimes identified with the Devil himself. Once he is said to have taken hold of a child by the back and set it down, saying, " So shall you sit until you are a year old." From this it comes that children have a hollow in each side of the hip, and cannot walk until the year is out.

II.—Trolls and Giants.

The Trolls in Heidar-skog.

KING OLAF TRYGGVASON was told that trolls lay on Heidar-skog, so that no one could traverse it. The king called his men together, and asked which of them would go and free the place. One of his vassals, Brynjulf of Thrandheim, a big and stately man, stood up and offered to go. He set out with 60 men, and on nearing the place they stayed all night with one named Thorkell, who showed them the way next morning, and said it was a great pity that the king should have no more profit of such men as they were. They rode on then till they came in sight of a great building, from which they saw three troll-women running; two of them were young, while the third and biggest was all covered with hair like a grey bear, and all three had swords in their hands. Then they saw a tall man, if man he could be called, and two boys with him. He had in his hand a drawn sword, so bright that sparks seemed to fly from it. A battle immediately began, in which the big man and the shaggy ogress dealt terrible blows, and in the end Brynjulf fell with all his companions except four, who escaped into the wood and returned to tell the story to the king.

Styrkar of Gimsar now spoke to his friend Thorstein Ox-leg, and asked if he would go with him to Heidar-skog. Thorstein said he was quite willing, and one

morning early they set out on snow-shoes (*skier*) up the
fell, nor did they stop until in the evening they came to
a shieling, where they proposed to pass the night. Styrkar
proceeded to light a fire, while Thorstein went in search
of water, with the pitchers in one hand and a spear in the
other. As he came near the water, he saw a girl with
pitchers; she was not very tall but fearfully stout. On seeing Thorstein she threw down the pitchers and ran off; he
also threw down his, and ran after her. Both ran their
hardest, and kept the same distance between them, until
they came in sight of a house, very big and strongly built.
Into this the girl ran, slamming the door behind her,
whereupon Thorstein threw his spear after her, with such
force that it went through the door. Then he entered
the house and found his spear lying on the floor, but no
traces of his girl. He went still further in, till he came
to a bed-closet where a light was burning, and there he
saw a woman lying in the bed, if woman she could be
called. She was both tall and stout, with strong features
and a colour both black and blue, in every way like a
troll. She lay in a silken shirt, which looked as if it had
been washed in human blood. The witch was sound
asleep, and snored terribly loud. Above her hung a
shield and a sword. Thorstein stood up on the bed-stock,
took down the sword and drew it. Then he lifted the
clothes off the hag, and saw that she was all covered with
hair, except a single bare spot under her left arm. Judg-
ing that iron would bite on her either there or nowhere,
he set the sword's point on that spot, and leaned upon
the hilt. It went right through her, so that the point of
it pierced the bed. The carline awoke then with no
pleasant dream, felt round about her with her hands, and
sprang up. In a moment Thorstein had put out the

light, and leapt over her into the bed, while she sprang
out on the floor, thinking that her assailant would have
made for the door, but as she reached it she fell on the
sword and died. Thorstein went up to her, and pulled
out the sword, which he took with him, and went on till
he came to another door, which ran up and down in
grooves, and had not been lowered to the bottom. There
he saw a big man with strong features, sitting on the
bench with all his war-gear hanging above him. On one
side of him sat a big woman, very ugly but not very old,
and two boys were playing on the floor, on whose heads
the hair was sprouting. The giantess spoke and said,
"Are you sleepy, father Ironshield?" "No, my daughter
Skjaldis," said he, "but thoughts of great men lie upon
me." He then called the boys by name, the one being
Hák and the other Haki, and told them to go and see
whether their mother Skjaldvör was asleep or awake. "It
is unwise, father," said Skjaldis, "to send young creatures
out in the dark, for I can tell you that I saw two men
running down from the fell this evening, who are so fleet
of foot, that I think there are few of our people who could
match them." "I think that of little consequence," said
Ironshield, "the only men the king sends here are those
that I have little fear of; I am afraid of one man only,
and he is called Thorstein, son of Orny, and comes from
Iceland, but I feel as if a leaf hung before my eyes with
regard to all my destiny, whatever be the reason." "It
is very unlikely, father," said she, "that this Thorstein
will ever come to Heidarskog." The boys now came to
the door, and Thorstein drew away from it. They ran
outside and in a little were followed by Skjaldis, who, on
reaching the outer door, fell over her dead mother. At
this she felt both cold and strange, and ran out of the

house ; at the same time Thorstein came up and cut off
her hand with the sword. She then tried to enter the
house again, but Thorstein warded the door against her.
She had, however, a short sword in her hand, and fought
with that for a time until she fell dead. At that moment
Ironshield came out with a drawn sword in his hand, so
bright and sharp that Thorstein thought he had never
seen the like. He immediately struck at Thorstein, who
tried to avoid the blow, but was wounded in the thigh.
The sword ran into the ground up to the hilt, and as
Ironshield bent down, Thorstein raised his sword and
hewed at him, striking him on the shoulder and taking
off both the arm and leg. Ironshield fell with that, and
Thorstein let little time elapse between his, blows, until he
had hewed off his head. After this he again entered the
house, but before he was aware of it he was suddenly
seized and thrown down. This, he found, was the old
hag Skjaldvör, now far more difficult to deal with than
before. She crouched down over Thorstein, trying to
bite his throat asunder, but at that moment it came into
his mind that He must be great Who had shaped heaven
and earth : many notable things too had he heard of King
Olaf and of the faith that he preached. He then of pure
heart and whole mind·vowed to embrace that faith, and to
serve Olaf while he lived, if he escaped whole and alive
from all this sorcery. Then as the hag tried to fix her
teeth in his throat, a ray of exceeding brightness came
into the house, and fell right into her eyes. At this all
strength and power forsook her ; she began to gasp
hideously, and then vomit sprang out of her and down
over Thorstein's face, so that he was nearly killed with
the evil smell that came from it. Some think it not unlikely that part of it had got into his breast, as it is be-

lieved that after that he was not quite of one shape always, whether this was caused by Skjaldvör's vomit, or by his having been exposed as a child. Both of them now lay between life and death, so that neither of them could rise up.

Meanwhile Styrkar was in the shieling, wondering what had delayed Thorstein. He threw himself down on the seat, and after he had lain there for a little, two boys sprang in, each with a sword in his hand, and attacked him at once. Styrkar caught up the seat-stock, and struck with it till he killed them both. Suspecting then what was detaining Thorstein, he went on till he came to the house, and found the two trolls lying dead there, but no signs of Thorstein. He vowed then to the maker of heaven and earth to embrace the faith that King Olaf preached, if he found his fellow alive and whole that night. Entering the house, he found him lying under Skjaldvör, whom he pulled off him, and then Thorstein rose up, though he was very stiff after all the struggle he had had with the trolls, and the embraces of Skjaldvör. They broke the old hag's neck, though that was not so easy, for her neck was terribly thick. Then they dragged together all the trolls, kindled a bale-fire, and burned them to ashes.

The Trolls and King Olaf.

IT is said that one time King Olaf went north to Hálogaland, which was so much over-run by trolls that men could stand it no longer, and sent word to the King. He came thither, and laid his ships at anchor, telling his men to remain quiet, and not go ashore until he himself went next morning. Two of the night-watch, however, found it dull on board the ships, and went ashore, and climbed up the mountain. There they saw a fire burning in a cave, at the mouth of which they took their stand. Beside the fire many trolls were sitting, and the men could hear how one of them, who seemed to be the chief among them, spoke up and said: "You must know that King Olaf is come to our land here, and intends to come ashore to-morrow, and come hither to our dwellings and drive us away."

Another troll answered and said, "That is an ill lookout, for I shall tell you that we once came together in this way. I had my home in Gaular-dal, a little south from my friend Earl Hakon, and it was an unpleasant change to me when this one came in his place, for the Earl and I had great fellowship with each other. One time when the King's men were disporting themselves near my dwelling, I disliked their noise and was ill-pleased with them, so I joined in their sports without their noticing me. Before I left them I had broken the arm of one, and on the following day I broke the leg of another, and thought things were looking very well then. The third day I again came to their sports, and intended to do mischief to some of them, but when I laid hands on one of them, he gripped me by the sides: I seemed to burn beneath his touch, and would fain have been away, but could not. Then I knew it was the King, and wherever he laid his hands on me I was burned, and have never been in such a wretched plight. The end was that I made my way down into the ground, and afterwards came away north here."

Then said another devil: "I came to where the king was present at a feast, and meant to beguile him with

drink, so I put upon me the form of a beautiful woman,
and stood in fine array beside the table with the drinking-
horn. During the evening the king noticed, me and held
out his hand towards me and the horn. I thought it was
all right now, but as soon as he had got the horn he struck
me such a blow on the head with it, that I thought my
skull would split, and had to betake myself to the nether
road. That is what I got by our meeting."

Then said the third troll : " I shall tell you how things
went with me. I went into a room where the king was
lying in one bed and the bishop in another, and put upon
me the form of a beautiful woman. 'Woman,' said the
king, 'come here and scratch my foot.' I did so, and
scratched his foot, and made it itch all the more. Then
the king fell asleep, and I raised myself up above him
and was about to spring upon him, but with that the
bishop struck me between the shoulders with his book, so
hard that every bone broke, and I had to make use of
the nether road. The bishop then woke the king, and
asked to see his foot. By this time there was a pain in
it, but the bishop cut out the spot and it healed afterwards. That is my recollection of him."

After hearing this the men went back to the ships, and
in the morning told the king and the bishop what they
had heard and seen. These recognised the truth of the
story, but the king ordered them not to do the like again,
saying it was very dangerous. After that they went up
on land and sprinkled holy water and sung psalms, and so
cleared away all the evil spirits.

The Hag of Mjóa-firth.

OUT from the farm of Firth in Mjóa-firth there lies a gill, called Mjóa-firth Gill, in which once dwelt a hag, who was in the habit of drawing to herself by magic the priests from Firth. This she did by going to the church while the priest was in the pulpit, and holding up one hand outside the window next to it ; then the priest went mad and said :

> " Take ye out of me stomach and groin,
> For go to the Gill will I ;
> Take ye out of me milt and loin,
> To Mjóa-firth Gill I hie ! "

Having said this, they ran out of the church and off to the gill, and no more was ever heard of them. Once when a traveller passed the ravine, he saw the hag sitting on a projecting cliff above him, holding something in her hand. He called out to her and asked, " What are you holding there, old wife ? " " I'm just picking the last bits off the skull of Sir Snjóki," said she. The man told this story, and his news was not thought good.

The priests went off there one after the other, until matters grew serious, for priests were slow to come to Firth when they knew of the wicked troll in the gill. At last it seemed impossible to get any one, but a certain priest offered to come, although he knew well enough how matters stood. Before he held his first service in Firth, he had instructed his congregation what they were to do, if they saw anything come over him while he was in the pulpit. In that case six men were to spring on him and hold him fast, another six men were to run to the bells and ring them, while ten should hold the door, and he selected the men who were to do these various things.   As soon as he had mounted the pulpit, the hand was held up outside the window, and waved about ; then the priest went mad, and said :

"Take ye out of me," etc.

With that he would have run out of the church, but the six men who had been appointed to that task sprang upon him, the other six rang the bells, and the ten held the door.   When the hag heard the bells she took to her heels, making a great gap in the churchyard wall with her feet, at which she said, "Stand thou never !"   She then ran off into the ravine, and has never been seen since.   The gap she made in the churchyard wall has never stood firm since, however well it has been builtup.

The Giantess's Stone.

CLOSE to Kirkju-bæ in Hróars-tunga there are some remarkable cliffs, known by the name of Skersl.   In these there is a cave, in which there once lived a troll-carl and a troll-carline.   His name was Thorir ; hers is not mentioned.   These trolls drew to them every year, by sorcery, either the priest or the shepherd at Kirkju-bæ, and this went on for some time, one or other of them disappearing every year, until there came a priest named Eirik.   He was the most spiritual of men, and by virtue of his prayers, succeeded in defending both himself and the shepherd so well, that all the attempts of the trolls were in vain.   So time passed until Christmas Eve, and late on that evening the hag at last despaired of getting

either the priest or the shepherd into her power. She
ceased her endeavours and said to her husband, " Now I
have tried till I am tired, to charm either the priest or
the shepherd hither, but I cannot accomplish it, for every
time that I begin my sorcery I feel as if there came
against me a hot breath that is like to burn every limb
and joint in my body, and so I always have to give over.
Now you must go and see about some food for us, for
there is nothing left to eat in the cave." The giant was
unwilling to go, but was finally persuaded into it by the
giantess. He set off out of the cave, and held west over
the ridge that has since been named after him, and called
Thori's Ridge (Thoris-ás), and so out on the lake, since
known as Thori's Water. Here he broke a hole in the
ice, and lying down there began to fish for trout. There
was a keen frost at the time, and when he thought he
had caught enough, and tried to rise up to go home with
his catch, he found himself frozen to the ice so firmly
that he could not rise at all. He struggled hard and
long, but all to no purpose, and there he lay on the ice
till he died. The giantess thought her husband long in
coming, and began to get hungry, so she too left the
cave and went over the ridge, in the same direction as he
had gone, and found him lying dead there on the ice.
She tried long to pull him up from it, but seeing that this
could not be done, she caught up the bundle of trout and
threw it on her back, saying at the same time, " This
spell and charm I lay, that henceforth nothing shall be
caught in this lake." Her words have taken effect, for
there has been no fishing at all there ever since. She
then held home to the cave, but just as she reached the
brow of the ridge, it happened at one and the same
moment that day broke in the east, and the church-bells

sounded in her ears. She turned into a stone on the top
of the ridge, which has since been called Skessu-stein
(The Giantess's Stone).

The Female Troll on Blá-fell.

ONE time the people in Thing-ey went wrong with their
calendar, and did not know when Christmas was. They
decided to send a man south to Skál-holt to get from the
bishop the information required, and one named Olaf
was selected for the purpose.—a fearless, venturesome
fellow. He rode up Bardar-dale, and south over Spreingi-
sand, and late in the day arrived at Blá-skógar. Not
wishing to stay there, he held on his way, and near sunset
saw a tremendously big female troll, standing on the
mountain named Blá-fell, which lies near the road. She
called to him with a hollow voice, and said,

" Olaf big-mouth !   I rede you, wry-mouth,
South will ye roam ?   To turn back home !"

Olaf answered her with

" Sit thou hale and well,   Hallgerd on Blá-fell !"

She called again hoarsely,

" Few have ever hailed me so ;   Fare-ye-well, my dearest jo !"

When Olaf reached Blá-skógar again on his homeward
journey, he again met the troll, and thought that she was
not half so fearsome as he had imagined. She then gave
him the famous " Troll-woman's Rime," and said, " If
Christ, son of Mary, had done as much for us trolls, as you
say he has done for you mortals, *we* would not have forgot the day of his birth." With that they parted, and
nothing uncanny was ever seen in Blá-skógar after that.

Gissur of Botnar.

IN Landsveit beside Mount Hekla lies a farm named Botnar, commonly called Lækjar-botnar, where there once lived a man named Gissur. One time in summer he had ridden to. the hill to hunt, taking an extra horse with him. When he thought he had a sufficient load on the horse, he mounted and rode homewards. As he came to Kjallaka-túngur over against the Troll-wife's Leap, he heard a terrible voice in Búrfell calling,

"Sister, lend me your pot."

An equally terrible voice east in Bjól-fell answered and said,

"What do you want with it?"

The troll-wife in Búrfell said,

"To boil a man in it."

The one in Bjól-fell asked,

"Who is he?"

The other answered,

"Gissur of Botnar,—Gissur of Lækjar-botnar."

With that Gissur looked up to Búrfell, and saw a troll-wife rushing down the slope, and making straight for the Troll-wife's Leap. He saw that she was in earnest with her words, and that the quicker he tried to save his life the better. He therefore let go the reins of the led horse, and whipped up the one he was riding, an unusually swift beast. He neither looked back nor slackened the horse's speed, but rode as hard as he could, yet he was sure that the troll was making up on him, for he heard always better and better her heavy breathing as she ran. He held the straightest way over Land, with the troll after him, hoping that the folk in Klofi would both see himself and her, when they came on to Mark-heath.

This luckily happened, and they were not slow in ringing all the church-bells in Klofi as Gissur came inside the home-field fence. When the troll saw she had lost Gissur, she hurled her axe after him, so that as he came up in front of the house the horse fell dead beneath him, the axe being sunk up to the shaft in its loins. Gissur thanked God heartily for his escape, but as for the troll, as soon as she heard the sound of the bells, she grew furious and ran away again with all her might. Her course was seen from various farms in Land, and she was holding much further east than to her own place, apparently up to the Troll-wife's Gill, where she was found a few days later dead from exhaustion, and the place was named after her. Her sister in Bjólfell was never known to do any harm to the district, and it is not very certain what became of her after this. Some think she must have shifted her abode from there to Troll-wife's Gill, as being too near human habitations where she was.

Jóra in Jóru-kleyf.

JÓRUN was a farmer's daughter somewhere in Sandvík-hrepp in Flói (S.W. of Iceland), young and promising, but considered to be proud. She kept house for her father. One day it so happened that a horse-fight was held near the farm, and her father owned one of the horses, which Jórun had a great fancy for. She was present at the fight along with other women, and saw that her father's horse was giving way before the other. With that she became so fierce and furious that she sprang at the other horse, tore off one of its hind legs,

and ran with this up Olfus River to Lax-foss, where she
tugged a huge rock out of the cliffs beside the river, and
threw it out to near the middle of the stream. On this
stepping-stone she then crossed over, saying :

> " Mighty is the maiden's stride ;
> Meet for her to be a bride."

The place has since been known as the Trollwife's Leap,
or Jóra's Leap. After this she held further up to Heingil,
where she took up her abode in a cave, since called Jóru-
hellir, and was the worst troll, doing harm both to men
and animals. From a height up there she kept a look
out for travellers, whom she robbed or killed, and became
so wicked a fury that she laid waste all the district round
about her. The inhabitants suffered so much from her,
that they assembled in force to put an end to her, but
could achieve nothing against her. While they were in
these straits, however, there was a young man who was
engaged in trade, and spent the winter in Norway. One
day he went before the king and told him of this monster,
asking him for advice as to how he could destroy the
troll. The king told him to come upon Jóra at sunrise
on Whitsunday morning, "for there is no being so evil
nor troll so powerful that they are not asleep then," said
he. "You will find Jóra lying asleep, face downwards.
Here is an axe that I shall give you," said the king,
giving him a silver-mounted axe, " and you shall strike
between the troll's shoulders. She will waken when she
feels the wound, turn herself round and say, " Hands
cleave to the shaft." You will say, " Then let the head
come off." Both of these sayings will take effect, and
Jóra will throw herself into the lake that lies not far from
Jóru-kleyf, with the axe-head between her shoulders.

The head will afterwards drive up into the river that will
be named after it, and there will the Icelanders afterwards choose their thing-stead." The man thanked the
king for his advice and for the axe. He went out to Iceland, followed all the king's directions and killed Jóra.
The axe came up into the river Oxar-á (Axe-river) where
the Icelanders set their Althing.

Loppa and Jón.

IN Bleiks-mýrar-dal, which is the hill-pasture of the men
of Fnjóska-dal (N. of Iceland), there is a hollow in the
fell on the west side of the river, called Loppa's Hollow
(*Loppu-skál*). This is said to take its name from an
ogress, who in old time lived there in a cave, and once
stole a young and promising man, named Jón, while he
was gathering moss along with others. Loppa took Jón
home to her cave, where her sister also lived, but no
more trolls. The two sisters were in the flower of their
age, and as Christianity long before this had spread over
all the land, and the trolls were dying out, they meant to
have Jón as their mate to perpetuate their kin. They
were therefore careful to treat him as well as ever they
could, and let him want for nothing that could increase
his strength. They often took him and rubbed him with
some kind of ointment, and tugged him out between
them, as well as howled into his ears, in order to make a
troll of him. They never left him alone in the cave, and
only one at a time went out to get supplies. So some
seasons passed, and Jón never saw the sun, nor got any
chance to escape, which he had a great desire to do,

though he concealed that from them. One time Loppa's sister disappeared ; Jón did not know what became of her, but she never came back. Loppa was greatly distressed at losing her sister, for she did not trust her fosterling. She had now to do all the work herself, and leave Jón alone, but she never stayed away so long that he could see a chance of escaping. He then feigned illness, and pretended to be very bad. Loppa was greatly vexed, and asked what would cure him. Jón said the most likely thing to effect a cure, was for him to get a shark twelve years old. Loppa promised to procure this for him, and set out for that purpose. Shortly after, she turned back to see if her fosterling was quiet, and found him so ; this made her think there was no fraud intended, and she went her way. In a little Jón rose out of bed, left the cave, and ran down to the river. There he found a stud of horses, one of which he took and rode down the dale, but it soon foundered, for Jón had grown so heavy that no horse could bear him. In this way he held on down to Illuga-stadir, having by that time spoiled three horses, and yet been compelled to walk most of the way. When he got to the south side of the farm, he heard Loppa calling to him from Mid-degis-hóll, and saying, " Here's the twelve-year old shark, Jón ! and thirteen-year too ; I went to Siglu-ness for it." Jón was overcome by exhaustion, but managed to reach the church, broke up the door with his fist, and told them to ring the bell. By this time Loppa was close to the farm, but on hearing the sound of the bell she turned back. Jón had grown so tall that his head touched the ridgepole of the church when he stood upright in it. He only lived for three days after, and was supposed to have died of exhaustion from the race.

Trunt, Trunt, and the Trolls in the Fells.

Two men were once out gathering moss, and lay by night
in a tent together.   One was asleep, and the other awake,
when the latter saw the former creep out.   He rose and
followed him, but could hardly run fast enough to keep
up with him.   The man made for the glaciers above, and
the other then saw a giant hag sitting on a glacier peak,
alternately stretching out her crossed hands and drawing
them in to her breast, and by this means she was charming the man towards herself.   He ran straight into her
arms, and she then made off with him.   The year after,
the people from his district were moss-gathering at the
same place, and the man then came to them, but was
very silent and reserved, so that scarcely a word could be
got out of him.   The folk asked him in what he believed,
and he said that he believed in God.   The next year he
came to the same folk again, and was now so troll-like that
they were afraid of him.   However, they asked him what
he believed in, but he gave no answer.   On this occasion
he stayed with them a shorter time than before.   The
third year he again came to them, and had now become
the greatest troll and hideous to look on.   Some one
however ventured to ask him in what he believed, and he
said he believed in " Trunt, trunt, and the trolls in the
fells."   After that he disappeared, and was never seen
again ; indeed no one ventured to go there for moss for
some years after.

Andra-rímur and Hallgríms-rímur.

SOME fishermen from the north were once journeying
south, and were caught in a very severe storm on the fells,
so that they went astray, and knew not where they were
going. At last they came to a cave-mouth, and went into
it until they were out of the wind and rain. Here they
struck a light, and made a fire with moss which they
pulled off the stones, and soon began to recover themselves and grow warm. They then discussed what they
should have to amuse themselves with ; some wanted to
recite Andra-rímur, and some to sing Hallgrím's psalms.
Further in from them they saw a dark cleft, looking as if
there was a new turn on the cave there. They then heard
a voice saying in the darkness,

> " Andra-rímur to me are dear,
> But Hallgríms-rímur I will not hear."

They accordingly began to recite Andra-rímur with all
their might, and the best reciter among them was one
named Björn. This went on for a good part of the evening, until the voice in the darkness said, "Now I am
amused but my wife is not : she wants to hear Hallgríms-
rímur." They now began to sing the psalms, and finally
came to an end of all the verses they knew. The voice
said, "Now my wife is entertained, but I am not." Again
it said, "Will you lick the inside of my ladle for your reward, reciter Björn ? " He assented to this, and a large
tub on a shaft was handed out with porridge in it, and all
of them could scarcely manage the ladle. The porridge
was good to eat, and three of them partook of it and enjoyed it, the other one did not venture to touch it. Then
they lay down to sleep, and they slept well and long.

D

Next day they went to look at the weather, and found it bright and clear, so they decided to resume their journey, but the one who had not ventured to eat on the previous night slept so sound that he could not be wakened. Then one of them said, "It were better to kill our companion, than leave him thus behind in the hands of trolls." With that he struck him on the nose, so that the blood flowed down all over him, but at this he awoke and was able to leave with his fellows, and they at last arrived safe at human habitations. It is supposed that this troll had charmed to himself a woman out of the district, and that to her their escape was due.

Hremmu-háls.

ON a farm east in Öræfi (S. of Iceland) lies a ridge called Hremmu- or Hremsu-háls. It is entirely a sandy ridge with fens on each side of it, and covered with small gravel, except for three large stones that lie in the middle of it. The largest of these is said to be a troll-hag, on whom day broke here, and the others a whale-calf and a bear. At the time when this happened, the parish priest had been sent for, to minister to an old woman in the district, who was a witch and had been in league with the troll. When she sent for the priest, she bade the messenger tell him not to be afraid of anything he might see on the way, or it would be all over with her. The priest's road lay over the ridge, and it was night when they crossed it. They saw a huge hag come up from the sea and make towards the fells, carrying a bear on her back, and a whale-calf in front. This was Hremma or

Hremsa. She took long strides and breathed heavily, nor did she notice the men till they met each other on the ridge. Then she looked up and glared at them, and at that the messenger was so startled that he fell down dead. The priest began to talk with her, and they continued talking until the hag looked up and cried, " Day in the east, but dead is the carline ! " meaning the old woman for whom the priest had been summoned. At the same moment the hag turned to stone. The priest afterwards said that he was not afraid, but had been a little startled when the man fell down dead by his side, and that must have hastened the old woman's death.

Bergthor in Blá-fell.

THERE was a man named Bergthor who lived in a cave on Blá-fell, along with his wife Hrefna. The land was all heathen at that time, which was in the days of the giant-ess Hít, after whom Hítar-dal is named. Bergthor was among the guests, when she invited all the trolls of the country to a feast in Hunda-hellir. After the feasting was over, Hít bade them devise some entertainment, so they tried feats of strength, and Bergthor always came out the strongest. Bergthor did no harm to men, if he was not meddled with, and was believed to be wise and far-seeing. After the land became Christian, Hrefna thought it unpleasant to live in Blá-fell and look over Christian habitations, and so much was the change against her liking, that she wished to remove their dwelling north over Hvít-á (White River). Bergthor however said that he did not mind the new faith, and would stay just where he was. Hrefna took her own way though, and removed north across the river, where she built herself a hall under a fell, a place since known as Hrefna's Booths. After this she and Bergthor only met when trout-fishing in White River Lake. Bergthor often went out to Eyrar-bakkar to buy meal, especially in winter when the rivers were frozen over, and always carried two barrels of it. One time he was going up the district with his load, and on coming up below the home-field at Berg-stadir, in Biskups-tungur, he met the farmer and asked him to give him something to drink. He said he would wait there while the farmer went to the house for it, and laid down his burden beside the berg or rock from which the farm takes its name. While waiting there he picked a hole in the rock with the pike of his staff, and when the farmer returned with the drink, he told him that he should use this hole to keep his sour whey in; water would never mix with it there, nor would it freeze in winter, and it would cost him dear if he did not use it. He then thanked the farmer and held on his way.

When Bergthor was far advanced in years, he came one time to the farmer of Hauka-dal, and said he wished to be buried in a place where he could hear the ringing of bells and saying of prayers, and therefore asked him to bring him to Hauka-dal when he died. For his trouble the farmer should have what he found in the kettle beside his bed; and the token of his death would be that his walking-staff would be found beside the door of the farm-house. The farmer promised this, and so they parted. Time passed, and no word was heard of Bergthor, until one morning, when the folks at Hauka-dal came down-stairs, they found a huge walking-staff at the outer door. They told this to the farmer, who said little, but went

outside and saw that it was Bergthor's staff. He then
had a big coffin made, and set off with some other men
north to Blá-fell. Nothing is told of them until they
reached the cave, where they found Bergthor lying dead
in his bed. They placed him in the coffin, and thought
him wonderfully light compared with his size. The
farmer noticed a large kettle standing beside the bed, and
gave a look to see what might be in it. He saw nothing
there but leaves, and gave no heed to it, thinking that
Bergthor had made a fool of him. One of his companions
however filled both his gloves with the leaves, and they
then carried Bergthor's body out of the cave and down
the mountain. When they had got down to level ground,
the man looked into his gloves and found them full of
money. The farmer and his men turned back at once to
get the kettle, but could not find the cave anywhere, and
it has never been found since. They had therefore just
to turn back again, and took Bergthor's body down to
Hauka-dal, where he was buried on the north side of the
church. The ring of his staff is said to have been fixed
in the church-door, and the spike of it to have been long
used for the church-mattock, and here ends the story of
Bergthor in Blá-fell.

The Origin of Dráng-ey.

IN former days two night-trolls, an old man and old
woman, had their home on Hegra-ness, but little was
heard of them until the following event happened. One
time their cow was in heat, and whether it was that they
had no one else to send, or that they trusted themselves

best, they went and led the cow themselves, not to let her miss her time. The man led her, and the wife drove her from behind, as is the custom. In this way they held with the cow out Hegra-ness, and out into Skaga-firth a good way, but when they still wanted no little distance of being half across the firth, they saw day beginning to dawn over the hill-tops on the east side of it. As it is sudden death to night-trolls if day breaks upon them, the dawning was their destruction, so that each of them became a pillar of rock, and are now those which stand there, the one out from Dráng-ey and the other in from it ; the former is the man, the latter the woman, and from that they are still called to this day Karl and Kerling. Out of the cow was formed the island Dráng-ey itself.

It is an ancient practice still observed, that all who go to Dráng-ey for the first time in spring, salute it as well as the Karl and Kerling. The captain on each boat begins by saying, "Whole and well, Dráng-ey mine, and all your followers ! Whole and well, Kerling mine, and all your followers ! Whole and well, Karl mine, and all your followers ! " Then each sailor in the boat repeats the same formula, though now perhaps more in jest than earnest.

The Size of Trolls.

IT is said that a troll-wife once thought of wading from Norway to Iceland. She was aware indeed of the fact that there were deep channels on the way, but she is reported to have said to another troll-wife, her neighbour, who tried to prevent her from going, " Deep are Iceland's

channels, but yet they can well be waded." At the same
time, she admitted that there was one narrow channel in
mid-sea, so deep that it would wet her crown. After this
she set out, and came to the channel that she was most
afraid of. There she tried to lay hold of a ship that was
sailing past, to steady herself in stepping over, but she
missed the ship and stepped too short, and so fell into the
channel and was drowned. It was her body that once
drove up on Rauda-sand, and was so large that a man on
horseback could not with his whip reach up to the bend
of her knees, as she lay stiff and dead on the shore.

A little above Mælifell in Skagafirth, is a strip of fen
between two ridges, called "the Hag's Bed," the story
being that a troll-wife slept there, and that this hollow is
her lair. It is evident where her head lay. The fen is
deepest where her shoulder and thigh-bone sunk in, for
she had lain on her side and drawn up her knees a little :
the mark of her shoes can also be seen. The hollow is
undoubtedly well on to two hundred fathoms in length,
and that shows of what size men have imagined the trolls
to be.

Trolls in the Færöes.

IT is said that the trolls are fain to get a human habitation to stay in and enjoy themselves on Twelfth Night.
North from Nugvu-ness in Borgar-dale, on the island of
Mikines, there is built a little house for the shepherds to
lie in at certain seasons of the year, as the pastures
are far from any habitations, and they have to watch the
sheep to hold them to their own ground, to keep them in

about the shelters, and help them when buried in the snow. One night a shepherd was making his way east to the pastures in Borgar-dale, when a fierce storm came on him at this spot, so he decided to seek shelter in this house, but as he drew near it he heard noise and din coming from the inside. He therefore went first to the window to peep in, and discovered that the house was crammed full of trolls, who made themselves merry, and danced and sang, " Trum, trum, trallalei ; it is cold in the fells among the trolls ; it is better in the house on the brae at Skála-vellir ; trum, trum, tralalei ; dance close to the door."

Worse, however, is said to have happened at Trölla-ness, the most northerly inhabited spot in Kalsö, for there they came on Twelfth Night every year, trooping from every direction, in such numbers that the inhabitants had always to flee to Mikladal, and stay there over the festival, while these gentry enjoyed them at Tröllaness, which got its name from them. On one occasion, it so happened that an old woman was unable to go away with the others, and so had to stay at home on Twelfth Night: she lay down under a table in the kitchen, and hid herself there so that the trolls might not see her. As the evening wore on, she saw them come thronging in at the door, like sheep being driven into the fold, so many that she could not count them. They straightway began to dance and play, but just as they were at their merriest, and the dance thundering at its hardest, the old woman grew frightened, and cried, " Jesus have mercy on me ! " When the trolls heard the blessed name, which they all hate and fear, they all began to howl, and shout, " Gydja has broken up the dance," and struggled to get out of doors as quick as possible, and have never since ventured to trouble the district by visiting Tröllaness. When the folk came north again from Mikladal, they expected to find old Gydja dead, but she was on her legs and could tell them how she had got on with the trolls, and how they disappeared when they heard the name of Jesus.

The Troll and the Bear.

IN Höiegaard in old days no one could stay over Christmas Eve. All the folk had to go down to the old farm in Rönnebæk, which has long been given up, and stay there till Christmas morning, for every Christmas Eve there came an ugly troll from Dragchöi, with a sackful of toads on his back, which he roasted at the fire in the sitting room, and ate one after another; but if any one ventured to stay there over night, he might be prepared to be torn in pieces by the troll. One time, just as the folk were leaving the farm, there came a man who went about with a bear, exhibiting it. They told him why they had to leave, and advised him also to get away from there; but the man begged to be allowed to stay overnight, and as he was bent on doing so they finally gave him leave. Towards evening, the troll came with his sack on his back, sat down by the fire, opened it and pulled out the one toad after the other, took each by a hind leg and held it over the fire till it was roasted, and then swallowed it. So one toad after the other went into him for some time, till he began to be satisfied. Then he turned to the man, and said, " What's your dog's name ? " " Toad," said the man. The troll took a toad, roasted it, and held it out to the bear, saying, " Toad shall have a toad," but the bear growled, and began to rise. "Yes," said the man to the troll, "just you take care, and not make him angry, or he'll tear you in pieces." The troll looked quite frightened, and asked, "Have you any more like him?" "Yes," said the man, "this one has five young ones, which are lying outside on the baking oven." The troll made haste to tie up the toads he had left in the sack, threw it on his back, and went out at the door in a hurry. Next morning, when the people of the farm came home, the man was lying all right in the bed, and the bear beside the fire, both quite comfortable. When the man told them how he had got on, they were very glad, and bade him come again next Christmas Eve, which he did, but the troll did not come, and has never shown himself there since.

Dyre Vaa and the Troll at Totak.

IN Vinje in Thelemark lies a lake called Totak, which seldom freezes before Yule. Beside this lake, on the farm of Vaa, there once lived a man named Dyre, who had the reputation of being afraid of nothing in the world. It happened once late on a Yule Eve, that the folks in Vaa heard something howling frightfully on the other side of the lake. The others were terrified, but Dyre went calmly down to the water to see what was going on. He took his boat and rowed over to the place from which the sound came. Although it was dark, he made out that it was a huge berg-troll that was shouting, but he could not see him. The troll immediately asked him who he was. "It's Dyre Vaa," said he, and in turn asked the troll

where he came from. "From Aas-haug," was the answer.
"And where are you going?" continued Dyre. "To
Gloms-haug, to my girl," said the troll; "will you set me
over?" Dyre agreed to do so, but when the troll set his
foot into the boat, it was like to sink. "Lighten yourself,
you great troll," shouted Dyre. "Yes, I'll do that," said
the troll. As they rowed over the lake Dyre said to him,
"Show yourself to me, and let me see how big you are."
"No, that I won't," said the troll, "but I will leave a mark
in the boat." Early on Christmas morning Dyre went
down to the lake to look for the promised mark, and
found in the boat the thumb of the troll's glove. He took
this home and it certainly was not small, for it held four
bushels good measure.

The Trolls in Hedal-skov.

ON a croft up in Vaage in Gudbrands-dal there lived in
old days a pair of poor people. They had many children,
and two of the sons, who were about half-grown, had
always to wander about the district and beg. In this way
they were well acquainted with all the roads and paths
round about; they also knew the straight way to Hedal,
and one time they decided to go there.

They had heard, however, that some falconers had built
themselves a hut beside Mæla, so they decided to go that
way and see the birds and how they caught them, so they
took the straight road over Lang-myrer. But by this
time it was so far on in the year, that all the dairy-maids
had gone home from the shielings, and they could nowhere find either shelter or food. They had therefore to

hold on the way to Hedal, but this was only a faint track,
which they lost when the darkness fell upon them, and
before they knew, they were in the thick of Bjöl-stad
Forest.   When they saw that they could not get on any
further, they began to break off branches and make a fire,
as well as to build a little hut, for they had an axe with
them.   Then they tore up heather and moss, and made a
bed of that.   Some time after they had lain down, they
heard some one snuffing loudly with the nose, and listened
attentively, to see whether it was a beast or a wood-troll.
The snuffing was repeated, still stronger than before, and
a voice said, " There is the smell of Christian blood here."
Then they heard steps so heavy that the earth shook beneath them, and knew that the trolls were out.

   "God help us ; what are we to do now?" said the
youngest boy to his brother.   .

   "Oh, just you stay under the fir-tree where you are,
and be ready to lift the bags and take to your heels as
soon as you see them come ; I shall take the axe," said
the other.

   At that same moment they saw the trolls approaching,
so tall and stout that their heads were as high as the fir-
tops, but they had only one eye between the three of
them, which they took turns of using.   They had a hole
in the forehead, in which they set it, and guided it with
the hand.   The one who went in front had to get it, and
the other two came behind and hung on by him.

   "Take to your heels," said the oldest of the boys,
"but don't run too far until you see what happens.
Since they have their eye so high up, they will have difficulty in seeing me when I come up behind them."

   His brother ran on ahead and the trolls followed him,
but the eldest boy came behind, and hacked at the hind-

most troll's ankle-joint, so that he set up an awful howl.
At this the foremost one was so alarmed that he started
and let go the eye, which the boy was not slow in snap-
ping up. It was as large as two quart-bowls laid together, and so clear that although it was a pitch-dark
night, it became as bright as day when he looked through
it. When the trolls discovered that he had taken the eye
from them, and done mischief to one of their number,
they began to threaten him with all possible evils unless
he returned it at once.

" I am not afraid of trolls and threats," said the boy ;
" I have three eyes now, and you three have none, and
two of you must carry the third."

" If we do not get our eye again this minute, you shall
turn to stock and stone," screamed the trolls, but the boy
thought it would hardly go so far as that ; he was afraid
neither of boasts nor of trolldom, he said, and if he was
not left in peace, he would hack at all the three of them,
so that they would come to creep on the ground like reptiles and vermin. When the trolls heard this they were
frightened, and began to speak him fair. They earnestly
begged him to give them the eye again, and he should
get both gold and silver and all that he could wish for.
The boy thought this was very fine, but he would have
the gold and silver first, so he said that if one of them
would go home, and bring as much gold and silver as
would fill his and his brother's bags, and give them two
good steel-bows as well, they should have the eye, but
until that he would keep it.

The trolls protested and said that none of them could
go, when they did not have the eye to see with, but at last
one of them began to shout for the old woman, for all
three had an old woman in common as well. In a little

he was answered from a crag far away to the north. The
trolls told her to come with two steel-bows and two
buckets full of gold and silver, nor was it long before she
was there. When she heard how things had gone, she
too began to threaten, but the others were frightened
and entreated her to take care of the little wasp ; she
could not be certain that he would not take her eye as
well. So she threw the buckets of gold and silver along
with the steel-bows to the boys, and went off home with
the trolls, nor since that time has any one heard of their
going about in Hedal Forest smelling after Christian
blood.

The Trolls and the Cross.

ON a man's land in Vivild there was a high bank in
which there lived three trolls. Every Valborg evening
they came out, and took something of what was nearest
them. The man who owned the ground had once forgot
two harrows and a plough on the field, and these they
took and burned, but they could not take anything that
was marked with the cross. Another Valborg evening it
happened that the ploughs and harrows were standing
outside, and the farmer was not at home. In order not
to lose them again, his man was sent out to make the
mark of the cross upon them. He went accordingly, but
when he came to the first, and was about to bend down to
make the sign, the first troll gave him a box on the ear.
He went to the other to try if things were the same way
there, and the second troll laid his hand on his neck,
dragged the coat off him and kept it. He then fled home

without accomplishing anything. The little boy then
came to his mother, and asked if he might go. "Can you
do it?" asked his mother. Yes, he was sure he could.
"You know what you have in your pocket?" Yes,
it was a piece of chalk and a pin of rowan-tree. Off he
went merrily, but when he had gone part of the way, he
began to think what he should do to get the better of the
trolls. He had the chalk in his pocket, so he first marked
a cross on his cheek, for the trolls were afraid of the cross,
and so he was sure to escape the box on the ear. Next
he considered that the second troll had taken the man by
the neck, so he wrapped the rowan-tree pin in his handkerchief and tied it on the back of his neck. With that
he had arrived at the first harrow, and bent down to make
the mark. At the same moment the first troll gave him
one on the ear, but the cross on his cheek burned through
his hand, so he screamed and ran away. When the boy
got to the second harrow and was bending down over it,
the second troll came and seized him by the neck, but
with that his hand withered. He had now to go and
make the cross on the plough, and having seen what effect
the rowan-pin had on the second troll, he decided to take
it and show it to the third one. As he came up, he held
the pin out, and said, "Do you know that? That is
a chip of Jesus' cross." Then the third troll turned to
coal, of which the boy took a bit home with him, and said
to his mother with great delight, "Did you see, I stood
against the trolls? and the chip I had was indeed a piece
of Jesus' cross as my grandfather said. When I grow big,
I can go wherever I please, for the trolls are afraid of me."

Dofri.

WHILE King Halfdan the Black sat in peace at home in the Uplands, it befell that much treasure and valuable things disappeared from his treasury, and no one knew who was to blame. The King was greatly troubled, for he thought that this would not be the only visit of the thief. He then had things so arranged with cunning devices and powerful spells, that whatever man entered the house to take the treasure would have to stay there till some one came to him. He guessed that the one who did the mischief would be both big and strong, so he ordered men to make ponderous fetters of the hardest steel, and twisted leaden bands. One morning early when they came to the treasury, they found there a huge giant, both tall and stout. They fell on him in a body, and put the fetters on him, but he was exceedingly strong, and sixty men were needed before he was secured with the fetters. Then they bound his hands firmly behind his back with the leaden bonds, and after that he became quieter. King Halfdan asked him his name; he said he was called Dofri, and lived in the fell that is named after him. The King asked whether he had stolen his gold; he admitted it, and asked for pardon, promising to repay it threefold, but the King said he would never pardon him, he should stay there bound until the Thing could be summoned, and there he should be condemned to a shameful death. He said too that he would give him no food, and whoever did so should lose his life. Then the King went home, and Dofri remained there in bonds.

Soon after this, Halfdan's son Harald came home, and learned all these tidings, and what his father had said.

He was then five years old. Going to where Dofri was
sitting, with a grim and gloomy look, Harald spoke to
him, and said, "Hard stead are you : will you accept
your life from me?" "I am not sure," said Dofri,
"whether, after what your father said, I ought to bring
you into so great danger." "What does that concern
you?" said Harald, and with that he drew his short
sword, which was of the best steel, and cut the fetters and
leaden bands off Dofri. He, as soon as he was freed,
thanked Harald for giving him his life, and betook himself off at once : he took no long time to tie his shoes,
laid his tail on his back, and set off so that neither wind
nor smoke of him was seen.

When Halfdan discovered this, he was so angry that he
drove Harald away, saying he could go and look for help
from the troll Dofri. Harald wandered about for four
days in the woods, and on the fifth as he stood in a clearing, worn out with hunger and thirst, he saw a huge fellow
coming along in whom he thought he knew the troll
Dofri. "You are in no good plight either, prince, as
things are now," said Dofri, "and all this, one may say,
you have fallen into on my account : will you go with
me to my home?" Harald agreed, and the giant, taking
him up in his arms, carried him swiftly along till he came
to a large cave. In entering this he stooped rather less
than he intended, and struck the boy's head so hard on
the rock that he was at once made unconscious. Dofri
thought it would be a terrible accident if he had killed the
boy, and was so deeply grieved that he sat down and cried
over him. As he sat shaking his head and making wry
faces Harald recovered, and looked up at him and saw
his mouth distorted, his cheeks swollen, and the whites of
his eyes turned up :—"It is a true saying, foster-father,"

E

said he, "that 'few are fair that greet,' for now you seem to me very ugly. Be merry, for I am not hurt."

Dofri fostered Harald for five years, and loved him so much that he could oppose him in nothing. Dofri taught him much both of learning and of feats of skill, and Harald increased greatly both in size and strength. There he stayed until the death of his father Halfdan, when Dofri sent him to succeed him as king. "I charge you," he said, "never to cut your hair or nails until you are sole king over Norway. I shall be present to assist you in your battles, and that will be of service to you, for I shall do all the more harm, in that I shall not be easily seen. Farewell now, and may everything turn out for your glory and good fortune, no less than if you had stayed with me."

The Giant on Saudey.

In Denmark lived a man named Virvill, who had a son called Asbjörn, surnamed "the Proud." It was the custom at that time for women called *völvur* (sybils) to go about the country and fore-tell men their fate, and the kind of season it would be, and other things that they wished to know. One of these came to Virvill, and was well received and entertained with the best. In the evening the sybil was asked to tell their fortunes. She said that Virvill would live there till old age, and be greatly esteemed; "but as for that young man that sits beside you, it is good for him to hear his fate : he will travel widely, and be most thought of where he is best known, and perform many exploits, and die of old age if he never comes to North Mæri in Norway, or further north in that country." "I expect," said Asbjörn, "that I shall be no more fey there than here." "You will not have the settling of that, whatever you may think," said the witch.

When Asbjörn grew up he visited various lands, and was highly esteemed by great men. His mother's folk were in Norway, in Hördaland and North Mæri, and among the former of these he stayed a long time. There he became friendly with an Icelander named Orm, a man of immense strength, and the two swore to each other foster-brotherhood after the old fashion, promising that if either of them was slain the longest-liver would avenge him. In the Spring Asbjörn said to Orm that he intended going north to Mæri to visit his kindred ; "I am also curious to know," he said, "whether the life will drop out of me the moment I get there, as the wretched witch said." Orm was willing, and they went north to Mæri with two ships, and were well received. This was in the later days of Earl Hakon. There Asbjörn learned that off the coast of Mæri lay two islands, both named Saudey, over the outer of which ruled a giant named Brusi, who was a great troll and man-eater. It was thought that he could not be overcome by mortal men, however many they were, but his mother was still worse to deal with, and that was a coal-black cat, as big as the biggest ox. Those on the mainland could get no good of either of the islands for these monsters. Asbjörn would fain have gone to the islands, but Orm dissuaded him, and they returned to Denmark.

The second year after this they came back to Norway, and spent the winter there: in the spring Orm went home to Iceland. Not long after that Asbjörn sailed north to Saudey with other 23 men. It was late in the day when they arrived there ; they went ashore and pitched their tent, but noticed nothing all that night. Early in the morning Asbjörn rose, and dressed himself, and taking his weapons went up on the island, telling his men to wait there for him. Not long after he had left them, they discovered that a fearsome cat stood in the tent-door, coal-black in hue and fearfully grim, for fire seemed to burn from her nostrils and mouth, and her eyes were fierce and cruel. At this sight they were greatly astonished and terrified. Then the cat sprang in upon them, and seized one after the other ; some she devoured and some she tore to death with teeth and claws. Twenty men she killed there in a little while and only three escaped to the ship, and immediately put off from the shore.

Meanwhile Asbjörn went on till he came to the cave of Brusi, and straightway turned into it. It was very dark inside so that he could not see clearly, and the first thing he knew he was caught up, and thrown down with a force that astonished him. Then he saw that the giant had come upon him, and was of a huge size. "Very eager were you to visit me here," said Brusi, "and now you will accomplish your errand, for you shall perish here with such torments as will hinder other men from coming to assail me." With that he stripped Asbjörn of his clothes, for he was so much stronger that he might do with him as he pleased. After this he put him to death in a most horrible fashion, while Asbjörn repeated verses recalling his old exploits and companions, and looking to Orm to revenge him.

When Orm heard of his death he came from Iceland to avenge it. He and his men landed on the inner Saudey in the evening and spent the night there. As he slept a

woman came to him, and said that she had the same
father as Brusi, but her mother was of mortal birth. She
told him all about Asbjörn's death, and how Brusi was
afraid of his coming, and had closed the mouth of his
cave with a rock that no man could move. To remove
this she gave him a pair of gloves, asking him to give
Saudey to her after he had overcome Brusi. When Orm
awoke he found the gloves beside him, and by means of
these was able to remove the stone, and to kill first the
cat and then the giant, whom he tortured by cutting the
" blood-eagle " on him. After that he burned the bodies
of both, and carried off from the cave two chests full of
gold and silver, the rest he left to Brusi's sister.

The Giantess's Cave in Sandö.

WEST from Sandsbygd there is a large cave in the earth,
called Gívrinarhol (the Giantess's cave), in which a
giantess lives. The story goes that a man from Sand
went down to the bottom of the cave to find the giantess.
He managed this successfully, and saw there a huge old
woman standing and grinding gold in a quern, while a
little child sat beside her playing with a golden baton.
The old woman being blind, the man ventured to go
cautiously up to the quern and took some of the gold for
himself. The giantess, though she neither saw nor heard
him, felt that some mischief was on foot, and said, " It is
either a mouse making meal, or a thief trying to steal—
or else this old thing isn't running right." The man now
went away from her with the gold, took the gold baton
from the child and struck it on the head with it, so that it

began to cry loudly. When the giantess heard this, she
suspected mischief, and, springing to her feet, felt for him
all round the cave, but found no one, for the man had by
this time got out of the cave, mounted his horse, set both
spurs to it, and rode home as fast as he could with the
gold.

The giantess cried as loudly as she could on her neighbour, told her of her trouble, and asked her to help her to
take the thief. She was not slow in getting to her feet to
run after him, and stepped across the lake so hard that her
footprints are still to be seen in the rock, one on each side
of the lake, and are called " the Giantess's footprints."
The man had got so good a start, that there was a long
way between them until he had reached Volis-myre,
when the giantess had got so close to him that she managed to catch the horse by the tail. She kept her hold
of that, and stopped the horse in its course, but the man
urged it on so hard, that it made one bound forward, and
the tail came off, for the giantess had a firm foothold and
was able to hold against it. The horse then fell and
threw the man forward off its back, but with that the
church came in view and the man was saved ; the giantess
had no more power over him, and had to turn back again.
One may still at Givrinarhol hear the blind old giantess
grinding gold in the deep cavern.

Oli the Strong and Torur the Strong.

In far back times there lived in Goosedale in Vaagö a giant
named Torur the strong, and in Miki-nes (Myggenæs) at
the same time dwelt a man called Oli the strong. Torur,

the dalesman, meant to kill the Mikines-man, and get the
island for himself, so he went up out of the dale on to
Liraberg, and from there sprang across the sound and
landed in Borgar-cleft at the eastern extremity of Mikines.
His footprints still remain in the cliffs on both sides of
the firth.   The Mikines man had his home in the west of
the island, so that Torur had a long way to go over hill
and dale before he found him, but it was not such a long
way for him, he could easily step west with his long legs.
The Mikines man saw him as he came striding down the
cliff, and fear fell upon him, for this big giant was terrible
to behold.   He therefore sprang to his feet, and ran
away west the island as fast as he could, but when he had
got to the westmost point there was not far between
them. Oli's heart began to come into his mouth, he grew
terribly afraid, and shouted in his extremity, " Split cleft !"
and then it was that Mikines-holm was separated from
the main island, and the sound came between them.   It
is evident from the cliffs on both sides of the strait, that
the holm and the island must have formerly been fast to
each other, for where there are caves in the cliffs of the
one, there are projecting rocks right opposite on the other.
When the giant saw this opening of more than twenty
fathoms wide before him, and the holm separating from
the island, he shouted, "Cleave what cleave will, I shall
leap after."   So he sprang across, and out there on the
holm the two began to fight, for Oli saw that he had now
no choice before him but to meet the giant and try his
might and main.   They wrestled long and fiercely, and
cast up the earth about their ankles ; the place is called
Trakk (treading) and no grass has grown there since,
though otherwise the holm is all thick with long grass
from the highest point down to the sea-cliffs.   At long

length the Mikines man brought the giant to his knees, knocked one of his eyes out, and threatened to kill him. But the giant was loath to lose his life, and began to beg himself off, promising Oli three rare things if he would give him his life. The first thing he would give him to save his life was a large whale, which would come every year into Whale-goe (Hvalagjógv) on Mikines ; the second was that a large tree should spring up in a cleft not far from that, called Woodcave-goe (Vidarhellisgjógv), and the third was a bird that would not settle or make its nest on any other isle on the Færöes except Mikines-holm. To these gifts, however, he attached the condition that no one who settled on the island in the future, and wished to have the good of them, should ever depreciate or mock them. Oli agreed to the conditions and accepted Torur's offer ; so the two were reconciled to each other, and lived together all their lives. When they died, they were buried in two grave-mounds in the west of the island, on the point that runs out toward the holm, and to this day the northmost of the two, where the Mikines-man is buried, is called "Oli rami," and the other, where the Dale man lies, has the name of "Torur rami."

The giant kept his promise well : every day during the hay-time the big whale came into Whalegoe, but it does not come now, for the men of Mikines forgot that they must not say any ill about it, and so mocked at it because it had only one eye (being a "döglingur"), and spoke ill of it because the flesh of it made them sick. So the whale disappeared and never came again.

The tree came in spring, but soon went the same way as the whale, for they abused the wood as being crooked and twisted, and wished it out of their sight, for they had to use it every year to build a chapel, and every spring, when the drift-wood came, this was blown down by the wind and carried over the cliff. They thought this gift was no good to them, and so it disappeared.

The bird, which was the third thing the giant had promised, was the solan-goose, which comes in large flocks to the holm and the rocks beside it ; but no Mikines man will speak an ill word about the solan-goose, to make them lose that, for it is a great help to those who have no good landing-place and can seldom get to sea to fish. If any one from the mainland ever happens to come to Mikines, and speaks ill of the bird, saying that its feathers have a bad smell, or anything of that kind, then the native who hears him makes it good, and says, "A good bird it is all the same, and a high-born bird that says *træl* (*i.e.*, thrall) to every man." The solan never settles on any other island than Mikines-holm, unless it is about to die, and then it may be seen flying all over the firths between the islands. It comes to the holm in the end of January, and stays there till about Martinmas, when the young are well fledged : then it is away all the early part of the winter.

Mikines.

ACCORDING to tradition Mikines was a floating island. A man in Sörvaag, who was in the habit of going out to fish, was very much afraid of the big whales out at sea, and having no beaver's scent to drive them away with, he used for that purpose bull's dung, which he threw into the sea when the whales came near the boat. Once as he sat in his boat and was driving along the west side of

Vaagö, he saw a large island come out of the mist. All
the fishermen drew up their lines, and rowed towards it
as fast as they could. The man from Sörvaag, who had
first caught sight of it, threw the dung up on a ness which
they came to, and then went ashore himself. The island
was made fast by the dung that was thrown up on the
ness, and from that it is said to have got the name of
Mykju-ness (muck-ness). Others however call it Miki-
ness from the "meikle" ness at the eastern extremity,
which has the name of Nugvu-ness.

Other traditions relate that there was once a giant,
who wished to live in the Færöes, but the islands he liked
best were too small, and so he thought of putting several
of them together. First of all he came to Koltur, and laid
it where it is now. Then he went to Skuö, to drag it up
beside Koltur, but the folk of Skuö asked him if he really
could think of living in the island that " Little Calf " had
owned. When the giant heard that a calf had owned
Skuö, he would not have it, and thanked them for telling
him this, gave them valuable gifts in return and went
away. To the north of the Færöes he next found a large
island, which he thought would be good for him to live
on ; so he brought it southwards through the sea, but
when he came right west from Vaagö, he was unable to
get it any further. He lay there for a week, striving to
get the island south to Koltur, but without success, he
could not move it out of the spot. Then he grew angry,
and said, " My life, my life, if I could have got the island
past here, I could easily have got this one under the sea,"
for he did not want anyone to have Mikines to live on
but himself. To this day men are said to have sometimes
seen an island north from Vaagö ; high fells are visible
on it, deep dales and white waterfalls. These are mainly

Sörvaag men, who have often seen it clearly while watching sheep on the out-pastures where the North Sea is in
view. No wonder though the men of Mikines are depressed
when word is brought out to them that anyone has seen
this island again ; who knows but what the giant is living
yet, and may sink Mikines to the bottom in order to get
his island brought south and fixed where he wishes it
to be ?

The Giant on Hestmandö.

ON Hestmandö in Lurö in Northland, lies a mountain
which at a distance resembles a horseman with a big
mantle over him. This mountain was formerly a giant
who lived at this place. Twelve miles further south, on
Lekö, in Nummedal, lived at the same time a maid whom
he wooed, but she was so proud that she gave him a
scornful refusal, and was besides so accomplished in all
kinds of magic that she transformed all his messengers
to stone, and they may still be seen in the reefs lying
around the northern corner of the island. Enraged at
this conduct, the giant bent his bow, intending to avenge
this insult. The mighty arrow flew forth and went right
through the high mountain Torgehatten, where one may
still see the great hole which the arrow made for itself
through the hard rock. "That straw came in the way,"
said the giant ; but impeded in its flight by this, the arrow
did not quite reach its destination. It fell down at the
maiden's feet on the northern corner of Lekö, and still
lies there in the shape of a large long stone. By mutual
trolldom they were both transformed to stone, and shall

sit thus and look at each other till Doomsday.   Even in our own day, a northland sailor seldom sails past without taking off his hat to the maid of Lekö.

The Raa-man and the Giantess on Mo-laup.

OUT of a cave in the high mountain, which rises above the farm of Mo-laup on the shores of Jörgensfirth in Söndmör, come sometimes fire and smoke, together with loud noises, which were formerly attributed to a troll who lived in the fell.   The story relates that a giantess or female troll had her abode here, and was wooed by the giant in Raamandsgill, which is in the neighbourhood. She sailed thither to have a look at her suitor, but on arriving there found him so little and raw (useless) that she in contempt spat upon him.   By this he was transformed to stone, and may still be seen on the mountain in the shape of a man, and is known by the name of " Raamand."   On the return journey she was overtaken by a violent storm, which nearly stranded her between the farms of Ness and Mo-laup, but by a vigorous push with one of her feet against the beach, the trace of which is still shown, she gave the boat such an impetus that it went right over the firth to the farm of Stavsæt.   Here it struck against a cliff, in which may still be seen the hole made by the collision.   With this both troll and ship sank, and formed there a blind reef, which is one of the best fishing places in the whole firth.

The Giant in Dunkeraberg.

IN Dunkeraberg in Fosen, there lived a giant of the name of Dunker. He once fell in love with a Christian girl, whom he carried off into the mountain. Here she sat in grief and tears, while the giant prepared the wedding feast. On the evening before the marriage Dunker drank merrily, and became very jolly. The girl, who often in vain had tried to get the giant's name from him and free herself thereby, for Christian folks can kill giants by calling their name, took advantage of the opportunity, got the troll to lay his head in her lap, and made him so happy, that at last he sprang up, danced, and sang :—

> "Hey, hey, Dunkeromdey,
> To-morrow first, Herr Dunker bold
> Within his arms his bride will hold."

Then the girl joyfully exclaimed, "No, poor Herr Dunker," and with that Dunker burst, and fell down so heavily that the mountain split, and the girl came out safe.

The Giant of Tindfell.

IN Tindfell, there has lived from time immemorial a giant of the largest kind. Once he was in a hurry and had no time to go up to the end of Tind Lake, so he thought it would be quite possible for him to stride over the little bit of water. For this purpose, he planted his foot on its west side, but was unfortunate enough to slip, and so made a great rift in the Fell. As he slipped in this way, he landed with one of his feet in the water, but deep as it is, it did not reach higher than his belt, and with the next step he was up in the East Fells, " I have been in many deep waters," said he, " but never in one deeper than that."

Another time he had got something in his eye that caused him pain ; his fingers, even the little one, were far too thick to poke after it with. After long searching he found a corn sheaf, with the help of which he got out the thing in his eye. It was a fir-cone. "Who would have thought that such a little thing could hurt so much," said he.

The Giant of Ness.

IN the district of Ness, in Vermeland, there once lived a giant who was on a friendly footing with a peasant on a neighbouring farm. One time, the peasant, along with another man, was returning from his work in the wood, when he saw the giant sitting beside a large stone. In this there was a cavity like a room, in which the giant lived.

" Will you exchange with me," said he to the peasant ; " I will give you six she-goats and a billy for a cow ? "

" Yes ! " answered the peasant.

Next morning, when the peasant's wife went into the byre, she saw that the cow was gone, and that there were goats in its place, and that was greatly to their advantage, for they had a good profit out of them when they killed them.

Once, when the peasant's folk were out in the field, they saw straight before them a cow in calf.   The peasant's wife was sorry for the heavy brute, and tied a woollen band round its body. In the evening the giant came to the farm, and bade the woman come out and loose what she had tied. The woman went along with him to the stone, and saw then that the cow was no other than the giant's wife, who had assumed this shape. She took the band off, and so delivered her. As a reward for this service, the giant bade her come with a sack, into which he poured as much silver coin as she could carry. One Easter evening the peasant went past the stone and sitting beside it he saw the giant, who said to him, " Will you come inside and take bread and milk with me ? "

" No," said the peasant, "if you have more than you can eat, keep the rest till to-morrow."

" Thanks," said the giant, "if I had known that sooner, I should be rich now."

After that time the giant was never seen again.

The Giant at Lagga-Kirk.

BESIDE Lagga Kirk, in Upland, there is a mound, where, according to tradition, trolls lived until the Reformation in the time of King Gustav, when the church, and the bell along with it, were shifted.

An old giant at that time was still living in the hill all by himself. A peasant in Lagga, named Jacob, came one morning to the neighbourhood of the hill, and heard the giant say, " Come in, Jacob, and eat porridge with me." But Jacob, who was rather surprised at this invitation, answered, " If you have more than you can eat, keep it till to-morrow." Then he heard the following mournful

words, "I can't stay here till to-morrow, I must go away
now, on account of this kling-klang, I can't bear to hear
it." "When will you come back again?" asked the
peasant. "When Lagga Firth becomes ploughed land,
and Ostuna Lake a meadow," was the giant's answer.

The Giant's Flitting.

CLOSE to Tolne Kirk in the neighbourhood of Fredericks-
havn lies a huge grave-mound called "The Berg," where
in far back days there lived giants of a tremendous size,
who ruled over all the little berg-folk that lived in the
other mounds round about. When folk were about to
build Tolne Kirk, they at first thought of placing it on
the "Stone mound," a mound in the neighbourhood of
the Berg, containing two grave-chambers, and surrounded
by about 40 large stones arranged in an elongated circle;
one of these is at least three to four ells in height. The
giants however would have no such neighbour as this,
and so every night they destroyed all that was built
during the day. The church had accordingly to be
moved further south to the spot where it now stands;
there it was beyond the reach of the trolls, for a wise and
holy man had consecrated the place before the building
was commenced. The church was finished in the autumn,
about the time that folk went for their herring to Sundby
beside Limfjord. A man from Tolne had been at Sundby
for herring, and on the homeward way he met, in Slag-
sted Forest, a man over ten ells in height, who was
pushing a wheel-barrow far larger than the peasant's cart.
On the barrow was piled a large quantity of luggage, and

on top of this sat an old giant, so old that three large iron hoops were fastened round his head to keep it from falling in pieces. " Well, are you getting home, Peter ? " said the troll. " Yes," said the peasant, " but how do you happen to know me?" "We have been neighbours for many a year," said the troll, "for I have lived in Tolne Berg well nigh on to two hundred years, but now I must flit, for they have built this blessed Church, and got that Ding-dong, and I can't bear to hear it. I am going off just now with my old father ; my wife and children are coming behind." The peasant then noticed for the first time that there were a great many others along with him, all carry-ing baggage, but before he could say a word they had all disappeared.

The Giant's Dam.

BESIDE Limfjord there is a small hill called Rön-bjærg, of the origin of which the following legend is told. In Himmerland there once lived a berg-man and his wife. The man went over to Livö and took service as a cattle-man, but wanted to get home to his wife every evening, and so had to wade across Limfjord. In no long time he grew tired of all this wading back and forward, so he and his wife decided to build a dam between Livö and Himmer-land, on which he might walk across. The arrangement was that on a certain evening they should begin work, each from their own side of the firth, and meet in the middle. The night however was so misty that they could not see each other, and that proved rather unfortunate, for when the man on Livö had got a sackfull of earth and was about to begin work, he heard some one blowing a

F

horn on the south side of the firth. Thinking that it was
his wife who was calling on him, he went in that direction
and deposited the earth. Meanwhile his wife over in
Himmerland had got her apron full of earth, and had
gone down to the right place on the firth, but there was a
hole in her apron, through which she let fall a handful
here and there, and so formed the three or four mounds
that are still to be seen. Just as she got down to the
firth, however, the mist began to lift, and she saw that
her husband had made his dam far out to the south, at
which she was so annoyed that she threw down all the
earth she had in her apron, and in this way Rön-bjærg
hill was formed. At the place where she took the earth
from, there is still a great deep hole, large enough to hold
a house.

The Giantess and the Ploughers.

A giant's wife went outside the mound to look about
her. Close by there were some people ploughing, so she
took up the horses, folk and plough together in her apron,
and went back into the mound to her husband, to ask
what this was that was wriggling in her apron. " Let
them go again," said he, "for they will drive us out in
time."

The Giant's Glove.

CLOSE beside Gudum Cloister, on the field belonging to
the parsonage, lie two mounds, one of which is of an
immense size and bears the name of Raa-bjærg mound ;

the other is much smaller. Of these it is told that in old days there was a giant, who had now and again to cross Oddesund, but he had so much trouble in getting ferried over it, that he conceived the idea of doing without a ferry by building a dam across the sound. Accordingly he went out on Cloister-heath, and filled his big glove with sand for that purpose. On the way to the sound, however, he was overtaken by mist and could not see where he was going, and so kept more to the east than he intended. This was not the only misfortune that befell him either, for as he was going along, a hole formed in the thumb of his glove and all the sand in it fell out; that formed the little mound. However, he went boldly on, holding the end of the thumb firmly with his other hand to prevent any more falling out, but another hole came in the part for the fingers, and all the sand in the glove rushed out. That was the origin of Raa-bjærg mound. The story says that out on the heath there is still a large hole from which he took the sand, and from what I have heard, it is of exactly the same size as both the mounds put together, and its circumference at the top is just the same as that of both mounds at the bottom. They are both overgrown with heather, and consist of sandy earth, which is remarkable enough, and points to the truth of the story, as they are surrounded on every side by good clay-land.

The Giantess and her Sons.

ON the fields of Hede-gaard in the parish of Vrads lies a long grave-mound, which goes under the name of "The Giantess." In this mound a giantess is said to be buried,

and away on the fields of Vinding, a little west from
Vinding Church, are two smaller mounds side by side,
where her two sons are said to lie. There was a big giant
who was angry with her, and pursued them. He first
caught up with the boys, who could not keep pace with
her ; these were killed by him and buried on the spot
where they fell. Four miles further west he came up to
her as well, and killed her on the spot where she now lies.
She was so stout that she could throw her breasts back
over her shoulders, and let the sons suck her as they ran
behind.

One time a man planned to dig through the mound.
On one side of it was a pool and on the other a hollow,
so he thought to kill two flies with one blow, namely, drain
the pool and dig through the mound at the same time.
But when he got into it as far as where the giantess's
knees would lie, he had the ill-luck that his cows died,
and believing that the digging must be to some extent to
blame for that, he gave up the undertaking.

III.—Bergfolk and Dwarfs.

The Origin of Bergfolk.

BERGMEN originated in this way, that when Our Lord cast down the wicked angels from heaven they could not all get to hell together, and some of them settled in the mounds and banks.

Brownies, bergmen, and such creatures originated in this way. When Our Lord cast the wicked angels down from heaven some of them fell on mounds and banks, and these became bergmen; some fell into woods and mosses, and these became fairies (ellefolk), while those that fell into buildings became brownies (nisser). They are just little devils, the whole lot of them.

The Oldest Man in Bankeberg.

THE girls from Ry were in the habit of meeting beside Slagelse mounds, when going out to milk their cows, which grazed on common pasture out beside Löve Moss. On one occasion several of the girls had assembled, and were dancing round one of the mounds. While the dance was at its height there came out of the mound an old troll, who danced along with them, and sang, "The barley's in ear, the ox has horns, and I am the oldest

man that lives in Banke-berg." The foremost girl, whose
hand the troll had hold of, exclaimed, "Christ preserve
us from the oldest man that lives in Banke-berg." He
let them go then, and the girls ran home as hard as they
could, some getting their milk-cans with them, and others
not.

A Meeting with Bergfolk.

" ONE evening I was driving along the high-road between
Kalundborg and Slagelse, and was just close to Agerup
Mill, when I saw on the road before me some little black
figures, which at a distance looked like a large crowd of
school-boys. As I was driving pretty fast I soon got
nearer them, and saw then that they were bergfolk or
brownies. They wore dark clothes, and each of them was
smoking a silver pipe. As I passed them they greeted
me with ' Evening, evening,' for that kind of folk cannot
say ' *Good* evening.' I saw them as plainly as I see you,
and I can remember that the sparks flew out of their pipes
now and again. I gave myself no time to return their
greeting, but laid on to the horses, nor did any of them try
to harm me. They must undoubtedly have been underground folk, going to a party in some of the mounds
round about."

Gillikop.

SOME Jutlanders once got hold of a little bergman. They knew of nothing better than to make him a Christian, and put him on a cart to drive him to the church, where he was to be baptised. As he sat there and peeped out, the peasants heard by the wayside a voice crying, "Whither away, Gillikop?" Then the little man in the cart answered, "A long way, Slangerop; I am going off to a little water, where I expect to be made a better man!"

Skalle.

IN olden times there were not so many who wanted to take farms on lease as there are now. There was then a certain farm, which in a short time had had many tenants, who had all gone wrong together. Some died soon, and others had become so poor that they could not pay the landlord what they owed, and were therefore thrown out of the farm. This had just happened to a tenant, and the landlord made one of his men take the farm (as landlords could do at that time, whether the man wanted to be a farmer or not). The evening that this man entered on the farm, he said, as he came in at the gate, "Well, good evening, Skalle." It was the farm he meant, because it was so bare (*skallet*) and desolate. But with that he heard a voice above the gate, which answered, "Good evening." The man was surprised at this, but immediately said, "If there is anyone here that

I can't see, I invite them to be my guest on Christmas
Eve."

On Christmas Eve, just as the peasant and his men
had finished their work in the stable, and had gone into
the house, but had not as yet got the candles lit, there
came a little man in to them, and said, " Good evening,
and a Merry Christmas to you all." " Who are you ? "
said the farmer. " I am the one you invited to come this
evening," said the little man. " Then please sit down at
the table," said the farmer, " and take a bite of meat."
The stranger sat down, and ate along with them. " Now,
I invite you to be my guest on New Year's Eve," said
the troll, for it *was* a troll. " O, thanks," said the farmer,
" but where do you live ? " " Just come to the outside of
your stable-door, and you will be sure to meet me," said
the troll.

On New Year's Eve, the farmer went to the outside of
his stable-door, and the troll immediately came and took
him down under the ground, to his dwelling. It was
pretty and nice there, thought the farmer. The troll
bade him sit down at the table, and they got boiled rice,
but just as they sat and ate, the troll snatched the dish
off the table. The farmer was a little astonished at this,
but he summoned up courage to ask " What's the meaning of that ? " " Don't you see, there's a drip comes down
on the table," said Skalle (for that was the troll's name),
" and that's the reason that no one can get on in the farm,
but if you shift the stable to another side of the yard, you
will become a rich man here."

The farmer did so, and after that got on splendidly, for
he had success both in crops and cattle, and became a
well-to-do man.

"We Others."

IN Erslev there is a farm called Höjgaard, which takes its name from a mound (höj) that lies near it. The farmer had once taken all the greensward off this, and carted it off to his dung-heap. In the gloaming, when the good-wife was about to go into the kitchen to light the candle, she found that she was unable to enter it, there was no room for her. She called on her husband, and asked him to come into the kitchen, but he could not manage it either, and yet he could see nothing. "What's the reason of this?" he asked. "Oh, it's WE OTHERS who live in the mound. You have taken our roof off, and the rain is coming in on us." They got leave then to stay in the farm for the time being, on condition of causing as little trouble as possible, the farmer promising to put the mound in good order again. He then took his whole dung-heap, and carted it up to the mound, where he spread it out and beat it well down. After that they saw no more of them, but there was great blessing and plenty on that farm, which has continued ever since, so that they are rich folks to this day.

The Key of Dagberg Dos.

THE bergman in Dagberg Dos had gone down one day to take a turn in Höne Moss, where the boys go with the cattle in the summer. While there he was so unfortunate as to lose the key of his money-chest, and it was impossible to find it again. He then stood on the top of the mound, and shouted every day to the boys—

> " The key of Dagberg Dos
> Is lost in Höne Moss ;
> Who finds it now for me,
> Much gold shall be his fee."

Finally one of the boys did find the key, and was eager enough to give it up and get the great reward, but we shall hear how well the bergman kept his promise. When the boy had got up on the mound, with the key in his hand, he thought he would just look what the cattle were doing, but when he turned round they were running about and straying in every direction. At this he was so startled that he threw the key from him, and ran down to them as fast as he could, and never got either gold or silver for finding the bergman's key.

A Birth among the Bergfolk.

THERE lived an old woman in Andrup, of the name of Ann Ovster (Ove's daughter), who was employed as a midwife. One time during the summer she had been attending the wife of the farmer of Lille-kræns, and while returning home was passing the two mounds between which his fields lay. There she noticed an unusually large toad, of the kind they call " padder," with white stripes on its back. To this she said in jest, " I shall come and help you too when you are in labour," never thinking that her words had any significance. Some time after this she heard a waggon come driving up one night and stop before her house. She hurriedly rose, wondering who it could be that had come for her, as she did not know of any one likely to want her services so soon. She

opened the door, and there entered a little man, with a
beard so long that he almost trod on it, who explained
his errand, and asked her to go home with him. "You
have made a mistake, my little man," said she; "you are
none of my folk." "Yes," said he, "you must come with
me, if you wish to be prosperous; you promised it to my
wife fourteen days ago." So she went along with him,
not daring to refuse. He drove on for a long time, as she
thought, and it was pitch dark too. Finally she entered
a long passage, and found a little, thick woman lying in
bed, and so wretched was the place that she had nothing
but straw to lie on. Ann aided her successfully, and she
was delivered of a pretty boy. "You are surely very
poor here," said Ann, while the man was outside. "No,
indeed, we are not so poor," said the woman. "There is
a jar standing in the window there; dip your finger in it,
and anoint your right eye with that." As soon as she
had done so, everything was changed; she was in a most
beautiful hall, and had never been in any mansion that
was so grand. The woman then, putting her hand into
a pot, gave her a whole handful of gold coins, and said:
"When my husband comes to drive you home, you must
spring off the waggon as soon as the horse seems to be
going through soft ground, otherwise you will not escape
him. You will be just at home then." In a little the
man came, and asked if they were ready. He drove off
with her again, and a long time passed, so that she fell
into a doze, but woke up with the horse dragging in mire
up to its sides. Then she sprang out at once, and stood
just at the end of her house.

In the following autumn the berg-folk came to help
themselves at Lille-kræns. In the evenings the folk were
in the habit of dragging the corn, and setting it up be-

tween the mound by moonlight. The old woman then saw the little man springing in front of her and taking every tenth sheaf. She thought this was too much, and said to him, "You mustn't do the like of that; that's stealing." He was surprised at this, and said to her, "Can you see me?" Yes, that she could. "Shut your left eye," he said: "can you see me now?" "Yes," said she. Then he understood that it was her right eye she saw him with, and poked it out. From that time forth she was one-eyed and could see him no longer.

"Life Hangs by a Thread."

Two girls were digging in a garden when one of them found a mole. "Kill it," said the other, but the one who found it said "No;" it would be a sin to kill it, it did no harm. They argued over this for a little, but the finder prevailed at last, and they let it go. Some days after, as the girl stood by the fireplace, there came to her a little man, and asked if she would visit them on Sunday; they were to have a christening, and would she carry the child, and bring the other girl with her? Both of the girls promised to come.

Next Sunday, at the hour appointed, they were dressed in all their finery, and the little man came to fetch them. He took them round behind the oven, where they saw a little hole they had never noticed before; into this the man went, and the girls followed. On entering this, they found a great company of little creatures assembled in a large room: this was the christening party, and they took the child to church, and had it baptized. On returning home from church, they sat down at table, as is the custom, but after having sat for a little the first girl happened to look up, and saw a huge millstone hanging over her head. She could see nothing that it hung by, and thought that it was quite loose, but on looking closer she discovered that it was hanging by a silk-thread. At this she was terrified and gave a scream, whereupon the woman asked her what she was frightened at. "Good reason to be frightened," said she, "with such a millstone hanging above my head ; if it falls I shall be killed." "Yes ; my life also hung by a thread the other day," said the woman, "for it was me that you dug up in the garden in the shape of a mole, and I thank you for sparing my life, but you need not be in the least afraid of the stone, it is only a deception to show you what danger I was in."

When the two girls were about to return home, the man came and gave each of them a quantity of shavings, thanking them for their trouble in coming. They returned by the same hole as they had entered, and on reaching the kitchen one of the girls threw away her shavings, and laughed a good deal at the little man's present. The other one, however, thought to herself, " If they do no good, they'll do no harm either," and laid them in a drawer beside her clothes. Some days later she wanted to look at her clothes, and on lifting them there was a great rattling in the drawer. She looked to see what this might be, and found that the shavings had turned to pure gold. Off she ran in great glee, and told this to the other girl, who was then vexed that she had thrown away so much wealth, but gone it was, and gone it had to be.

The Bergman's Christian Wife.

IN the big sandhills along the shores of the North Sea
there lived bergfolk in old days, as well as in the inland
mounds. These little creatures are only three or four
feet high, with big clumsy heads, broad faces, big round
noses, and red hair, and always wear a red woollen cap.
These mannikins tried to ally themselves by marriage
with the folks in Raa-bjærg, but although they had
great stores of silver and gold, and the inhabitants there
are known to be ahead of all the other Jutlanders in their
regard for money, yet there was no one who would willingly enter into kinship with them, so they often carried
off a girl or a child. So it happened at Kande-steder ; a
girl disappeared one evening while getting supper ready
in the kitchen, and nothing could be heard of her. About
a year afterwards, as her mother was standing beside the
fireplace, also preparing the supper, a large stone was
pushed aside in the chimney or hearth, and out of the
hole came a troll, who told her to follow him as his wife
was in labour. In her alarm the woman dared not scream,
and followed him. It was to her own daughter, who was
with child to the bergman, and under these circumstances
a Christian woman cannot be delivered, until she has a
Christian woman beside her. When the bergman had
gone out, the daughter said that she was very well off,
but longed to see her relatives. "When you are about
to go home," she added, "he will give you something for
your trouble, but you must not take what seems to you
to be money, for that is only leaves ; take flints and
shavings." Accordingly, when he came with a drawer full
of gold and silver coins, and told her to take as many as
she pleased, she said, "No, they are too fine for me ; may

I not rather take some flints from the other drawer?"
"You are surely mad," said the troll; "what do you
want with flints?" "Oh, I have often to strike fire in
the mornings, so I will take them and some shavings."
"Well, take them then," said he, "but the one who taught
you *that* did not strike you on the mouth." Her son-in-
law then led her up into the kitchen again, where her
husband and children were greatly surprised to see her,
having long sought for her in vain, for she had been
absent about eight days. In her hand she had two of the
coins, which were now only pieces of peat, whereas her
apron was full of old crowns and ducats. When she had
told her husband the whole story, he said, "Well, it's a
pity that Karen is gone, but her advice was not so foolish,
and the journey not so bad after all." And in that he
was right, for he and his family became the richest people
in the parish, and so are their descendants to this very
day.

Working for the Bergfolk.

THERE was once a girl at service with the midwife in
Vallö, who always complained of having such pains in
her arms, as if she was quite killed with work, and yet
her place was an easy enough one. One time the midwife had been sent for, but as she was driving past a
mound, there came out one who took her out of the
waggon, away from the man who had been sent for her,
and carried her down through the mound to a large cave
below it, where she had to assist a woman. When this
was done, she noticed a girl standing and grinding malt

with a quern, looking exactly like her own maid, and even wearing a pelisse the very same as one she had given her. She talked a little to the girl, who said that she was *so* tired, and had a great deal to grind yet before she would be finished. Meanwhile the woman slyly cut a piece out of her pelisse. In the morning her own maid was lying asleep in her bed, but by and bye she came, and complained that some one had cut a piece out of her pelisse. Her mistress now brought the piece she had cut, and it fitted exactly, so she told the girl that it was no wonder her arms ached, seeing that she had to stand and grind away at the troll's quern by night. With that she told her the whole story, and advised her to repeat the Lord's prayer, and cross herself every evening on going to bed, before she laid herself down to sleep. This proved effectual.

Maid Ellen.

ON the estate of Skovs-gaard in Humblè parish, there lived in the sixteenth century a pirate, who lived a wild and savage life, and was feared by every one. With him lived his sister Ellen, who was mild and good, and tried to influence her brother, but without effect, although he was very fond of her. One day she went out into the forest with two friends, and on coming to a little mound Maid Ellen sat down, and told the others to go on a little and come back to her, as she was tired and wished to rest. They left her alone there, and on their return Maid Ellen was gone; the grass was all trampled, and they found one of her gloves on the top of the mound. They

ran to the house and told this to her brother, who immediately took fifteen of his best horsemen with him, and
some musicians, and betook himself to the mound. Around
this they began to ride, playing the meanwhile, and this
went on for 40 days and nights. As soon as the one
party grew tired others took their place, until on the 40th
night the mound was suddenly lifted on four pales, and a
troll came out leading Maid Ellen by the hand, and saying that here she was now, and they might stop all the
noise and music. They rode home with her then, and
the troll-mound looked just as before, but round about it
(it now bears the name of Ellens-bjærg) there are still
traces of a path. She brought with her out of the mound
a silk gown that she was sewing at, but in the haste with
which she left, she only took one sleeve with her, and she
could nowhere get the cloth matched again. She also
brought with her a silver knife and fork, which are still
preserved in Taasinge Castle, and have the property of
stopping blood.

When her brother died, his ghost went about, and they
had to send for the priest to exorcise him, but the dead
man asked him so difficult questions that he nearly lost
the day. Among other things, he asked where our
Lord was, when he was neither in heaven nor on earth.
The priest stood and could give no answer, but Ellen,
who was sitting at a window on the second floor, under
which they were standing, answered that then he hovered
over the waters. When her brother heard this, he began
to sink into the earth, but found time to call out to her,
"If I had thought that of you, little sister, you should
have remained in Ellens-berg."

There is still a hollow where she came out of the
mound, and neither leaf nor grass grows on it to this day.

G

It was on the seventh Wednesday in Lent that she was brought out, and every year after that a sermon was preached on that day in Humblè Church, for which Skovs-gaard had to pay ten dollars to the priest of that parish. Not so many years back the service was dropped, because no one came to it latterly, but the payment is still made to the priest every year.

The Changeling and the Egg-shell.

A WOMAN'S child was once changed by the troll-folk, and instead of a beautiful fair-haired bairn, she got a little dumpy creature, with a big head, and little eyes as black as coal. The poor mother had recourse to a " wise woman," who gave her the following advice. She should first try whether the child was really a changeling, and if was so, she should threaten to throw it into the heated baking-oven, and then its real mother would come and take it away. The woman therefore set the changeling down on the hearth, while she went about saying to herself that now she would start to brew. She then took seven egg-shells filled with water, and set them on the fire beside the child, after which she hid herself near at hand, to see how the changeling would behave at this. It looked long at the egg-shells in which the water was boiling, and then exclaimed in amazement:—"Long have I lived and much have I seen. I have seen Rold Forest seven times burned down, and seven times grow up again, but never have I seen anyone brew in egg-shells." The woman then came out of her hiding-place and said: " Then you are old enough now, you little troll! Into

the oven you shall go." But immediately there appeared
a little grey female with the woman's child on her arm,
which she gave her, while at the same time she seized the
changeling and said, " I have never treated your child as
you have treated mine ! "

<hr>

The Changeling and the Sausage.

IN Rold Forest, beside Hobro, there lived a married
couple who had only one child, a boy of eight or nine
years old, but he was no bigger than a child of three. He
had a large head and thick speech, and was as ugly as
sin, but neither the man nor the wife could see this, for of
course everyone thinks well of their own children.   One
harvest the man had a litter of little pigs, and as these
were so cheap that year that it would not pay to sell
them, they roasted them and ate them themselves ; they
wrapped them up in a piece of canvas, plastered this over
with clay, and laid them in the glowing ashes, and when
they were sufficiently roasted, they could flay canvas, clay
and hair off them, and then take out the inside.   This
then made a beautiful roast, which they ate with great
satisfaction.   One day they had laid one of the little pigs
in the ashes to be cooked in this way, and had gone out
to the harvest, leaving it to be ready when they came
home again.   The child was left poking about at home,
and in raking among the ashes it found the pig.   At first
it was greatly puzzled as to what this could be, but finally
made up its mind that it was a sausage.   At this it was
greatly delighted, leapt and sprang round the room, crying out, "Sausage, have you ears ? sausage, have you

eyes? sausage, have you a tail? I have lived so long
that I have seen Rold Forest cut down twice and grow
up thrice, but never have I seen such a sausage!" It
kept on shouting this and leaping about, till finally it
crawled up on a rafter, and was sitting there repeating
the same words, when the man and his wife came home.
The woman heard it and said, "Now I know why the
child is never growing any bigger; it is a changeling, but
I'll soon get rid of it." She entered the house, and called
to the little fellow to come down, as she wanted to talk
to him. He did so, and she took him and gave him a
good thrashing, and threw him out of doors. There he
lay and howled at the pitch of his voice, and after a while
there came an ugly little woman with a child on her arm,
which she threw to the woman, saying, " There you have
your youngster; I have been better to it than you have been
to mine." When she had said this she disappeared with
the changeling, but the woman's own child was quite
ruined by the troll-folk, and died soon after.

The Troll's Wedding.

EAST from Ronnebæk there lay a little mound which was
called Dragehöi; it is now levelled with the ground, but
within living memory it was an ancient grave-mound,
where a girl once found a clay vessel with ashes and
bones in it. Formerly every Christmas Eve it stood
raised on four fiery pillars, and the trolls could be seen
dancing inside. The little trolls who lived in this mound,
often resorted to a small farm close by, which now is
given up. There they often borrowed various articles,
especially for festive occasions. Thus one of the trolls,

named " One-Leg," came once to the farmer's wife, and
told her he was to be married, and therefore wanted to
borrow dishes, ladles, and many other things. The woman
lent him what he wished, but asked in return, that she
might be allowed to see the bridal procession. "One Leg"
promised that she should be allowed to see it, but at the
same time it would cause her a little unpleasantness. On
the wedding day, as the household sat at dinner, the
woman saw the little bride with her following, come
dancing through the room, and as " One Leg " came hopping behind them, she could not help laughing out loud,
and still more did she laugh when " One Leg " came past
her children, who were sitting eating out of a clay dish,
and struck out with his leg, so that the dish went on the
floor. The farmer, who could see nothing, except that the
dish fell on the floor, became angry, and gave his wife a
good box on the ear because she laughed at the children
spilling the good food, and breaking the dish ; but the
woman could not even then stop her laughing until the
procession was out of the room.

Sten of Fogelkärr.

STEN of Fogelkärr in Svarteborg parish was a good
marksman. One day he went out hunting, and came to
the neighbourhood of a knoll. There he caught sight of
a pretty young girl, sitting on a stone outside the mound ;
and, as he at once determined to have the pretty maiden
for his wife, he threw his fire-steel between her and the
mound, so as to get her in his power. Then he heard a
long laugh from inside ; this was the pretty girl's father,
the *bergbo*, who now opened the door, and asked the

hunter, "Will you have my daughter?" to which Sten answered "Yes." As she was quite naked, he took his coat and wrapped her in it, carried her home, and had her baptised. But before he left the mound, her father gave him these orders: "When you hold your wedding with my daughter, you must brew twelve barrels of ale, take bread for that, and the flesh of four oxen, and bring it to the berg here where I live; when the wedding presents are to be given, mine shall not be wanting." The berg-man honourably kept his promise, for as the wedding party sat at table, and the presents were, according to old custom, being collected from the guests, the roof was suddenly lifted up, and a large purse of money thrown in ; along with it the old man's voice was heard : "Here's my wedding gift, and when you want your dowry, you must drive to the mound with four horses and get your share." This was done, and when Sten, says the story, came to the berg with four horses he got several copper kettles, the one bigger than the other. He also got "brand" cattle, of which good breed descendants were long afterwards found in that place. Sten became there-after a rich and powerful man, and had many strong and handsome children by the wife he found in this way. Even yet there are said to be families in the district, who trace their descent from Sten of Fogelkärr and the berg-woman.

The Bergman's Daughter of Dagberg-daas.

THE Bergman of Dagberg-daas had a daughter who was married to a smith in Mors. The smith was bad to the

woman, and often beat her, until finally she got tired of
this, and once, when he laid hold of her, she, instead of
growing yellow with vexation, seized a horse-shoe which
was lying on his anvil, and broke it in two, right in front
of the smith's nose.

The smith now had considerably more respect for the
woman's powers, and did not try her patience further.
But as rumour told strange things about her, she was not
at all respected by the good folk in the neighbourhood;
she had to mind her own business, and even in church no
one would sit by her side. One Sunday, just as the
people were standing in the churchyard waiting for the
priest, she too was standing there, but in a corner by
herself. All at once, she pulled her husband by the coat,
"Listen, goodman," said she, "my father is coming to
visit me to-day, but he is angry, I can see that by the
mist over the sea, which goes before him." The mist
parted, and the Bergman came up on shore, and was of
so terrible an appearance that many a one of those who
saw him, would willingly have crept into a mouse-hole for
fright.

"Well, my daughter," said he to her, "I think people
must be made to have a better opinion of you: I believe
I can bring that about. We will try tossing them in the
air a bit; whether will you throw them or catch them?"
"Catch them," said the woman, for she was afraid that
otherwise he would handle them too roughly. The Bergman now began to lay hold of the church-goers, one after
the other, and throw them over the roof of the church,
while she caught them on the other side. From that time
forth, all the rest had to do as the smith had done, and
treat his wife rather differently.

"Viting is Dead."

A MAN from Levring had been in Viborg, and when
nearing home on his return journey, was about to walk
up a steep slope by the side of his cart, when he heard a
cry from a mound, "Won't you tell Black-eye that Viting
is dead?" The man was greatly frightened, but arrived
home in safety. As he drove up to the door, his wife
came out, and asked whether he could see to find the
house. Yes, said he, that was not so bad, but he had
been somewhat frightened in coming past the mounds
outside the village, for there was some one there that
shouted, "Tell Black-eye that Viting is dead." As he
said this to his wife, there arose a cry in the yard, "Oh! is
Viting dead?" The man and his wife went in and could
see nothing, but later on in the evening, when the wife
went out to take the barm off the ale, she found in the
vat a large silver cup. Black-eye had no doubt been busy
taking some of the ale, but on hearing of Viting's death
had run home, and in his confusion had forgotten to take
the cup with him. The old man who told this story says
that the silver cup is still to be found on a farm in Levring, and that he himself has drunk out of it. It has been
there for more than 150 years.

"Tell Finkenæs that Jafet is Dead."

THE south-eastern farm in the village of Vissing, beside
Randers, is called Pil-gaard. The tenant of this was out
driving one day in winter, and on his way home in the
evening was passing Os-höj. Beside this he saw some

one standing, who beckoned to him and shouted, " I say, make haste and drive home, and tell Finkenæs that Jafet is dead." " What do you say?" said the man. The stranger repeated his shout, until the man finally got hold of the curious names, but thought no more about it after he reached home. It was cold weather, and when he entered the house he blew on his hands, and complained of the cold. " You will soon get some warm kail to your supper," said his wife. Just at that same moment the man noticed a stranger sitting beside the stove, and asked him if he would also have some. The person thanked him, and sat down at the table. The man blew on his kail, and said, " They are hot yet." At this the stranger remarked, " You said it was cold when you blew on your hands to warm them, and now you blow on the kail to cool them ; can you blow both hot and cold with one mouth?" The man said he could. " Then you are my master," said the other. " Where do you come from?" asked the man, who just then remembered the incident at the mound ; "perhaps you are from Os-höj, and are called Finkenæs." Yes, that was his name. " Well, as I came past the mound, there was a person standing outside who shouted to me to tell Finkenæs that Jafet was dead." " What! is Jafet dead?" shouted the stranger, threw down his spoon, and out at the door. A week later he came again, and told the farmer that because he brought him such good news, and because he and his forefathers had never disturbed the mound, he would bring it about that Pilgaard should never want an heir, nor pass into the hands of strangers, but there would only be one heir always, or two at most. This has held good for at least five generations back.

Bröndhöi.

A MILE from Sorö lies Pedersborg, and a little further
away is the village of Lynge. Between these two villages
there is a mound called Bröndhöi, which is said to be inhabited by trolls. Among these there was once an old
jealous troll whom the others called Knurremurre ("the
grumbler,") because he was often the cause of dissension
and disturbance in the mound. This Knurremurre had
once discovered that his young wife had a good understanding with a young troll, and the old fellow was so
angry at this that he threatened the other's life, so that
he found it best to flee from the mound, and betook himself in the shape of a red cat to the village of Lynge,
where he ingratiated himself in this form with a poor
cottar of the name of Plat. There he lived for a good
while, got every day his porridge and milk, and lay the
whole blessed day in an armchair behind the stove. One
evening Plat came home, and just as he entered the room,
the cat was lying in his usual place, scraping porridge out
of a pot and licking it off his paws. "Well, good-wife,"
began the man, "I'll tell you what happened to me on
the road. As I came past Bröndhöi, a troll came out
and called to me, saying, "I say, Plat, tell your cat that
Knurremurre is dead." At these words the cat rose up
on its hind legs, let the pot roll away and said, as it crept
out at the door, "What! is Knurremurre dead, then I
must hurry home."

Skotte.

BESIDE Gudmandstrup in Oddsherred, there is a mound
called Hiule-höi. The berg folk who live in it are well-

known in the villages round about, and if any one forgets
to make the sign of the cross on their ale barrels, the
trolls from Hiule-höi slip in there to steal the ale. Late
one evening a peasant was coming past the mound, and
saw it standing on red posts, and under it there was
music, dancing, and a grand festival. The peasant
stopped to look at their merry-making, but just as he
stood and marvelled at it, the dance stopped and the
music ceased, and amid much lamentation he heard a
troll cry, " Skotte has fallen into the fire, come and help
him out." The mound then sank, and the whole merriment was at an end.

Meanwhile, the peasant's wife was at home all alone,
and as she sat and span her tow, she had not noticed that
a troll had crept into the next room by the window, and
was standing by the ale barrel, drawing ale in his copper
kettle. The door was open, and the troll was keeping an
eye on the woman. Just then the man entered the room,
feeling quite strange by reason of what he had heard and
seen. " Well, goodwife," he began, " I'll tell you what
has happened to me," (the troll was all attention), " as I
came past Hiule-höi I saw a big troll-festival, but just as
it was at its best, some one shouted ' Skotte has fallen
into the fire, come and help him out.' " On hearing this,
the troll who stood beside the ale barrel was so alarmed
that he let the kettle fall to the ground, left the ale running and hurried out at the window as fast as he could.
At this noise the people understood well enough what
had taken place, and finding the copper kettle, they took
it as payment for the ale spilt, and that same kettle, it is
said, was to be seen for many years after, in the villages
round about.

Plough-irons made by Bergfolk.

ONE evening as a man was driving past the eastern
Mölgaard mound, he heard some one calling on him.
At first he was alarmed and drove on, but it presently
occurred to him that he was in want of two plough-irons,
so he called out to the troll-folk, and asked if they would
make them for him before his return. They promised to
do so, and when he came back to the mound there came
out of it two little fellows, carrying two red-hot plough-
irons, which they threw into the back of his cart, with the
words, "Just fix them on when you get home : they'll fit
all right." The man was rather scared, and feared they
would set fire to his cart, but on reaching home he tried
them, and found them better than any he had ever had.
After six or seven years had passed they began to crack,
and he sent them to the smith, not daring to take them
back to the mound, as he had never paid them for making
them. As soon as the smith laid them in the fire they
turned to coal, whereas if the man had been wise enough
to lay them down on the mound, he would have got them
back whole and sound.

The Borrowed Petticoat.

ON Mors in Jutland there stands a mansion called Overgarth, in which there once lived a lady, Fru Mette by
name. A little bergman came to her one day, and said,
" Fru Mette of Overgarth, will you lend Fru Mette of
Undergarth your silk petticoat to be married in ? " This
she did, but as it was a long time before it was brought
back, she went to the mound one day, and called from

the outside, "Give me back my petticoat." The bergman then came out, and gave her the petticoat, all covered with drops of wax, saying, "Since you have asked for it, take it as it is ; but if you had waited a few days, there would have been a diamond on it for every spot of wax."

The Bergfolk's Ale Barrel.

EAST from Nörre-tang in Ulfborg there is a mound with bergfolk in it. One of their women came to the farm one evening, and asked for the loan of a barrel of ale. The farmer's wife asked where she came from. "Don't you know me?" said she : "we have been neighbours for so many years !" She then explained that she came from the mound, and got the ale. In a few days she came back to repay it, and said, "So long as you refrain from looking into the barrel, so long shall it continue to give out ale ; and your race shall be prosperous to the fourth or fifth generation, because you lent to me." The barrel did continue to yield ale for a long time, but finally curiosity got the upper hand, and the woman must have a peep into it, cost what it would. She found it full of mould and cobwebs, and after that all was over with the ale.

The Nisse in the Ale Barrel.

IN old days there lived Nisses (bergfolk) in a mound in Fyen, and one evening they took counsel as to where they should steal some ale which they wanted. Some said they should go the clerk's, but the others said it was too thin, and finally it was agreed to take it from the cooper, for his was so rich.   On arriving there they crept in at the window of his ale-cellar, where they went round and tasted the ale, and finally found a barrel with ale in it, which they proceeded to drag off with them.   The cooper, however, was awake and heard the noise in his cellar, and went down to see what was the cause of it. All the nisses then crept out at the window again, except one who could not get away so quickly as the others, and therefore had to creep into an empty ale barrel that stood there.   The man, seeing the point of a red cap sticking up out of this, put the bung into the barrel and went his way.   On telling his wife what he had done, she made intercession for the nisse, but the man answered that he would teach the thieving pack to leave his ale in peace. So the poor nisse had to sit in the barrel overnight, but there was no pin in the tap-hole, and this was so big that he could get two of his fingers out at it, and with these he managed to make the hole so large that he could put out one of his legs.   In the morning then, what did the cooper see but the nisse in the barrel, hopping off across the yard on his one leg?   When he got over the gutter, the barrel fell in pieces, and the nisse bolted for the mound as fast as he could.   From this he got the name of Halte-kok.   When he reached the mound, and told the other nisses what had befallen him, they decided to revenge themselves, and they did so, for the following night they went and took the taps out of all the cooper's ale barrels, and let all the ale run out.

The Bergfolk at the Wedding Feast.

IN Maal-bjærg there lived a nisse, who was king over a great part of the berg-folk round about.   One time there was a great wedding in Kjöl-by, and after the bridal party had set out for the church, a herd-boy was lying by the side of this mound, when he heard a great uproar get up inside it, and shouts of "Give me my hat!   Give me my hat!"   He was a bold-hearted fellow, this same herd-boy, so he also shouted, "Give me one too!"   "There's none left but father's old one," was the answer.   "Give me that then," said he.   He got the hat and put it on, and with that the dwarfs came up, and made for Kjöl-by, and the boy went with them, thinking he had just as good a right as they had.   When they came to the scene of the wedding, the guests were just sitting down to the table, so the dwarfs stuck themselves up between the guests wherever they thought fit, and all began to eat.   As a result there was not enough food for all, which the cook could not understand, as she had prepared as much as at other times.   When they had finished eating, they prepared for dancing, in which the trolls also joined, dancing with their own women.   When the people had danced for some time, some one happened to knock the herd-boy's hat off, and there he stood in his old clothes.   They then wanted to know how he came there, and he told them the whole story, but could not understand how they could not see him before.   As he was coming to the farm he had said "good day" to the folks he passed, but these could see nothing either.

Stealing Music.

"ONE year there was a summer festival at Anders Ander-
sen's, and I played to the dancers—that time they had
the summer festival from Volder-mass (May 1st) until
they 'rode summer out of town' on St. John's Day, and
those who 'went off' paid the musician his fee on Our
Lady Day, and so all was over for that summer. They
danced in the southern length of the village barn, and I
played to them in the afternoon in a way that was a
delight to hear. In the evening they danced by moonlight (for it was full moon), and had all the doors and
windows open. All at once the fiddle became as dumb
as a clog. I waxed my bow and scraped away again, but
it was all the same. I tore and scraped at it, but there
was no more music in it than in an old wooden shoe.
They were dancing 'mollevit,' and I know that at any
other time I could play that till everything rang again,
but now the fellows tramped and stamped quite out of
time, for they could hear no music. When I came home,
Karen was lying awake and said to me, 'It was awful
the way *they* danced and performed under the loom there
all evening. They danced reels and they danced 'mollevit,' and I thought that you sat at the end of the table
and played to them, for I could hear both the tunes just
as clearly as if you were sitting there. Now and again
one of the little things would jump into the air, clap his
wooden shoe and say, 'He thinks he is playing to them
over there, but we are taking his music.' 'Yes, now I
can understand why the fiddle would not sound,' said I,
and went off to my bed."

The Berg-woman's Bread.

IN Volstrup, in Hörmested parish, there was once a large farm, which was split up half a century ago. Long before that time there were once two men, belonging to the farm, ploughing on the fields that lie between it and the large mound to the east. When they came to the east end of the field, close to the mound, they could feel the smell of bread-baking coming from it, and immediately noticed lying there a bread shovel which was broken. From this they guessed that the troll was not at home, and that his wife was in perplexity how to get the bread into the oven, since her shovel was broken.

Fortunately, one of the men had a few nails in his tobacco pouch, and with these he mended the shovel. The other man, who stood and looked on, said then, " Now we shall want some hot bread from the berg-wife for our trouble." " I ask for nothing," said the other. After the men had gone home for dinner, and came back to their ploughing, they found, when they came to the east end of the field, a little tray with two small loaves on it, lying beside the mound. The one who had asked for the bread, was now afraid to eat of it ; whereas the other, who had mended the shovel, ate his, and found himself very well after it. The first, on the other hand, put his in his pocket, to be able to show the girls at the farm the troll-wife's bread. But when he got home, he suddenly took ill and died. He ought not to have despised the bread which he himself had asked for, and still less to have made fun of it. The loaf (a stone shaped like a loaf) was preserved in Volstrup, for many years after, until the farm was burned down, in the beginning of this century.

H

The Old Man of Hoberg.

IN Gotland lies a high mound, known by the name of Hoberg, in which for a long time there lived a powerful berg-troll, who, from his place of residence, was called the "Old Man of Hoberg." Not far away there lived a poor farmer who had intercourse with the troll, from which he thought he might derive some advantage. Many, indeed, assert that those who wish to have good luck in hunting or fishing, should employ such unlawful means, and form connections, with the beings that haunt the woods and lakes.

It so happened that this farmer's wife gave birth to a child, and when it was to be baptised, the farmer was quite puzzled as to whom he should ask to stand god-father to it. The farmer's boy noticed that something was weighing on his master's mind, and being desirous to know what ailed him, the following conversation took place between them.

"I think," said the boy, "that you ought rather to be happy just now, than go and look glum : you have now got an heir, and yet you go about and mope."

"What you say is true enough," answered the farmer, "but, for all that, there is something, that not without good reason troubles and vexes me, and that is, that I now ought to invite some godfathers to the baptism, according to use and wont. Now, if I pass over the Old Man of Hoberg, who has done me so much good, as you very well know, he will be so offended that I can never expect him to do me any further service, however great necessity comes upon me. On the other hand, if I do invite him, he is well enough able to eat up all my food, so that I perhaps would come to stand before the other guests in shame and disgrace, for you know well what a fearful eater and drinker he is, so that it is almost impossible to satisfy him, especially for such a poor man as I am."

" I know that that is the case," said the boy, "but keep your mind easy ; I shall manage things in such a way that there will be no difficulty about what you are so much afraid of. I shall go to him now, and invite him to the feast, but shall talk to him so cleverly that he won't come."

" If you can manage that," said the farmer, " you will do me so great a service that you will, in all justice, deserve to be praised for it, and may expect a reward if you come back with your errand well discharged."

His boy then asked him for a sack, and started on his way to the Old Man of Hoberg. He presented himself before him, and said, " My master sends you his greeting, and asks if you will be so good as to oblige him with some fish, as you have previously been in the habit of doing when he has asked you. This time though, he wants no small ones, nothing but big ones."

" And what is his reason," asked the Old Man, " for wanting only big fish, and no little ones this time ; he has always been quite content with what he could get, big and little mixed."

"Well," said the boy, "he is going to have a christening party, for he has been blessed with a son and heir, and for that reason I have also been sent to invite you to be one of the godfathers."

This greatly delighted the Old Man of Hoberg. " For as old and as gray as I am," said he, "no one has ever done me that honour yet ; give him my compliments, and

thank him from me, for his invitation, and say that I shall
come,—but, I say, who are to be god-fathers besides?"

"St. Peter," said the boy.

"Ah," said the Old Man, "then I am not quite sure if
I can come ; for I have heard that St. Peter is an obstinate
fellow, and for that reason we perhaps might not get on
very well under one roof; but all the same, as your master
has done me the honour to invite me, I shall come, and
see how we can agree together. But are there to be no
more god-fathers?"

"O, yes," said the boy, "Our Lord too."

"Then, I can scarcely come," said the Old Man, "for
St. Peter and I might perhaps have got on together in
the same house, but scarcely Our Lord and I. But, all
the same, since my neighbour has done me the honour, I
shall come, for no one has ever paid me such a compli-
ment before, for as old and gray as I am. But I shall
just set myself in a corner, and see how things go on.
Are there to be any more god-fathers?"

"No," said the boy.

"Then which of the god-mothers is to carry the child?"

"The Virgin Mary," said the boy.

"He is cutting a mighty dash with his god-fathers and
god-mothers," said the Old Man. "I suppose he has engaged some musicians when he is going such a length
with the rest of it."

"Yes," said the boy, "the DRUMMER is to be musician."

"I was really thinking of coming," said the Old Man,
"even although St. Peter and Our Lord were coming, as
he had done me the honour to invite me, but when the
DRUMMER is coming" (by which he understood and meant
thunder), "then I simply won't come, I tell you flat, for a
fortnight ago I was at a party, and, as I was going home,

the clouds came over the sky, and the DRUMMER began
to beat his drum so hard that I grew frightened and
started to run home as fast as ever I could ; but just as I
got to my outer door, he threw one of his drum-sticks
after me " (by this he meant a thunder-bolt), "and broke
one of my thigh-bones, which I feel painful yet, and so I
daren't encounter him in any way. If I were to come
just now, he would perhaps break my other leg for me
this time. So give my regards to your master, and thank
him for the invitation, but say that I can't come—but, I
say, is it the custom to give presents to the child on such
occasions ? "

" O, yes," said the boy, " those who want to be like
their neighbours always give something."

" Come this way then," said the Old Man, " and I will
also send some presents, although I am not coming myself, for I will not be the least in any thing." So he took
the boy with him down into a cave, where there stood
chests filled with dollars and other silver coins, told him
to hold the sack open, took a shovelful of dollars and cast
them into the sack. After he had done this, he asked the
boy if it was customary to give more.

" Well, I have seen some who gave more," said he.

" In no way will I be the least," said the Old Man, and
thereupon took another shovelful and threw it into the
sack, asking as before, if it was customary to give more.

" O, yes," said the boy, " I have seen one person who
gave more."

" Then I won't be the least," said the Old Man, and
again he took a shovelful and threw it into the sack, and
still asked if any one was in the habit of giving more.

" No," said the boy, " I have never seen any one give
more ; " for he had now as much as he could carry, other-

wise he would certainly have said " yes " once again to
the Old Man's question, and so have got him to pour
another shovelful of dollars into the sack.

"Now, go home with that," said the Old Man, "and
come back again, and you shall have the fish."

The boy did so, and in this way he had rendered his
master a great service, since by his cleverness he had not
only contrived to prevent the Old Man of Hoberg from
coming to the christening, but also had got a respectable
present from him.

Bergfolk Militia.

WHEN there was war with England, and the English
fleet tried to seize upon Bornholm, the underground folks
are said to have behaved very bravely.   An English fleet
lay off Povlsker parish, and the inhabitants of Bornholm
had therefore to keep watch on the south coast.   One
night there was only one man on the watch, and before
he knew of anything the English began to fire.   At first
the man did not know what to do, but he then heard
voices saying, " Fire, fire."   (The underground folks cannot shoot until a Christian man has first done so.)   The
man obeyed and fired off his rifle against the English,
and immediately heard round about him " paf, paf," and
saw how the hats flew off the heads of those on board the
ships.   The English turned and fled in hot haste.   At
this same time many are said to have heard the underground folks piping, drumming, and rattling their sabres
and guns, and have often seen and heard them drilling
on Rispe-bjærg.

They have also cavalry, who have been seen riding

about after sunset. Some say that their horses have only
three legs, but others have seen the tracks of four feet on
the newly fallen snow.

The Herd-boy and the Bergman.

A FARMER on Tyholm, who always treated his servants
badly, had once a little herd-boy, whom he regularly
thrashed for the smallest fault, so that the boy was naturally very much afraid of his severe master. One evening,
when he brought home some cattle, it so happened that
a black ox was missing. The farmer was furious, and
gave him a good thrashing, after which he drove him out
of the farm, saying, "Don't you come home again before
you find that ox." It was a dark night and the boy was
very much frightened for ghosts ; the church lay close at
hand, and he had heard so many stories of people who
walked after death. So he went out on the open fields
and cried, until he came to a mound, out of which he saw
a little man come and make straight for him. He was
frightened in earnest now, and screamed loudly, but the
little man said to him, "What are you crying for, my
little boy ? " "Oh, I have lost an ox, and I daren't go
home before I have found it, or the man will kill me."
" No, that he won't ; just come with me, and it may be
that I shall be able to help you." The boy followed the
little man into the mound, and the latter gave him a
spoonful of porridge. "Oh, that was rare porridge," said
the boy. "May I not have another spoonful ? I seem to
grow so strong with it." "Yes, of course you may," said
the little man, and gave him another spoonful. "I should

like to have yet another," said the boy. "Well, take it
then, but you must promise me three things: firstly, that
you will go home and not bother yourself about the ox :
secondly, that when you go home and the man comes out
to you and threatens to strike you, you shall go to the
stone that the horses are tied to, pull it up, and throw it
at him; then he will let you alone; and thirdly, you must
promise me never to do harm to any one with your
strength." The boy promised all this to the berg-man,
and went home again. His master came out and asked
whether he had found the ox, and was about to strike
him for not having done so, when the boy went up to the
stone, pulled it out of the ground and threw it at him.
The farmer retired inside as quickly as possible, and after
that never tried again to strike the boy who had now acquired such strength. Next day the boy found the ox
lying quietly in the churchyard.

The Bergfolk's Present.

IN a mound a few hundred ells straight east from Grön-
bæk farm in Haarup there lived bergfolk. The little
folk were often seen going about beside the mound, and
sometimes when they had an entertainment the mound
stood on glowing pillars. At that time there stood a
house to the south of the farm, the well of which may still
be seen. The housewife there lived on a good understanding with the berg-folk, who one day presented her
with a skirt, which they said she might put on every day
without wearing it out, and it would even become more
beautiful the longer she used it, only she must never enter
a church with it. One Sunday morning, as she was

sweeping out her house, she heard the bells of Linaa Kirk ringing, and thought it was high time she was setting out. She looked down at her skirt, which had now become really beautiful, and thought that she had nothing finer to go in than that. She hastily made herself ready, and went to church without thinking of the berg-folk's warning, but as she entered the porch of the church the beautiful skirt disappeared, and she was left with her plain underskirt, and had to hurry home again. After that she saw no more of the berg-folk, and regretted deeply having disobeyed them.

The Bergman's Beetles.

So far as I know, my nurse assigned the following incident to the mounds that lie beside Tuesböl. One Sunday a girl was going past them on her way to church. It was a winter's day, and there lay a thin coating of snow on the ground, but it was bright sunshine. She looked up to the south side of this mound, which faced the sun, and saw that it was all covered with dung beetles. " That is strange," thought she, " but no one will believe me when I tell it, so I will take a few of these beetles with me," and accordingly she put a few of them into one of her gloves. It happened as she expected ; folk laughed at her when she told of this strange sight. " Well, you'll see them here," said she, and shook out her glove, but now they were gold pieces. They were not slow in making for the mound then, but when they got there the bergman had got all his beetles gathered in.

The Red Stone on Fuur.

ON Fuur lies the Red Stone, a crag of rough-grained sandstone, from twelve to sixteen ells high, with a deep hole in it close to the ground. Here the berg-folk hold their goings-on, so that no one dares to come too near the Red Stone after sunset. Once, on a dark and rainy October evening, two boys were herding sheep on the braes round about, and on account of the bad weather sought shelter in a hole in the crag. The boldest of them wished to examine it more closely, and although advised against it by the other, tied a rope round his body, and went further in. He was away a long time, and finally, his comrade heard a faint crying from the nether depths, pulled the rope and brought it out, but with the end of it burned. The boy was never seen nor heard of again.

Another time, a man came riding past it, late in the evening. The moon was shining brightly, and by its light he saw little figures busily moving backwards and forwards. He looked closer and saw that it was the berg-imps, carrying their golden treasures out to some little hillocks to air them. The man happened to have his gun with him, and knowing that if one could manage to shoot three times over them the treasures would be his, he fired the shots. He ought now to have left the treasure lying till day had dawned, and the elves, who naturally avoid the light, had hidden themselves in the depths of the stone; but he was so greedy for the treasures that he straightway put them into a sack, and rode off as fast as he could. The little fellows set out after him, and while he was still upon the road between the banks, he was caught up by a little man with a long beard, on a horse no bigger than a cat, but headless. The little man stopped him, and asked whether they should not let their horses fight each other. " No, God forbid," said the other in a fright. Then the berg-sprite offered to let his little black dog fight the other's, or, preferably man against man ; but to every proposal the man answered with his " God forbid," and hurried off home as hard as he could. When he got inside, it seemed to him as if all at once it began to storm and howl in the house, and that it was in flames in every corner. The man, who guessed the reason, took the sack and threw it out in despair. " You have quite enough yet," said a thin, little voice outside, and next morning he found a heavy silver cup, which had fallen down behind the chest of drawers, and made him a wealthy man as long as he lived.

The Silver Cup from Dagberg Daas.

IN Dagberg Daas there formerly lived a berg-man with his family. It happened once that a man who came riding past there took it into his head to ask the berg-woman for a little to drink. She went to get some for him, but her husband bade her take it out of the poisoned barrel. The traveller heard all this, however, and when the berg-woman handed him the cup with the drink, he threw the contents over his shoulder, and rode off with the cup in his hand, as fast as his horse could gallop. The berg-woman threw her breasts over her shoulders, and ran after him as hard as she could. (The man rode off over some ploughed land, where she had difficulty in following him, as she had to keep the line of the furrows). When he reached the spot where Karup Stream crosses the road from Viborg to Holtebro, she was so near him

that she snapped a hook (*hage*) off the horse's shoe, and
therefore the place has been called Hagebro ever since.
She could not cross the running water, and so the man
was saved. It was afterwards seen that some drops of
the liquor had fallen on the horse's loins and taken off
both hide and hair.

One-leg and the Stolen Goblet.

A LITTLE over a mile south from Slagelse, on the left
side of the road between Skörping and Flakke-bjærg, on
the fields belonging to the village of Skörping, there
stood some years ago a mound, now almost entirely
levelled, known as Barnet. A peasant from Flakke-
bjærg was riding home from Slagelse one evening, and
on approaching Barnet he saw the whole mound standing
on four glowing pillars, while on drawing nearer he could
see a crowd of little creatures dancing merrily about beneath it. The man stopped for a little to look at the
sport, and while doing so one of the trolls came hopping
out to him on one leg, bringing a large goblet, which he
offered him to drink from. The man pretended to drink,
but poured the contents over his back, and some of these
falling on the horse's loins took off both hide and hair.
He kept hold of the goblet and rode off, the troll following. He rode as hard as he could, but midway between
Barnet and Flakke-bjærg the troll had almost caught up
to him. There lived, however, an old female troll in
Hö-dysse, which stands on the fields of Flakke-bjærg,
and she had come to be on bad terms with the troll in
Barnet. She therefore came running and called to the
man, ".Off the smooth and on the rough, then One-leg

can never catch you, and make for the holy place!"
Thereupon the man rode into the ploughed land, and
right across the fields, where the troll had to run up one
field and down the other, and was left a little behind.
The man made straight for the church, rode close up to
the churchyard wall, and quickly sprang off the horse's
back to the inside of that, but the troll was then so close
behind him that he had very nearly got hold of him.
When he saw that the man had escaped, he hurled the
horse over the wall after him, and broke all its ribs.

The goblet was afterwards given by the man to the
church, where it is said to be still used as a communion-
cup. When the trolls saw that One-leg did not get hold
of the man, one of them hurled a huge stone at Flakke-
bjærg church, but it fell short and dropped into the
stream at the foot of the slope. It is a stone of four or five
ells in thickness and the same in height, and the impression of the troll's fingers are still plainly to be seen.

The Bergfolk pass over Limfjord.

ABOUT half a Danish mile east from Lundby lies a farm,
which is called Loen, where there has been a ferry across
to the lime-kiln which lies opposite. From this kiln
many of the people in Vendsyssel got their lime. Many
travellers crossed over there, as they did not require to
show a passport, which they had to do at Lundby. In
consequence of this, there was a great traffic at this point
in olden times. One day there came to the ferry a man
with some bundles under his arm, and asked the ferrymen to take him over for payment, but he would not
have all the bundles taken over at once. The ferrymen

were quite willing, but were not a little surprised when they got out from land, for the boat sank so deep that the water almost came into it. In this way the man was ferried over three times with his bundles, and each time they were almost sinking, so heavy a load had they with them ; yet the ferrymen could see nothing except the man, and some insignificant bundles. When they had finished the work, and been paid for their trouble, the stranger asked them if they would not like to see what they had sailed with, for it was certainly a long time since they had carried over such loads. The ferrymen were naturally eager enough, as they could not in the least understand what it was they had taken over. Then the stranger took his hat and put it on the head of the chief ferryman, who now to his great astonishment could see that it was just like a little market of bergfolk, nisses and elves. After that, each of the other ferrymen got a turn of the hat and saw the same thing. Then the stranger told them that he was a human being like themselves, but that before his baptism he had been carried off from his parents by the berg-folk, and had been with them ever since, and had now been compelled to help them to get over Limfjord. He told them also that they had come there to be taken across, since no pass was required, whereas at Lundby they could not get over without it. The ferryman asked him why they wanted to cross. The man said, "Christianity has grown too strong for them, and they can stay here no longer, so they are departing for the heathens' land."

Reimer the Ferryman's Aerial Voyage.

AT Ottesund Ferry on Limfjord there is said to have
lived a ferryman of the name of Reimer.   He had gone
to Copenhagen to get licence to ferry over the Sound.   It
took a long time to get the thing properly arranged, so
that it was only on Christmas Eve that he got finished
with the Lords of Council.   As he went along the street
there and wished within himself that he was at home that
evening, and was greatly vexed that he was not so, he
met a little old man in a grey coat, who addressed him
by name, and asked " Wouldn't you like very much to
get home this evening yet ? "   Yes, of course he would,
but it was impossible.   " O, no," said the little man, "if
you will do me in return a service that I shall shortly
have need of, which you can easily render, and for which
I shall also pay you richly, you shall be home this very
evening, at supper time, quite unharmed."   Yes, but
Reimer would first like to know what service he was to
do to the stranger.   " Just this," said he, " that you, and
your ferrymen, one night shall carry cargoes for me from
the south to the north side of the Sound, and for that you
have now a licence, and legal permission."   Well, there
was no objection to that, Reimer said, but what means
of conveyance were they to have ?   " We shall both
mount my horse," said the little man, "you will sit behind
me ; the horse is only a little one, but I know how to
guide it."   Outside one of the city gates they both
mounted the little horse, and then went through the air
like a flash of lightning, without meeting anything until
two hours after they had begun their journey ; then Reimer
heard a clink, as if two pieces of iron struck each other.
" What might that be ? " he asked.   " O, nothing except

that the beast's hind shoe touched the spire of Viborg Cathedral," said the little man. Soon after Reimer dismounted in his own courtyard, and his guide disappeared that same moment.

Pleased to be home again, Reimer forgot his promise in a few day's time ; but one evening the little man came and reminded him of it. He made haste then to get all his things ready, and waited quietly till such time as the promised service should be required of him. After some time had passed, his travelling companion came to him one evening, as it was growing dark, and told him to come now, with all his men. The ferry-boats came and went the whole night, and many heavy chests and boxes were ferried over, but they saw no people except the one man. When they had finished, the bergman took a basket, opened one of the chests, and out of it filled the basket with chinking coin, gave it to Reimer, and said, "Take that for your trouble and goodwill towards one that you know not, but don't thank me for it. I suppose you would like to know what you have ferried over to-night ; there you can see it," taking the cap off his own head, and putting it on Reimer's. Thereupon he saw the whole beach swarming with little dwarfs of both sexes, many thousands of them, at least. Quite terrified, Reimer snatched the cap off his head, and asked the old man, "But where are you going to with all this?" "Further north," said the bergman. "Why so?" asked Reimer again. "Because Christianity is pushing further and further up from the south," said the old man, "but will hardly get up to the Ice Sea in my time, so we are going there."

The Bergman in Mesing Bank.

IN old days there lived a bergman, in a bank beside
Mesing Mill on Hindsholm. On the same bank there lay
a house, the people of which had always bad luck with
their calves. Every time they tried to rear one, it took
ill and died ; the reason for this, however, was that the
calves' stall was right above the bergman's table, and the
wet dripped down into his room, and caused him great
annoyance, so he always put an end to the calves. The
people of the house did not know the reason of their misfortune, but one day they had a visit of a man who, when
they spoke about their calves, advised them to shift their
stall, and they would find that the calves would thrive
well enough. They followed his advice, and from that
time forward they were not only successful with their
calves, but everything else went remarkably well with
them, so that the farmer became a man of means. The
man, however, who had given him the good advice was
the bergman himself, who often took upon himself human
form, and went about among folk. For a time all went
well, but then Dr. Martin (Luther) came into the country,
and the bergman could stay there no longer for the ringing of bells, and singing of psalms, for these kind of folk
cannot bear that. So he went to Norway and lived in
Dovrefell. There he often went about in the coast towns,
and enjoyed himself, particularly when he met any one
from Denmark. Once, in Bergen, he met with a merchant
from Kerteminde, and on hearing where he came from,
asked him to take a parcel to the afore-mentioned farmer,
at Mesing Mill. The merchant promised to do so, and
the farmer received the present, which consisted of a
beautiful belt, set with gold and precious stones. The

I

belt was for his wife, who was delighted with it, but her husband thought that it was not suitable to the rest of her dress, and to their position in life. One day they were going to a party, and the woman wanted to try on the beautiful belt, but her husband said, " There is no use in that, it only looks bad when a common woman like you, in your home-made clothes, goes about with such a belt ; folks will only make a fool of you when they see you." The woman, however, thought that she would just like to see how the belt would look on her. " You will see that best," said the man, " if you go out and fasten it round the tree in front of the window there." The woman did so, and as they now stood and looked at the magnificent belt, the tree began to shake and rock— stronger and stronger, till it finally tore itself loose from the earth, and took its way northwards through the air. Both the man and his wife thanked Our Lord that she had not the belt on, for then she would have flown off to Dovrefell. How the bergman was pleased to get a big ash tree instead of the woman, there is no one here that knows.

Dwarfs in the Færöes.

DWARFS are short and thick ; beardless, but not at all ugly. They live in large stones or in mounds at the bottom of high rocks ; such dwarf-stones are to be found in many places all over the islands. The dwarfs are well-disposed, but cannot bear any quarrelling near their dwelling ; at that they get angry and go away. The large dwarf-stone on Skuö is cleft in two, because two boys happened to quarrel and fight while beside it ; then the dwarfs fled and split the stone. They are excellent smiths, and it was from them that men first learned to harden steel in water; before that they beat out the iron and worked it by hammering it while cold. Their tools can work by themselves. The dwarfs' power lies in the belt which they wear round their waist; if that is taken from one he is powerless, and can be compelled to make whatever one asks of him, and to give valuable things to get back the belt. Under the stones in which they live, there may often be seen ashes which are swept out of their smithy.

In Goosedale stands a cliff inhabited by dwarfs, inside which they are sometimes heard working. A poor man, who had once gone north to Tongue to set up peats, saw the cliff open and the dwarfs at work inside it. He went nearer to look at them, when one of them came to the door, and said, "Inquisitive were you, for as poor as you are; but you shall have this knife;" and with that he threw out to him a knife, so sharp that it cut everything that touched its edge, however hard it might be.

The Dwarfs in Smithdale.

IN Smeddal, on Fille-fell, where there has once been an iron-work, dwarfs had their smithy in old days, and prepared all the iron that they used, but when the church music from Thomas Kirk, which stood at the eastern end of the dale, sounded in the ears of the dwarfs, they withdrew further up into the fells, leaving their tools and their other things behind. Second-sighted folk can still see huge bars of iron, heavy anvils and tongs, lying under the cliff, but it is useless to try to remove them. Now

that the church has been pulled down, it is maintained
that the dwarfs again potter about in their old haunts.

The Last Dwarfs in Iceland.

THE poet Gudmund Bergthor's son was all paralysed on
one side, and this was variously attributed to his mother
and nurse having quarrelled violently over his cradle, or
to his mother's imprecations, which took effect on him
and made him a cripple all his days. Gudmund is
generally reputed to have been one of the most powerful
of those poets in whose verses lie magic powers (*krapta-
skáld,*) but he did not use his gift merely to injure others,
as he often saved men from the attacks of ghosts and evil
spirits by means of it, and only came a little short of
healing his own infirmity. A man named Andrès Jónsson, who lived near Gudmund's home at Hóls-búd, is said
to have told the following to a friend in the north.
"When I was about twenty years old I heard Gudmund
say that now there were only two dwarfs left in Iceland,
one of whom lived in some cliffs north on Lánga-ness
strand, while the other was his dear neighbour, and lived
in a stone not far from Hóls-búd. The latter had an
ointment that could cure him of his infirmity if he could
only get it, but he was afraid that it would never be his
fortune to rid himself of the powerful spells under which
he had innocently fallen."

One summer, on a holy day, when all or most of the
others had gone to church except Gudmund and Andres,
Gudmund said to him, "Now I will make a bargain with
you, friend, for I have always found you faithful and
secret ; you shall carry me east from the house to the big

stone that stands there, which I shall point out to you."
Andrès was willing, and carried him to the stone, setting
him down over against it as he was directed. Gudmund
seemed to him then so earnest that he could not look
into his eyes. He told Andrès to go home again and
not come to him before mid-evening, nor tell anyone
where he was, no matter who asked after him or what
they might want. Andrès promised all this and went
home. Soon after mid-day a man came to Hóls-búd in
great excitement, and asked for Gudmund. Andrès said
he knew nothing about him, he was not at home, and had
perhaps got himself taken to the church, as he often did,
what did he want with him? The man answered, " My
daughter at home is tormented by an evil spirit or a
ghost sent to trouble her. He came upon her last night,
and she is like a mad thing. I wanted to ask Gudmund's
help and advice, knowing that he would not refuse me
his assistance where the life and welfare of my daughter
was at stake, and I call upon you in the name of all the
saints to tell me the truth, for he must be told about her
condition." Andrès tried to get out of it as long as he
could, and made many excuses, but all to no purpose,
and at last he had to agree to see what Gudmund would
say. He went to the spot where he had left him, and
saw that Gudmund had succeeded in charming the dwarf
out of the stone, and close up to himself, with a large box
of ointment in his hand. On seeing the man appear, the
dwarf was so startled that he went back like lightning
into the stone, which immediately closed up again.
Gudmund felt this deeply, and said that he would never
have the good fortune to escape from his hard lot; " I
am destined," said he, " to bear my weakness to the grave,
and the Lord's will be done, for now no human power can
avail to bring the dwarf out again."

IV.—ELVES OR HULDU-FOLK.

The Origin of the Elves.

ONE time God Almighty came to Adam and Eve. They received him heartily, and showed him all their household possessions, as well as their children, whom he thought very promising. He asked Eve whether they had no more children than those she had just shown him. She said "No ;" but the fact was that Eve had not got some of the children washed, and was ashamed to let God see them, so she kept them out of the way. God knew this, and said, "That which has been hid from me shall also be hid from men." These children now became invisible to mortals, and lived in holts and heaths, in knolls and stones. From these are the elves descended, but men are descended from those of Eve's children which she showed to God. Mortal men can never see elves, unless they wish it themselves, but they can both see mortals and give mortals power to see them.

The Elves' House.

GUDMUND MAGNUSSON tells of his ancestor Olaf Sigurdsson, that in his young days he was once out looking after sheep, somewhere in Skagi in the North of Iceland. It was thick mist ; Olaf had walked far, and had grown thirsty. Coming to a farm house, he knocked at the door, and a woman came to it. Olaf asked her for something to drink, and she went in to get it, while he remained standing outside. Looking into the passage, he saw many things that he had never seen before, though others were quite familiar, but what seemed most curious to him, was that everything which is usually made of *iron* was here made of *clay*. It now dawned upon him that this was an elf-house, and with that he took to his heels and ran away, but before he had gone far, the woman called after him, and he dared not but stop. "Ill have you done," said the woman, "in not even waiting to get the milk. You might well understand that I should do you some mischief for that, but so much good fortune has been granted you, that no spell of mine will have any effect on you. At the same time, I shall see to it that your cowardice is visited on your children." The woman said no more, and Olaf ran off with his heart in his mouth. Her spell, however, apparently had its effect; Olaf was a great man all his days, but some of his children were weak-minded.

A Fairy Birth.

AT Skúms-stadir, in Landeyar in the district of Rángár-valla, there once lived a farmer, who had a good-looking wife and many children. One evening during the winter he was out in the stack-yard, while his wife was inside preparing food. There came to her then a man she had never seen before, and asked her to help his wife, who was in labour. She tried hard to get out of it, saying that she had never waited on a woman, but he only pressed her the more, until she agreed to go with him. They went on together, until they came to a high knoll, which opened up at their approach. The man went in first, and the woman after, but she took care to lay her gloves on the mound above the door, in order to ensure her return. On entering the mound she saw nothing but a bed, and in it a woman in great pain. She passed her hands over her, at which she felt some relief, and soon after gave birth to a child. The farmer's wife took the child, and gave it all the usual care and attention, after which the man opened a box, and took out of it a stone, which he asked her to rub round the eyes of the child. The woman did not understand what this meant, but thought to herself that it could hardly do her any harm, though she rubbed one of her own eyes with it, and this she did without the man being any the wiser. Then she saw other people going about in the mound, and some sitting at work, but kept this to herself. The fairy-man then saw her home again, and thanked her for coming with him.

The following summer the farmer went to Eyrarbakki with his wares, and was accompanied by his wife. On the return journey, they stopped for the night beside Egils-stadir on Thjórs-á. All had gone to rest, but the farmer's wife could not sleep, and by and by she pulled aside the edge of the tent, and looked out. There, with her second-sighted eye, she saw a man come to the meal-sacks which belonged to the travellers; these he opened and took a handful out of each, which he put into a bag that he carried under his arm. When he had nearly filled the bag, the woman spoke to him, saying, "Why are you doing that?" He looked at her in surprise, and said, " How can you see me?" and with that he blew upon her,

so that she plainly felt it, and from that time she could
see no fairies.

Baptizing a Fairy-child.

ONE time long ago, while a party was gathering Icelandic
moss at Reyk-hólar, a girl disappeared in a thick mist
that came upon them, nor was she found again all that
summer.   A wise man was then asked to search for her
by means of his magic arts, and find out where she had
gone to, and bring her back.   This he succeeded in doing,
and after her return her master, the priest, never let her
be left by herself.   One time, however, it happened that
she was sent out into the church, and before long her
master went to look for her, suspecting that something
had happened ; when he entered the church she had disappeared.   He then looked about him, and saw a man in
a red kirtle riding away with the girl behind him.   Time
went on and nothing was heard of her, until the priest's
wife dreamed that the man who had carried off the girl
came to her, and brought her greetings from his wife, with
the request to baptize the child that would be found lying
in its cradle before the church door when she awoke ; the
priest should have for his fee the vestment that was over
the cradle.   The priest's wife then awoke, and found
everything as she had dreamed it.   The cradle was at the
place stated, with the child in it, and over it a costly
priest's vestment and a linen surplice.   The priest baptized the child, and it was put back in the cradle as before.   He kept the vestment, but laid the surplice over
the cradle again.   A little later both cradle and child had
disappeared, but the surplice was left behind.

The Changeling.

ONCE there was a double household at Sogn in Kjós, and one of the men had a son, who was thought not to have all his wits. He learned nothing and never did anything, but lay continually in bed, though he was always ready enough for his food. It was generally believed that he was a changeling, but for long this was uncertain. One time, however, when he was of age to be confirmed, every one had gone out of the room except a woman, who was lying in her bed with a child beside her. After all had gone out, she heard the lad begin to yawn loudly, until she at last began to be terrified at the way he went on. Then she heard him begin to toss about in the bed and stretch himself, and next she became aware that he had stood up in the bed, and stretched himself till he reached almost up to the roof of the room. This was so built that it had short beams between the rafters, and as he yawned and brought his face near one of these, the beam came right into his open mouth, so that his upper jaw rested above it, while the under one lay below it. At the same time he became so ugly and horrible to look at, that the woman was mortally afraid, and cried out in terror, knowing herself to be alone in the room with him. As soon as she did so, he shot down again into his bed, and was in his usual shape when the folk came in again. After this it was thought that there was no doubt of his being a changeling.

The Father of Eighteen Children.

ONE summer all the folk on a farm were in the fields except the housewife, who was left at home with a child

of three or four years old.   The boy had thriven well up
to this time, and was in every way a promising child.
Having a good deal to do, his mother had left him for a
little, while she went out to wash her milk-dish in a stream
not far from the house.   On her return, whenever she
spoke to the child, it cried and howled in a way that surprised her, for hitherto it had been so good and quiet.
From this time it never spoke a word, and was so fretful
and cross, that the woman could not understand the
change in it.   It grew no bigger, and seemed a perfect
idiot. Greatly vexed at this, she consulted her neighbour,
who was believed to be a wise woman.   The latter, after
hearing all her story, said, "Don't you think, my dear, it
is a changeling?   I expect it must have been exchanged
when you left it alone on that occasion."   "I don't know,"
said the mother; "can you tell me any plan to find that
out?"   "I shall try," said the neighbour.   "Some time
you must leave the child all alone by itself, and let something strange happen in its sight.   It will speak then,
when it sees no one near it, and you must listen and hear
what it says.   If you think its words strange and suspi-
cious, then beat it unmercifully till something happens."

With this they parted, and the woman returned home,
thanking her neighbour for her advice.   Arrived at home,
she set a little pot in the middle of the kitchen floor.
Then she took a number of sticks, and tied them, one to
the end of another, until the upper end of them reached
up into the chimney.   To the lower end she then tied the
porridge-stick, and let the whole thing stand in the pot.
These preparations made, she brought the child, and left
him alone in the kitchen, while she went outside, and
stood listening where she could see into the kitchen from
behind the door.   Before long she saw the child begin to

walk round the pot with the stick in it, looking at it, and finally heard it say, "Now I am as old as may be seen by my beard, the father of eighteen children in the elf-world, but never have I seen so long a stick in so little a pot." The woman now entered the kitchen with a fine switch, took the changeling and thrashed him long and unmercifully, while he howled terribly. After she had done this for some time, she saw a strange woman coming into the kitchen with a beautiful boy in her arms, with which she played, and said to the woman, "We behave very differently: I dandle your child, and you beat my husband." Having said this, she set down the child, which was the housewife's real son, and left it there, while she took with her her husband, and the two immediately disappeared.

Making a Changeling.

KRISTIN, who lived at Minni-Thverá (apparently in Skagafirth district) about 1830-1840, told of her mother, who was second-sighted, that she was once out on the meadows with Kristin's grandmother, and saw two women coming down from the mountain, leading between them a man who was carrying something. On coming near, they took the bundle off the carl, and she then saw that it was a cradle covered with red. They then took the carl and began to beat him, while he grew less and less till he was quite a little fellow. They took him again, and squeezed him till he was as small as a child in the cradle. Then they laid him in the cradle, spread the red cloth over him, and made for the farm, carrying the whole thing between them. The girl told her mother what she had seen, who immediately ran home and got to her child's cradle, which she had left standing in front of the house, before the fairy-women reached it. When the latter saw this they took the child they were carrying out of the cradle, slapped it, beat it and drove it on before them. With that the carl quickly began to grow big again, until he was just as he had been originally, and held with them up into the fells, where they all disappeared.

The Child and the Fairy.

AT Heidar-bót in Reykja-hverf, in the district of Thingey, it happened one evening that while a woman was in the byre, one of her children went out of the house, intending to follow its mother thither. On going out at the door, it saw her standing in front of the house. She signed to it in silence, and clapped her thigh, walking off slowly and still beckoning it to come. Above the farm are some pointed cliffs known as the "Steeples." The woman made her way to these, enticing the child to follow her, and finally disappeared with it into one of the steeples, for it was not the child's mother at all, but an elf-woman. When the mother returned from the byre, she missed her child and made enquiry after it, but those in the house thought it had been with her. Its parents were panic-struck; a party was gathered and search made, but it could not be found, wherever they sought for it. At Sand there lived a man named Arnor, who was reckoned a wizard. To him the mother went to ask counsel, and arrived there late in the day. Arnor invited her to stay all night, and this she accepted. He asked her all about the child's disappearance, and she told him all the facts. That evening, about the same time, Arnor took a knife and cut three triangular pieces out of the floor of the room. As he cut the last one, a loud crash was heard. He then replaced the pieces on the floor, and told the woman that she might sleep soundly all night, for the child had come back. Next day she went home and the child had come, but it was thought strange that one of its cheeks was blue, and never afterwards lost that colour. The child was now asked where it had been, and told about the woman who had enticed it up to the Steeples, and carried it in there, whereupon it saw that she was not its mother. It tasted no food there, because it all seemed to be red. The evening that Arnor cut the pieces out of the floor, there fell three stones out of the mountain, all three-cornered. At the last of these, the fairy took up the child in a great rage, ran with it to the farm, and gave it a good slap in the face at parting ; that was the noise that was heard after the last piece was cut out, and for this reason one of its cheeks was blue. The child's name was Gudmund, who afterwards lived there in the north, and had a daughter named Elizabeth, whose descendants lived in Eyafirth.

Carried off by the Fairies.

In the east of Iceland, it happened that a farmer's daughter disappeared from her home, and could not be found though searched for far and wide. Her parents were greatly distressed, and the farmer went to a priest, whom he knew to be wiser in many things than other men. The priest received him well, and the man begged him to devise some plan, that would enable him to know whether his daughter was alive or dead. The priest then told him that she had been carried off by the elves, and that he would have no pleasure in seeing her again. The man however would not believe this, and asked the priest to help him to get her back, and in the end, by reason of the man's persistence, the priest fixed an evening on which he should come again to him. This the man did at the time appointed, and after all had gone to bed, the priest called him outside, where there stood a horse saddled and bridled. The priest mounted this, and told the man to get on behind him. They then rode off, nor did the man know how long they had ridden, till at last they came to the sea. The priest rode out into the sea for a considerable distance, until they came to some high cliffs. Up under these he rode, and onwards until he stopped at a place in front of the cliffs. These opened up then, and it seemed just as if there was a house-door in them : inside there was a blazing light that made everything perfectly clear, and there the man saw people going to and fro, both men and women. Among these he saw one woman, who had a face of a bluish colour, with a white cross on the forehead. The priest asked him how he liked the one with the cross. " Not well," said he. " Yet this woman is your daughter," said the priest, " and I shall get her, if you wish, but she has now become like a troll from living with these folk." The man said he did not wish it, and asked the priest to leave as quickly as possible, for he had no heart to look on this any longer. The priest turned about his horse, and rode home the same way again, without any one knowing of their journey. The farmer went home again next day, sad and sorrowful, and no more is told of him.

The Girl and the Elf-brothers.

THERE was once a married couple who had a daughter, who disappeared every evening in the gloaming. Her mother did not care much for her, and spoke little to her; but on the farm there was an old woman, who was very fond of the girl. The daughter would never tell her mother where she went to, but when the old woman asked her about it, she told her that a little way off on the farm there was a mound to which she went. Two brothers lived in it, and were glad to see her, but she was not pleased that she never saw a Bible there. Time passed till the girl was confirmed, and went to the altar on the following Sunday. In the evening, the old woman told her to go to the mound, and see how she would be received. She did so, and on her return said that they had received her kindly, but refused to kiss her, saying that a black spot had come upon her lips. Thus time passed, until a man came to ask her hand. He received this at once, and she went away with him. Three years later, she came to visit her parents again, and the old woman told her to go to the mound, and see how things were there. She did so, and returned in a very short time. "How are things going on there?" asked the old woman. "Well enough," said she; "but I saw only one of the brothers, and he told me the other had died of grief." She went home again with her husband, and there the story ends.

Ima the Elf-girl.

THERE was a man named Jón Gudmundsson, who lived at Beru-nes in Reydar-firth. Many stories were told of him after his own days, for he was believed to be wise in many things, and mixed up with magic arts, like many others at that time. He was brought up at Beru-nes, and herded sheep when he was grown up. One time, it is told, he was watching the ewes at the head of a glen in the hill above the farm, when there came to him a young girl, who was very pleasant with him. He asked her name, and she said it was Ima, and that her father and mother lived in the hill there. She was wonderfully familiar with Jón, and told him all about her father's house. Among other things, she told him that her father had a book, in which there was much marvellous lore, and from which one might learn much; anyone who read it would become a poet with magic powers in his verse, and few things would come on him unawares. Jón asked her whether she could not procure the book for him, but she said that that was almost impossible, her father guarded it so carefully. Jón then pressed her to get a loan of it for him for a little time. She answered that she was ready to do· most things to win his love, and would try to procure the book ; but if her father came to know of it, it would probably cost her her life. She stayed with Jón until he drove his sheep home in the evening, and next day she came with the book, and bade him keep good faith with her, as she would come for it in a fortnight. Jón promised this, and was very nice with her in every way. At the appointed time, Ima came and asked him for the book, saying that both her own life and his were at stake, if this came to be known. Jón replied that he could not want the book, and would never let it go. Ima threw her arms round his neck, and begged him with tears not to break his promise to her ; but he said that neither prayers nor entreaties would help her, he would not let the book go.

K

" You do ill in this," said she, "when my life depends on it ; but all the same I cannot deal with you as you have deserved, so much do I love you." So she parted with him sorrowful and angry, and their meeting-place has since been known as Imu-botnar.

After this, and a little before Christmas, Jón dreamed one night that a man came to him and addressed him, saying that he had come to warn him of the danger that was hanging over him. Everything had now come out about the book that Ima had lent him, and they were coming to him for it on Christmas Eve. " Her father means to kill you. There will be four of us, the carl, the carline, Ima, and I. I warn you of this because I am tired of life ; I was of the race of mortals, but was taken away by the elves. About midnight on Christmas Eve they will enter the house. You must sit up on the dais with a large knife beside you, and as soon as you hear them come to the door of the room, you must spring up, go down into the passage, and kill the one that comes first, and then the others in turn. I will put myself but little forward, and will protect you as well as I can against the attacks of the others. You will succeed in overcoming them, and I shall be severely wounded, and do you remember then to put me quickly out of pain, for I wish to live no longer. When you have killed them, you must drag them out of the house and burn them, and be finished with this before daybreak." After this the man disappeared, and Jón awoke. Everything went as he had been told in the dream, after all the others had gone to church on Christmas Eve, and Jón was left at home alone. He mentions the incident himself in the introductory verses to one of his ballads.

The Elfin Fisherman.

IT is told that in former days a farmer lived at Götur in
Mýr-dal, who in the season went out to fish beside
Dýr-hólar island. One time, as he was returning from
the sea, and crossing the mires on his way home, he came
in the twilight upon a man whose horse had fallen, and
could not be got up without assistance. The farmer did
not know the man, but helped him up with his horse.
When this was done, the stranger said to him, " I am
your neighbour, for I live in Hvamms-gil, and am just
returning from the sea, like yourself, but I am so poor
that I cannot pay you for your assistance as it deserves.
However, if you follow my advice, you shall have this
good of me, that you will never have to go on a useless
journey to the sea, but only on the condition that you
never set out until you see me do so. If you observe this,
you will never fail to get out to fish whenever you go
down to the shore." The farmer thanked him for his
counsel, and for three years he never set out unless when
he saw his neighbour do so, nor was he ever unsuccessful
in getting out to sea all that time. One day, however,
it happened that the weather in the morning was splendid
for fishing, and all went down to the shore at once, but
the farmer could not see his neighbour, though he waited
long for him. Finally he could stand it no longer, and
went off without seeing him, but when he got to the shore
all the boats had gone. That day all the boats were
caught in a storm, but the farmer escaped by not getting
one in the morning. During the following night he
dreamed that his neighbour came to him, and said, " You
got this much good of me, that you did not go to sea to-
day ; but because you set out without seeing me, you will

not require to wait for me any more, for I do not mean to let you see me again after this, since you did not follow my instructions."

The Elfin Cow.

ONE time when a farmer in the West Firths went into his byre, he saw standing there a grey cow which did not belong to him. He bit the cow's ear so that it bled, and thus it became his, and could not go away again.

During the night his wife dreamed that a woman came to her, and said, " Your husband did ill to mark my cow as his own, and leave me without any support for myself and my children, seeing that I had no other cow giving milk this winter. For your sake I will do him no harm, but only on condition that he shall give me one share of his fish every time he goes to sea, all through the winter up to Cross-mass (May 3). This he shall lay aside un-cleaned, and I will come for it. I also want the cow's calf, when that comes." The farmer's wife agreed to all this, and the woman went away. The wife told her husband all the talk she had had with the elf-woman, and begged him not to break any of the promises she had made. To this he agreed.

When the cow calved, the calf disappeared at once. All winter the farmer's wife laid the evening milk of the cow in a place out of the way, and in the morning the vessel was always empty. The cow gave a great deal of milk, and many fine calves were got from it, whose descendants are said to be still in the district.

The farmer had good catches when he went out fishing during the winter and spring, and always laid aside a share of the fish when he divided them in the evening ; in the morning they had disappeared. On the day after Cross-mass he did this as usual, but in the morning the fish lay there untouched, and henceforward he kept them to himself, nor did the elf-woman ever come near him again.

The Elf-woman in Múli.

WEST under Barda-strönd, in the parish of Flatey, lived a man named Ingimund, whose grand-children are still alive. He was a well-to-do man, hard-working, and of a determined nature. On his lands was an island-meadow, called Múli, which had to be left untouched, and never had been mown, though there was abundance of grass on it. Ingimund was annoyed to see so much grass on the meadow, and not have the use of it, till at last he could stand it no longer, and told his men to mow it. His wife bade him let it alone, but he never heeded, and had it mown against her wish ; he got a great quantity of hay off it, and thought he had done well in mowing it. In the autumn, however, his wife dreamed that a woman came to her with a sorrowful look, and said, "Your husband did ill in mowing the island that I live in, for I have had to kill my cow that I lived by. He will be spared on your account, but he shall bear my mark for having made me kill my cow." Then she went away to Ingimund, who slept in another bed, and said, "You owe it to your wife that I do not give you your just reward for not giving heed to her, and having the meadow mown when she told you not to. I have had to kill my cow on account of that, and I will make you remember it." Then she grasped his arm and said, "You shall have no harder punishment than this." She went away then, and he awoke with a pain in his arm, which afterwards withered up, so that he could never work with it again.

Fairies' Revenge.

ABOUT the beginning of this century, a man and his wife lived on a farm in Eyjafirth; the man's name is not given, but the woman's was Ingirid. They were very well off, and had many grown-up children. The husband was considered rather greedy, but the wife was liberal, and not of a sparing disposition.

One time, in the end of winter, the farmer was coming into the house, when he noticed his wife in the pantry, filling a vessel with sour milk. " Ingirid again," he thought, "giving away to somebody," and paid no more heed to it. On entering the house, however, he found his wife there, and was at first surprised, then angry; declared that it had been some thief, hoped she might never thrive, and consigned her to the lowest depths. Ingirid took it more calmly; said it must have been some hungry person, and that he should not go on like that, but her husband only grew angrier, and rushed to the pantry. There he found the door locked, and no trace of any one having been near it, so he quieted down and the matter dropped. The following night, Ingirid dreamed that a woman came to her, and said she had done well in saying little about it, although she had come quietly into her pantry; but her husband had behaved differently, and she was afraid that her own husband would pay him back for it. She therefore begged her not to have her two eldest sons at home on the first night of summer, and to remember that well. Then the woman disappeared, but Ingirid remembered the dream. For three nights she had the same dream, and the fairy woman seemed very anxious about this, which was the only thing she spoke about. After this she entirely disappeared, and it came on towards summer. The last Wednesday in winter Ingirid sent her sons away, so that they should not be at home that night. When the byre was entered on the first morning of summer, the two best cows were found lying dead in the stalls, and it was supposed that the fairy had intended to kill the farmer's sons in revenge, and, not being able to get hold of these, he had killed the cows rather than nothing.

The Two Sisters and the Elves.

Two grown-up sisters once lived with their parents, who petted one and were harsh to the other. One time during winter, it so happened that all the people about the farm wanted to go to even-song, and along with the rest the daughter who was thrust aside was very anxious to go ; but as some one had to stay at home, she was made to do so, though it was greatly against her will. When all the others had left the place, she began to clean the whole house up and down, and set lights in every corner. This work finished, she invited the huldu-folk to visit her, going round all the farm repeating the usual formula, " Come all ye that care to come," etc. Then she went inside, and sat down to read the Bible, and never lifted her eyes from it until day dawned. No sooner had she sat down, however, than a crowd of elves entered the

house, all dressed in gold and fine clothes. They laid on
the floor all kinds of precious things, and offered them to
the farmer's daughter ; they also began to dance and invited her to join them, but she paid no heed to them.
This went on till morning, when the girl looked out at
the window, and said, " God be praised ; the day has
come now ! " When the huldu-folk heard God named,
they hurried off and left all their treasures behind.

When the others came home, and her sister saw the
valuable things she had come into possession of, she
envied her greatly, and said that next year she would
stay at home herself. New Year's Eve again came round,
and the spoilt daughter stayed at home ; she was very
eager for the coming of the elves, so she lighted all the
house and invited them to come. They came then, as
finely dressed as before, piled their treasures on the floor
and began to dance, inviting her to join them. This she
did, but in the dance she broke her leg and went out of
her senses, while the huldu-folk went off again with all
the treasure.

The Elves' Removal.

IN 1819 there was on the farm of Stóru-akrar, in Skaga-
firth, a young fellow named Gudmund, about twenty
years of age, who acted as shepherd. On the morning
after Twelfth Night he let out the sheep before daybreak,
and drove them to the dale where they pastured when
weather permitted. Arrived at the dale with his sheep,
he saw a caravan making its way along, in which were
both men and women, as well as children; the women and
children were seated in cars, while the horses were loaded

with luggage. Gudmund never thought but what the travellers were of his own species, although he was surprised that any one should be removing at that time of year, and also at their being seated in cars. He was desirous to speak with them, and ran from his sheep to do so, but these people made haste out by some cliffs to avoid him. Gudmund managed to get opposite to them, but could not get talking with them, as there was so great a distance between him and them, and he had also begun to doubt what they were. They then arrived at the cliffs and unloaded the horses. He seemed to see several doors open and lights burning·inside; the folk went up to these, the women and children entered, and the men carried in the luggage. Then he heard ringing of bells and singing, but could not make out a word, and when he arrived at the cliffs they were all shut up again, and the cars, in which the women and children had seemed to be seated, were only stones before his eyes. He saw now what kind of folk they were, and wished to get away as quickly as possible, but grew so sleepy and powerless, that he had to lie down there and sleep. When he awoke again day had dawned, and he rose, but had again to lie down beside the cliffs and sleep. When he next awoke it was clear daylight, and he recovered his strength, although still somewhat confused. He returned to his sheep, and took them home in the evening. People thought him strange for some time after this, but it gradually passed away.

The Huldu-folk in the Færöes.

THESE are tall of stature ; their clothes are all gray, and their hair black ; they live in mounds and are also called

" elves." There is an ", elf-howe" in Nord-strömö, south from Haldors-vik. They live like other folk, go out to fish, and have sheep and cattle, which go in the pastures among other cattle. They can make themselves and their property invisible to mortal men, and hence it is often said, when one is searching for anything, that a "hulda has hid it." They are eager to get children, who have not been baptised, taken out of the cradle, and to leave their own instead, but the latter remain mere idiots. Little children, who go out alone, often disappear, carried off by the huldu-folk ; sometimes they are afterwards found far away from any habitation, and have then told that a big man brought them food while they were away. Huldu-girls often fall in love with Christian men, and try then to tempt them, and draw them to themselves ; if they are out on the pastures, thirsty and tired, then the mound opens and the girl comes out to offer them ale or milk to drink, and unless they blow off the froth (for in that lies the charm), they forget everything as soon as they drink, the fairy gets power over them, and carries them off with her into her elf-howe.

The Dulur Fishing-bank.

ONE time in old days there was a famine in the Færöes ; a disease had carried off the sheep, the corn had not ripened, and no fish could be got in the sea. The distress is said to have been greatest in Vaagö, for it was a long time since they had caught anything at the good fishing-banks west in the sea, or anywhere else—they tried it often but came back quite empty. On this island, then, a poor man was going about, heavy and sad at heart, lamenting his distress ; he had many children, and could not see how he was to get a bite to put into their mouths. As he went about in this sorrowful mood, and complained of his hard lot, in having to starve his children and die of hunger himself, he met a huldu-man, who asked him what ailed him that he seemed so heavy-hearted. The man told him how badly off he was, and the huldu-man answered that it was a shame he should suffer such distress, for there was plenty of fish, if they had only been able to find them, and he would now tell him the marks to find the fishing-place by :—"the stream in Dal, the mound on Harda-völl, the river in Tang,—fish here shall you fang—bitten iron and trodden,—he that fishes not then is fey." When the huldu-man had said this he suddenly disappeared, without explaining these dark words and unknown names. The man, however, carefully remembered what had been said, and began to ponder over it, till at long length he thought he had some idea where the fishing-place ought to be. Old folks in the district knew the names, and could tell him where the landmarks were to be found. There still remained to find out what the huldu-man had meant by "bitten iron and trodden." It finally struck him that "bitten iron" might be the bit of a bridle, and "trodden iron" a horse-shoe, so he took these and made his hooks of them. When he had got this done, they manned a fishing-boat, and took their bearings after what the man had made out of the huldu-man's words. He gave all the boatmen hooks which he had made from the horse's bit and shoe, and they let them down. They had struck the right spot, and had not sat there more than a little while, before the boat was laden with fish almost to sinking. They then rowed home rejoicing, and the bank is still called the Dulur (*i.e.*,

hidden,) after the huldu-man, and is regularly frequented.
On their way home, the Vaagö men rowed past a boat
they did not know, but it was a huldu-boat, the captain of
which rose from his seat, and said to the man, " A lucky
man are you ; well were the words explained and well
was the bank found." The boat disappeared from view,
and was never seen again ; but the Vaagö fishers were
glad to have something to give to their wives and children that evening and afterwards.

The Man from Gása-dal in the Huldu-boat.

THERE is no level beach at Gása-dal in Vaagö, only
rocks fifteen fathoms high facing the sea. The place is
thus badly situated for fishing, as no boat can lie under
the cliffs during winter, on account of the breakers. This
accordingly prevents them from keeping a large boat, as
it would be too hard work to drag it to the top of the
cliffs, and so the men of Gása-dal share the fishing-boats
of the men of Bö, and go out with them.

One night, when the weather was promising, a man
from Gása-dal left home to go east to Akra-nes, where
the men from Bö were to put in to land, and take him on
board. When he came east to Skards-á, he saw a boat
rowing in to Akra-nes, and being unwilling to keep them
waiting long for him, he started to run down to them as
fast as he could. He saw then that there were seven men
on board, and an empty place for him on one of the seats,
but he could not recognize the men, as the darkness had
no more than begun to clear away. He had no suspicion
but that everything was as it ought to be, sprang quickly
into the boat, and they at once pushed off from the shore.

The man sat down in his accustomed place, and put out
his oar, but on looking about him found that he knew no
one on board, and began to suspect that it was huldu-
men he had got among ; however, he showed no dismay,
and rowed as stoutly as they did. They held north round
the island to Ravna-múli, a bank frequented by the fishermen on the west coast of Vaagö. The huldu-men baited
and threw out their lines, but the man from Gása-dal sat
still and said nothing, for although he had brought his
line with him, his hooks were at Bö, and he had no bait.
The foreman on the boat asked him why he did not cast
his line ; he answered, "I have no *crook* and no *bite*."
The huldu-man at once gave him both hooks and bait,
and the hooks had no more than reached the bottom
when he felt a pull, and drew up a large fish, which, as
soon as he had killed it and laid it down in the boat, the
foreman took and marked, and every fish he caught was
marked in the same way. When they had got the boat
laden with fine fish, they rowed home again, and put to
shore at Akra-nes, at the same spot where they had taken
the man on board. As he had fished all day on his own
account, they threw ashore every fish that had been
marked. When he had got ashore, and had received his
catch out of the boat, he noticed that he had left his knife
in it, and called out to them, "Sharp by thigh is left behind." The huldu-man caught up the knife and threw it
at him, but did not strike him, whereupon he cried "A
curse on you, but you are a lucky man." They then
pushed off from the land again, and the foreman said,
"Hound that you are, you never said thanks to me for
the boat." It is not good, when huldu-folk are near on
the sea or on land (and who knows that?) to name knife,
sword, axe, bait, smoke, etc., by their proper names, but

by other words such as " sharp," " bite," " house-shadow,"
and the like.   Neither is it good to thank the huldu-folk
when they do one a service, for then they have power to
do one some mischief.

The Huldres in Norway.

THE huldres are women as beautiful as can be imagined,
who live in the mountains and graze their cattle there.
These are often fat and thriving, brindled, or light in
colour.   They themselves, when they appear to men, are
dressed in grey clothes, with a white cloth hanging over
their face, and the only thing they can be recognised by,
is the long tail that drags behind them, which, however,
they for the most part generally manage to conceal.

If one hears them play among the mountains, it is so
enchanting that one can scarcely contain one's self for
joy.   This music is called the Huldre's tune, and there
are many peasants who have heard it, and learned it, and
can play it again.

Now it once happened at a sæter, or mountain shiel,
that a man, who was working there, lay down on the
ground to rest.   He had scarcely fallen asleep, before it
seemed to him as if he was in such a beautiful meadow,
that he had never before seen its equal ; mountain lilies
grew round about in fairest bloom, and in the midst of
them lay a farm, one of the finest he had ever seen.   He
went into this, and saw in it a whole little family, all
dressed in grey.   The father was an old man with a long
beard, but altogether a dainty creature.   " Sit down and
eat with us," said the old man.   " Yes, thanks for the invitation," said the man, "but I must first say my grace," and

he began to take off his hat and fold his hands. "No, no," said the old man, "we don't use these tricks here, and if you would lay aside your knife and your silver pin, I should be very much obliged ; I don't like all that show ; " for so long as one has silver and steel about him these creatures have no power over him. "No, thanks," said the man,-"I keep them always about me and don't like to part with them." "As you please, my son," said the old man ; "wouldn't you like to have one of my pretty daughters though ?" "Thanks," said the man ; "but I am married already." "Oh, indeed," said the little one, "that needn't cause you any trouble, for you will never see her again, but live for ever down here with us, in pure joy and pleasure." The man grew a little uncomfortable at this, but stuck to his refusal. "Well," said the old man, "if he won't be good friends with us he may as well go to the door ;—out with him, my lads." So they laid hold of the poor peasant and threw him out, and with that he awoke, and was mortally ill after it.

The Huldre's Tail.

ONE time a huldre was present at a gathering, where everyone wanted to dance with the pretty stranger, but in the midst of the merriment, the young fellow who was dancing with her, caught sight of her long tail. He immediately guessed what she was and was frightened, but kept his presence of mind, and did not betray her, but only said at the end of the dance, "Pretty maid, you are losing your garter." She immediately disappeared, but afterwards rewarded him with fine presents and success in his cattle-rearing.

A half-grown lad from Vermeland was once in the
forest, busied with charcoal burning, when there came to
him a beautiful woman with long hair falling down her
back.   She greeted him in a friendly manner, and began
to talk to him, and he was quite enchanted with her
beauty ; but as they sat and talked, he looked behind her
and caught sight of a long tail.   "What's this I see?"
he cried in amazement ; "that's a rare train you have."
She became quite angry at the joke, and said, "I wished
you well, my lad, but now no one shall ever love you, I
shall take care of that, and everything shall go against
you."   With that she disappeared, and the lad immediately fell into a fatal illness.

The Huldre's Husband.

IN Nordland the story is told that a smart fellow got
hold of a huldre in the wood, by laying the barrel of his
rifle over her.   She was baptised, and became his wife.
They lived very well together and had a child, but suddenly one evening as the child was playing on the hearth,
where the woman sat and span, while the husband was
doing something else, something of her wild nature came
over her, and she, in a savage mood, said to him that the
child would be splendid to spit and roast for supper.   The
man was scared, and the woman, who noticed that she
had made a bad mistake, checked herself and entreated
him to forget it ; but he didn't.   The frightful words were
always in his ears ; he got by them an ugly glance into
his wife's true nature, and the peace of the home was destroyed.   From being a good husband he became irritable,
often taunted his wife with her savage proposal, cursed

his folly in marrying her, and struck and beat her.   So
things went on for a time, while the woman suffered and
sorrowed.   One day she went to the smithy in all friend-
liness to look at her husband working, but when he began
as usual, and they finally came to blows, she, to give him
proof of her superiority, caught up an iron rod and twisted
it like steel wire round her husband, who had then to give
in and promise to keep the peace.

The Bride's Crown in Numme-dal.

IT is not much beyond living memory, since a grown up
fellow from Opdals Annex in Numme-dal came upon a
merry huldre wedding, as he went past a deserted sæter.
Through a window he saw that everything went on
among the berg-folk the same as at ordinary weddings,
but his attention was most attracted by the bride, both
for her beauty and her beautiful dress, the finest part of
which was a massive bridal crown of shining silver.   He
looked at the bride so long that he fell in love with her,
and did not think twice of depriving the wedding guests
of their merriment, and the bridegroom of his rich and
beautiful bride.   He quickly drew his knife, and cast it
through the window over her head, upon which the others
disappeared like lightning, leaving only the fair one sitting, bound fast by the spell of the steel.   The two soon
came to an understanding, the fairy bride followed him
home, and finally, after being baptised, went with him to
the altar; but her beautiful bridal dress was spoiled by
an ugly cow's tail, which only disappeared little by little.
They lived long and happily together, and the costly
silver crown is still preserved at Mæra-bru.

L

Fairies in the house.

SOME people who know no better, say that they have
heard the Goa-nisse go about and sweep the house, when
in reality it was only the *raa*, imitating the work of
mortals. The *raa* can never be seen, but every night they
may be heard working in workshops, in houses that are
being built, or in large kitchens, and even spinning with
the spinning wheels, when these have been laid aside for
any length of time. For this reason, every orderly woman
is careful to remove the distaff from the wheel and tie it
up firmly, so that the fairies have to let it remain in peace.
Otherwise, these fairies do neither good nor ill, beyond
befooling some ignorant people into going to see what it
is, that is working in this way ; but in that case nothing
more happens, than that everything becomes quiet, until
the inquisitive person has gone his way. Then the fairies
begin anew.

In Kristianstad there was a bake-house which was full
of fairies, who went about in it every night as if they had
been human beings. There was a stable-man named
Jöns, who had always to awaken the baker at two o'clock
in the morning, so that the bread could be ready by six.
One morning the baker was allowed to oversleep himself,
and was furious at Jöns. The servant asked the stable-
man how he had so far forgot himself, especially when he
got up at that time at any rate, to look to the horses.
Jöns answered her, that when he went to awaken his
master at two o'clock, there was a light in the bake-house,
and fire in the oven, and he had plainly heard them rolling out the dough inside. He never took any thought
about the fairies, but supposed that it was the bakers already at work. It was rather simple of Jöns, to allow

himself to be fooled in this way by the fairies, for he knew
best himself how things stood in the bake-house.

It is a good sign when the fairies are heard working
actively in houses, ships, mills, and other buildings while
they are being erected, but if they are heard lamenting,
some accident is sure to happen, such as a workman
getting injured, or other unfortunate occurrence.

The Wood-fairy.

"In my young days," said a wood-cutter, "I saw the
wood-fairy with my own eyes; she had a red knitted
jacket, a green bodice, and blue gown. She ran past me
with her long yellow hair flying loose about her; she was
pretty in the face, but behind she was as hollow as a
baking-trough. A thick vapour can sometimes be seen
rising from the flat rocks, and one knows that she is boiling her clothes; and often during thunder loud noises
can be heard coming from them, as if a whole load of
stones were emptied down; this is her beating her clothes.
She can sometimes be seen with a child on her arm; my
own father saw this, and had heard that she had a husband, although she is given to enticing men to her. It is
not easy to find out the husband's proper name, for some
say that she is in the habit of calling on Erik, while others
think that she and the "hornufve" are a couple.

"Many years ago, it happened that a man, who was
burning charcoal in the thick forest, was several times
visited by a wood-fairy, who wished to warm herself at
his fire. He was annoyed at this, and threw a burning
coal at her. Then she screamed, 'Ture Koppar-bonde,
the man took red hot and burned me.' Others say that

she screamed, ' Svante, Svante, the man burned me.'
He was then heard saying, ' Self answer and self have ! '
But whatever his name was, and whatever answer he gave,
a terrible noise was heard in the forest, so that the charcoal-burner took to his heels, and ran away as fast as he
could, and so escaped the danger.

" I know a man myself, who saw her sitting, combing
her hair ; he was wrong in the head for a long time after
that sight. It might, however, have been worse for another
man that I heard tell of. He had gone out to look for
his master's cows, and searched for them till late in the
evening. By this time he had gone astray, and had found
no cows. He then saw a light at some distance further
into the forest, and went towards it, in the belief that
some human beings lived there. There was a house, sure
enough, and the door was open, so he entered and bade
them good evening. At the end of the table, with her
back against the wall, sat a woman, whom he took to be
the good-wife, and asked her whether he could stay there
overnight. 'That may well be,' said she, 'you can lie
in the bed that is made up in the room there.' He
thanked her, and began to undress, and in doing so happened to throw his clasp-knife on the coverlet. He then
thought he heard a splash, as if the knife had fallen into
water, but tired as he was, he sat down on the bed, saying : ' So, in Jesus' name, now I have gone enough to-
day.' As he said this, he sank into a pool, so that the
water splashed up over him. At the same instant the
house, and everything in it had disappeared, and the man
found himself sitting in a pool of water in the forest, while
his clothes were hanging on a bush beside him. He
could thank the name he had named, that he escaped as

he did ; for had he lain down in the wood-fairy's bed, her
husband would soon have come and torn him to pieces.

"A generation ago, it happened in Stene-stad that a
peasant, who was out in the forest in broad daylight,
looking to his cattle, found a lamb lying by itself beside
a bush.   He took it up gently, and carried it home to his
house, where his wife petted it all she could, and let it lie
under the stove.   Later in the day the man again went
out to the forest, and heard a piteous voice, which said,
'My child! my child!   Where is my child?'   The man
could see no one, and went home again.   There he told
what he had heard, and wondered who it could be that
was crying in this way for the child.   'That was my
mother,' cried the lamb, and made out at the door, across
the yard, and into the forest.   They knew then that this
was the wood-fairy's child, which she had changed into
the shape of a lamb, and which they had taken care of.
As thanks for this they had great luck with their cattle,
which were always much finer than their neighbours."

The Peasant and the Wood-fairy.

THERE was once a peasant, who was always equally cool
and collected, whether things went with him or against
him, so that no one was ever able to startle him, or make
him either laugh or cry ; they might say what they
pleased, he had always his answer ready, and had the last
word with them,   He had been at work in the woods all
week, and was going home on Saturday evening, when
he met the wood-fairy, who tried to get the better of him.

"I have been at your house," said she.

"Then you weren't at home that time," said he.

" Your wife has had a child," said she.

" It was her time then," said he.

" She has got twins," said she.

" Two birds in one egg," said he.

" One of them is dead," said she.

" Won't have to cry for bread," said he.

" They are both dead," said she.

" That's only one coffin then," said he.

" Your wife is dead as well," said she.

" Saves her crying for the children," said he.

" Your house is burned down," said she.

" When the tail's seen, the troll is known," said he.

" If I had you out at sea," said she.

" With a ship under me," said he.

" With a hole in it," said she.

" And a plug in that," said he.

The Wood-man.

IN the forest there are quite different beings from those
out on the plain.   In the woods round about the farm of
Skaber-sjö the wood-man is found.   He does not the
slightest harm, but just comes into houses to warm himself.   The worst of him is, that he takes up so much
room, and always wants to lie before the stove.   He has
tremendously long legs, but if one gives him room, he
disposes them round about him as well as he can, and if
he is received in a friendly way, he comes dragging whole
trees, and wants to lay them on the fire.

The Danish Ellefolk.

ADAM first had a wife named Lillis, who could fly and
swim, and when she bore children, it was by the half-score
at a time. They were all elle-folk, tiny little things.
They got their name from their mother, because she had
all these l's in her name.

The ellefolk live in mosses, banks and mounds, under
alder-trees and in alder-thickets. They wear white
clothes, and always turn their backs to the wind. The
women are hollow behind like a dough-trough, and a
good way to get rid of them is to refer to this, by saying,
" Let me see your back," or, " Let me see whether you are
the same behind as before."

Their children have helped mortal children to drive
home the cattle in the evening, and said that they lived
under the elder tree in the garden. A peasant once
found in the wood a boy of two or three years old, and
brought him home with him. The boy grew well, but
had an unusually large head, and would never speak.
One day the man was in the wood again, and saw a
woman with very long breasts who was running about,
and calling out one name continually. He told this on
his return home, whereupon the boy exclaimed, " That
was my mother ! " He was then taken back to where he
was found, and was never seen again.

The ellefolk also carry off children, or entice them to
follow them. Those who have once been with them are
never right in their minds after it, and always wish to go
back again. Even meeting with them, and talking to
them brings on sickness of body and mind, those who are
thus affected being said to be " elf-shot " or " earth-shot."
The men try to entice girls away with them, and often

came to them when milking ; the girls then take various plans to disgust them and get rid of them. One of them used to meet a girl when she went to milk the cows, until she told of him at home and was advised to ask him to turn round ; when he did this, his back resembled a stump of alder-tree. An elf-girl once came to a forester as he sat in the wood; she offered him a pancake, and sat down on his knee. He looked at it, and at her, and was at a loss what to do, but finally took his knife and cut a cross on the cake, whereupon both it and the girl disappeared. They even chase human beings, but must stop when they come to cross-roads. Eating a piece of bread and butter is a safe-guard against their attack. In one district it is the practice for mowers to sharpen their scythes before laying them aside, otherwise the elf-women can make them fall in love with them through these.

They can be heard singing in the woods with the most beautiful voices, and have music which has been known to have effect on horses. They are often seen dancing, either in the alder thickets or in the mounds, which are raised for the occasion. A herd boy was once invited by an elf-girl to join the dance, and next morning his body was found lying beside the mound ; he had danced till he died. Another never grew any bigger all his life ; another was only rescued by the prompt action of a plough-man in carrying him off. Such boys always wish to go back to them. They have been known to pay mortals to dance with them, but when these get tired of it and refuse to go any more, the elf-women revenge themselves.

They are greatly given to stealing, especially articles of food, and cats, which must not be left alone in the house. Once when they had stolen a woman's bread, her husband dug in the moss after them, but could not find

them. In revenge they plagued him till he died. To
protect anything against them, the mark of the cross is
sufficient, and it is extremely dangerous to annoy them
in any way, as they are sure to have their revenge.

The Elf-King.

IN Stevns Herred reigns the elf-king, and he, it is well
known, cannot bear any other king to set his foot in the
district, although this has really happened several times.
Neither can he endure any foreign foes, and in this respect
he has been better able to enforce his will, as was shown
in 1807, when the English entered the country as enemies.
When they tried to enter Stevns, and in order to do so,
had to cross Pram Bridge, they could get no further than
to the middle of it. Here they had to stop and turn back,
none of them daring to go further, as an invisible power
seemed to force them back. They had therefore to be
content with visiting the villages on the other side of the
river from Stevns, where they plundered and pillaged
largely, while Stevns was completely spared.

In olden times the elf-king carried music with him
wherever he went, but in later times nothing of the kind
has been heard. A woman from my native district was
going over a meadow, through which runs the stream
that divides Stevns from Fakse Herred. On reaching
the other side of the meadow, she sat down to rest beside
an alder stump, but had scarcely sat there a moment,
before there came a rushing sound through the air, and
she saw the meadow heaving up and down as if with a
whole troop of horsemen riding after each other, and
heard music along with them. In the midst of all this,

the woman became so frightened, that she sank to the ground in a swoon, but when the tempest was past, she was quite well again. It must assuredly have been the elf-king riding past with music, and in full equipment.

When King Frederick the Sixth once paid a visit to Dragsholm, a beautiful large watch dog of a rare breed died suddenly on the very night that he stayed there. This mishap was attributed to the elf-king's revenge, who was said to have taken up his abode in the alder wood beside the castle, and was angry at another crowned head daring to enter his kingdom.

An Elf-Child's Birth.

IN Tjörring there lived an old woman, called Maren, who was sitting spinning very late one evening, when she heard a voice from under the floor, saying, " To bed, Ma, to bed !" She paid no more heed to this, and continued to spin, as she had much to do. In a little she heard the same voice again, saying the same words, and adding, " You don't know what I have suffered for what you have spun this evening." Maren now understood what was the matter, and made haste to get into bed and put out the light. The fact was that there lived elle-folk under her floor, and one of the women was about to give birth to a child. But this can only take place above ground, and as she could not come up so long as the wheel was going, and the light burning, she had to let Maren know in this way of the pains she was suffering on her account. It must have been the case that the elle-folk's outer door was just in the old woman's room.

The Changeling and the Stallion.

THERE was a farmer in Vendsyssel, whose wife had a child.   After she was going about again, she one day went out into the kitchen, and when she came back there were two children lying in the cradle, nor could she tell in the least which of them was their own.   They were perplexed at this, and the man went to make his moan to the priest, who answered that in such a case he could do nothing, and they would have to get "wise folk" to help them.   The man then went to one of these, who was wiser than any other person.   "You have a stallion, of course?" said the wise man.   "Yes," said the farmer.   "Then you must lay both the children on the dung-heap outside your stable-door, then go in and put the bridle on the stallion, and let it go out by itself."   "That will never do," said the man, "for as soon as the bridle is put on it, it flies out and never looks at the ground, but only at the mare, and might just as readily trample to death the right child as the wrong one."   "No fear of that," said the wise man, and so the farmer let out the stallion as he had been directed.   As soon as it got outside, it took one of the children in its teeth and threw it into the mire.   The woman then took the other child, and carried it into the house.   As soon as she had gone, the elf-woman came, and said it was a great shame of them to throw her great-grandfather into the mire, for he was 160 years old, and with that she picked him up and ran off with him, as if he were a child.

The Elf-woman at Fred-skov.

OLD Peter Hendrick relates that in his youth, while he served on a farm in Rönnebæk, he was one day cutting

grass up in Fredskov. It was about midsummer, and
that day there were two girls with him in the wood. It
was in the south-east corner of the wood, but beside a
moss. At mid-day after eating the dinner he had brought
with him, he laid himself down all his length to sleep. A
little behind him, the two girls sat resting themselves, but
before he had fallen asleep, he saw all at once a woman
come out of the alder bushes in the moss, and stand
straight in front of him, beckoning him with her hand.
The girls who were with him called to him " Do you see
her, Peter ? " But he cried, " Away with her," and just
as he cried it, the fairy turned about and disappeared in
the bushes, while at the same time there was a loud peal
of thunder, which rumbled like a cart going over a cause-
way. Peter says that the fairy was very pretty while she
stood in front of him, and was dressed in shining gold,
which glittered in the sun, but when she turned about she
was hollow behind, and mis-shapen, and to look at her
then was like looking into a black pot. He thinks it was
great good luck that he did not rise and give her his
hand, for then he would have had to go along with her.
He relates that this was what happened in his young
days to a man who still lives in Myrup, of the name of
Rasmus Hansen. He was one day out on the meadow
beside the peat moss, cutting grass, and as he stood there
the fairy woman came and beckoned on him. As soon
as he went to meet her, she took him by the hand and
went off with him, far over moors and mosses, and Rasmus says that he danced with her in this way for a long
time, and can remember nothing except that he constantly heard music, and constantly danced about with the
fairy.

What he lived on he does not know, but at last, one

day when he was beside Myrup again, the fairy let him
go, and he came home.   It was then three weeks since he
had disappeared, and in that time he had grown so thin
that he could scarcely be recognised again.

The Elf-Girl and the Ploughman.

LARS JENSEN, who lived in Stubberup, served in his
young days on Mose-gaard, in Dalby, on the fields of
which are two small woods, one of them consisting for
the most part of dwarf alders.   It was in early summer,
and they were holding the hay-festival.   Lars was a
terrible fellow to dance, and it was almost daybreak
before the party broke up, so he said to the boy, "You
can go and lie down and I'll shift the cattle."   He went
out to these, which stood in or near by the alder wood,
and after shifting them he lay down in the grass, being
very tired, and fell asleep.   Just as the sun rose, he
awoke, and saw a beautiful young woman, dressed like a
peasant-girl, standing over him and pulling at his buttons.
He thought it was one of the girls from the party, and
said, "Why can't you let me sleep in peace?" but he then
was more familiar with her than he should have been, and
only afterwards discovered that something was wrong.
From that time forward he had to visit her in the wood
every night, and could never have peace to stay in his
bed.   If he did not go at a certain time every evening,
she came herself to fetch him.   At last things went so
far that she came for him at mid-day, and the people
about the farm often saw her outside the window, and
when she came there he had to go, but she never got so
much power over him as to be able to keep him.   She

often pressed him to go home with her, and he would get
many glorious things to see, but he would not do this, as
he was afraid that their men-folk would do him some
mischief. She assured him that there was no fear of
that ; if he would only go with her he would have a good
time of it, and if he was not content with her he could
get her sister, who was much prettier than herself, and
many other promises she made, but could not prevail with
him. This continued until the autumn, and he grew
afraid that he would not be able to oppose her much
longer. He then applied to the priest, who came and
sent him to bed, gave him the sacrament, and spread the
chasuble over him. They were sure that she would come
now, and so she did, and wanted to take him with her,
but could not. The priest told her that she might take
him now if she could, and if not, she could have nothing
to do with him thereafter. She had thus to go away
again, and from that time forward Lars Jensen was free
from her. It must have been an elf-girl, but she was not
hollow in the back, as some folks say they ought to be.

An Elf-charm Cured by Melted Lead.

IN the parish of Mern there are two farms known by the
name of Skalsby. Fifty years ago one of them was inhabited by Rasmus Bosen's widow, who had it in life-
rent, and had a son, Peder Rasmussen, who managed it.
Every time they were to bake, they had to go into the
wood and steal sticks to bake with. At that time a
girl called Bodil served on the farm, and had to help in
this. The son and the ploughman got the wood, the one

cutting it and the other dragging it off, while the girl had
to keep watch and see that the forester did not come
upon them.   One time they were out for this purpose,
and had finished their work, but when they looked for the
girl she had disappeared.   Peder called on her, but got
no answer, and they were afraid she had lost herself.
He called again, and this time she answered him, but
from another part of the wood altogether.   They found
her then, but she was quite wrong in the head.   She
would not go home with them, saying that she was going
to a ball in Lange-mose, so they had to take her and drag
her home by force.   They put her to bed, and understood
well enough what was wrong with her, so they got a
woman brought who could melt lead over her, and in that
way she was made well again.   (This consisted in melt-
ing lead, and pouring it into a vessel of water held over
the sick person's head.   The figures which it formed in
the water explained the trolldom).   So long as she lived
she could well remember what she had seen, and told
about it.   As she went about in the wood and listened,
she thought that all at once it became strangely clear
round about her, and then there came two little fellows,
each of whom took hold of one of her hands.   They told
her that they lived out in Lange-mose, and that the one
was called Svip (Glance) and the other Glööje (Glare-
eye).   They earnestly begged her to come and dance
with them, as the elle-folk were to have a ball that night.
She went with them for some distance, and was very
pleased to walk and talk with them ; then she heard
Peder Rasmussen calling on her, and was unwilling to
answer the first time, as she did not want to separate
from the boys, but when he called the second time, she
thought she could not help answering.   No sooner had

she done so than the boys were gone, and all was pitch-dark round about her, until the men came and found her.

Curing an Elf-charm.

A GIRL from a farm in the village of Galten had to shift the sheep to a sheltered place on the fields, as the weather was very severe, so she took them down beside an alder thicket, but there she came among some little creatures, and remained with them until far on in the night. She told afterwards that there were some who played while the others danced, and she danced with them. There were both men and women, and they wore red sleeves. Towards morning she came home and went to her bed. When they called on her to rise and milk the cows, she got up, but could neither speak nor open her mouth, which seemed to be all twisted together. When they could not get a word out of her, they grew frightened, and sent for a wise man, who lived in the alder-wood at Laas-by. He said that she had danced with the elle-folk, and they must now take her back there. A man should go on each side of her, and she herself ride on a broom-handle. When they got so far that she could see the elle-folk, they must bring her back again. He then forced her mouth open with a silver spoon, and they set out. At last she could see them, and gave a scream, and said, "There they are!" With that she would have run off to them, but the men kept hold of her, and dragged her back with them. She was now freed from them, and told the whole story, but never liked to talk about it afterwards, and was a little strange ever after. I can remember her as an old woman.

The Elfin Dance.

THE thicket at Havers-lund was full of elf-girls, and in the village lived a man who had a good-looking son, named Tammes (Thomas). The elf-women had a loving eye for him, and he often heard their song and music, and watched their dance, when he drove the cattle down to the fold late in the evening. He often stayed away for a long time, and then his father scolded him, but his longing only grew all the greater. Finally, late one evening, he ventured so near that they formed a circle round him, and he came home no more. For three years his parents waited for him in vain ; then they heard tell of a wise woman, who was said to be able to help them, so they got her down there one evening, and waited outside the thicket with anxious attention. Finally the dance stopped, and the elf-girls disappeared, leaving something lying on the ground,—it was Tammes, but he was dead. They had danced him to death, and the blood was flowing from his nose and mouth. After this nothing succeeded with Nis Tamsen, whereas everything had gone well with him while his son was with the elf-girls. This happened about the year 1700.

The Lady's Beech.

IN the middle of the fields of Kokke-dal, three and a half Danish miles from Copenhagen, stands an enormous beech-tree, which serves as a landmark for the Sound, and is called "The Lady's Beech." A large forest formerly stood here, and some girls, returning from their

work in the fields, were once passing this way in the
evening, when there suddenly arose a violent storm,
accompanied by thunder and lightning.   They all ran to
reach home with the exception of one, who sought shelter
under the large tree.   Here a white-clad figure appeared
to her, and revealed to her that she should one day become
mistress of Kokke-dal, but she must promise never to give
her consent to this tree being felled.   Some years later
the owner of Kokke-dal happened to see her, fell in love
with her, and asked her hand.   She remembered the
prophecy, and gave her assent.   The whole forest has
been felled since that time, but each owner is bound
down to leave this tree standing.

Thefts by the Elves.

In Ginnerup, beside Krei-bjærg, there are many mounds,
in which there formerly lived elle-folk.   My mother's
mother has told that they were so given to stealing, that
one could hear them come by night, and fill their metal
pots out of the dough-troughs, but when a cross was made
over the dough they could not take it.   This was therefore usually done, and the practice is still kept up without
thinking of the reason of it.   One time when an elf-woman
came to Mads Bakke's farm, and was about to fill her
metal pot with dough, the man came over her with an axe,
whereupon she ran away and left the pot, which was long
kept on the farm, until it was once left outside at night,
and in the morning it was gone.

     They were worst, however, for unbaptised children, and
on this account a cross was made above and below the
cradle, on both ends and on both sides.   One night two

fairies came to carry off a child, which lay in a cradle thus protected. "Take it out at the end," said the one. "I can't," said the other, "there's a cross on it." "Take it out at the side, then." "No, I can't do that either ; there are crosses everywhere." So they had to go away again.

The Charcoal-burner and the Elf-girl.

A CHARCOAL-BURNER from Ry was lying one night beside his heap, in the middle of the North Wood there. The fire crackled away outside his hut, in which the man lay at full length, keeping an eye on the burning pile, to see that it did not burn down to ashes. At twelve o'clock at night there came an elf-girl, who sat down in front of the fire, and turned her face to the man, while she showed her legs and pointed to them saying, "Do you know leg-pip ?" The man answered "Do *you* know brand-stick ?" and with these words he took a stick from the burning heap, and struck at her legs with it. She then shouted so that she could be heard over the whole wood, "Red, red elf-lad, elf-girl burned bad !" With that the wood cracked as if about to fall, and from all its corners the elves came streaming in hundreds. The man ran home the whole two miles as fast as he could, while the elves ran after him with brands from the charcoal heap. He was very nearly giving in, but got under cover in a house that he was passing, and was safe, as the elle-folk dare not go under a roof. Next day, along with some others, he went to the wood to see his charcoal, and found it scattered in all directions to the distance of half a mile. The man never did any good after this, but slowly wasted away and died, and was believed to have been bewitched by the elves.

V.—NISSES OR BROWNIES.

The Nisse.

OF Nisses there existed in old days an immense number, as almost every farm had its own one. In later times their number has greatly decreased. They are no larger than little children, are dressed in grey, and wear on their heads a red peaked cap. For the most part they have their abode in barns and stables, where they help to look after the cattle and attend to the horses, to some of which, however, they show the same partiality as they do towards different persons. There are thus many instances of how the nisse has dragged the hay from the other horses' mangers to the one which he is fond of, so that in the morning this one stands well-fed, beside a full manger, while the others have got almost nothing. He likes to play tricks ; sometimes lets loose all the cows in the byre, or scares the milk-maids, sometimes by blowing out their light, sometimes by holding back the hay so firmly that the poor girls cannot get a single straw out, and then when they are exerting all their strength, he suddenly lets go, so that they fall their whole length. This amuses the nisse mightily, and at such tricks he laughs loudly. If he likes the owner of the farm, he looks after the house's welfare, and tries to drag hay and other things from the neighbouring farms, by which there sometimes arises quarrelling and fighting between the nisses on the several farms, so that the hay and straw has been seen flying about their ears.

As they are always very serviceable to those whom they like, but full of spite and revenge when they are despised or mocked, it is not to be wondered at that people on certain occasions seek to gain their favour. On Christmas Eve and Thursday evening it is the custom in many places to set in the barn sweet porridge, cakes, ale, etc., which he likes to partake of, if they are to his taste, for he is sometimes rather particular. Scorn and contempt he cannot stand, and as he is very strong, in spite of his size, his assailant often comes off badly. A peasant who met a nisse on the highway one winter evening, and in an authoritative tone ordered him out of the way, was thrown right over the fence into the snow by the offended little man before he knew where he was. A servant girl, who made fun of him when she brought his food into the barn on Christmas Eve, had to dance with him so vigorously that she was found next morning lying breathless in the barn.

They love moonlight, and in the winter may be sometimes seen amusing themselves driving little sledges, or leaping with each other over the fences, but although they themselves are lively, yet they do not always like noise and disturbance in their neighbourhood, especially on vigils or Thursday evenings. In general, the nisse is well liked, and in many places is called "A Good Fellow."

The nisse lives in church steeples, and over church ceilings, but if any one becomes friendly to him and receives him on his farm, he is there both early and late, and helps with the work, especially in the stable ; during the night, he steals grain round about, wherever he can find it, and brings it into the barn, so that prosperity

always comes where he makes his abode. But although
he helps those that make friends with him, he deals badly
with those who send him away. In the time when Captain
Tage owned Rönne-bæks-holm, and was a severe and
strict master, whom all were afraid of, there lived in
Brandlev, on a farm which then belonged to Rönne-bæks-
holm, a farmer of the name of Ole Hansen. When all
the rest had difficulty in paying their landlord what they
owed, he found it quite easy, and his farm was fully
stocked with everything. Nor would he stand any nonsense from Captain Tage, who also preferred to avoid
any talk with " Big Hans," as he called him. This Ole
Hansen had a nisse on his farm, who helped him in every
way. Ole told the girl, that when she went out in the
morning to clean the byre, she was not to be afraid of
the little fellow who would come to help her. " You
must be friendly with him," said he, " and he will do more
than half the work for you." Next morning, when the
girl went to the byre, the little fellow came and helped
her, and she, as her master had told her, was friendly
with him, so things went very well. Some time after this
she was in company with some other girls, who had the
same task as herself, and these complained that it was so
hard work to clean the byre. " It is very easy for me,"
said she, " for the little fellow who comes about our farm
does the most of the work for me." Next morning the
other girl on the farm came and wakened her, where she
lay asleep in the middle of the court-yard, asking her if
she was wrong in the head that she was lying there. The
girl knew well enough that it was the nisse who had
carried her out, as a punishment for talking about him to
the other girls ; and after that she never spoke of him,
until she had been some years married, and was living

on a farm in Rönne-bæk. One day her husband came in and told her that the little fellow had come to him in the stables, and offered him his services, but the woman bade him not to accept them by any means—they should far rather be poor with honour, than get goods and gold dishonestly. So the man let the nisse go away, and refused his help, but after that they never had any luck with their cattle, and finally became so poor that they had to leave the farm.

The nisse, who comes to farms, wears a round blue cap sitting close to his head, and a white frieze smock. One evening when a young fellow was seeing a girl home to a house in Rönne-bæk, which lay near a farm where a nisse lived, he saw a huge load of grain coming down the road; it was bigger than the biggest load of hay, yet there was no horse to it, but the nisse was under it, and carried the lot. When this arrived at the farm, the young fellow and the girl both saw the entrance lift itself up, so that the load could get in, and then come down into its place again.

In Rönne-bæk not so long ago there was a farmer, who wished very much to have a nisse on his farm, and as he knew that one must always look for him at cross-roads, he went to these several times, but the nisse never came. At last the nisse did come on one occasion, and the man invited him home with him, but the nisse refused, saying that the farmer did not have true faith in him or in his master.

To Catch a Nisse.

As every one was eager to have a nisse attached to his farm, the following plan was formerly made use of to catch one. The people went out into the wood and felled a tree. At the sound of its fall the nisses all came running as hard as they could to see how folk did with it, so they sat down beside them and talked with them about one thing and another. When the wedges were driven into the tree, it would often happen that a nisse's little tail would fall into the cleft, and when the wedge was driven out, the tail was fast, and nisse was a prisoner.

Down in Böge-skov (Beech-wood) lived two poor people, who, as they lay awake one night, talked of how fine it would be if a nisse would come and help them. No sooner had they said this than they heard a noise in the loft, as if some one were grinding corn. " Hallo ! " said the man, "there we have him already." " Lord Jesus, man, what's that you say ? " said the woman ; but as soon as she named the Lord's name, they heard nisse go crash out of the loft, taking the gable along with him.

The Nisses in Gedsby.

THERE is a man in Gedsby known as " The Noltosse," but his proper name is Arnold. Of late he has been greatly plagued by nisses. Some people say that he must have offended them by levelling a mound on his field, in which he is said to have found a quantity of human bones, which he sold in Nyköbing instead of burying them. Others say that he has always had an old nisse on his farm, and that they formerly were very good friends ; so much so, that with the nisse's help he once, in digging up a mound, found a pot full of ashes, but which became full of pure silver coin as soon as he got it home. But all agree in this, that he had afterwards fallen out with the nisse or nisses—for some say that there was only one, others that there were several—and that he then felt the want of them. There was no one on the farm that could see them, except a girl from Möen, who was somewhat *aparte*, and could always see them. Some say that she had become so because the nisse had breathed upon her.

The Noltosse's father-in-law, a very old man, was one day going through the kitchen, but just as he had shut the door, and was going past the kitchen-table, a large weight, which was lying on it, rolled off and struck him on the heels. He lifted it and laid it on the table again, but as soon as he turned to go away, it rolled after him again and struck him on the heels. He took it up again, although he was surprised that it would not lie still, but he had only got a few steps away from the table when it came rolling after him just as before. He could now see that there was something uncanny about it, so he went away and let the weight lie.

Once the Noltosse sent his servants to make malt, but when they came to clean the mill, it was quite full of old slippers and wooden shoes. They began to throw these aside, but as fast as they cleared them out, the slippers and shoes jumped in again, till at last they went in tears to their master, and told what had happened. He ran down in person to the mill to see what was the matter, but the slippers and shoes flew about his ears, and slapped him so hard that he had to hurry away.

It happened also, one day, that he had got two sacks of rye meal from the mill, and there was to be a baking. The one sack of meal was made into dough, but every time they put a loaf on the peel to push it into the oven, it disappeared from amongst their hands.

No one could imagine where the loaves went to, but

they did not go into the oven.   So things went with the
one sack of meal.   The Noltosse then told the servants
to bake up the other sack, which was standing in the
brew-house, for they could not do without bread.   When
they went for the meal, however, it was not to be found.
It was found at last, though ; it was scattered all over the
courtyard, and the sack it had been in was thrown into a
corner.   The nisses there had also a habit of mixing up
all the grain in the barn-loft, so that he could not get it
separated again.

One day, when he and all his folk were sitting at table,
the porridge suddenly disappeared, and in its place the
table was covered with old slippers and shoes, which
danced about and slapped their ears.   No one could see
how it came about, except the girl from Möen ; she said,
" Just look, the nisses are eating all our porridge ! "   The
same girl also saw them one day in the stable ; they were
neat little fellows, with red caps on their heads.   Two of
them were springing about among the straw, and three
of them danced in the hay-basket.   " Just come and see
how neat they are ! " she called to the other folk, but
these could not see them.

Once the Noltosse tried to get rid of the nisses, and
gave " Wise Christian " a bank-note for that end, but the
latter made the mistake of scattering flax-seed round the
farm *before* the nisses had left it.   As these could not
cross the flax-seed, they had to stay on the farm, and
then they became real wicked.   Finally, they say, he got
the Mormons to exorcise them, and they removed to a
neighbouring farm.

Father and Son.

A farmer in Dybböl stood on a very friendly footing with some little nisses, who lived in the neighbourhood, and these continually brought so much to the farm that there was great wealth there. When the man died, a little nisse came one day to his son, and asked whether he would stand in the same relation to them as his father had done. The son would not answer this, unless the nisse could tell him where his father was. The nisse could easily do that, for he was with them. " No," said the son, " in that case I will have nothing to do with you." The nisse replied that if he would not deal with them, he must resign himself to their taking away again all that they had brought in his father's life-time. The son begged that this should not happen all at once, but little by little, and the nisse promised this for his father's sake. After that time there came great poverty on the farm and it has been there ever since.

The old Bushel.

ON a farm there lived a little nisse, but the proprietor was not very good to him, for he never gave him porridge with butter in it on Christmas Eve, or other Saints' eves. Neither did the owner have any luck ; everything went back with him, and he had finally to sell the farm, and buy a little place in the neighbourhood. But his man, who had served on the farm for several years, longed very much for the little nisse, with whom he had always had a chat every day ; so even now, after they had left the farm, he went over as soon as he found time, to have

a talk with his little friend. One day when he came
over, the nisse asked him how his master was getting on.
" Pretty poorly," said the man, " he will not be successful there either." " Then," said the nisse, " you must tell
him to come over here, and ask the person who bought
the farm from him, whether he may take away the old
bushel which stands at the back of the chimney, as he
forgot to take it with him when he removed." " Oh, but
we didn't forget it," said the man, " we didn't want to
take it with us." " Yes, but that's what you must say, all
the same," said the nisse. The man went home and told
his master what the nisse had said to him, so the farmer
went over to the new owner of the farm, and asked for the
old bushel which stood at the back of the chimney, as he
had forgot it. " Yes, that you may have with pleasure,"
said the other ; " we don't use it at any rate, *we*'ve got a
new one." When the man got home with his bushel, it
went in pieces in his hands, but at the same time a whole
lot of money fell out on the floor. There had been a
double bottom in the bushel, between which the money
had lain. The man was greatly delighted, for there was
so much of it that he could buy his old farm back again,
and so he did. After that time he never forgot to put
down rice-porridge, with butter in it, for the nisse, and
even sprinkled a good layer of cinnamon and sugar over
it, and ever after all went well with him.

The Nisse's Parting-Gift.

OUT in Vester-egn lies Skop-hus, which had many acres
of land, but hardly any of them were cultivated. One
time the farmer had been in Viborg, and as he came home

again he saw a nisse sitting on his garden wall.   He took
him in with him, and gave him both food and drink, so
that he took a fancy to stay there always.   From that
time forward several acres of land were taken in from the
heath every year, without anyone knowing exactly how
it happened, and in several years time there were fertile
corn-fields where formerly only heather had grown.   The
man's wife, however, was not at all good to the nisse,
although it was he who had helped them to become well-
to-do people.   One day when her husband was at Viborg,
she ordered nisse to procure a thousand dollars for each
of her children, otherwise she would take him and throw
him into the fire.   He long refused, but finally there was
a rumbling and a tumbling, and all the money lay on the
kitchen-floor.   The woman gathered it up, put it in a
bag, and buried it in the garden.   A little later the man
came back from Viborg, and found nisse sitting on the
garden wall where he had first seen him.   He asked him
why he was sitting there, and invited him in to get a
drop from the keg, which he had just got filled, but nisse
answered that he was going back to his own folks again,
and told how he had been treated by the wife.   "You
have been kind to me," he added, "and I will say farewell and thanks to you.   Here are some little stones for
you, which I will give you as a parting gift."   With that
nisse was gone, and from that time things began to go
back with the folks in Skop-hus.   The land fell back into
heath again, and the children died, one after another.
After they were all dead, and the riches completely gone,
the woman went out to the garden to dig up the money
that she had hid there.   She found it too, but when she
touched it, it turned to stones.   At this she was so angry
and vexed, that she fell down dead on the spot.   The

man was now left alone, and one day he thought he
would have a look at the little stones which the nisse had
given him at parting, and when he opened the drawer
and touched them, they turned into gold coins.

Nisse Kills a Cow.

IN Toftegaard there is said to have been in former days
a " Gaardbuk," or " Little Nils," who brought luck to the
house, and they never neglected to give him every evening, in the stable, a bowl of porridge with butter in it.
One evening the girl had put the butter pretty deep into
the porridge, and the " Gaardbuk," who thought she had
forgot it, was so angry that he left it untouched, and
went and wrung the neck of a red cow which stood in the
byre. Getting hungry, however, he finally set to work
on the porridge, when he found the butter, and regretted
what he had done.   He then took the dead cow on his
shoulders and carried it over Rybrook to a byre on Jets-
mark, and took in its place another red cow, which resembled the dead cow to a hair, and brought it to the
byre in Toftegaard.

Nisse's New Clothes.

A PEASANT had on his farm a nisse, who did much
service in his stumpy coat and red cap. When the man
came home from Skanderborg or Horsens in the evening,
he only needed to throw the reins from him and hurry
in to the fireside. Nisse took out the horses, led them
into the stable, fed them and watered them, all with the

greatest care. Now, there came a severe winter, and the peasant's wife was sorry for the nisse, so she got good thick clothing made for him—among other things, a long-skirted coat, instead of the old stumpy jacket. One day the peasant went to market, came home late, threw the reins from him as usual, and went off to bed. He heard, indeed, the words, " O, the poor horses! O, my good new coat!" but never thought it meant anything. Next morning he found his horses lying dead before the cart, frozen to death, for nisse had been afraid of soiling his coat.

The little Harvesters.

THE slopes of Fjelkinge-bank are divided between the different proprietors in the village, and of one of these lots—a field which, so far as I remember, is called Orme-lykke-krog—there is found the story that in old times, when the corn on it was ripe for harvest, the peasant who owned it brought a large dish of boiled rice and a barrel of ale out to the field, a little before sunset, and after that went quietly home again. When he came back next morning, the rice was eaten and the ale was drunk, but the field was very nicely harvested, and the corn bound in sheaves and set up in stooks. This had gone on for many years, without anyone knowing exactly who the harvesters were, or daring to find out. Then the farm was taken over by the old man's son and his wife, and the latter had no peace, until she found out whether it was human beings who did the harvest, or good nisses, as was universally asserted and believed. So one year, after the rice and the ale had been taken out to the field as usual,

she betook herself thither in all secrecy, and hid herself behind a stone. Towards midnight she saw three mannikins,
wearing grey blouses and red caps, coming into the field.
One of them carried a sickle, and began to cut the corn
rapidly. Another was provided with a rake, and gathered
the corn into sheaves, after which the third bound them
and set them up in stooks. The work went on quickly,
and in a very short time the whole field was harvested,
after which all the three began to eat the rice and drink
the ale, which also was finished very quickly, so that they
soon had demolished the lot. Then the woman rose up,
and said to the little fellows, " Well, you are the smartest
harvesters I have ever seen, and many thanks for your
trouble ; " but at the same moment all the three disappeared, and from that day forward the peasant has waited
in vain to get his field harvested by the nisses.

Nisse's Rest.

ON a farm in Dokke-dal, in the parish of Mov, there
lived some years ago a man who was commonly called
Peder Skelund. On this farm lived a nisse. The farmer
had a little pony, which the nisse liked very much to ride
upon.

One time, towards spring, when the fodder in the barn
was like to go done, the ploughman one day said to the
nisse, that as there was so little to feed the horse with, he
would have to give up his usual ride. " Don't you trouble
yourself about that," said the nisse, " I shall hit upon a
plan." In the evening he asked the man to go with him,
and after having provided themselves with a good long
rope, they betook themselves over Vild-mose to South

Kongerslev. In this village there lived a man, who had
his whole barn-floor covered with unthreshed oats. Nisse
took the half of this, and tied it up in the rope, after which
the two set out for home again. When they had got
down on Vild-mose, the man began to get tired, and asked
the nisse whether they should not rest a bit. " Rest ? "
said the nisse, " what's that ? " " Oh, to lay down your
bundle on the ground and sit down on it," said the man.
They did as he proposed, and after the nisse had seated
himself, he found it so comfortable that he exclaimed, " If
I had known that a rest was such a fine thing, I would
have taken the whole floor-ful."

Fights between Nisses.

In Dalum, two miles from Odense, there stands an old
bridge called Nisse-böved bridge, which only comes in sight
when the water is very low. It owes its name to two
nisses, who lived in two farms, lying on different sides of
the river, and stole from each other in turn.

The ploughman on one of the farms was in the barn
one day, when he heard one of the nisses puffing and
blowing, as he dragged at the hay in the loft. The man
kept quite still, and the nisse, who did not know he was
being watched, at last exclaimed, half aloud, " O, fie, how
I sweat ! " " Ay, fie, how you steal ! " shouted the man,
and laughed. Soon after this, as he was standing in the
peat-moss belonging to the farm, he saw the two nisses
come along, each with a bundle of hay on his back. They
met right in the middle of the bridge, and as they could
not pass each other for the hay, and neither would give
way to the other, they finally came to blows. As the hay

hindered them from getting a proper hold of each other, they threw it into the river, and each tried to throw his opponent the same way, but in this they were unsuccessful, and parted to all appearance good friends.

In the evening the same man had been away from the farm, and it was late when he came home, so he had a lantern with him. As he came to the farm gate, he saw the two nisses sitting there, one on each post. As he tried to pass them, the one shouted to him " Light high!" He held up the lantern, but at the same moment got a good box in the ear from the other nisse, who shouted, " Light low !" He lowered the lantern, and again from the opposite side received as sound a slap with the order " Light high !"   And this went on till it struck him to put out the light. This was, no doubt, the nisses' revenge for his having been eye-witness to their fight on the bridge, and for having ventured to call them thieves.

Another ploughman came past two nisses who were fighting, one evening, and instead of helping the one belonging to his own farm, he ran home as fast as he could ; but the nisse had seen him, and was mad that he had not helped him, and determined to revenge himself.   Next night, after the man had gone to bed, the nisse came and lifted him, and carried him out into the farmyard, with the words, " Now you I'll maul till cock shall call ;" and threw him about on the dung-heap, until there was not a spot on it where he had not lain.   Then said the nisse, " Well, if there's no more land, there's water at hand," and gave him a kick which sent him flying into the pool beside the dung-hill.

Nisses Fighting in the Shape of Wheels.

IN Salling there are two large manors, one called Böl and the other Asgaard.   On each of these there was a nisse, and they were distinguished as the Böl nisse and the Asgaard nisse.   When fodder was scarce, these nisses went and fetched it from the smaller farms round about, so long as there was any to be got, and when that failed they stole from each other.   This went on for a long time, but finally each of the nisses began to notice that just as much rye as he took, so much barley was he short of, and neither of them could understand how this came about, until one night when each met the other with a heavy burden.   Then the matter became clear to them, and in their anger they threw down the grain, and began to fight in earnest.   This ended in the Böl nisse getting three of his ribs broken, and his back well thrashed to the bargain, after which he had also to go home empty-handed, as the Asgaard nisse took the whole lot off with him, and that was the worst of it all.   When the Böl nisse came home, he went in to the stableman and told how badly he had fared, finishing up by saying that if the man wanted his horses to be fat, and the fodder to be sufficient, he must help him in this quarrel.   The stable-man promised to do what he could.   "You must take the dung-fork here then," said the nisse, "and when you see a fiery wheel with twelve spokes come in at the barn-door, and another wheel with only eight spokes come against it, then strike as hard as you can at the one with the twelve spokes, for the one with the eight in it is me." When evening came, the man took the fork and went out to the barn.   Towards midnight a fiery, red-hot wheel came rolling into the courtyard, and another came out at

the barn-door to meet it. The two met in the court, and
dashed against each other with such force that two spokes
flew out of the wheel that had the eight.   When the man
saw this, he used the fork as best he could, nor was it
long before he knocked a couple of spokes out of the
other one.   He kept hammering away at it then, with the
little wheel helping him, until only four spokes were left
in the big one.   Then the two wheels ran against each
other so hard that the big one sprang backwards high
into the air, and flew over the top of the barn, and was
seen no more.   After this there was plenty of fodder at
Böl, while they were always short of it at Asgaard, and,
as the man said, could not be any better until they got
their wheel patched up again.

The Nisses' Visits.

ON the farm of Nörgaard, in the parish of Brovst, the
nisses were frequent visitors.   They were little creatures,
with fiery red hair, somewhat malicious, but otherwise
very good-natured.   Sometimes, however, they could be
real wicked ; for instance, they occasionally sat on the
roof and combed their hair above the pots that sat on
the fire, but this was nothing compared with all the luck
and good fortune they brought to the house.   The
woman in the house had a son who was changed by the
fairies before he was baptized.   The changeling was very
ugly, but the woman tended him just as carefully as if he
had been her own.   The changeling's mother often visited
her son, and promised the woman in the house that
things should go well with her children because she
tended him so well.   The son who had been carried off,

also came home often to see his mother.　He would go
into their sitting-room, where he examined everything,
but never spoke a word, and then returned to Brovsthöi,
where the nisses had their proper home.　The woman
once said to another one, that she didn't think the nisses
had long time to live.　"How so?" said she.　"Well, I'll
tell you," said the other; "folk are so wise now that they
make a cross upon everything, and so the nisses can't
thrive."　After that the nisses did indeed disappear little
by little.

Nisse and the Girl.

ON Ox-holm there was once a Gaardbuk, and it was the
custom on that farm that every girl had her cow to look
after.　One day the Gaardbuk came running to the window, and shouted to one of the girls: "Hurry out as
quick as you can, your cow has got a calf."　Then he
hastened into the byre, and put on the shape of a new-
born calf, but when the girl came out he again assumed
his own shape, and began to laugh.　The girl was
annoyed that he had made a fool of her, and gave him a
good blow on the back of the neck with a fork.　Then
she went in and told how he had fooled her.　"But I
gave him a good whack, too," she added.　"That's a lie,"
shouted the Gaardbuk, "for you gave me three."　"I
never did," said the girl; "I only gave you one."　"But
you did, though," said he, "for there were three prongs
on the fork."　There was no more of it just then, and the
girl went quietly to bed, but in the morning when she
awoke, she was lying on a plank across the ridge of the
barn.

Nisse as a Calf.

ON an estate there was once an old cattle-man, who looked after the cows. One evening a cow was expected to calve, and the cattle-man was to keep awake, to give a look to it now and again. When he went out the cow had calved, and "Boo," said the calf. "That's rare," thought the old man, and picked up the calf carefully to take it to the calf-stall, but to his great astonishment the calf began to laugh at him, for it was the nisse who had turned himself into a calf to have some sport out of the old man. "I'll pay you back for that," said the latter, and nisse said, "All right." Next day passed and the evening came, and the man had again to watch the cow —"Yes, quite correct, the cow has calved *now ;* it isn't the nisse this time," and with that he laid hold of it and put it in the calf-stall. "Ha, ha, ha," laughed the nisse, "I've completely cheated you twice now." The old man thought, "I'll see, then, whether I can't trick you the third time, my friend." The third evening things happened the same way. When the old man came out the cow had calved, and the cattle-man took the calf and threw it out as far as he could into the midden-hole. "I'll show you who'll be fooled the third time," said the old man, but with that the nisse, who was not far away, began to laugh and clap his hands, for it *was* the calf this time. The old man now saw that he was fooled again, and gave up trying to revenge himself on the nisse.

The Nisses and their Horses.

A MAN in Nörre Ökse had two nisses on his farm, and had also two pretty, bluish-grey horses. One evening the nisses had heard the man say that he would go to market on the following morning and get the horses sold. This they could not bear, and when the farmer got up in the morning the horses were gone, and were nowhere to be found, so they were not taken to market that day. Finally the man found his horses. The nisses had got them dragged up into the loft above the cowhouse, and there they were standing safe and sound.

The Nisse and the Ghost.

IT happened at a parsonage that a new man came at term-time, and the priest went round with him to show him the place. In the middle of the stable there was an empty stall, while the horse that should have stood in it was standing behind the others. The man said it was strange to have it standing there ; it ought to be in line with the others when there was a stall for it. " No horse can stand tied in that stall," said the priest. The man thought he would try that. " No, you must not," said the priest ; "it has been tried often enough, but the horse continues to work away till it is covered with foam, if it cannot get loose." The man said no more about it just then, but some time afterwards he tied it up there, and then lay down on the floor above, to watch through a hole he had made in it. After he had lain there for a little, there came a white figure up into the stall and placed its hands on the horse's forehead, which immediately broke loose. The ghost now lifted a stone in the stall, while the man lay and watched it. There was, however, a nisse on the farm, who came creeping up just at this moment, and said, " What is it you are lying there and looking at?"

"Hush, be quiet!" said the man; but nisse was inquisitive, and went creeping over to the hole in the loft to look down, but with that the man caught him by the legs and threw him down on top of the ghost.   There arose a fearful disturbance then, and the man was so frightened that he slipped out, got to his room, and locked his door. Well on in the night the fight came to an end, and then nisse came to get at the man.   He called on him in the name of many people, and tried all possible means to get in ; but the man had got such a fright that he dared not open the door, and next day told the priest what had happened. "That is a bad business," said he, "and you must take care never to let him in, for he will have his revenge. He will even come and call on you in my name, but you must admit no one, and in the end he will get tired of it and go his way."   This, indeed, was how it ended at last.   The place in the stall was then examined and a quantity of money found there, and after that was lifted, the horse could always stand in the stall.

" Light High, Light Low."

IN Tylstrup lies a farm which has a nisse on it. Two ploughmen served there, one of whom was very fond of the nisse, while the other found his greatest delight in annoying him.   Once he took away his porridge from him.   " You'll pay for that," said the nisse, and when the man woke next morning, he found that the nisse had placed a harrow over the ridge of the barn, and then laid him upon the sharp spikes.   " You'll pay for that yet," thought the man.   Some time passed, and the other man asked the nisse to sew something for him, for he was a

tailor to trade. It was a bright moonlight night, so the
nisse took needle and thread, seated himself on top of
the haystack, and began to sew. Just as he was hard at
work, there came a shadow over the moon, at which the
little fellow became impatient, and cried, " Light! light
high !" The man who teased him was, however, standing
down below with a flail in his hand, and when he heard
the shout, he brought this over the nisse's legs. Nisse
thought it was Our Lord who thus punished him for his
imperious shout, and said very humbly, " Light high,
light low ; light just as you please, Lord !"

Nisse's Removal.

THERE was a man who was greatly embarrassed with a
nisse that he had. He had been keeping his money in a
bushel, which sat up in the loft, and the nisse went and
stole out of it. Finally, the man decided to remove from
that house, thinking that there was no other way of
getting quit of the nisse. He accordingly got that place
sold, and bought another, to which he proceeded to
remove his belongings. As he walked along beside the
loaded cart, the nisse stuck his head out of an empty ale-
barrel, the bung-hole of which was turned to that side,
and shouted down to the man, " It's fine weather we're
removing in !" When the man discovered where the
voice came from, he was both frightened and angry, for
he had thought he was rid of him now, so he took the
barrel and pitched it into a dam beside the road. When
he had got settled down in his new abode, and went up
to the loft one day to turn over his corn, he also took a
look into the bushel, and found that there was just as

much money in it as there had previously been, so that
the nisse had stolen none of it after all.   But as he had
been unjustly treated, the man never saw him again.

The last Nisse in Samsö.

IN Dean Hammer's time there were nisses in Kolby
parsonage.   The narrator often saw one sitting and
grinning under the eaves, especially when a cow calved,
or anything of that kind was going on.   He was always
on a friendly footing with the nisse, who took the charge
of foddering the horses which the man used, so that he
did not require to keep awake to see to them.   Another
man, who also served at the parsonage, was a person that
the nisse could not bear, and always threw him head-first
out of the loft when he went up into it in the morning to
throw down the corn ; the sheaves were then thrown down
on top of him.   When Dean Hammer removed to Besser,
the nisse removed also, going in a barrel to Tafte-gaard,
with a man called Knud Lille-tyv (little thief).   Thereafter he drove about with this man and helped him to
steal, until, with the nisse's help, Knud piled up a large
fortune.   The last nisse on Samsö was on Tafte-gaard.
A number of years ago, in 1854, the said nisse left the
island and went to Norway, where nisses are still to be
found.   He went off with the declaration : "We can't
stay here for your crisses and crosses, and the big ding-
dong in Tranbjærg Church.

The Church Nisse.

IN Besser Church there lives a nisse, who has his bed in a bundle of rags in the church loft, but on Sundays, and other times when the bell is rung, he hides himself in a mound a little way off. One evening when the bell-ringer came to ring the curfew the nisse played him a little trick. When he started to pull the bell, not a sound did it give out, and he then discovered that a large bundle of rags was tied to the tongue of it. As he stood and wondered at this, he saw looking over the bell a little grinning face with a red peaked cap above it.

The Ship Nisses.

THERE had been a heavy storm in the North Sea, and many ships had been on the point of sinking. When the weather had improved, two ships met out there, and came so near to each other that those on board could call out and enquire where the others came from, and so forth. At the same moment they heard two nisses shouting to each other from the top of the mast on either ship, asking how they had fared in the storm. The one said, " I have had enough to do to hold the fore-stay, otherwise the mast would have fallen." When the crew looked up to see where the voice came from, the nisse let go the stay, which fell to the deck, and then he began to laugh with all his might. The crew had now something else to do than look for him, as the mast nearly fell overboard, and while they were busy putting it to rights again the nisse saw his chance to creep down into the hold, where they could not find him.

Old Tyge Hansen in Lundö sailed with a yacht for Per Rönbjærg in Skive. He had a Gaardbo-nisse on board, and they could tell by him when they were to have storm, or head-wind, or the like ; at such times he was very busy with one thing or another, went creeping about, and tried to get everything put right. At other times he had his abode in the fore-castle. One time Tyge Hansen was sailing from Skive to Aalborg, and had favourable weather to sail north in ; but all the same the yacht would not work with them ; they could make no progress with it, and so had to sail into Baads-gaard Vig, instead of keeping to the west of Lundö. Next day they had such a storm from the north-west that it was clear that their anchors and tackling could not have held, had the ship been out at sea. The nisse knew this, and therefore kept them back in this way. They had him always on board, but could not see him except by night. One time Tyge Hansen himself was sitting at the helm, when the nisse came and told him that Per Rönbjærg's wife was dead. Tyge asked him at what hour she died, and he answered, " Two o'clock." This was afterwards found to be perfectly correct.

The Swedish Tomte or Nisse.

A PEASANT family in Skaane were in the habit of placing food every day on the stove for the Tomtes, who are there called Nisses. This came to the ears of the parish priest, who searched the house, and tried, meanwhile, to convince the people that such nisses did not exist. " How, then, should the food disappear every night ? " asked the good-wife. " O," said the priest, " I can tell you that.

Satan takes all the food and collects it in a kettle in hell, and in that kettle he thinks to boil your souls to all eternity." From that day no more food was set out for the nisses.

When building or joiner's work is going on, it is said that the tomtes have been seen, while the workmen were at dinner, going about on the erections, and working with little axes. When a tree is felled in the forest, it is said, " The man indeed holds the axe, but the tomte fells the tree." When the horses in a stable are well attended to and in good condition, the saying is, " The man lays the fodder in the manger, but it is the tomte that makes the horse fat."

The Nisse and the Dean.

THE Goa-nisse is not a good being like the little Vättar. Whoever wishes to have to do with one, must engage him on Christmas Eve. For every year he serves, he must get a joint of his master's body; first the little finger, and so on till the whole person has become his property.

Many years ago there was a young priest up in the forest districts who had a Goa-nisse, and that although his father was dean in a rich pastorate down on the plains. The dean came at last to hear of the tales that were common about his son, and decided to visit him in person on Christmas Eve and see how the case actually stood. The son was a little put out when his father entered the house that evening, but the dean merely asked to be shown his household when they sat down at table. The son could not well refuse this request, and when the dean had entered the servants' hall, he saw at once a little fellow, with a red, peaked cap, sitting at the bottom of the table. He asked the son what kind of a person this was, and received the answer that it was one who worked for day's wages. The dean then turned to nisse himself, and asked if this was true ; the latter dared not impose on the dean, and answered " No." The son then said that it was a servant who had yearly pay, and the dean again asked nisse if this was true. " Yes," said he, " I get a bowl of porridge and milk every evening." The dean wanted to know what he did with this, seeing that he was a creature who did not resemble human beings in the matter of food and drink. The nisse then pointed him to a stone out in the yard, and said that all the porridge and milk lay under that. The dean then wanted to know how he, who was so little, could drag so much grain and other articles to the farm. The nisse then made himself so long that he had to stand in the room doubled up four times.

"Well," said the dean, "since you have shown me how long you can become, I command you now to show me how little you can be, for out here you must go." With that he took an awl, and bored a hole in the lead of the window, whereupon the nisse became as slender as a thread, and crept out at the hole lamenting. From that time forth he dragged away from the young priest all that he had previously dragged thither, and more than that.

Vättar.

A WOMAN near Landskrona was satisfied that vättar lived in her house, although her father had been com-

monly accused of acquiring his wealth by the assistance
of a nisse. It was said that her mother gave the Goa-
nisse a new jacket and peaked cap every year, and a
bowl of porridge and milk every Christmas Eve, but this
must have been pure slander, for her mother was a priest's
daughter, and a pious woman like her daughter. In that
house, among the nine children and the numerous
servants, vättar could easily thrive, for order and disci-
pline reigned there. One night the woman awoke, and
missed her little child which she had lying on her arm.
She kindled a light, and began to search for the little
one, which she found lying asleep under the bed, with its
mother's shoe for a pillow. It was so red and warm and
full that the woman easily saw that a little vätte-mother
had given it suck.

On that farm they were also very careful, as all decent
folks are, that the vättar should thrive there. No boiling
water was allowed to be poured into the drain, for through
that the vättar come out and in to a house. If at any
time, such as at washings and cattle-killings, it was
necessary to pour out hot water, no one would venture to
do so before the vättar had first been warned in the usual
words, "Watch yourselves, good vättar, and not get
scalded."

In other places, where people had been careless with
hot water, they have seen the vättar (who come up and
play with the little children, when these are alone) make
their appearance with their heads tied up and badly
scalded. It often happened in old days that the vättar
came up through the floor by night, and held parties in
the room while the inmates were asleep. If any one
wakened then, it was necessary to keep perfectly quiet
and still, otherwise the party broke up and the vättar

disappeared.   Still worse was it if one happened to laugh
at the little ones, who, in all respects, behaved like human
beings.   At their parties they burned the so-called
" vätt-lights," which look like little petrified wax-candles,
and are often found among the stones and pebbles on the
beach.

No one has ever heard of the vättar and the Goa-nisse
living in the same house, nor is this so remarkable either,
for the vättar are good little beings who only watch over
the peace and friendship of the house in which they live,
while the nisse draws to it earthly possessions, and that
too from the property of other men.   Such riches may
well last for a time, but there goes with them no real luck
for the children and grandchildren.

Marjun in Örda-vík and the Vættrar.

VÆTTRAR are beautiful, little, good spirits who live in
houses beside good people.   These enjoy good-luck, and
receive assistance from them all their life-time, so that
everything goes well in that house where the vættrar are.
Happy is he who is their friend, for neither trolls nor
elves (huldufolk), nor any living thing under or on the
earth, can injure him.

Marjun in Ördavík, on the east side of Suderö, who
came there from Kollafirth, on the east side of Strömö,
is said to have been one of the most powerful witches
ever known in the islands.   She was an extremely clever
and capable woman in every respect, and was enormously
rich, having abundance of cattle and sheep, and all kinds
of wealth, and no wonder either,—the vættrar lived with
her.   She had on her farm a witless boy, whom she

employed in summer to drive the sheep away when they came in about the home fields, and this was all that the natural was fit for.   During Marjun's life-time Turkish pirates came from the south to plunder the Færöes.   They landed also on Suderö at Hvalbö, and after plundering and laying waste the northern part of the island, proceeded towards the south of it for the same purpose.   Marjun saw them coming south over the ridge and bearing down upon Ördavík, but she was not frightened like those who fled before them to the hills, and hid themselves in caves and holes, and hung black cloth in front of them.   No, Marjun sent out the witless boy with the watch-dog, and told him to chase these men off the farm.   He had no thought of any mischief, poor fellow, and so went without fear and with a light heart to do what his mistress told him, just as he always did. He went running towards the pirates with his little dog, as if they were nothing but a few scared sheep, which would run away whenever he came near them.   Meanwhile the wise woman stood beside the wall of the house, and pointed her hand at the Turks.   When these now saw a little wretch of a boy coming so boldly to meet them with a little dog, and an old woman standing so confidently under the wall, they were astonished, and thought to themselves that these two could not be so weak as their numbers might imply, but had something in secret to defend themselves with, which might cost them .dear.   So it is said that they were afraid to go further south on the island, and turned straight back to Hvalbö.   From there they took away with them two girls who were related to Marjun, on hearing which she said that before' her blood was cold (*i.e.*, before the seventh generation from her was dead), this would be avenged, and the Turkish people come under the rule of a king from another country.

Marjun in Ördavík had good luck with her in everything she undertook, and all went well with her; all this came from the fact that the good vættrar lived in her big byre. Nor did she forget to set down a pail of milk for them every time the dairy-maids milked the cows. The vættrar rewarded her for her kindness, and she had never any want of milk so long as they lived there; and no sickness ever came upon cattle or sheep while they watched over them. It was not necessary for the maids to stay overnight in the byre when a cow was expected to calve, for if she calved during the night with no one beside her, the calf was not lying on the ground when the maid went in next morning, but stood in the stall, tied with a silk band under the cow's belly so that she could lick it. The girl who came out to see to the cows had then to take the silk band off the calf immediately, and lay it on the cross-beam, and after that the vættrar took it back again. So Marjun was kind to the vættrar who did her so much good, and often earnestly exhorted her son to bear in mind, when he became farmer there after her, that it was well to lodge the vættrar, and he must always give them house-room; and if he did away with, and pulled down the big byre, it would bring hurt on himself and others. Marjun died, and her son, who was now farmer in Ördavík, heedless of his mother's warnings, tore down the byre. Then the vættrar left, wishing evil on him and all his kin in Ördavík,—a sudden death they should all meet. The same day that this happened, a man was going north the island from Vág, and when he came to Manna-skard, he met a tiny little woman coming down the narrow pass, leading two little children, one in each hand, and carrying

a third on her back.   As he passed them he heard her
say, "Avenged shall it be, that we had to leave ;" and
avenged it was, for one evening, when the three brothers
were out line-fishing south along the coast, they struck
the reef under Tjaldar-víks-hólm, the boat capsized, and
every one on board was lost.   Marjun also had three
daughters, who were at Ördavík ; they died soon after of a
violent plague which went over the district, and all this
was revenge on the part of the vættrar who had to leave
the place.

VI.—WATER-BEINGS.

Mermen and Mermaids.

THE mermaid is described as being golden-haired, and possessed of human shape down to the waist; below that she is like a fish, tail and all. Icelandic fishermen believe that they sometimes see her, for the most part north about Gríms-ey. She especially has her eye on young men, and comes on board the boat to them, if they happen to be nodding, but the 'Credo' in the old Graduale is a good defence against her.

The merman (marbendil) lives at the bottom of the sea, and never appears above the surface, unless when fished up. In Landnáma-bók it is told that Grím, one of the early colonists, went out fishing one winter with his thralls, taking with him his little son. The boy began to grow cold, so they put him into a seal-skin bag, which was drawn tight round his neck. Grím caught a merman, and said to him, "Tell us all our fortunes, and how long we have to live, otherwise you shall not get home again." "It matters little for you to know," said the merman, "for you will be dead before spring; but your son will take land and settle, where your mare Skalm lies down under her load." More than this they could not get out of him.

Mermen have been caught in this way not unfrequently, and have also been found driven dead on shore, or in the stomachs of sharks. When they are caught alive, they always want to get back to the same spot as they were taken at; they are of few words, and give little heed to men. Once some fishermen from Höfdi on Latra-strönd caught a woman on one of their hooks, and took her home with them. She said she lived in the sea, and was busy screening her mother's kitchen chimney when they caught her. She continually entreated them to take her out to sea again, and let her down at the same place as they got her, but they would not. She remained there for a year, and sewed the vestments that have been in Lauf-ás ever since. At the end of the year she was taken out to sea again, for they saw that she would never be happy on land. She promised to send some cows up on shore, and told them to be ready to receive them whenever they appeared, and burst the bladder between their nostrils, otherwise they would immediately run back into the sea. Not long after this, twelve heifers came up out of the sea, and proceeded to Höfdi. They were all sea-grey in colour; six of them were caught and greatly prized, the other six escaped.

"Then Laughed the Merman."

THERE is an old Icelandic saying, frequently made use of, "Then laughed the merman," the origin of which is said to be as follows. Once a fisherman caught a sea-creature, which called itself a "marbendil"; it had a big head and long arms, but resembled a seal from the waist downwards. The merman would give the fisher no information of any kind, so he took him ashore with him, sorely against the merman's will. His young wife came down to the sea to meet him, and kissed and caressed him, at which the man was delighted and gave her great praise, while at the same time he struck his dog for fawning on him. Then laughed the merman, and the fisherman asked the reason why he did so. " At folly," said the merman. As the man went homewards, he stumbled and fell over a little mound, whereupon he cursed it, and wondered why it had ever been made upon his land. Then laughed the merman, who was being taken along against his will, and said, " Unwise is the man." The man kept him prisoner for three nights, and during that time some packmen came with their wares. The man had never been able to get shoes with soles as thick as he wished them, and although these merchants thought they had them of the best, yet of all their stock the man said they were too thin, and would soon wear through. Then laughed the merman, and said, " Many a man is mistaken that thinks himself wise." Neither by fair means nor foul could the man get any more out of him, except on the condition that he should be taken out again to the same fishing bank where he was caught ; there he would squat on the blade of an out-stretched oar, and answer all his questions, but not otherwise. The man took him out there, and after the merman had got out on the oar-blade, he asked him first what tackle fishermen should use, if they wished to have good catches. The merman answered, " Bitten iron and trodden shall they have for hooks, and make them where stream and sea can be heard, and harden them in horses' tire ; have a grey bull's line and raw horseskin cord. For bait they shall have bird's crop and flounder bait, and man's flesh in the middle bight, and fey are you unless you fish. Froward shall the fisher's hook be."

The man then asked him what the folly was that he laughed at, when he praised his wife and struck his dog. " At *your* folly, man," said the merman, "for your dog loves you as its own life, but your wife wishes you were dead. The knoll that you cursed is your treasure-mound, with wealth in plenty under it ; so you were unwise in that, and therefore I laughed. The shoes will serve you all your life, for you have but three days to live."

With that the merman dived off the oar-blade, and so they parted, but everything turned out true that he had said.

> " Well I mind that morning
> The merman laughed so low ;
> The wife to wait her husband
> To water's edge did go ;
> She kissed him there so kindly,
> Though cold her heart as snow ;
> He beat his dog so blindly,
> That barked its joy to show."

The Merman and the Mermaid in the Færöes.

THE merman (marmennil) is like a human being, but considerably smaller in growth, and with very long fingers. He lives at the bottom of the sea, and annoys fishers by biting the bait off the hooks and fixing these in the bottom, so that they have to cut the line. If he is caught, he is so dexterous that he can loose the thread that ties the hooks to the line, and so escape from being brought up, and taken on board like any other fish. One time when he tried to play his tricks at the bottom of the sea, he was rather unlucky, for just as he was about to lay hold of the line of Anfinn from Eldu-vík, with intent to make it fast, Anfinn gave a pull, and caught the merman by the right hand. With one hand he could not free himself from the line, and so was drawn up; a cross was made upon him, and he was taken home. Anfinn kept him in his house on the hearth-stone, but had to remember every evening to make a cross on the four corners of this. He would eat nothing but fish-bait. When they went out to fish, they took the merman with them, and had to recollect to make the mark of the cross on him, when they took him on board the boat. When they rowed over a shoal of fish, he began to laugh and play in the boat, and they were sure of a good catch, if they put out their lines then, especially if he dipped his finger into the sea. Anfinn had the merman with him for a long time, but one day the sea was pretty stormy when they launched the boat, and they forgot to make the cross on him. When they had got out from land, he slipped overboard, and was never seen again.

The mermaid is like a human being above the waist, and has long brown hair like a woman, which floats round about her on the sea, but her arms are shorter. Below the waist she is like a fish, with a scaly tail. If she turns towards the boat when she comes up out of the water, a storm is sure to come, and then it is a case of rowing home as fast as possible, and so try to escape being drowned. But if the merman comes up beside her, it will be good weather. The mermaid sings so sweetly that men lose their senses with listening to her song, and so they must thrust the thumbs of their gloves into their ears, else in their madness and frenzy they will leap out of the boat into the sea to her.

The Merman and Mermaid in Norway.

WHEN the weather is calm, sailors and fishermen sometimes see mermen and mermaids rise up out of the sea.
The former are of a dusky hue, have a long beard and
black hair, and resemble a human being above the waist,
but below it are like a fish.   The latter, on the other
hand, are fair and like a beautiful woman above, but
below they have also the shape of a fish.   The fishers
sometimes catch their children, whom they call Marmæler,
and take them home with them to get knowledge of the
future from them, for they, as well as the old ones, can
foretell things to come.   Now-a-days, however, it is very
rare to hear mermaids speak or sing.   Sailors dislike to
see these beings, as they forebode storm and tempest.
To try to do them harm is dangerous.   A sailor who once
enticed a mermaid so near that she laid her hand on the
gunwale, and then hacked it off, was punished for his
cruelty with a terrible storm, from which he only escaped
with the greatest difficulty.

The Fisher and the Merman.

ONE cold winter day a fisherman had gone out to sea.
It began to grow stormy when he was about to return,
and he had trouble enough to clear himself.   He then
saw, near his boat, an old man with a long gray beard,
riding on a wave.   The fisherman knew well that it was
the merman he saw before him, and knew also what it
meant.   " Uh, then, how cold it is ! " said the merman as
he sat and shivered, for he had lost one of his hose.   The

fisherman pulled off one of his, and threw it out to him.
The merman disappeared with it, and the fisherman came
safe to land.   Some time after this the fisherman was
again out at sea, far from land.   All at once the merman
stuck his head over the gunwale, and shouted out to the
man in the boat,

> " Hear, you man that gave the hose,
> Take your boat and make for shore,
> It thunders under Norway."

The fisherman made all the haste he could to get to land,
and there came a storm the like of which had never been
known, in which many were drowned at sea.

The Merman and the Calf.

AN old woman in Stradil tells the following story after
her grandmother.   Once, when no ship had been wrecked
for a long time, and the merman thus had not got his
victim, he went up on shore, and cast his hook into the
cows which went about on the sandhills.   Just beside the
sea there lived a peasant, who had two pretty red calves
that he did not want to lose, so he coupled them together
with rowan tree, and the merman had no power over them.
All the same he fixed his hook in them, but he could not
drag them down into the sea, and had to let go his hook,
with which the calves came home in the evening.   The
man took it, guessing it was the merman's, and hung it
up beside the stove, where it hung till one day, when only
an old woman was left in the house.   Then the merman
came and took his hook, and turning about to the old
woman, said in his own imperfect speech, " Two red cows'
first calves ; rowan tree to couple ; man couldn't drag

them ; man has lost many good catch since." With that
he went away with the hook, and never tried to take
cattle on the beach again.

The Dead Merman and the Sand-Drift.

A DEAD body was once washed ashore on the Danish
coast, and buried in the churchyard of Nissum. No
sooner had this been done than the sand began to blow
over the country from the beach, and this continued for
three days, growing always the longer the worse. People
now began to think there was trolldom in the matter, and
applied to a wise man for advice. On his learning that
the sand-storm had begun immediately after the burial
of the dead body from the sea, he declared that this was
undoubtedly a merman, and that his burial in Christian
ground had caused the drifting. They must instantly
dig him up again, and see whether he had sucked his
fore-finger into his mouth past the second joint. If he
had done this there was no help for it, but if not they
should bury him in the sandhills, and the drifting would
cease. They accordingly dug him up again, and sure
enough they found him lying with his finger in his mouth,
but he had got it no further than the second joint. They
then buried him in the sand-hills, and the drifting ceased.
After that all bodies washed ashore were buried in these
hills, down to quite recent times.

The Sea-Sprite.

THE sea-sprite is seen after sunset standing on out-lying
reefs, and when men row out to fish he calls upon them

and asks to be taken on board the boat. Sometimes they have taken him on board, and set him on one of the seats to row with the others ; during the darkest part of the night he can row against two at the least, so strong is he. He is good at finding the fishing-ground when it is not clear enough to see the land-marks, but he grows smaller and smaller as day approaches, and fades away into nothing when the sun rises out of the sea. They have made the sign of the cross on him, but as the eastern sky grew redder and redder before the sun, he begged more and more piteously to be let go. One time they would not let him away, but when the sun rose he disappeared, and his pelvis was left lying on the seat, for the sea-sprite is said to take to himself a human pelvis, and this is left behind if the sprite himself disappears. He can also produce ocular deceptions : sometimes he seems like a man, sometimes like a dog. He is of a dark-red colour, and hoots and howls so that it can be heard a far way off. Fire flies from him when he is on shore. He has only one foot (or tail), but can hop a long way with it, and his tracks have been seen in the snow. When he meets a man on land he tries to drive him out into the sea.

The Shepherd and the Sea-Folk.

ONE time there was a rich yeoman who had a large and splendid house, with a sitting room all panelled from floor to ceiling, but it had the defect that any one who stayed there on Christmas eve was found dead next morning. It was, therefore, difficult to get any one to stay there, for no one wished to remain at home that

night, and yet it was necessary for some one to do so.
Once the yeoman had got a new shepherd, as he did frequently, for he had many sheep and required an active
man to look after them.   The yeoman told the man
honestly of this bad point about the farm, but the shepherd said he did not mind such trifles, and was quite as
willing to come to him for all that.   He came to him
accordingly, and they got on very well together.   Time
passed until Christmas came, and the yeoman and all his
household went to evensong on Christmas eve, except the
shepherd, who was not making ready to go to church.
His master asked why this was.   The shepherd said he
meant to stay at home, as it was impossible to leave the
farm to itself, and let the cattle want their food so long.
The farmer told him never to mind that, no one could
venture to stay there on Christmas eve, as he had said
before, for every living thing then about the house was
killed, and he would not have him risk it on any account.
The shepherd professed to think this all nonsense, and
said he would try it.   When his master found he could
not persuade him, he went away with the others, and left
him there alone.

The shepherd, when left to himself, began to think
over his design, and decided that he had better be prepared for all emergencies, as there was plainly something
wrong.   He kindled a light in the sitting-room, and made
it quite bright.   Then he looked for a place to hide himself, and loosening two planks of the panelling at the end
of the room, he crept in there, drawing them into their
places again so as to leave no trace.   There he stood
between the panelling and the wall, being able to see
all that went on in the room through a chink in the
boards.

No long time after he had thus disposed of himself, he saw two unknown and very grim-looking men enter the room, and look all round it. Then one of them said, " The smell of man ! the smell of man ! ". " No," said the other, "there is no man here." They then took lights, and looked everywhere in the room, high and low, till at last they found a dog that was lying below one of beds. Him they took and wrung his neck, and threw him out at the door. The shepherd saw then that it would not have done for him to come in contact with these fellows, and thanked his good fortune that he was where he was. After this the room began to fill with people, who proceeded to lay the table, and had all their table-service of silver—dishes, spoons, and knives. Food was then served up, and they sat down to it, making great noise and mirth, and were there eating, drinking and dancing all night. Two, however, were set to watch and tell if they saw any man on the move outside, and whether day was about to dawn. Thrice during the night they went out and said they saw no one coming, and that it was not yet day. When the shepherd thought that it must be dawn, he seized both the loose boards, sprang out into the floor with the greatest violence, clapped the boards together, and yelled with all his might, "Day! Day!" The strangers were so startled at this that they tumbled out, heads over heels, leaving all their belongings—table, table-service, and clothes which they had put off during the night to be all the lighter for dancing. Some were hurt and some trodden under foot, while the shepherd continued to chase them, clapping his boards and shouting "Day! Day!" till they reached a lake a little way from the farm, into which they all dived, and then he saw that they were "sea-folk" or "water-dwellers." After that he went back home, dragged out the dead ones, and killed the half-dead, and then burned up the bodies. When his master came home, he and the shepherd divided between them all that the visitors had left, and from that time forward nothing strange happened there on Christmas Eve.

The Origin of the Seal.

SEALS originally come from mortals who have intentionally drowned themselves in the sea. Once in the year, on Fastern's Eve, they can take off their skins, and enjoy themselves as human beings, with dancing and other amusements, in caves and on the flat rocks beside the beach.

A young man in Mikladal had heard of this, and there was pointed out to him a place not far off, where they assembled on that night. Towards evening he slipped away to this, and kept himself concealed, until he saw the seals in great numbers come swimming up, take off their skins and lay them on the rocks. He noticed that a most beautiful girl came out of one of the seal-skins, and laid it a short distance from where he had hid himself, so he slipped up and took possession of it. They danced and played the whole night, but when day began to dawn, every seal went to look for its skin. The girl was distressed when she missed hers, and traced it to the man from Mikladal, but as he, in spite of her entreaties, would not give it back to her, she had to go home with him. They lived together for many years and had several children, but he had always to take care that his wife should have no chance of getting hold of her seal-skin, which he therefore locked up in his chest, and always carried the key about with him. One day he was out fishing, and as he sat and fished out at sea, he discovered that he had left the key at home, and called out to the others, "To-day I have lost my wife." They pulled up their lines and rowed home in all haste, but when they reached the house, the woman had disappeared, and only the children were left. To prevent these coming to harm when she had left them, she had put out the fire and laid away all the knives. Then she ran down to the beach, put on the skin and plunged into the sea, where a male seal came up by her side,—he had all the time been lying out there waiting for her. Whenever these children came down to the beach, a seal might often be seen to rise and look towards land, and it was believed that this was their mother. So a long time passed, and it happened that the man intended to go into a large cave to kill seals. The night before this took place, he dreamed that his former wife came to him and told him that if he went on this expedition, he must take care not to kill the big seal at the mouth of the cave, for that was her mate, nor the two young seals at the back of the cave, for these were her two young sons, and she described to him the colour of their skins. The man, however, gave no heed to the dream, but went with the others, and they killed all the seals they could lay their hands on. The spoil was divided when they came home, and the man got for his share the big seal and the hands and feet of the two young ones. In the evening they had boiled the head of the big seal, and the flippers of the young ones for their supper, but when these were set on the table there was a great crash in the kitchen, and his former wife came in like a fearful troll, snuffed at the dishes, and cried, "Here lies

the head of my mate, the hand of Hárek, and the foot of
Fridrik, but it shall be avenged on the men of Mikladal ;
some of them shall perish on the sea, and some fall down
the cliffs, till their number is so great that they can reach
round the whole island of Kallsö, holding each other by
the hand." After uttering this curse she disappeared and
was never seen again, but to this day some are always
being lost on the dangerous waters and cliffs in this neighbourhood, and it is also said that there is always a lunatic
on the south farm in Mikladal. The number of those lost
must, therefore, still be insufficient to stretch round the
island.

Nykur or the Water-horse

NYKUR lives both in rivers and lakes, and even in the sea.
In shape he most resembles a horse, generally grey in
colour, but sometimes black ; all his hoofs point backwards, and the tuft on the pastern is reversed. He is,
however, not confined to this one shape, but has the property of being able to change himself at once into other
forms at his pleasure. When cracks come in the ice in
winter, and cause loud noises, it is said that Nykur is
neighing. He begets foals, just like stallions, but always
in the water, although it has happened that he has got
mares with foal. It is the mark of all horses that are
sprung from Nykur that they lie down when they are
ridden, or bear packs, over water that wets their belly.
This property they have from Nykur, who haunts lakes
and rivers that are difficult to cross ; he then appears
quite tame, and entices people to ride across on him.
When any happen to mount him he rushes out into the

P

water, lies down there, and drags his rider down with him.
He cannot bear to hear his own name, or any word
resembling it; at that he changes shape, and springs into
the water.

In Gríms-ey, in the north, it is believed that Nykur
lives in the sea there, and neighs whenever he knows that
the inhabitants have gone to the mainland for a cow. His
neigh drives them mad, and they spring into the sea and
are drowned. To this also points the fact that it is only
of late years that the men of Gríms-ey have ventured to
keep a cow on the island.

Nykur does work as a Grey Horse.

ONCE the farmers of the parish had to build a wall round
the churchyard at Bard (some say Holt) in Fljót (N. of
Iceland). One day they had all come to the work early
except one man, who was thought rather evil-disposed.
Not before mid-day did they see him coming, leading
after him a grey horse. On his arrival he was assailed
by those who had come early, for coming so late to do his
share of the work. The man calmly asked what he was
to do, and was set to work along with some others to
bring turf for building the wall, with which he was well
enough pleased. His grey horse was very fierce towards
the others, bit them and kicked them, till at last no horse
could stand before him. The men tried putting heavier
loads on him, but that did no good, for he went with
loads half as heavy again just as easily as before, and
never stopped till he drove off all the other horses, and
was the only one left. The man then put on his back as
much as all the other horses together had taken at each

journey, and after that he went quietly and carried all the material needed for the wall. When this work was finished, the man took the bridle off the horse beside the new-built wall, and struck him over the loins with it just as he let him go. The horse not liking this, threw up his heels and struck the wall with them, thus making a great gap in it that could never be filled up afterwards, however often it was built again, until at last they came to use it as a gate to the church. The last seen of the horse was that as soon as he was loose, he set off and never stopped till he landed in Holt Lake, and all were sure then that this had been Nykur.

Nennir.

ONE time a herd-girl was searching after sheep, and was very tired with walking so far. She then, to her great delight, came upon a grey horse, for which she made a halter with her garter, laid her apron on his back, and proceeded to mount him. But just as she did this, she said " I don't think I care to (*nenni*) go on its back." With that the horse started violently, dashed out into a lake near hand, and disappeared. The girl now saw that this was Nykur, for it is his nature that he must not hear his name, otherwise he goes off into his lake, and his other name is *Nennir*. The same thing happens if Nykur hears the Devil named.

One time three or four children were playing themselves near their home on the level banks of a lake. They saw there a grey horse, and went to look at it. Then one of the children mounted it, and the others followed, one by one, till only the eldest was left. The others told it to come up too, the horse's back would be long enough for them all to sit on. The child would not go, however, and said it did not care to (ekki *nenna*). With that the horse started and dashed into the lake with all the children on its back. The one that was left went home and told what had happened, and all knew that this must have been Ny-kur, but neither he nor the children were ever seen again.

The Long Horse.

IN the middle of the town of Ryslinge there was in old days a morass called Tange's Kjær, and the name is still given to a dam which by draining has taken the place of the morass. One evening, many years ago, some young girls from Ryslinge had been out at a farm in Skirret, to help the woman there to card her wool, and it was pretty late before they started to go home. They followed the path from Skirret to Ryslinge, which went through the morass. The girls were frightened as to how they were to get over this dangerous spot, but on coming to it they found there an old lean horse, so lean that one could count its ribs. The boldest of the girls immediately mounted on its back, and the others followed her example, for the more that mounted it the longer grew the horse. They then rode into the morass, but when they had got half way over, the foremost girl looked behind her, and when she saw that they were all on one and the same horse, she was so scared that she cried out,

"Jesus Christ's cross !
We are sitting all on one horse."

As soon as this was said, the horse suddenly disappeared, and the girls were left standing in the middle of the bog, and had to wade to land.

Nykur in the Færöes.

NYKUR lives in lakes, where he has his abode deep down
at the bottom of the waters, but he often comes up on
shore, and it is no good thing to meet him. Sometimes
he is like a pretty little horse, and looks quiet and tame,
and so entices folk to come near to him, and clap him
and stroke him on the back ; but as soon as they happen
to touch the tail, they stick fast to him, and then he lets
no one go, but drags them down with him to the bottom
of the water. Sometimes he appears in human shape, as
a fine young fellow, to entice girls to go with him, and
promises them mirth and play in his hall, if they will but
follow him ; but if they get a suspicion of who it is that
they are giving themselves over to, they have only to
name him by his right name, "Nykur," and he loses all
power over them, and must let them go and return all
alone to his lake. It is said that Nykur can also assume
the shape of all four-footed beasts, but he cannot get the
point of a wether's horn made on himself. So long, however, as he keeps his own shape he is like a horse, and it
has happened that men have got power over him by cutting a cross on his back, and have then employed him to
drag large stones down from the hills with his tail, to
build walls or houses with, such as may still be seen at
Húsavík in Sandö, and at Eid in Österö. The huge
stones gathered there bear witness to his great strength.
On Takmyre, in Sandö, lies a huge rock, which they
would have had him draw to Húsavík, but his tail broke,
and the stone stands there with part of the tail still to be
seen adhering to it.

The Nök or Neck.

THIS water-troll resides mainly in rivers and lakes, but sometimes also in fjords. He requires a human sacrifice every year, and therefore in every river or lake where a Nök has his abode, at least one person is lost every year, and when one is to be drowned, the Nök is often heard shouting with a hollow and ghostly voice, " Cross over." These foreboding cries, in some places called " ware-shrieks," are also sometimes heard like those of a human being in a death-struggle.

The Nök can change his shape to resemble all kinds of things, sometimes a half-boat in the water, or a half-horse on land, sometimes gold and valuables. If any one touches these, the Nök has power over him, and is especially greedy for little children, but is only dangerous after sunset. On approaching a water at that time, it is not amiss to say, " Nyk, nyk, needle in water ! the Virgin Mary threw steel in water : you sink, I float !"

Although the Nök is a dangerous troll, yet he sometimes finds his master. In Sund-foss in Gjerrestad, says the story, there lived for a long time a Nök, who was often the cause of people being lost, when they rowed up or down the fall. The priest, who feared danger from this Nök, took with him on his journey four stout fellows, and made them twice row up the foss with all their might, but each time they were carried back without getting over it. When they rowed up for the third time, they saw the priest, at the head of the foss, plunge his hand into the water and pull out of it a creature which looked like a little black dog. The priest then told them to row further up the stream, while he set the Nök between his feet and remained quite silent. As they neared the cairn beside

Tvet, he charmed the Nök into it. Since that time no
one has been lost in Sund-foss, whereas two have been
drowned beside the cairn of Tvet, where cries are often
heard as of people in danger of their lives.

Not much better did the Nök in Bahus fare. In Norland he transformed himself into a horse, and went on the
bank to graze, but a wise man, who saw that there was
something on foot, cast so ingenious a halter on him that
he could not get free again. He kept the Nök beside him
the whole Spring, and worked him well, for he ploughed
all his fields with him. At last the halter gave way by
accident, and like a shot the Nök sprang into the lake,
and took the harrow along with him.

The River-Horse.

THE river-horse (bäck-hästen) is very malicious, for, not
content with leading folk astray and then laughing at
them, when he has landed them in thickets and bogs, he,
being Necken himself, alters his shape now to one thing
and now to another, although he commonly appears as a
light-grey horse. A good long time back a peasant got
the better of him. The river-horse wanted to get the
man on his back, when he would soon have carried him
out into the stream ; but the peasant was wiser than that,
for instead of mounting him he put a bridle on him, and
Grey-coat had to go home with him. He now got something else to do than go about and play tricks, for the
peasant harnessed him to the plough and to a heavy
waggon, so that he had to use all his strength, and the
bridle was never taken off him for a single minute so long
as the peasant remembered about it. One day, however,

he forgot what kind of horse he had and took off the bridle, whereupon the river-horse went off like a shot, and was never again seen in that district.

He also changes himself sometimes to other animals. On one occasion a servant-girl went into the cow-house, and found there a new-born calf. It was a winter day, so she took the calf and carried it into the house, where she laid it beside the stove. Her master and mistress were delighted with this, as they had not been expecting one, and asked the girl whether it was a bull or a cow. She did not know, and when she proceeded to find out, the calf sprang up and laughed, "Ho, ho, ho!" and dashed out of the house.

It is certain that the river-horse still exists, for it is no more than a few years back that a man in Filborna district, who owned a light-grey horse, was coming home late one night, and saw, as he thought, the horse standing beside Väla brook. He thought it strange that his man had not taken in Grey-coat, and proceeded to do so himself, but just as he was about to lay hold of it it went off like an arrow, and laughed loudly. The man turned his coat, so as not to go astray, for he knew now who the horse was.

In Kristianstad there was a well, from which all the girls took the drinking-water, and where a number of boys always gathered as well. One evening the river-horse was standing there, and the boys, thinking it was just an old horse, seated themselves on its back, one after the other, until there was a whole row of them, but the smallest one hung on by the horse's tail. When he saw how long it was he cried, "Oh, in Jesus' name!" whereupon the horse threw all the others into the water.

A worse thing about the river-horse is that he has a

great passion for women who have just given birth to a
child. He then puts on the appearance of the genuine
husband, and tries to share her bed ; but however he may
change his shape he cannot get rid of the horse's hoof,
and by this the wife can distinguish him from her real
husband. If she does not look to this, and allows herself
to be deceived by him, she becomes wrong in the head
from that day forward. No woman, however, receives
these ugly visits unless the midwife or some other person
has been so careless as to wash her linen in some stream
or river, and dry it in the open air, for through this the
river-horse (or river-man, as one may call him) gets power
to enter the house.

The River-Man.

LIKE the trolls and the wood-fairies, the river-man belongs
to the fallen angels, and like these also he desires to play
wicked pranks on mankind, so he changes his shape at
pleasure. A story is told of a young girl who engaged
herself to an agreeable young man, and the two were in
the habit of meeting beside a stream. The river-man
took advantage of this, put on the shape of her betrothed,
and met the girl several times. She found, however, that
he behaved differently from his usual conduct, and complained to her parents. These suspected mischief, and
told her that the next time she met him, she should pretend to be very friendly with him, and so get out of him
the way to protect herself against the river-man. She
took their advice, and he was foolish enough to say to her,
that whoever carried on their person, " wall-stone, sausage-
bone, and the white under ground,' would be safe from

him. The girl then searched for a stone from a clay-covered house-wall, a bone-splinter from a meat-sausage, and a garlic-root ; these she carried about with her, and so put an end to his tricks.

The river-man plays music in the rivers and streams. His music is wondrously beautiful to hear, but dangerous to listen to, for one can lose their senses by standing and hearing the dance to the end. Many village musicians have been known, who have learned from him to play this elf-dance, and have sometimes played the first parts of it at Christmas parties and elsewhere. This might be done without any danger either to themselves or the dancers, but if the player had not sense enough to stop at the end of the third part, but began to the fourth and last, then it was too late. At the third part both old and young danced like mad, but now the musician and tables and benches danced as well, and could not stop so long as life was in the people, unless some one from outside entered the room, and cut all the strings of the violin across with a knife.

Necken is Promised Redemption.

IN the songs which were composed in old times about Necken, he is represented, like all the elf-folk, as worthy of sympathy and compassion, and the country people always listen with a feeling of melancholy to the sorrowful Necken's song, in which he laments his hard fate.

> " Oh, I am ne'er a knight, though so I seem to you,
> I am the wretched Necken, that dwells in billows blue,
> In fosses and thundering torrents.

> " My dwelling it lies beneath a bridge so low,
> Where no one can walk and where no one can go,
> And no one can remain till the morning."

Among the most common and most widely-spread stories of Necken is the following. A priest was one evening riding over a bridge, when he heard strains of most melodious music. He turned round, and saw upon the surface of the water a young man, naked to the waist, wearing a red cap, with golden locks hanging over his shoulders, and having a gold harp in his hand. He knew that it was Necken, and addressed him thus : " Why do you play your harp so merrily? Sooner shall this withered staff that I hold in my hand grow green and blossom, than you shall get redemption. The unhappy Necken threw his harp into the water, and wept bitterly. The priest turned his horse again and rode on his way, but lo, when he had gone a little way, he noticed that round about the old pilgrim's staff that he had in his hand green shoots and leaves had come forth, mingled with the most beautiful flowers. This seemed to him to be a sign from heaven, to preach the comforting doctrine of Redemption after another fashion, and he hastened back to the still mourning Necken, showed him the flowering staff, and said, "See, now my old staff is green, and blossoms like a rose ; so also shall hope blossom in the hearts of all cre-ated beings, for their Redeemer liveth." Comforted with this, Necken seized his harp again, and joyous tones sounded over the banks the live-long night.

" The hour is come, but not the man."

IT was the Nök, or another water-troll, who late one even-ing shouted from the lake beside Hvide-sö Parsonage, " The time is come, but not the man." As soon as the priest heard of this, he gave orders to watch the first man who came with intent to cross the lake, and stop him from going further. Immediately after this, there came a man in hot haste, and asked for a boat. The priest begged him to put off his journey, but as neither entreaties nor threats had any effect, the priest made them use force to prevent his crossing. The stranger became quite helpless, and remained lying so, until the priest had some water brought from the lake from which the cry came, and gave him it to drink. Scarcely had he drunk the water, when he gave up the ghost.

In southern Vend-syssel in Denmark the river-man is also known as the Nök. The river Ry there takes one person every year, and when it demands them, it calls, " The time and the hour are come, but the man is not yet come." When this cry is heard from the river, folk must beware of going too near it, for if they do so, they are seized by an irresistible desire to spring into it, and then they never come up again. There are many who are said to have heard the cry, among others a girl who was going along its bank with a dog by her side. When she heard the call, she cried out, " Not me, but the dog," which immediately sprang into the stream and was drowned. She also saw a little man with a large beard running about in the river ; this was the Nök, from whom the cry no doubt came.

In Odense river there is also a river-man, who requires his victim every year, and if one year passes without any one being drowned there, he takes good care to have two in the year following. It is said that two little boys were once playing on the bank, when one of them fell into the water. The other tried to help him out, but just as he got hold of his comrade's hand, a voice was heard out of the river, " No, I shall have both of you ; I got no one

last year," and with that this boy also slipped into the
water and both were drowned. Some men, who were
witnesses of the accident from the opposite bank, hurried
with a boat to lend their aid, but came too late. The
bodies were never found either, the river-man had kept
them.

The River-Man.

THERE was a river-man in a stream which runs on the
south side of Maarup-gaard in Fjaltring. The man on
the farm was well acquainted with him, and the river-man
gave him permission to pasture his cattle along his possessions. Finally, however, they fell out, as the river-man
thought that the farmer was coming too close to him ; so
he decided to play him a trick. The meadow had just
been mown, and a pair of bullocks were pasturing on it,
one of which he resolved to take when it came down to
drink. One of them had a piece of a tether round its
neck, and as it bent down its head to drink, the river-man
fixed his gold hook in this, and tried to drag it down into
the stream. The bullock, however, dragged the hook
from him, and ran straight home with it. The farmer
came out into the yard, and saw this big gold hook hanging at the bullock's neck, so he took it off and hung it up
in his parlour. In a little the river-man came and asked
it back, but the man said, "No ; it is hanging in a place
that you cannot take it from." "Oh, never mind," said
he, "you can just keep it for the services you have done
me in time past ; I wanted you to have it as a reminder
of me, and there is a blessing along with it, for you and
your descendants will never come to poverty so long as

you have it." This has been fulfilled, for there has always been prosperity on that farm, as far back as any one can remember.

The Kelpie.

IN Gerrestad, they formerly used to set down a bowl of gruel, or something of that kind, beside the mill, so that the kelpie might increase the meal in the sacks. For a long time he lived in Sand-ager-foss, where a man had a mill. Whenever he tried to grind corn, the mill stopped, and the man, who knew that it was the kelpie who caused this annoyance, took with him one evening some pitch in a pot, under which he lighted a fire. As soon as he had started the mill, it stopped as usual. He then pushed down a pole to drive away the kelpie, but in vain. Finally, he opened the door to look out, but right in the doorway stood the kelpie, with open mouth, which was so big, that his under-jaw rested on the threshold and the upper one on the lintel. " Have you ever seen anything gape so wide ? " said he to the man, who straightway caught up the pot of boiling pitch, and threw it into his mouth, with the words, " Have *you* ever felt anything taste so hot ? " The kelpie disappeared, roaring loudly, and has never been seen since.

Sea-Serpents.

IN the fresh-water lakes and rivers, as well as along the coasts of Norway, are found monstrous sea-serpents, which, however, differ in respect both of their appearance and magnitude. According to the general belief, they are born on land, and have their first abode in forests and stone-heaps, from which, when they are full-grown, or have tasted human blood, they make their way down to inland lakes, or to the sea, where they grow to a monstrous size. They seldom show themselves, and when they do, they are regarded as omens of important events. In most lakes and rivers of any importance these monsters have, according to tradition, been seen some time or other rising from the depths of the waters, and thereby foretelling some great event. In the fresh-water lakes none have shown themselves within living memory, but they are sometimes seen in the firths when it is perfectly calm. In Snaasen Lake is found a large serpent, which yearly demands a human life, and in Sælbo Lake there exists one which has lain there since the Deluge. When once it turns itself, it will break down the mountain that now dams in the lake, and the result will be that Trondhjem will be overflowed. Some time after the black death, says tradition, there came two large serpents from Foksö past By and down into Lougen ; one of them is said to be still there, but the other, a couple of centuries ago, tried to go down the river to Gulosen, and was killed in the waterfall, and drifted over to Braaleret, beside By-nes in the neighbourhood of Trondhjem, where it rotted and gave out such a stench that no one could go near the spot.

The Sea-Serpent in Mjösen.

IN Mjösen there once lived a sea-serpent, and one time, when it was fine summer weather, it came to the surface to sun itself, throwing the water into the air, while it reared its head above a reef. Its eyes were large, and glowed like a carbuncle; a long mane like sea-tangle hung down its neck; and its body, covered with scales which glanced with a thousand colours, stuck up here and there. As it was unable to go away again, and lay and beat its head upon the reef, there was a monk, a daring fellow, who shot an arrow into one of its eyes. It died in terrible convulsions, so that the waves became both red and green with blood and venom, and finally it drove ashore at Pulstö on Helge-ö. It lay there and rotted till the stench became so intolerable, that the inhabitants had to cart wood and burn it up. They afterwards set up its ribs, which were so high that a man on horseback could ride under them.

VII.—Monsters.

Gold—Thorir and the Drake.

In the days of Harald, the Fair-haired, Thorir Oddson came from Iceland to Norway, and was sent by his uncle Sigmund there to his friend Ulf, north in Hálogaland. One day Thorir and his comrades were out fishing and came home late. Ulf went to meet them, and when they had fixed up their boat for the night, Thorir saw a fire like the light of the moon, over which hovered a blue flame. He asked what light that was. "Better not enquire into that," said Ulf, "it has no human origin." "Why should I not know of it," said Thorir, "though it is caused by trolls?" Ulf said it was a grave-mound fire. Thorir still questioned him, and at length Ulf told him about it, saying, "There was a berserk named Agnar, who made this mound and went into it with all his ship's crew, and much treasure besides. Since then he guards the mound by his trolldom, so that no one may come near it. Many who have come to break into it have died, or some other mishap has befallen them, and we do not know whether the troll is alive or dead." Said Thorir, "Now you have spoken well, and it is more manly to get treasure there, than row out to the fishing. I shall venture it." Ulf tried hard to prevent him, as well as all his comrades, but Thorir declared he would go all the same. Ketilbjörn alone was willing to go with him, none of the

Q

others being bold enough. To reach the mound they had
to ascend a hill-slope, and on their coming up on this,
there broke upon them such a violent storm that they
could not stand before it. They had a rope between
them, and Thorir went on foremost as long as he could,
but finally the storm lifted both of them and threw them
down the slope. The rope caught round a large stone,
and they were now so exhausted that they lay there till
they fell asleep. Thorir dreamed then that a man
came to him, big of body, dressed in a red kirtle, and
having a helm on his head and a sword in his hand. He
wore a broad belt to which was fixed a good knife, and
had gloves on his hands ; the man was majestic and
stately. He thrust at Thorir with the point of his scab-
bard, and spoke to him angrily, bidding him wake up,
and saying, " There is the making of an ill man in you,
when you will rob your kinsmen, but I will do to you
better than you deserve, for I am your father's brother
and by the same mother as him. I will give you presents
to turn back and look elsewhere for treasure. You shall
have from me this good kirtle, which will shield you from
fire and weapons, and along with it the helm and sword.
I shall also give you gloves such as you will not get the
like of, for your followers will be free from wounds if you
stroke them with these. You shall also wear them when
you bind up any man's wounds, and all the pain will soon
go out of these. I shall leave here my knife and belt,
and these you shall always have with you. I shall also
give you twenty marks of gold and twenty of silver."
Thorir seemed to himself to answer that he thought this
too little from so near and so rich a kinsman, and said
that he would not go back for any little bribe, "nor did I
know," said he, " that I had trolls so near of kin to me

until you told me, and you would have no hope of mercy
from me, were it not for our kinship." Agnar said,
" Long will it be ere your eyes are filled with treasure,
and you may well excuse me for loving my wealth, for
you will love it well too before all is done." Thorir said,
" I care not for your prophecies of ill, but I will accept
your offer of showing me where I may look for greater
treasures, if you wish to beg off your own." " I will
rather do that than quarrel with you," said Agnar.
" There was a viking named Val, who had much gold.
This treasure he took into a cave north beside Dumbs
Sea, and he and his sons brooded over it then and became
flying-dragons. They have helms on their heads, and
swords under their arms. Now here is a cup, of which
you shall drink two draughts and your comrade one, and
then happen whatever may." Then Thorir awoke, and
found all these things that Agnar gave him lying there
beside him. Ketilbjörn awoke also, and had heard all
their talk, and seen where Agnar went ; he advised Thorir
to take this offer. Thorir then took the cup and drank
two draughts of it and Ketilbjörn one; there was still
some left in the cup and Thorir set it to his mouth and
drank it off. Again sleep fell upon them, and Agnar returned and blamed Thorir for having drunk all that was
in the cup, saying that he would pay for this drink the
latter part of his life. He also told him many things that
befell later, and gave him directions how to win the cave
of the viking Val.

After this they woke and went home. They told Ulf
what had befallen them, and bade him direct them to
Val's cave. Ulf tried to prevent their going, and offered
them money to desist, saying that no one who had gone
had ever come back, and he would like ill that those men

should be lost whom his friend Sigmund had sent him. Thorir, however, was bent on going at any cost, and soon after with his comrades set out and held north along Finnmark till they came to Blesaberg, which was the name of the fell where Val's cave was. It lies north, beside Dumbs-haf, where a great river falls from the mountain into deep chasms and so out into the sea. Thorir knew then that they had reached the spot to which he was directed. They went up on the fell, and made the preparations that Agnar had taught him. They cut down a great tree, and laid it with its branches hanging over the mountain's edge, piling up stones on its root; then they took a cable and fastened it to the branches. Thorir then offered his comrades the chance to go and keep all the treasure they got, but none of them had any hope of reaching the cave, even though there were no other danger than that, and bade him give up the attempt. "That shall not be," said Thorir, "rather will I try it myself, and have all the treasure that can be found." The others said that they would make no claim on it; he would have plenty to do if he got it. Thorir threw off his clothes and equipped himself lightly, putting on the kirtle he got from Agnar, and taking the gloves, belt and knife, and a slender line that Agnar gave him. He had a javelin that his father gave him, and with this he went out on the tree; from there he shot the javelin across the river and fastened it in the wood on the other side; after that he went down the rope and let the line draw him away under the waterfall. When Ketilbjörn saw this, he declared he would go with Thorir, and let one fate go over them both; so he too went down the rope, followed by Thorhall and Thrand. Thorir had by this time reached the cave, and drew in those who came down. A rocky projection ran out to the sea in front of the waterfall, and up this came Björn and Hyrning, the tent being beside this projection, because no one could stay near the waterfall on account of the shaking and spray. Thorir and his men kindled a light in the cave, and went on till the wind blew against them, and the light went out. Then Thorir called on Agnar for aid, and straightway there came a great flash of light from the door of the cave, by which they went on for some way, until they heard the breathing of the dragons. As soon as the light came over the dragons, they all fell asleep, and then there was no want of light, which shone from the dragons and from the gold they lay upon. They saw swords there with the hilts ready to their hand; these Thorir and his comrades seized at once, and then leaped over the dragons and thrust them under their shoulders to the heart. Thorir got the helm taken off the largest dragon, but at that moment it seized Thrand and flew out of the cave with him, the others following one by one and casting fire and much venom from their mouths. Those who were outside now saw light flashing from the waterfall, and ran out of their tent, while the dragons flew up out of the chasm. Then Björn and the others saw that one of them had a man in its mouth, and supposed that all who entered the cave must be dead. The biggest dragon, which had the man in its mouth, flew furthest, and as they came up over the ledge of rock Björn sprang up and thrust his inlaid spear into it. When it received the wound, there sprang from this a great quantity of blood into his face, so that he died suddenly, and the blood and venom fell on the foot of Hyrning, where it caused such pain that he could scarcely stand. As for Thorir and his comrades, they got great treasure in the cave, so that there was sufficient for many men in gold and precious things. It is said they stayed three days in Val's cave, and there Thorir found the sword Horn-hilt that Val had borne. Thorir then climbed up the rope first, and afterwards drew up his fellows and the treasure. He took Hyrning's foot and stroked it with the gloves, and all the pain left it at once. They then divided the treasure, Thorir receiving the largest share, and returned to Ulf.

In his later days Thorir, being hard pressed by his foes, took the two chests in which he kept this treasure, and with these on his arms sprang into a deep chasm and was never seen again. It was supposed that he had lain upon his gold-chests and turned into a serpent, for long afterwards a dragon was seen flying down into the ravine in which he disappeared.

Björn and the Dragon.

ONE summer Björn of Hítardal, in the west of Iceland, sailed from Norway to England, and remained there two winters with Knut the Mighty. While he followed this king and was sailing with him off the English coast, a flying dragon flew over the ships, swooped down upon them, and tried to seize a man in its claws. Björn, who was standing by, covered the man with his shield, through which the dragon's claws almost pierced. Then Björn caught the dragon's tail with one hand, and with the other gave it a stroke of his sword behind the wings, cleaving it in two, so that it fell down dead. King Knut rewarded Björn with much money and a good war-ship, with which he set sail for Denmark.

Dragons in Norway.

STORIES of dragons which fly through the air by night, and vomit fire, are fairly common, and in various places all over the country there are still shown holes in the earth and in the hills, out of which they are seen to come flying like blazing fire, when wars or other troubles are to be expected. When they return to their dwellings, where they brood over immense treasures (which they, as some say, have gathered by night, in the depths of the sea) there can be heard the clang of the great iron doors that close behind them. As they are fierce and vomit terrible fire, it is dangerous to meddle with them. Under Akers Kirk, which rests on four golden pillars, there lies a dragon brooding over immense riches, which, within living memory, shortly before the last war, has been seen to come out of a hole beside the church. At innumerable other places there have been, and still are seen fiery dragons with long tails. That they are not invincible however, can be seen from an old story which relates that a priest of the name of Anders Madsen, (supposed to have lived about 1631), shot a dragon which lay upon silver, in the so-called Drage-fjeld beside Tvede-vand,

Dragons in Denmark.

DRAGONS brood over gold in the mounds. They are fiery in front like a baker's oven, and have a long tail behind. If any one throws an edged tool over the dragon, the gold will come rattling down to them. There was a man who tried this, but the dragon filled his whole farm-yard with horse-dung instead of gold ; perhaps that one

didn't have any. It is also said that one can compel a
dragon to give up its gold, by throwing a stone at its tail,
as it comes flying. The tail then falls down as gold, with
the exception of the one spot which the stone strikes ;
that remains unaltered, but when the stone strikes the
dragon, it gives forth a shriek which kills the man who
threw the stone, if he hears it. In the parish of Saltum,
there was a man who saw a dragon. A girl on the farm
was grinding with a quern at the time, and he told her to
turn it round as fast as possible, which she promised to
do. When the dragon came, he threw a stone at it, and
was fortunate enough to strike the tail. He at once stuck
his fingers into his ears and thrust his head under the
quern ; by this means he escaped hearing the shriek, and
got the tail, which was of pure gold. The girl heard the
shriek, but it could do her no harm. Some said that
when a dragon was seen, a bunch of keys should be
thrown over it, and it would let go its treasure, but the
person must be able to hide himself immediately, otherwise it would kill him with the falling gold.

The Dragon Disturbed.

IN the parishes of Ugilt and Taars, there lie some
mounds called Ilbjærge. In the largest of these a dragon
brooded over an immense treasure. Folk, of course,
wished to get hold of this, and one time twelve stout fellows would make an attempt to dig it up. This had to
be done on a Thursday at midnight and in deep silence.
The first and second Thursday they dug on without finding anything, but the third one they struck a large copper
chest, full of gold, and with thick rings on the sides and

ends. With immense labour they finally got the chest
up on the edge of the hole, and set it down there to rest
themselves before carrying it further, but one of the fellows forgot about the silence, and exclaimed, "See there;
now we have it." With that the chest fell back again,
and they could hear that it rolled much further down
than they had dug. The fellow was left standing with
an iron ring in his hand, and that was all they got of the
treasure. The ring was fixed on the inner side of the
door of St. Catherine's church in Hjörring, and is there to
this day. When the chest sank, the dragon, spouting fire
and venom, flew out of the hole and shrieked—

> " If I may not in Stue-höi be,
> You never will drive me from Sjörup Sea."

It then flew off, and dashed down into Sjörup Lake, in
Taars parish, so that the water foamed and boiled around
it. After it had taken up its residence here, it used to go
to some mounds a short distance away, and all along its
path, the grass was burned as if by fire. When Kristen
Kristensen took the farm there, he decided to build a
smithy right in the dragon's path. The neighbours tried
to dissuade him, but he built it where he wanted it. After
it was erected, a violent storm arose one night, and in the
morning the building was level with the ground. In spite
of the neighbours' warnings, he again built the smithy on
the same spot, and one night it was burned down. It
was, of course, the dragon who had set fire to it, because
it did not want its path blocked. The man built it a third
time on the same spot, and that smithy stands there to
this day. The dragon had to give in, and has never been
heard of since.

The Charcoal-burner and the Dragon.

SÖREN MELDGAARD from Haarup was watching his charcoal heaps, a little east from where Sejbæk station now stands. At that time there was a large forest there ; there were beeches with eighteen or twenty branches, and four ells in circumference. While there, he saw, coming over the heath, a shape like a headless ox and of a tremendous size, which came striding towards him. He never would believe that there were such spectres down there, although the other burners had said that they could not get their piles left in peace, as there was something that came and scattered them. He had laughed at this, and sworn that it was nothing but sheer lies ; but when this spectre came, he said, " Have mercy, Mister Satan." Then there arose a howling and screaming in the air, and the piles were scattered all round about, but he himself received no harm. It was a dragon which came flying from Osterskov, and passed over the lake near by.

The Lindorm in the Churchyard.

LINDORMS have their abode in waste places, but sometimes go over the country, and lay themselves round church-towers. It happened once that a lindorm laid its head close to the church door, so that no one dared to enter the church, and still less to try to drive it away. During the day it ate grass and turf, and gnawed the wooden crosses off the graves, as well as any young shoots or plants it could find, but by night it was quiet. As the people were afraid that, as soon as it got finished with the churchyard, it would begin to what was outside it, they sought for good advice.   They were first advised to poison it with tobacco, and this they hung up in little bundles on some stakes round the churchyard, but the lindorm only butted at these, and ate none of it.   They would then try to shoot it, and this of course must be done by moonlight.   They planted heavy ordnance against it, and were successful in killing the lindorm, but at the same time they spoiled both church and steeple. So big was the monster, that it took them three days to get the pieces of it carried off and buried, and it was half a year before they got the church put in good condition again.

The Lindorm and the Bull.

THERE was once a girl in Tjörne-lunde, who went out to milk her master's cows, and as she went across the fields, she saw a little brindled snake creeping among the grass. She thought it was so pretty, and took it home with her, and kept it in a little box.   Every day she gave it sweet milk and other dainties, such as she could get for it. After some time had passed, it grew so big that it could no longer stay in the box, but crawled after the girl wherever she went.   Even when she went out to the field to milk the cows, it went with her, and drank out of the pail.   Her mistress did not like this, and told the girl that unless she took means to get the snake killed, it would be an unfortunate thing for her.   So indeed it turned out, for it was soon evident that it was a young lindorm.   It grew larger every day, and finally it would not be content with what was given it, but lay outside the

village, and ate up the cattle and whatever else it could
find, and became a terrible monster.

There was in the village a "wise woman," who told
them to feed up a bull on sweet milk and wheaten bread.
This was done, and after the bull had been reared on this
for two years, it was taken outside the village to fight the
lindorm. It could not hold its own with it, however, and
had to be taken home for another year, in order to become strong enough. Meanwhile the lindorm had become
so voracious, that a cow or an old horse had to be driven
out to it daily, otherwise it took one for itself. When the
bull was three years old, it was so big and strong that it
was fit to gain the mastery over the lindorm. While the
fight was in progress, the lindorm struck a stone with its
tail, so hard that it left a deep furrow in it. After the
bull had overcome the lindorm, it was so furious that with
its horns it tore up a large pool, which is still to be seen
to the east of the village. No one could go near it, the
folk even crept up on the housetops with fright, so it had
to be shot. Considering that the bull had done such a
feat in delivering the village and killing the lindorm, the
inhabitants named the place after it, and called it Tyrs-
lund (Bull's Grove), but this has since been changed to
Tjörne-lunde (Thorn-groves). On a farm close by is
still to be seen the stone, with the mark of the lindorm's
tail in it.

The Lindorm and the Glazier.

IT happened once, many generations ago, that the bodies
which were laid in Aarhus Cathedral disappeared time
after time, without anyone knowing what the cause of

this could be. It was then discovered that a lindorm had its hole under the church, and went in by night and ate the bodies. It was also found out that it was undermining the church, so that it would soon be liable to fall in ruins, and against this danger help was sought for in vain. At last there came a wandering glazier to Aarhus, who on learning the straits into which the town had come, gave his promise that he would help them. He made for himself a chest of mirror-glass, with only a single opening in it, and that only large enough for him to thrust out his sword through it. He had the chest placed on the floor of the church during the day-time, and when midnight came, he kindled four wax candles, one of which he placed at each corner. The lindorm now came creeping through the choir-passage, and on seeing the chest and beholding its own image in the glass, it believed it to be its mate, but the glazier thrust his sword through its neck, and killed it at once. The poison and blood, however, which flowed from the wound, were so deadly, that the glazier perished in his chest.

The Lindorm and the Wizard.

ON Bogö they had at one time a terrible number of snakes, vipers, and creeping things of that kind. At Sort-sö in Falster there lived a man who could clear out such pests, and to him the folk of Bogö sent a message, asking him to come and free them from all this. Accordingly he came over to Bogö and made a bargain with the inhabitants, taking upon himself the task of destroying all this vermin, if they for their part would assure him that there was no lindorm in the island. No one

knew of any such creature being there,' but the man had
a feeling that there was one, and so he had three iron
chests made, one inside the other with a space between
each. These chests he took down to the beach right opposite Stubbe-köbing, and then lighted a huge fire, in
which all the snakes, vipers and other reptiles were to be
burned, and as soon as the fire blazed up, all these did
come and crawl into it. The man, however, could feel
that a lindorm was on its way to the fire now, so he laid
himself in the innermost of the three chests, and told the
bystanders to close him up in them. They did so, and
then hurried aside, knowing that something was far
wrong. Then came the lindorm, and crawled round the
fire three times before entering it. He had to be burned,
but he had power to take the man along with him, and
this he did, wrapping himself round the chest and dragging it into the fire along with him. When he had
entered the fire, however, the men of Bogö came with
fire-hooks and whatever else was handy, and pulled out
the chest, which they then dragged down to the beach
and opened, and so the man was saved. He received his
payment, and went home to Sort-sö.

After a year or two had passed, he took a fancy to see
whether he had cleared out all the reptiles on Bogö, and
went over there again. He went down to the beach to
see the place where he had kindled the fire, but there a
mishap befell him. One of its sharp bones which lay hid
among the ashes pierced his thin shoe and entered the
sole of his foot. The wound swelled up, and finally
caused his death. He had, however, cleared out the reptiles over there so well that fifty years ago there was
neither snake nor viper on Bogö. What there may be
now, I don't know. Where the lindorm was buried there

is now a landing-stage called Linde-bro, after this very lindorm.

The Lindorm in Klöv-bakke.

IN Klöv-bakke, north from Thisted, there lies a monster lindorm. There was once a doctor in Thisted who undertook to dig it out, if the people would only do as he wanted them, and there were plenty who offered to help him in the work, as otherwise it might come out upon them some day, for of course it would break out some time, and then terrible things would happen. The doctor had a little bottle with some kind of blue drops, and that was the only thing that could kill the lindorm, and even that could only do it if they could hit it on the right spot; in that case three drops were enough, and if they were of no avail, neither would a greater number help. The doctor showed the people where the lindorm's neck lay, and where they were to dig; then he kindled three fires beside the mound, and said to them, " Now, I shall stand here beside the hole, with the bottle in my hand, so as to be able to pour the drops on the neck, as soon as it comes in view. Whenever the lindorm feels them, he will come out of his hole and make the earth shake, but he must go through the three fires, and if his tail falls before he gets through them, everything will be well, and we shall be freed. But if it does not fall, things are wrong, and the drops have not gone home, and you must look after yourselves if you can, for it will go out into the world, and nothing will stand before it. There will be mischief so great that one can hardly imagine it,—the whole world almost will be laid waste. Now you know it before it happens." But after this information the digging did not go very far; they slipped away one after the other, and since that time there is no one that has dared to meddle with the lindorm in Klöv.

The King of the Vipers.

A MAN in the district of Silkeborg once found a viper-king. It was a tremendously big serpent, with a mane like a horse. He killed it, and took it home with him, and boiled the fat out of it. This he put into a bowl and set it aside in a cupboard, as he knew that the first person who tasted it would become so clear-sighted that they would be able to see much that was hid from other people; but just then he had to go out to the field, and thought that he could taste it another time. He had however a daughter who found this bowl with the fat in it, while her father was out in the field. She thought it was ordinary fat, which she was very fond of, so she spread some of it on a piece of bread and ate it. When the man came home, he also spread a piece of bread with it, and ate it, but he could not discover that he could see any more than he did before. In the evening, when the cows were being driven home, the girl came out and said, " Look, father, there's a big red-speckled bull-calf in the black-faced cow." He could see well enough then that she had tasted the fat of the viper-king before him, and had thus got all the wisdom, in place of himself.

The Basilisk.

WHEN mead has been kept in a barrel for twenty years without being opened, a basilisk is formed there. It once happened in Randers, where there was a great store of mead, that a barrel was forgot in the cellar, and when it had lain there a long time, a basilisk was produced. It first drank the mead, until there was no more left; then it began to growl, and the noise grew louder and louder, until the folk in the house heard it. They could not understand what was the matter with the barrel, but there was a " wise man " who knew all about it, and he advised them to get it buried in the ground, otherwise the time would soon come when the animal would break it in pieces, and come out, and such a monster no one could overcome. They did as he advised, and since that time nothing has been heard of that basilisk.

The Grav-so or Ghoul.

THIS monster is properly a treasure-watcher, and lies and broods over heaps of gold. For the most part it has its abode in mounds, where a light is seen burning by night, and it is known then that the treasure lies there. If any one digs for it, he may always be certain of meeting a ghoul, and that is hard to deal with. Its back is as sharp as a knife, and it is seldom that any one escapes from it alive. As soon as one begins to dig in the mound, it comes out and says, "What are you doing there?" The treasure-hunter must then answer, " I want to get a little money, and it's that I am digging for, if you won't be angry." With this the ghoul must content itself, and they

R

make a bargain. "If you are finished," it says, "when I
come for the third time, then all you find is yours, but if
you are not finished by then, I shall spring upon you and
destroy you." If the man has courage to make this compact, he must lose no time, for if the ghoul comes for the
third time, before he has finished, it runs between his legs
and splits him in two with its sharp back. Old Peter
Smith in Taaderup, who is now dead, had the reputation
of having got his wealth in this fashion ; he and another
young fellow were desirous of digging for treasure, and
went one night to a mound where they knew that there
was a ghoul. When they began to dig, it came up and
asked what they wanted, and then fixed a certain time
within which they were to be finished. They worked now
with all their might, and finally got hold of a big chest
which they dragged out as fast as they could, but before
they had got quite clear of the mound,—Peter Smith had
still one of his legs in the hole—the ghoul came for the
third time and managed to rub itself against Peter's legs.
Although it only touched him slightly, he had got enough
for all his life, for however wealthy he was, his legs were
always so feeble that he could neither stand nor walk.

The Nidagrísur.

THE Nidagrísur is little, thick and rounded, like a little
child in swaddling clothes or a big ball of yarn, and of a
dark reddish-brown colour. It is said to appear where
new-born illegitimate children have been killed and
buried, without having received a name. It lies and
rolls about before men's feet to lead them astray from
the road, and if it gets between any one's legs, he will not

see another year. In the field beside the village of Skáli on Österö stands a stone, called Loddasa-stone, and here a nidagrísur often lay before the feet of those who went that way in the dark, until once a man who was passing and was annoyed by it, grew angry and said " Loddasi there," upon which it buried itself in the earth beside the stone, and was never seen again, for now it had got a name.

The Were-wolf.

WHEN a woman is about to become a mother for the first time, and is afraid of the pains of childbirth, she can escape from these if she chooses. She must go before daybreak to some place where there is a horse's skeleton, or the membrane that encloses a foal before its birth. If she sets up this, and creeps naked through it three times in the Devil's name, she will never feel any pains, but to her first born there clings the curse, that it becomes half a brute ; if the child is a boy, he will be a were-wolf, if a girl, she will be a night-mare. This can be prevented, however, if any one discovers the woman while she is performing the charm, and hinders her from completing it ; then the child goes free, and the woman herself becomes the were-wolf.

Early on the morning of Tuesday in Whitsuntide a man at Pedersgaard, beside Kalve-have, was going along a dike between a forest and a field, in which the cows were at grass. He could see that the servant girls must be in the field, as their milk-pails were standing there, but the girls themselves were not to be seen. The mare had just foaled, and was busy licking its young one. He then caught sight of the girls a little way off from the milking-place, quite naked and in the act of creeping through the foal's caul, one by one. The man immediately cut a long supple hazel-switch, untethered one of the other horses, sprang on its back, and rode down upon the girls, whom he drove home to the farm, naked as they were. They had to leave the place after that. This happened within the present century.

The children who are born in this way are just like other children, except that their eyebrows meet over the nose, but they are also born with a little hairy lump between the shoulders. The mother carefully keeps this concealed, while the child is little, but when it grows up, she lets it know the meaning of the mark, so that it may be careful not to expose it in the presence of others. When the child is full grown, the curse comes out in it, and the animal nature breaks forth. As soon as darkness falls, the unfortunate being retires from human presence, the spot between the shoulders expands until the whole body is covered with hair, and at the same time assumes an animal shape, either of a were-wolf or a night-mare, according as it is a man or a woman. If the were-wolf can succeed in tearing a child living out of its mother's body, and killing it, or eating its heart, the curse is at once removed, and he is henceforward like other men. Many assert, however, that this only happens if the child is a male, and some say that it requires the heart's blood of twelve to free the were-wolf.

When a were-wolf goes about, it hops on three legs, while the fourth sticks out behind it like a tail. Dogs are always furious against it, and run howling and barking after it ; as it has only three legs, they have no difficulty in overtaking it, and it has to seek refuge among thick

bushes and thorns, where the dogs will not venture to
follow it. If a man is a were-wolf, it is always easy to
see when the dogs have been after him, as his face is then
so badly scratched and torn.

In the shoemaker's house in Taaderup there has lived
a were-wolf within living memory. Andrew Weaver's
mother served, in her youth, with the parish clerk in
Tingsted, and she often saw in the evenings how all the
dogs of Taaderup and Tingsted came running and barked
at the were-wolf. She could never see the wolf itself, indeed, but saw how all the dogs snapped and growled at
it. The priest's old cattleman could also tell a great deal
about the were-wolf in Taaderup, and could see him in
the shape of the dog with three legs.

The were-wolf, however, can be freed if any one has the
courage to say to his face 'You are a were-wolf,' but if
the were-wolf then answers, " Now you can be that just as
long as I was," then the other is doomed to become one,
until he has the good fortune to be freed from it. It is,
therefore, very seldom that they are delivered in this way,
as folks are afraid of bringing the spell upon themselves.

It is also told that there was once a man who had been
in Stubbe-köbing with his wife, and was driving home
late in the evening. When they came to a hollow way,
he got out of the waggon, gave the woman the reins, and
went into the forest, telling her that if anything came to
her while he was away, she had only to strike out well
with his handkerchief, which he gave her. A little after
the man had gone there came a were-wolf, which tried to
spring into the waggon beside the poor woman ; however,
she did as her husband had told her, and struck out boldly
with the handkerchief. The were-wolf then attacked the
waggon, and bit the shafts and everything else he could

reach, but did no harm to the woman. Finally he ran
away, and not before time, for she had only a rag of the
handkerchief left. Soon after this the man came back
and seated himself again, and the woman told him how
she had defended herself against the furious beast that
came while he was away. "You did quite right," said
the man, and they drove home. Next morning as they
sat at breakfast, the woman saw some threads of the
handkerchief among her husband's teeth; "Jesus, man,"
she cried, "you are a were-wolf." "Thanks," said the
man, "I shall never be so again, since you have said it to
me so openly."

The Night-mare.

VANLANDI, the son of Svegdir, took the kingdom after
his father, and ruled over Uppsala; he was a great
warrior, and went over many lands. He stayed one
winter in Finland with King Snow and got from him his
daughter Drift to wife. In the spring he went away, and
promised to come back again in three years, but he did
not come in ten. Drift then sent for the sorceress Huld,
and bargained with her either to bring Vanlandi back to
Finland by means of her witch-craft, or else to kill him.
When the charm was performed, Vanlandi was at Uppsala,
and became eager to go to Finland, but his friends and
advisers prevented him, saying that his eagerness must be
due to some magic of the Finns. He then became heavy
with sleep, and lay down to slumber, but he had not
slept long before he called out and said that Mara was
treading him. His men came to him, and tried to assist
him, but when they took hold of his head, she trod his

legs, so that they nearly broke ; then they turned to his feet, and she depressed his head, so that he died.

Marra resembles a beautiful girl, but is the worst kind of troll. During the night-time, when folks lie asleep, she comes in and lays herself above them, pressing so hard on the breast that they can neither draw breath nor move a limb. She puts her fingers into their mouth to count their teeth, and if time is given her to do this, they at once give up the ghost. They must therefore try to get her away from them and drive her out, and if they are able to call out, " Jesus," she must flee, and disappears at once. Folks often seem to themselves to lie quite awake and see Marra enter the room, come forward to the bed, lie down above the bed-clothes, and proceed to feel in their mouth for their teeth, and yet they can do nothing to defend themselves against her. In the evening she may be in the room and yet not be seen, but this can be found out by taking a knife and rolling it up in a handkerchief or garter, which has been twice folded in two. The knife is then passed from one hand to the other three times round the body, repeating these words,

" Marra, Marra, minni,
 Are you in this place ?
Have you still the blow in mind,
That Sigurd Sigmundsson unkind
 Once gave you in the face ?

" Marra, marra, minni,
 Are you in this place?
Out you go into the cold,
Bearing both the turf and mould,
 And all that's in this place ! "

If the knife is lying inside the fold of the doubled cloth or garter when it is opened up again, then Marra is

inside, and the same ceremony with the knife and cloth
must be repeated to get her driven out again.   It is also
said to be a good plan to prevent her coming up into the
bed, to place one's shoes at bed-time so that the heels are
turned to the bed, and the points out to the floor : then
Marra will have difficulty in getting into it.

·

A Girl as Night-mare.

THE Marre is some unknown person who is secretly in
love with one.   There was once a man who served on the
farm of Taanum beside Randers, and with whom a girl
in Helstrup was in love, but he would have nothing to do
with her.   On account of this she used to come and lie
heavy on him by night, so that he could not remain in
bed for her.   He complained of this trouble, and some
people advised him to place his wooden shoes the wrong
way beside the bed when he went into it in the evening.
He did this, and heard the shoes rattling during the
night, but his visitor could come no further.   One evening
he took a scythe, and made it fast to the front of the bed ;
then he heard her say—

> " Ah, woe !
> The snow is white, and the blood is red,
> Ere I reach Helstrup I shall be dead."

In the morning this girl was found lying dead in her bed.

A Night-mare Caught.

THERE was once a young fellow who was ridden by
" Marre " every night, and although he sprinkled flax-seed

outside the door, and placed his shoes the wrong way before his bed, it was all of no avail, and he was at a loss what to do. He asked a wise woman for advice, who at once said that she knew what would help him. " When you go home," she said, " you must stop up all holes and chinks that there are in your room ; the keyholes and windows must also be made fast. When that is done, you must bore a little hole in the door, and cut a pin to fit it exactly ; this hole you must leave open to-night, but as soon as Marre has come in by it, spring to it and put in the pin, then she is in your power." The man did as the woman told him. During the night Marre came in by the hole, which he immediately stopped up, to her great alarm. She went round about from keyhole to window, and made herself both small and thin to get out, but every place was closed fast, so that she could not get out, however many tricks she tried. When she saw that all her trouble was in vain, she besought him to take the little pin out of the door, and let her go as she had come, and she would never come again. Meanwhile he had been standing looking at her, and saw that she was a pretty girl, so he would not let her go in that way, but asked if she would be his sweetheart, and everything would be all right. " Yes," said she, " if you will really marry me, the mischief is over ; let me out now like any other person." She was a girl from the next village, and when he knew that, he let her out at the door. Shortly after they had their wedding, and she was never Marre again.

The Night-mare on Horses.

IT is often the case that in the morning the horses are found standing in the stable dripping with sweat, although they have been there the whole night. In that case it is Marre who has ridden them, and it is generally very bad for the horses. Marre also often plaits the horses' manes and tails into "Marre-locks," which it is impossible to comb out. Sometimes Marre selects one horse in the stable, and confines herself to that; thus the priest Heynet had a horse called Young Holger, which Marre rode every night, so that it was covered with foam when they went to feed it in the morning. In spite of that, Young Holger was the most thriving of all the priest's horses. The surest means to hinder Marre in this is to fasten a chopping knife on the horse's back, edge upwards. When she, as usual, tries to spring up on the horse's back to ride, she cuts herself in two, and will never again plague man or beast. But as it is well known that Marre is a human being, who is condemned to act as she does, whether she will or not, there are few that care to use this means, as they thereby deprive a fellow-creature of life. At Korselitse there was, many years ago, a big white horse, which every night was ridden by Marre. On a farm in the neighbourhood there was a girl who was said to be a Marre, and the man suspected that it was she who rode the horse. To put a stop to this he fixed a knife on its back one evening, and when he came in the morning to feed it, the girl was hanging in two pieces, one on each side of the horse, and had thus met her death.

If one takes a bucket of cold water and throws it over any one who is plagued with the night-mare, the person who is in love with him will become visible, and one can then discover who it is. A story is told of a queen, who was a great lover of horses ; in particular she had one horse which was dearest of all to her, and filled her thoughts both sleeping and waking. The stable-man had noticed several times that there was something wrong with the horse, and came to the conclusion that it was being ridden by a night-mare, so one time he seized a bucket of water and threw it over it, and lo and behold, the queen herself was sitting on its back !

In another instance, where the horses were plagued by the night-mare, and this same process was adopted, there was disclosed a naked woman, who said, " Oh, why did you do that ? Now I must cross both sea and salt water to my little children." The people helped her to reach home again, and she never came back as Marre.,

VIII.—Ghosts and Wraiths.

Thorgils and the Ghosts.

THORGILS of Flói, in the south-west of Iceland, went from there to Norway at the age of sixteen, and incurred the enmity of Gunnhild, "the kings' mother," by refusing to become one of her son's retainers. To escape her anger, he went on a trading voyage, and in the autumn found himself in the south of Norway, where he took up his quarters with a widow named Gyda and her son Audun. Gyda was a woman skilled in magic arts, but both she and her son treated Thorgils with great hospitality. After a time Thorgils shifted to the house of a great man named Björn, where he was also well received. The household there went to bed very early, and Thorgils asked the reason of this. He was told that the father of Björn had died shortly before, and that his ghost walked, so that they were frightened for him. Often during the winter Thorgils heard something hammering on the thatch, and one night he rose up, and went out, axe in hand. Before the door stood a ghost, big and grim. Thorgils raised his axe, and the ghost turned away towards the burial-mound, but when they reached that he turned to meet him. They wrestled with each other, Thorgils having let go his axe, and the struggle was both hard and fierce, so that the earth was torn up by their feet, but longer life was fated for Thorgils, and in the end the ghost fell on his back, with Thorgils above him. The

latter, after recovering himself a little, managed to reach
his axe, and hewed the ghost's head off, commanding
him henceforward to harm no man ; nor indeed was he
ever heard of afterwards. Björn thought highly of Thorgils for having helped his household so much.

One night a knock came to the door. Thorgils went
out and found his friend Audun there, asking his assistance ; his mother Gyda, he said, was dead, and there
had been something strange about her death. "All the
men have run away, too, no one daring to stay beside
her. Now I want to bury her, and do you come with
me." "So I shall," said Thorgils, and went off with
Audun without the knowledge of Björn. On reaching
Audun's farm they found his mother lying dead, and
dressed the body. "You, Thorgils," said Audun, "shall
make for my mother a coffin with a hearse beneath it,
and fix strong clasps on it, for it will take it all to do."
When all this was done, Audun said that now the
coffin must be disposed of. "We shall drag it away,
and bury it, and put as much weight as possible
on top of it." So they set out with it, but before
they had gone far the coffin began to creak loudly ; then
the clasps broke, and Gyda came out. They both laid
hands on her, and required all their strength to master
her, strong as they both were. The plan they took then
was to carry her to a funeral pile which Audun had prepared ; on this they threw her, and stood by till she was
burned. Then said Audun, "Great friendship have you
shown me, Thorgils, and manly courage, as you will do
everywhere. I shall give you a sword and kirtle, but if
ever I ask the sword back, I wish you to let me have it
and I shall give you another weapon as good." With
this they parted, and Thorgils went back to Björn, who

had by this time missed him, and was greatly distressed,
saying he had lost a good man, "and it is a pity that
trolls or evil spirits have taken him. We shall honour
him, however, by drinking to his memory, though I am
afraid it will be no merry feast, for we have now searched
for him for many days." In the midst of this Thorgils
came home, to the great delight of Björn, who then began
the feast anew.

Thorolf Bægifót.

THOROLF BÆGI-FÓT (the cripple) came home in the
evening and spoke to no man, but sat down in the high-
seat and took no food all evening. He remained sitting
there when the others went to bed, and when they rose
in the morning he was still sitting there—dead. The
housewife sent a message to Arnkell to tell him of Thorolf's death, so Arnkell with some of his men rode up to
Hvamm. On reaching it he learned that his father was
sitting dead in his high-seat, and that everyone was
frightened, thinking they saw a look of displeasure on
Thorolf's face. Arnkell entered the hall, and kept along
the side of it till he came behind Thorolf, charging everyone to take care not to approach him in front until he
had closed his eyes, nostrils, and mouth. Then he laid
hold of his shoulders, and had to exert all his strength
before he could bring him down. After that he threw a
cloth over Thorolf's head, and laid him out as was the
custom. Thereafter he had the wall behind him broken
down, and took him out that way. He was then laid in
a sledge, to which oxen were yoked, and these drew him
up into Thórs-ár-dal, not without great effort, till he came

to the place fixed upon for him. There they buried
Thorolf in a mighty cairn, after which Arnkell rode home
to Hvamm, and took possession of all his father's property
there. He stayed there three nights, during which nothing
happened, and then went home.

After the death of Thorolf many men thought it bad
to be outside after the sun had set, and as summer went
on they became aware that he was not lying quiet, and
none could remain in peace outside after sunset. Over
and above this, the oxen which had drawn him became
" troll-ridden," and all the cattle that came near his cairn
went mad and roared till they died. The shepherd at
Hvamm often came home chased by Thorolf. In the
autumn it so fell that neither shepherd nor sheep came
home, and when search was made next morning, the
shepherd was found dead not far from Thorolf's cairn.
He was all black as coal, and every bone in him broken,
so they buried him beside Thorolf ; of the sheep that had
been in the dale some were found dead, while some ran
to the hills and were never found again. If birds settled
on Thorolf's cairn they fell down dead. The hauntings
grew so terrible that no man dared to pasture the dale.
At Hvamm loud noises were often heard outside at night,
and the hall was often ridden. When winter came,
Thorolf often made his appearance about the farm, where
he mostly attacked the housewife ; many were distressed
at this, and she herself nearly went out of her senses.
The end of it was that the housewife died from his
attacks, and was also taken up to Thórsárdal and buried
beside Thorolf. The people began to run away from the
farm after this, and Thorolf now began to go so widely
about the dale that he laid waste all the farms in it, and
so outrageous were his hauntings that he killed some

men, and all these were then seen in company with him. Folk complained greatly of all this trouble, and thought that Arnkell ought to amend it. Arnkell invited to himself all those who cared to come, and wherever he was no harm was ever received from Thorolf and his followers. So much were all men afraid of Thorolf and his hauntings, that during the winter no one dared to go on any errand, however pressing. In spring, when the frost was out of the ground, Arnkell obtained help, to which he was entitled by law, to shift Thorolf from Thórsárdal to some other spot. They went to his cairn, fifteen in all, with sledge and tools, broke open the cairn, and found Thorolf undecayed and looking hideously grim. They lifted him out of his grave and laid him in the sledge, to which two strong oxen were yoked, and these drew him up on Ulfars-fells-háls. By that time they were exhausted, and others were taken to draw him up to the ridge. Arnkell intended to take him to Vadils-head and bury him there, but when they came to the brow of the ridge the oxen became furious, tore themselves free, and ran down off the ridge, keeping along the slope above the farm of Ulfars-fell, and so down to the sea. By that time they were utterly exhausted, and Thorolf had become so heavy that they could take him nowhere. They got him however to a little headland near hand, and buried him there ; it has since been known as Bægifót's Head. Arnkell then had a wall built across the headland above the cairn, so high that nothing but a bird on the wing could cross it, and the marks of which may still be seen ; there Thorolf lay quiet all the days of Arnkell's life. After Arnkell's death Thorolf began again, and haunted Ulfars-fell. The farmer complained to his superior, Thorodd Thorbrandsson of Kárs-stad. With a number of men

Thorodd went to the cairn, where they found Thorolf
still undecayed, and most like a troll in appearance ; he
was black as Hell and as thick as an ox, nor could they
move him until Thorodd had a plank pushed under him,
and with this they got him out of the cairn.   They rolled
him down to the beach then, heaped up a large pile of
wood, set fire to it and rolled Thorolf into it, and burned
the whole to ashes, though it was long before the fire
would fasten on Thorolf.   There was a strong wind
blowing, and the ashes were scattered far and wide, but
all of them that they could they raked out into the sea,
and went home when they had finished this work.

The Ghost of Hrapp.

HRAPP was a man hard to deal with in his lifetime and
vexatious to his neighbours.   When dying he called his
wife and said, "When I am dead I will have myself buried
in the hall door, and you must set me down there standing so that I may the more carefully look over my homestead."   After this he died, and everything was carried
out as he had directed, but ill as he was to deal with
while living he was still worse when dead.   He haunted
the place and is said to have killed most of his household
and caused great trouble to all who lived near there.
At length the farm was laid waste, and Hrapp's wife went
west to her brother Thorstein.   Folk had recourse to
Höskuld and told him of their trouble, asking him to devise some way out of it.   Höskuld said he would do so,
and went with some men to Hrapps-stad, where he had
Hrapp dug up and removed to where there was the least
chance of sheep pasturing or men journeying.   Hrapp's
hauntings then ceased for the most part, but his son

s

Sumarlidi, who took possession of the place again, had
not been there long before he went mad and died soon
after.

These lands afterwards became the property of Olaf
Pá, whose herdsman came to him one evening and told
him to get another man to mind the cattle and give
him something else to do.   Olaf refused to do so,
whereupon the man threatened to leave.   "Then you
have a grievance," said Olaf; "I will go with you this
evening when you tie up the cattle, and if I find any
good reason for it I will not blame you."   Olaf took in
his hand his gold-mounted spear, and left the house along
with the herdsman.   There was some snow on the ground,
and when they reached the cattle-shed they found it open.
Here Olaf told his man to go in, and he would drive the
cattle in to him.   The man went to the shed-door, but
before Olaf knew he came running back into his arms.
Olaf asked why he acted like this.   He answered,
"Hrapp is standing in the door, and tried to lay hold of
me, but I am tired of wrestling with him."   Olaf went
up to the door, and thrust at him with his spear, but
Hrapp seized the head of it with both hands and twisted
it, so that the shaft broke.   Olaf was about to spring at
him then, but Hrapp went down where he came up, and
so they parted, leaving Olaf with the shaft and Hrapp
with the head.   Olaf and the man then tied up the cattle
and went home, Olaf telling him that he would not blame
him for complaining.   Next morning Olaf went to where
Hrapp had been buried and had him dug up; he was
still undecayed, and there Olaf found his spear-head.   He
then had a bale-fire made, on which Hrapp was burned,
and his ashes taken out to sea.   Thenceforward no one
was hurt by Hrapp's hauntings.

The Ghost of Klaufi.

KLAUFI was brought from Norway to Iceland as a child, and grew up with a relative, Thorstein, in Svarfadar-dal. When he came to manhood, he was five ells and a hand-breadth in height ; his arms were both long and thick, and his grasp powerful ; he had protruding eyes and a high forehead ; his mouth was ugly, his nose small, his neck long, his chin big, and his cheek-bones high ; his eye-brows and hair intensely black ; his mouth open, dis-playing two projecting teeth, and his whole frame gnarled and knotted.

Klaufi was killed by the sons of Asgeir, with the assis-tance of his mistress, Ingöld the Fair-cheeked, and his body was dragged to the back of the house. Ingöld then went to bed, while the sons of Asgeir (who were her brothers) went away. As soon as they were gone, Klaufi came to Ingöld's bed, but she had them called back, and they then cut off his head and laid it beside his feet.

The next evening after this, while Karl the Red, son of Thorstein, Klaufi's foster-father, was sitting by the fire with eight of his followers, they heard something scraping on the house, followed by this verse :—

> " I hold me on house-top,
> Hitherward looking ;
> Hence am I hoping
> For help to avenge me. "

" That is very like the voice of our kinsman Klaufi," said Karl, "and it may be that he thinks himself greatly in need of help. It strikes me that these lines portend some great tidings, whether they have come to pass yet or not." After this they all went out, fully armed, and saw a man of no small stature, south, beside the wall. This was Klaufi ; *he had his head in his hand*, and said :

> " Southward and southward,
>   So shall we wend now."

They followed him then, and he led them to where the
sons of Asgeir had taken refuge.   Then he stopped, and
knocked on the door with his head, saying—

> " Here 'tis and here 'tis ;
>   Why should we further ? "   .   .   .

One morning Karl was standing out of doors, along
with a Norseman named Gunnar, who had wintered in
Iceland.   Karl looked up at the sky, and changed colour.
Gunnar asked the reason of this.   " No great matter,"
said Karl ; " it was something that I saw."   " And what
was that ? " asked Gunnar.   " I thought," said Karl, " that
I saw my kinsman Klaufi ride in the air above me.   He
seemed to be riding a grey horse, which was drawing a
sledge behind it.   In it I seemed to see you Norsemen
and myself, with our heads sticking out, and I suppose I
changed colour when I saw that."   " You are not so
stout-hearted then as I believed," said Gunnar ; " I saw
all that, and look now whether I have changed colour in
the least."   " I do not see that you have," said Karl.   As
they spoke thus, they heard Klaufi reciting a verse in the
air above them, adding the words, " I expect you home to
me this evening, Karl."

Gunnar decided that he and his fellows would go to
their ship that day, and Karl went with them, after in-
structing his wife what to do in case he should not return.
On the way they were attacked by his enemies, and all of
them fell.

When Karl's son (born after his father's death, and so,
according to custom, also named Karl) had grown up,
Klaufi still continued to walk, and did great hurt both to
men and cattle.   Karl thought it a great pity that his

kinsman should behave like this, and had him dug up out of the mound he was buried in. The body was still undecayed, and Karl burned it to ashes on a stone beside Klaufi's old home. The ashes he put into a leaden case with two strong iron bands on it, and sank this in a hot spring to the south of the farm. The stone that Klaufi was burned on sprang in two, and his ghost troubled them no more.

Sóti's Grave-Mound.

HRÓAR, son of Harald, earl of Gautland, made a vow at the Yule feast, that before another Yule he would break in the grave-mound of Sóti the Viking. "A great vow that," said the earl, "and one that you will not carry out by yourself, for Sóti was a mighty troll in his lifetime, and a greater one by half now that he is dead." Then Hörd, son of Grímkell, from the south-west of Iceland, stood up and said, "Is it not fitting to follow your customs? I swear this oath to go with you into Sóti's grave-mound, and not to leave it before you do." Geir swore an oath to follow Hörd, whether he went there or elsewhere, and never to part from him unless Hörd willed it. Helgi also swore an oath to follow Hörd and Geir wherever they went, if he could do so, and to esteem no one higher while they were both alive. Hörd answered, "It may be that there will not be long between us, and take you care that you do not bring death on both of us, or even on more men besides." " So would I have it," said Helgi.

When spring came, Hróar prepared to go to Sóti's mound along with eleven other men. They rode through a thick forest, in one part of which Hörd noticed a little by-path leading away from the main road ; this path he followed till he came to a clearing, in which he saw a house, both large and fair. Outside it stood a man in a blue-striped hood, who saluted him by name. Hörd took this well, and asked his name, " for I do not know you," said he, " though you address me familiarly." " I am called Björn," said the other, " and knew you as soon as I saw you, although I have never seen you before, but I was a friend of your kinsmen, and that will stand you in good stead with me. I know that you intend to break into the grave of Sóti the Viking, and that will not be easy for you if you draw alone in the traces ; but if matters go as I expect, and you cannot manage to break into the mound, then come to me." With that they parted, and Hörd rode on to catch up with Hróar.

They came to the mound early in the day, and began to break into it, and by evening had got down to the timbers, but in the morning the mound was as whole as before, and so it happened next day also. Then Hörd rode to visit Björn, and told him how matters stood. " Just as I expected," said Björn ; " I was not ignorant of what a troll Sóti was. Now, here is a sword that I will give you, which you will stick into the hole you make in the mound, and see then whether it closes up again or not." With that Hörd returned to the mound. Hróar said that he wished to go away, and deal with this fiend no longer, and several others were also eager to do so. Hörd answered, " It is unmanly not to keep one's oath ; we shall try it yet again." The third day they proceeded again to break into the' mound, and got down to the timbers as before, whereupon Hörd stuck the sword he had got from Björn into the spot. They slept all night, and on coming to the mound in the morning they found that nothing had happened. The fourth day they broke through all the long timbers, and the fifth day they opened up the door. Hörd bade them beware of the wind and stench which issued from the mound, and stood himself at the back of the door while it was at its worst. Two of the men died suddenly with the bad air which came out, through being too curious, and neglecting Hörd's advice. Then said Hörd, "Who will go into the mound? I think he ought to go who vowed to overcome Sóti." Hróar was silent, and when Hörd saw that no one was prepared to enter the mound, he drove in two rope-pegs. " Now," said he, " I shall enter the mound, if I shall get three precious things which I choose out of it." Hróar said he would agree to this for his part, and all the others assented. Then said Hörd, " I will have you to hold the rope, Geir, for I trust you best." Hörd found no treasure in the mound, and told Geir to come down beside him, and bring with him fire and wax, " for both of these have a powerful nature in them," said he ; " and ask Hróar and Helgi to look after the rope." They did so, and Geir went down into the mound. At last Hörd found a door, which they broke up, whereupon there was a great earthquake, the lights were extinguished, and a great stench came out. In the side-chamber there was a little gleam of light, and there they saw a ship with treasure in it ; at its stern sat Sóti, terrible to look upon. Geir stood in the door, while Hörd went up and was about to take the treasure, when Sóti said :—

" What hastened thee,
Hörd, thus to enter
The mould-dweller's house
Though Hróar bade thee ?

Ne'er have I wrought
The wielder of swords
Aught of harm
In all my days."

Hörd answered—

" For this I came   That never on earth
    To cope with the thane,   In all the world
    And spoil of his wealth   Will wickeder man
    The weird old ghost,   His weapons use. "

With that Sóti sprang up and ran upon Hörd, and there
was a fierce struggle, for Hörd was much inferior in
strength.   Sóti gripped so hard that Hörd's flesh ran
together in knots.   He then bade Geir light the wax-
candle, and see how Sóti took with that, but as soon as
the light fell on Sóti he lost all strength and fell to the
ground.   Hörd then got a gold ring taken off Sóti's arm,
so great a treasure that it is said that never has so good
a ring come to Iceland.   When Sóti lost the ring, he
said :—

" Hörd has reft me   Golden burden.
    My ring so good,   Yet it shall be
    More lament I   The bane and death
    The loss of that   Of thee and all
    Than all of Grani's   Of them that own it. "

" You shall know this," said he, " that the ring shall be
your death, and that of all that own it, unless it be a
woman."   Hörd bade Geir bring the light and see how
friendly he was, but Sóti plunged down into the earth
and would not abide the light, and so they parted.
Hörd and Geir took all the chests and carried them to
the rope, and all the other treasure that they found.
Hörd took also Sóti's sword and helmet, both of them
great treasures.   They now pulled the rope, and discovered that the others had left the mound, so Hörd
climbed up the rope, and then drew up Geir and the
treasure after him.   As for the others, when the earthquake took place, they all went mad except Hróar and

Helgi, and they had to hold the rest. When they found each other there was a joyous meeting, for they seemed to have got Hörd and Geir back from the dead again.

Kjartan Olafson's Gravestone.

KJARTAN OLAFSON is buried at Borg in Mýrar. His grave lies across the choir-gable, stretching north and south, and is fully four ells long. On the grave lies a thick pillar-stone, bearing a runic inscription. The runes on it are much worn, and some of them quite illegible. The stone itself is broken in many pieces, and this is said to have been done by a farmer at Borg. One summer he was about to set up his smithy, and wanted suitable stones for his forge, so he took Kjartan's stone, broke it in pieces, and built his forge out of the fragments. In the evening he went to bed; he slept alone in a loft, while his man slept in the common sitting-room. During the night the latter dreamed that a man came to him, stalwart and big of stature. He said, "The farmer wants to see you to-morrow as soon as you get up." In the morning the man woke and remembered his dream, but gave no heed to it. Between 8 and 9 o'clock he began to think the farmer long in rising, and went to him where he lay in bed, and asked if he were awake. The farmer answered that he was; " but listen," said he, " I dreamed last night that a man came up into the loft here. He was tall and stalwart, well-made and very handsome in every way. He was in dark clothes, but I could not get a look at his face. I thought he said to me, ' You did ill when you took my stone yesterday, and broke it in pieces. It was the only memorial that kept my name alive, and even this you

would not leave to me, and that shall be terribly avenged.
Put back the pieces on my grave to-morrow, in the same
order as they were before ; but because you broke my
stone, you shall never put a sound foot on the earth
again.' As he said this he touched the clothes on me,
and I awoke in fearful pain, but I thought I saw a glimpse
of the man as he went down out of the loft. I expect,"
said he, " that this was Kjartan, and you shall now take
his stone and lay the pieces on the grave just as they
were before." The man did so, but the story says that
the farmer was never in sound health again, and lived all
his days a cripple.

The brothers of Reyni-stad.

IN the autumn of 1780 Haldor Bjarnason, who then had
Reynistad, sent his two sons to the south of Iceland to
buy sheep, as many of these had died in the north during
the preceding year. Bjarni went first, along with a man
called Jón Eastman, and later on was followed by his
brother Einar, then only eleven years old, with a man
called Sigurd. While in the south Bjarni unintentionally
offended a priest, who cursed him in the lines,

> " Let thy soul for hunger howl,
> Homeless ere another Yule."

These words were fulfilled, for as the four of them tried
late in autumn to cross the mountains towards the north
they were lost, together with their guides and all the
sheep and other valuables.

The winter passed without anything being heard of
them, but the folk at Reynistad first began to suspect

how things had gone, when the sister of the two brothers
dreamed that Bjarni came to her and·said—

> " No one now can find us here,
> 'Neath the snow in frosty tomb ;
> Three days o'er his brother's bier
> Bjarni sat in grief and gloom."

In the spring a traveller going south found their tent,
and thought that he saw there the bodies of both the
brothers, and of two other men.   Later travellers saw
only two bodies, and only two were found when a party
went from Reynistad to take them home.   They were
those of Sigurd and the guide.   After long searching
they found, much further north, one of the hands of Jón
Eastman, along with his harness, all cut to pieces, and
his riding horse with its throat cut.   It was supposed
that he, being the hardiest of the four, had held on so far,
and when he gave up all hope of reaching the inhabited
districts, had himself killed his horse to shorten its
misery.   Of the brothers no trace could be found, nor of
the valuables they had with them.   Then their sister
dreamed that her brother Bjarni came to her again and
said—

> " In rocky cleft we brothers crushed are lying ;
> Ere this in the tent we stayed,
> All beside each other laid."

From this it was suspected that some one, who had gone
that way in spring, had stolen all the treasure off the
brothers' bodies, and then hid the latter somewhere.   A
search was made, but in vain.   Finally a wizard was employed to see whether he could find out anything.   He
performed his ceremonies in an outhouse at Reynistad,
and thought he saw the bodies buried in a lava hole with
a large stone above them, and a slip of paper with runes

on it under the stone, nor would the bodies be found, he
said, until this had decayed into nothing. This he could
see clearly at the time, but when he went to look for
them, everything became confused as soon as he got up
into the uninhabited districts. The bodies were finally
found in 1845 in Kjal-hraun, and under a flag-stone, as
the wizard had said.

Parthúsa-Jón.

THERE was a man east in Múla-sysla called Jón, who
was not well liked.   He was believed to have some
knowledge of magic, but never used it for anything but
mischief. He came into collision with a certain Magnus,
and threatened him, and as Magnus was defenceless himself, he went to the south country to ask help from a
wizard there. As soon as he had set out, Jón wakened
up a ghost, and sent him after Magnus, with orders to
kill him on Spreingi-sand when he was coming home
again. Magnus arrived safely at the wizard's, who said
that this was a difficult task, for the ghost was powerfully
enchanted ; but he must remember never to look behind
him on the sand, whatever he heard going on behind his
back.   In that case he was out of all danger, but if he
was so unfortunate as to look back, then he must take
care never to go out of sight of his farm afterwards, for
his life would depend on that.   Magnus promised to be
on his guard, and rode off along with his companions.
When they came north to Spreingi-sand they began to
hear terrible noises behind them, which were not so loud
at first, but steadily increased till at last they passed all
bounds. Sometimes there were howlings and growlings,

sometimes shrieks and screams, so that none of them had
ever heard such noises and uproar. They knew their
danger if they looked back, and restrained themselves
well for a long time, but at last the noises were heard
close behind him, and Magnus could not help looking
round. He then saw eighteen phantoms fighting against
one, which they were preventing from reaching Magnus
and his fellows, but as soon as he looked round everything disappeared.

On reaching home, Magnus followed the wizard's advice, and never went further from the house than he had
been told ; but one summer night he awoke and heard
the sheep coming in about the farm.¹ He ran out to drive
them off, but having no dog with him, the sheep only
went very slowly before him. There was a ridge close to
the farm, and in his eagerness to drive them over this,
Magnus did not notice that it shut out his view of the
farm. As soon as he had got over it the ghost came and
killed him ; at least he was afterwards found there stone-
dead, black and bloody.

After this Jón grew very heavy in spirits and strange,
could never bear to be left alone, and so on, and this was
believed to come from his knowing that he had caused
the death of Magnus.

Next winter Jón was travelling with another man, and
when they least expected it, there came upon them a
blinding storm. They were far from any dwellings, but
near them there was a pasture-house, and Jón said he felt
so ill that he would not attempt to reach any homestead,
but rather try to get to the pasture-house and lie there
till the storm ceased. They managed to reach it safe and
sound, and as it was now evening, they lay down in the
stall. Jón told his companion not to mind although any-

thing strange happened, and he would come to no harm.
The other asked what he expected, but Jón only said that
he would find out in the morning. Then he seemed to
fall asleep, but the man could not sleep for thinking of
what Jón had said. After some time he heard something
tug at Jón, and apparently drag him down the stall, but
as it was pitch dark in the house he could not see what
was going on. Then he heard Jón utter sounds from
which he guessed that he was awake ; then began great
strugglings, nor was the man long in being convinced
that the other person was much the stronger of the two.
Now and then he could hear Jón moaning and groaning,
and guessed that he was going down before his opponent.
Then he heard the wall being beaten as if with a soft
bag, and supposed that this must be Jón that was being
so hardly used, but dared give no sign. This went on
for a little, and was followed by the horrible sound of one
choking, after which all was still. The man supposed
that Jón was now dead, and in a little he heard him being
torn asunder, there being a sound as of breaking of bones
and tearing of tough cloth. After that these pieces began to be thrown over all the house, and this went right
on till morning, by which time the poor man was more
dead than alive with terror. As soon as it began to grow
clear, the man rushed out of the house, reached the nearest homestead in safety and told what had happened.
Some men went to the place, and found scraps and tags
of Jón all over the inside of the house, all crushed and
squeezed to fragments.

No one knew for certain how this had actually happened, as Jón had many enemies, but it was thought most
likely that it was the revenge of Magnus. After this the

pasture-house was discontinued, and called Part-hús,
from the parts of Jón that were found there.

The Cloven-headed Ghost.

AT Merkigil there are pasture-houses where formerly
there was a farm.   One time a farm servant there, named
Jón, was in the sheds as it was getting dark.   He had
given the sheep their hay and was about to go home, but
strangely enough could not find the door.   He felt and
felt all round, but could not get the door at all.   This
went on for a little till Jón grew frightened, and did not
know what to do.   Finally he took the plan of going up
into the stall, taking out his knife and throwing it straight
forward.   He heard it strike in the door, and thought he
was all right now.   Down he went out of the stall, found
the knife, and opened the door, but as soon as he came
out he saw a man sitting right in front of him.   He was
of a huge size, apparently some six ells in height.   There
was a red stripe down his face, and he was holding his
cheeks in his hands.   Jón did not like this spectacle, and
hesitated to go out, so he stood still and looked at the
man.   The latter seemed rapidly to decrease, till at length
he was only of ordinary size.   Jón thought now that there
was no good to be looked for from him, grew desperate
and rushed out.   As he sprang past the man, the latter
let go with his hands, whereupon the skull split in two,
and half of it fell on each shoulder.   This did not increase
Jón's courage, and he ran home as fast as his feet could
carry him.   It is said in old stories that the farmer who
once lived there had his head cloven to his shoulders, and
it is supposed to have been him that frightened Jón.

"One of Us."

ON a farm in the north of Iceland there lived a man and his wife, who were very rich in money. One spring the man died and was buried at the parish church, which was on the next farm. The wife kept on the farm, and nothing happened all that summer, but in the autumn the man began to haunt the place, and his ghost killed both sheep and cows, while the house was ridden every night. At length the only man left on the farm was the shepherd; he had been a favourite with the farmer, and the ghost meddled least with him. However, on Christmas Eve the shepherd did not come home from the sheep, and when they searched for him, they only found some shreds of him beside the sheep-house. No one would take service with the widow now, and she had to remove with all her belongings. The following spring she was anxious to work the farm again, for it was a good one, so she got a man to look after it for the summer. All went well until the nights began to grow dark again, when the ghost began anew, and finally the overseer ran away. The woman was unwilling to leave before it was unavoidable, but now "good rede was dear." There was, however, in the district a merchant from the south of the country, who was terribly lazy, but a good workman when he liked. In her strait the woman applied to him, begging him to try to work the farm for her all winter. He was quite willing, but only on condition that she should marry him if everything went well during that time. As the woman was rather pleased with the man, she agreed to this, and he went to her farm. Whenever it grew quite dark, it was almost impossible to live there; sometimes the house was ridden and sometimes beaten

from the outside, but the greatest uproar went on in the
store-room. The overseer now went to the nearest trading
village, and bought a large quantity of sheet-iron and
white linen. The iron he hammered and shaped till at
last it exactly fitted his whole body. Then he pierced
holes in it, and got the woman to make him a suit of the
white linen, with the iron plates sewed inside it. Next
night the ghost came, and began to ride furiously on the
house-top. The man put on his iron suit, picked up a
horse-hair rope, and ran off to the churchyard. Going
straight to the ghost's grave, he found it open and dropped
the rope into it, keeping hold of one end. Then he threw
earth on himself, and sat on the edge of the grave playing
with a dollar-piece. Toward morning the ghost came
back. " Who are you?" he asked. " ONE OF US," said
the man. " There you lie," said the ghost. The man
persisted that he was so, whereupon the ghost felt his
breast, and said that he was certainly as cold as a corpse,
but he was lying all the same. Still the man denied this,
and the ghost seized him by the arm, but finding it cold
as ice he said, " Cold arms but powerful ; you must be a
ghost, but why do you sit here?" The overseer answered
that he was as well there as anywhere else ; he had been
reduced to a single dollar, and it was all the same to him
where he amused himself with it. The ghost then asked
him to draw the rope up out of the grave, but he refused,
saying that he had put it there just because he wanted to
meet him : he knew that the other was a rich ghost, and
wished to propose that they should enter into partnership. He himself was a very strong ghost, as the other
must have felt by his arm, and they could have everything their own way if they combined, but in return he
wanted to have a share in the other's money. The ghost

T

for a long time refused to agree to these terms, and asked
the man to pull up the rope, which he flatly refused to
do. In the end the ghost gave in, and appointed a meeting next night in the store-room at his widow's farm, for
there he had half a bushel of money hid in the northmost
corner. After this the man drew up the rope out of the
grave, the ghost went into it, and it closed over him.

The overseer now went home, dug up the floor in the
corner of the store-room and found the money, which he
appropriated, as may be supposed. The sitting-room on
the farm was up a stair, and was entered by a trap-door. In
the evening the overseer spread a raw hide at the bottom
of the ladder, and made the sign of the cross all round
about it. This done, he waited upstairs for the ghost.

During the night the folk heard a terrible uproar in the
room, so that everything danced about. Then something
came along the passage with great violence, and broke
down all the doors in it. Finally the ghost made his appearance, and sprang over the hide on to the ladder, but
just as he got nearly up into the room, the overseer drove
a bed board against his breast as hard as he could, so that
the ghost fell backwards down the ladder with a crash,
and landed on the hide. He could not get any foothold
there, nor get off it owing to the crosses, and so was compelled to go into the earth where he was. The overseer
then had holy water sprinkled where the hide had lain,
and the ghost was never seen again. He then married
the widow, and was a most enterprising and successful
man ever after.

Stefán Ólafsson and the Ghost.

IT was generally believed that the men of Hornfirth were so enraged at the priest Stefán Olafsson, on account of a satire he composed on them, that they sent to him a ghost to take vengeance on him for this. An old woman, still alive, tells a story in proof in this, which she heard from a man in her young days. His story she gives as follows :—

"One winter evening when I was shepherd with Sir Stefán, I was lying on my back in my bed, which was nearest to the outer door, when I heard a noise out in the passage, just as if some one was dragging a hide along it. All who were in the house were asleep, except the priest, who was lying in his bed up in the loft, smoking his pipe. It was moonlight and quite clear in the room. After a little while, I saw a man, to all appearance, enter and come as far as the door, where he stopped and leaned against the door-post without saying a word. Then I heard the priest say, 'What are you after?' 'To meet with you,' it said. 'Why don't you come nearer then?' he asked. 'I can't,' said the ghost. 'Why not?' 'You are so hot,' said the ghost. 'Then stand there and wait for me, if you dare,' said the priest, and with that he sprang out of bed and made for the stranger, who did not care to wait for him, but hurried down stairs with the priest after him. I heard them go outside, and being curious to know more about this, I slipped downstairs and out of doors, where I could hear them down in the meadow below the home-fields, whither the priest had followed him. I heard him call to the ghost and bid him wait for him, and when he would not do so he told the fellow to meet him there again. I ran in then, wishing to con-

ceal the fact that I had seen this, lay down again and
pretended to sleep. The priest came in immediately
after, and I pretended to awaken. 'Did you see the
stranger?' he asked. 'No,' said I. 'Will you venture
to go and get me a light for my pipe then?' said he.
'Yes,' said I, and went for it, though not without some
fear."

Another story told of the Hornfirth ghost is to this
effect. Late one evening the priest wanted a book which
was lying on the altar in the church, but the night being
dark no one would venture to go for it, so he had to go
himself. When he reached the altar and was about to
lift the book, he heard some one in front of him say in a
hollow and ghostly voice :—

> " Upon the day of doom
> The dreadful trump shall sound."

The priest answered :—

> " And all men up shall come
> From out the yawning ground."

With that he seized the book, and returned to the door
of the church. Then he heard it say :—

> " O hour of awful strife ! "

and answered again :—

> " O day of light and life ! "

and went out, locking the door behind him. When he
entered the house, the folk thought they could see that
he had been frightened. Many add that he became weak-
minded after this, and could not be cured of it until the
plan was adopted of lifting the thatch off the sitting-room
and drawing him up through the roof, but it is more commonly said that he drove away the ghosts by his poetry.

Jón Flak.

THERE was a man named Jón, commonly called Jón Flak. He was of a curious disposition, and not well liked by his neighbours, who found him given to annoying them without their being able to pay him back. When Jón died, the grave-diggers, out of mischief, dug his grave north and south. He was buried at the back of the choir in Múli churchyard, but every night after this he haunted the grave-diggers, repeating this verse :—

> " Cold's the mould at choir-back,
> Cowers beneath it Jón Flak,
> Other men lie east and west,
> Every one but Jón Flak ;
> EVERY ONE BUT JÓN FLAK."

He never stopped this till he was dug up again, and laid east and west like other folk.

According to another version, Jón had a þad wife, who caused him to be buried in this position out of spite. Others say it was not done intentionally, but because the weather at his funeral was so bad that they were glad to get him buried in any way.

" Pleasant is the Darkness."

IN old times, and even right on to our own day, it was the general custom to hold night-watch over a corpse, and this was generally done with a light burning, unless the night was clear right through. Once there died a wizard who was ill to deal with, and few were willing to watch his body. However, a man was got to undertake the task, a strong and stout-hearted fellow. His watching went on all right so far, but on the night before the coffining the light went out a little before daybreak. The dead man then sat up and said, " PLEASANT IS THE DARKNESS." " That matters little to you," said the watcher, and made this verse :—

> " Shining now is all the earth,
>   Up has run the day ;
>   That was candle and thou art cold,
>   And keep thou so for aye ! "

With that he sprang upon the corpse, and forced it down on its back again, and the remainder of the night passed quietly enough.

Biting off the Thread.

THERE was a wizard named Finn, who was so full of sorcery and wickedness that all were afraid of him. When he died, no one, either man or woman, would put him in his shroud and sew it round him, as was then the custom. At last one woman ventured on the task, but was only half-finished with it when she went mad. Then another tried it, and paid no heed to how the corpse behaved. When she was nearly finished, Finn said, " You have to bite off the thread afterwards." She answered, " I mean to break it and not bite it, you wretch." Then she broke the thread, snapped the needle in two, and stuck the pieces into the soles of his feet, nor is there any word of his having done any mischief after that.

The Dead Man's Rib.

WHEN Eirik Rafnkelsson was priest at Hof in Alptafirth, he had a maid servant named Oddny, who was en-

gaged to a man in the same district. One time when a
body was buried in Hof churchyard, the gravediggers saw
Oddny come to the grave and poke about among the
earth ; but after a little she went away again, and they
paid no heed to her. Next night, however, Einar dreamed
that a man came to him, and asked him to get him back
his bone, which Oddny had taken out of the earth the
day before. The dead man said he had asked Oddny
herself for it, " but she will not give it up, and says she
never took it at all ; " and with that he disappeared.
Next morning the priest accused Oddny of having taken
a human bone out of the earth, and told her to give it
up ; but she would not take with this, and became so
angry that the priest did not press the charge. Next
night the dead man came again to the priest, and begged
him, as hard as he could, to get back the bone from
Oddny, for he wished to have it above everything. When
the priest woke in the morning, he arose and went to
Oddny, who was washing clothes in a stream near the
house, and again demanded the bone from her. She
denied flatly that she had taken any bone, but the priest
seized her, tore open her clothes, and found in her bosom
a man's rib wrapped in grey wool. He then gave the girl
a whipping, took the bone, and put it back into the grave.
He also told Oddny's sweetheart what she had done, and
asked him to consider whether he would have her after
that, but he did not mind it and married her. Nothing
ever happened to her afterwards, nor did the dead man
ever visit any one above ground again.

The Skull in Garth Churchyard.

THE following incident took place fully sixty years ago
(about 1830), and is remembered by persons still alive.

One time when there was a burial in the churchyard of
Garth in Kelduhverf (N.E. of Iceland), there stood by,
among others, a woman named Hólmfríd, wife of Grím,
the farmer of half of Víkingavatn in the same district.
In digging the grave a large quantity of bones was
thrown up, and among them a remarkably large skull.
Hólmfríd went to look at the bones, and, turning over
the skull with her foot, said, "How like a seal's skull it
is ; it would be interesting to know who the man was,"
and other words to the same effect. After the funeral
had taken place in the usual way, every one made their
way home.

At this time, the beds in farm-houses stood on a floor
of boards, running along both sides of the room, while
the passage up the centre was left unfloored. In many
cases a similar piece of flooring ran across the end of the
room furthest from the door, and this was sometimes
higher than that along the sides. This was the arrangement at Víkingavatn, and there was also a large rafter
stretching across the room. Hólmfríd's bed, where she
slept with her three-year-old child, was either across the
inner end of the room, or at least further in than this cross-
beam. When she fell asleep that evening, she dreamed
that a huge head came hopping in at the door, and made
its way along the passage in the middle, looking very
stern. In it she recognised the big skull she had seen
during the day, and was so frightened that she started up
in bed. On falling asleep again, the same thing happened, but the head this time was more venturesome, and

came hopping along the whole length of the room, and tried to get up into the bed. She put out her hands to thrust it away, and woke up in the act of pushing her child out of bed. It had been lying in front of her, so she now put it behind her, and fell asleep again. No sooner had she done so than a man of immense size entered the room, came forward to the cross-beam and laid his hands on it, saying in ghostly tones: "If you want to know my name, it is Jón, and I am son of Jón, and used to live in Krossdal." At this she was greatly alarmed and started up for the third time, and seemed to see this giant leisurely pass out at the door : after that she saw nothing more and slept all the rest of the night.

When this came to be talked about later, old people remembered a father and son in Krossdal, both named Jón, who had both died in the famine of 1783-84. The younger had been a very big man, and the story seemed to fit him exactly.

The Priest Ketill in Húsavík.

IN the north there was a priest named Ketill Jónsson who lived at Húsavík. He had a number of coffins dug up out of the churchyard, and said he did so because there was so little room there, and these coffins were only taking up space, the bodies being completely decayed. One time it so happened that three old women were in the kitchen, busy burning the coffins, when a spark flew out of the fire and lighted on one of them. It soon set her clothes on fire, and then those of the other two, as they were all standing close together. They burned so furiously that they were all dead before people came up and put out the fire. During the night the priest dreamed that a man came to him, and said, "You will not succeed in making room in the churchyard, although you go on digging up our coffins, for now I have killed your three old women to avenge ourselves, and they will take up some room in the churchyard, and still more will I kill, if you do not cease this conduct." With that he went away, and the priest awoke, and never again did he dig up any coffins out of the churchyard.

The Ghost's Cap.

ON a farm beside a church there lived, among others, a boy and a girl. The boy was in the habit of trying to frighten the girl, but she had got so used to it that she was not frightened at all, for whatever she saw, she supposed it to be the boy's doing. One time the washing was lying out in the churchyard, among the articles being a number of white night-caps, which were then in fashion. In the evening the girl was sent out for it, and ran out to gather it together. When she had nearly finished, she saw a white figure sitting on a grave in the churchyard. Thinking to herself that it was the lad trying to frighten her, she ran up and pulled off the ghost's cap, supposing that the boy had taken one of the night-caps, and said, "You won't manage to frighten me this time." When she went in with the washing, however, she found the boy in the house, while on going over the clothes there was found to be a cap too many, and it was earthy inside. Then the girl was frightened. Next morning the figure was still sitting on the grave, and no one knew what was to be done, for none would venture to take the cap to the ghost. They sent round all the district for advice, and one old man declared that it was inevitable that some mischief would happen from this, unless the girl herself took the cap to the ghost and set it silently on its head, with many persons looking on. The girl was then forced to go with the cap, and set it on the ghost's head, which she did very unwillingly, saying when she had done so, " Are you pleased now ? " The ghost started and struck her, saying " Yes ! Are YOU pleased ? " With that he plunged down into the grave, while at the blow the girl fell to the ground, and when they ran and lifted her she was dead. The boy was punished for having been in the habit of frightening her, for it was considered that all the trouble had been caused by him.

The Ghost's Questions.

ONE time long ago a young fellow named Thorlak was crossing Eski-firth heath on his way to school at Hólar. Passing a deep ravine he heard a dim and ghostly voice calling out to him, " What is your name ? Whose son are you ? Where do you come from ? Where are you going ? and, How many nights old is the moon ? " The youth answered at once, " Thorlak is my name ; I am Thord's son ; I come from Múla-sýsla ; I am going to Hólar school : and nine nights old is the moon." The story says that if Thorlak had made a slip anywhere in this, the evil being would have got power over him.

" My Jaw-bones."

THERE was once a priest who was in the habit of taking
all the bones that were thrown up in the churchyard,
when a new grave was dug, and burning them.   On one
occasion when bones had been thrown up in this way,
they were gathered up by the priest's cook, by his orders ;
but as they had got wet, either with rain or snow, she
could not burn them at once, and had to set them up on
the hearthstone beside the fire to dry them.   While this
was doing, and the cook was busy with her work in the
twilight, she heard a faint voice from somewhere near the
hearth saying, " My jaw-bones, my jaw-bones !"   These
words she heard repeated again, and began to look round
the human bones that were lying beside her on the hearth
to see what this meant, but could find no man's jaw there.
Then she heard it said for the third time, in a still more
piteous voice than before, " Oh, my jaw-bones, my jaw-
bones !"   She went again and looked closer, and then
found the two jaw-bones of a child, fastened together,
which had been pushed close to the fire and were beginning to burn.   She understood then that the ghost of the
child which owned the jaws must have been unwilling to
have them burned, so she took them up and wrapped
them in linen, and put them into the next grave that was
dug in the churchyard.   Nothing strange took place after
that.

" Mother Mine in Fold, Fold."

ONE time a servant-girl on a farm had given birth to a
child, and exposed it to die, as not seldom happened in

Iceland, while severe penalties—banishment or even
death—were imposed for such offences. Some time after
this, it so happened that one of the dances, called *viki-
vaki*, once so popular in the country, was to be held, and
this same girl was invited to it. But because she was not
well enough off to have fine clothes suitable for such a
gathering as these dances were, and was at the same time
a woman fond of show, she was greatly vexed that she
had to stay at home and be out of the merry-making.
While the dance was going on elsewhere, the girl was
engaged milking ewes in the fold along with another
woman, and was telling her how she had no clothes to go
to the dance with. Just as she stopped talking, they
heard this verse repeated under the wall of the fold :—

> " Mother mine in fold, fold,
> Feel not sorrow cold, cold,
> And I will lend you dress of mine
> To dance so bold,
> And dance so bold."

The girl thought that in this she heard the voice of the
child she had exposed, and was so startled at it that she
was wrong in her wits all her life after.

"That is Mine."

IN olden times there was a burial vault for the nobility
under the choir of Sönder-omme Church. Once, when
the church was undergoing repairs, one of the masons
wagered with his comrades, that he would venture into
the church by night, and go down into the vault for one
of the skulls from the decayed bodies that lay there. He
won the wager, for at midnight he descended into the

vault, and took the biggest skull he could find.   But just
as he had laid hold of it, and was about to go, he heard
a rough, harsh voice saying " THAT IS MINE."   " Oh, if it
is yours, I won't take it then," said the mason, and lifted
another which was not quite so large, but now he heard a
woman's soft complaining voice say, " That one is mine."
He threw it down also, and took the smallest he could
find, but now a thin childish voice called out, " *That is
mine.   That is mine.*"   " I don't care," said the mason,
" I'd take it even if it were the priest's."   He ran out of
the church with it, and so won his wager, but after this
he never had any peace.   He always thought that an
innocent little child ran after him wherever he went, and
cried, " That is mine.   That is mine."   He became strange
and melancholy, and did not live long after.

The Three Countesses at Trane-kær.

IN Trane-kær castle there is a room, which in old times
was so much haunted, that no one could stay in it over-
night.   A stranger once came to the place, and laid a
wager that he would lie in this room over-night, without
the ghosts doing him any harm.   He did lie in the room
and things went well until mid-night ; but then there
arose noise and disturbance, as if everything was being
turned upside down, and before he knew of it, he was
lying on the paved space outside the house.   After this,
the castle was even worse haunted than before, until at
last no one could stay in it over-night, and there was no
other way left than to get the ghosts laid.   Word was
sent to the priests in Snöde and Böstrup, and these promised to come on the Saturday evening following.   The

two of them drove together in a carriage to a knoll beside
the highway, north from the castle. Here they made the
carriage stop, and warned the coachman not to drive
away, whatever happened, until there came one who could
say, "Drive on, in Jesus' name." From here they went
up to the castle, and there the ghosts of the three countesses came to meet them. One of the priests had not yet
got his gown and collar on, and the foremost countess
held up her hand and shouted, "What do you want?
You have no business here." The priest, however, hastily
put on his gown and collar, and now they began to tackle
the ghosts. One of these reminded the priest of Böstrup
that he had once stolen two skilling's worth, but he
immediately threw the two skillings to her, and so that
was paid. The priests, however, were unable to stand
their ground, being only two against three, and were
driven back from the castle, and down towards the highway. If they had not got help then, they would have
fared badly.

That same evening, the priest of Trane-kær was lying
in his bed, and said to his wife that there came such a
strange restlessness over him ; he thought he ought to go
somewhere, as there was something not right going on,
but he could not tell what it was. His wife said that he
really must not go out so late ; so he lay for a little then,
but finally said that he could not help it, he must go, for
he could feel now that two of his brethren were in danger
of their lives. He hastily put on his gown and collar,
and went down to the highway, where the three countesses were driving the two priests before them. He came
just in the nick of time, for the priests were almost helpless. They had indeed got the countesses sunk in the
ground up to their knees, but one of the ghosts had

slipped behind them and was *looking through them* from
there, so that the priest from Snöde was already withered
on one side, and never recovered again.   The priest of
Trane-kær now lent a hand, and the ghosts had to give
in, as they were now one to one.   The countesses were
laid, and there was peace again in the place.   None of
the priests, however, got over that night.   The one from
Snöde was mortally ill when he reached home, and did
not live long after it.   When the Böstrup priest heard of
his death, he said, " Then my time will also come soon,"
and he died soon after.   The Trane-kær priest got off
best, but after this time he never mounted the pulpit, but
always stood in the choir-door when he preached.

The Ghost at Silkeborg.

AT Silkeborg there was the ghost of a man, who had
been foully murdered ; most people say that it was Captain H——'s servant, who had been first killed and then
drowned.   The curate in Linaa tried to lay him, but he
was too powerful for him, for it is not easy to lay the
ghost of one who has been innocently murdered.   " No
worthless wretch, but God's bairn," said the curate, when
he came home after a vain attempt.   The priest in Gjöd-
vad, Morten Regenberg, had then to take up the matter,
"for he was the man that could do it," say the peasants.
All the same, he was unsuccessful on the first two occasions on which he tried it ; the ghost was too much for
him also, knocked the book out of his hand and could
not be got to speak, and so long as it kept silence the
priest could not get the better of it.   Regenberg was not
the man to give in, however, and would try conclusions

with it a third time. He therefore ordered his man to yoke the horses and drive to Silkeborg, first laying a new horse-collar in the carriage. On the way to Silkeborg the priest got down and went aside, after giving the man orders to wait for him, and not drive on for any person except the one who said, "Drive on now in the name of Jesus." The Evil One now tempted the man to drive off and leave the priest in a fix. He sent to him one in the priest's likeness, but as he only said, "Drive on now," the servant saw that it was not the right person and would not obey him. So it went with others that the Evil One sent to him, but finally there came one with the proper words, and this was the priest himself. When they came to Lille-Maen beside Silkeborg, he ordered the servant to put the horse-collar round his neck; this he did in order to befool the ghost and get him to speak, and for this reason he wanted his man to look like a priest. The plan worked well, for as the man went forward and the priest came close behind him with his book, they met the ghost, who, on seeing the man, could not refrain from saying, "If you are to be priest this evening, I shall play fine pranks with you." The priest, who had previously forbid his servant to say a word, then stepped forward and said, "If he is not, I am." With that he began to read out of the book, and as the ghost had now spoken, he got the upper hand of it. He then ordered his man to turn the carriage, take off one of the wheels, lay it in the carriage, and drive home. The man thought they would be over-turned, but dared not disobey, and the carriage ran well enough on the three wheels, for the reason that the ghost had to do service for the fourth one; the priest had forced it to this, when he got power over it. They drove in this way to Resenbro, when the man received orders to put the fourth wheel on again, and they drove home. The priest had accomplished his difficult task, and the ghost was laid.

A Ghost Let Loose.

IN Bjolderup, beside Aabenraa, there is a farm where the cattle-house was once badly haunted. Every evening there came a man with red vest and white sleeves, who went about among the cattle and made a noise. Two large oxen, which were tied up in one of the stalls, were let loose every night by the ghost. For a long time no one could understand why this should have begun all at once ; but at last it occurred to them that the floor in the stall, where these two oxen stood, had lately been relaid, and on that occasion a stake was pulled up from the middle of the stall. A ghost must have been laid there in old days, and set free again when the stake was pulled out. There was no other resource then but to send for a "wise" priest to lay it again, but the ghost was difficult enough to deal with, "for he was now so old and so wise."

Exorcising the Living.

THERE was once a very clever priest in Stillinge ; he had gone through "the black school," and was an expert in that line, as the following story shows. He almost always wandered about under the open sky. Even by night he could often be seen walking backwards and forwards in his garden, or in the churchyard, or the church itself, and sometimes even in distant parts of the parish. When any

of his parishioners met him by night, he never entered
into conversation with them, but went silently on his way.
His wife, says the story, was much annoyed by this night-
wandering, and devised many a clever plan to get him
off it, but all in vain. At last she wondered whether it
would be possible to frighten him from it, and this she
resolved to try.

At this time there served on the parsonage a big,
strong, daring fellow, who was afraid of nothing. He
was taken into her counsels by the priest's wife, and promised to assist her. One night, when the priest was
going about as usual, the fellow took a sheet over him
and went out to frighten his master. He sought him in
the garden, but not finding him there, he went up to the
church. There he found the door open, and guessed that
the priest was inside. When he got inside the door, he
saw him coming down from the altar, deep in thought, so
he remained just where he was, as the priest could not
pass him without seeing him. As soon as the priest
caught sight of the white figure, he stopped and said in a
loud voice, "If you are a human being, speak ; if you are
a spirit, sink!" The man laughed to himself, and was
not going to be fooled in this way, so he stood silent and
motionless. The priest snatched "the book" out of his
pocket, and began to read in all haste. The man shud-
dered, for he felt himself beginning to sink, but he was
so determined that he made not a sign until he had sunk
down to the middle of his breast. Then he began to
entreat for himself, and begged the priest to forgive him
for having tried to play a trick on him. The priest was
horrified at what he had done, but said, "No ; it can't be
undone now, or we should both be lost. Down you must
go, but you can come up elsewhere."

The priest read on, and the man had soon entirely disappeared, but immediately afterwards he came up unharmed, in a sheep-cote belonging to a farm that lies a
little to the west of the church.   He came up out of the
ground with such force that he went right up through the
roof of the outhouse.   After that time there was always
a hole in the roof there, which could never be closed up.

The Tired Ghost.

MY grandfather told that, in his young days, he was
driving from Frederiksund late one evening, when all at
once he felt that something crept up into the waggon
behind him, although he could see nothing, and the waggon then became so heavy that the horses could scarcely
drag it.   This continued until he came to Gerlöv church,
where he distinctly felt something dump off the waggon,
which then became so light again that the horses ran with
it as if it were nothing.   He explained it in this way, that
it was a ghost who was making his way home to Gerlöv
churchyard, but had got tired on the way, and had
climbed up into the waggon until they reached the church.

The Long-expected Meeting.

WHILE they were once digging a grave in Assing Churchyard, they turned up a body which was not decayed,
although no one could remember of any one having been
buried at that spot.   They took the dead man, and set
him up against the wall of the church, where he remained
standing for some time.   One day the people in the

Nether Kirkton, which lies close by, were in the house taking their afternoon meal, when the ploughman said to the good-wife, " The dead man up in the churchyard ought to get a bite too. He has had to go without food for so long, that he may well be in want of it." " Well, I shall cut a slice for him, if you will take it to him," said the woman. The man was willing, and went over to the churchyard with the piece of bread. Handing this to the corpse, he said, "There is a bite for you ; you may well be hungry for it, seeing you have had to wait so long." No sooner were the words out of his mouth, than the dead man was on his back, and he was compelled, whether he liked it or not, to carry him four miles west over the heath to a farm there. When he entered with his burden, it was already evening, and the people were so scared that they ran out into the kitchen, with the exception of an old old woman, who lay in a bed beside the kitchen-door, and had done so for many years. The ploughman ran after them, but when he had entered the kitchen, he felt that the body was off his back. He now spoke to the others, and told them what had happened to him, and that the dead man had left him just as he came through the door. They became a little bolder after this, and would go back into the room and see what had happened. When they had opened the door, they saw nothing but a few handfuls of ashes, which lay in a little heap before the old woman's bed. She herself was dead. No one ever got to know what the dead man had to talk with her about ; but they could understand that they had both been waiting to meet each other, and on that account neither could he rot in the ground, nor she die. Now that this had happened, he had fallen into a little heap of ashes.

The Dead Mother.

ABOUT sixty years ago it so happened that the wife of the
priest in Väsby was sitting up late one evening, waiting
for her husband, when she heard the most pitiful cries
coming from the churchyard.   She readily understood
the meaning of these, and hastily got together a bundle
of such clothes as would be required for a newly born
child, and threw them over the churchyard wall.   There
was silence for a little after this, but the cries then began
anew, and the priest's wife understood that the dead
woman had borne twins, and required more clothing for
them.   She had no more children's clothes, but took all
the linen and woollen cloth she could get hold of at the
moment, and threw this over to the woman, who immediately became quiet.   When the priest came home, she
told him the story, but he would not believe it.   His wife
maintained its truth, however, so he spoke to the deceased
woman's relatives and asked leave to open the grave, to
satisfy himself whether the story was true or not.   They
agreed to this ; grave and coffin were opened, and there
lay the dead woman, with a child on each arm, wrapped
in the self-same clothes that the priest's wife had thrown
into the churchyard.

The Service of the Dead.

A GENERATION back a woman in Mariager had decided
to go to the early service in Mariager Church.   It began
at eight o'clock, and this was during the winter.   About
four o'clock the woman woke up and put on her finery,
and thinking it was near the proper time, made haste to

the church. The door was open, light streaming from all
the windows, and the organ playing. She hastened inside, and made for her seat, but was surprised to find that
she scarcely knew a single person in the church. The
priest, who stood by the altar, had also been dead for
many years. She was quite scared at this, and would
have run out again, but could not rise from her place. In
her confusion she looked round, and recognised a friend
in the seat behind her, who had also been dead for many
years. This friend bent over to her, and whispered to
her to unfasten her cloak, and be ready to run out of the
church as soon as the priest said " Amen " in the pulpit,
and before he had pronounced the benediction, otherwise
she would fare badly. The woman could not rise until
the priest had said " Amen," but she then ran out as fast
as she could. Just as she got outside the door, it slammed
behind her with a fearful crash, catching her cloak fast,
but doing her no harm. When the people came to the
church in the morning, they found the cloak caught in
the door. The part outside was whole, but that which
had been inside, was torn into little pieces, which lay
scattered all over the floor of the church.

The Perjured Ghost.

ON the estate of Palstrup lived a squire who had a great
desire to possess some fields which lay close to his own
ground. He employed every means to assert his claim
to these fields, and carried on a law-suit about them for
a long time. In the end the matter was to be decided by
oath. The squire had a servant, whom he bribed to give
his oath for him, and the latter put leaves in his hat and

earth in his boots, so that when the authorities visited the
disputed ground, he gave his oath that he stood on Palstrup earth and under Palstrup leaves. In this way the
lands came to belong to Palstrup. Before long, however,
the servant died, and could then be heard going about in
the fields by night, lamenting and saying, "Skovsborg
north-field and Dössing north-field are won to Palstrup
with great wrong: O woe and woe! O woe and woe!"
Finally the squire died also, and came about the farm
every night, making such noise and uproar that the people could scarcely stay there for fright.

Night-Ploughing.

IT has sometimes happened that people have been heard
and seen ploughing during the night time. These are
men who in their life-time have cheated their neighbours
by ploughing some of their land on to their own, and who,
after death, must go and plough, as if to return what they
had taken away ; but this they cannot accomplish unless
the living help them to put right the wrong they have
done. Such stealing of land could be very easily carried
out in old times, before the ground was marked off ; now-
a-days it seldom happens.

One evening a man was busy ploughing part of his
neighbour's field on to his own. He said to the lad who
was driving the plough for him, "When I am dead, I must
plough back again what I am ploughing to-night. Will
you help me then?" The lad said he would. Some
years passed, and the man died. Meanwhile the lad had
grown up and served as ploughman on another farm.
One evening as he was threshing, he saw his late master

on the other side of the beam that lay across the barn.
The ghost leaned his arms on the beam, looked at him
for a little, and said, " Will you come and help me now,
as you promised ? " The man went with him, and when
they had got outside the court-yard the ghost said, " Now
you can take the short cut across the field, I must go
along the road." When the man got to the field where
the ploughing was to be, he found the other there already,
with horses and plough. The man took the reins, and at
first they went quite slow, but got faster and faster, till at
last he had to run to keep up with the plough, and was
afraid that he would lose his wind. Fortunately it was
soon finished, and when they came to the end of the field
the whole thing suddenly disappeared before his eyes,
and he went home again, glad to have got off so well.

It is no pleasant thing to come across such night
ploughers, and no easy matter to defend one's self against
them. They are, indeed, for the most part, heard far
away, shouting and driving their horses, and sometimes
one can hear the ploughshares and wheels creaking ; but
as soon as they notice that any one is about to cross the
place where they are ploughing, they take good care not
to be discovered before they have him in their power.
Some say that these night ploughers can bewitch those
who come near them, so that they can neither hear nor
see. If they do get hold of any one, he must be very fortunate to escape from them before the cock crows. This
can only happen when the man thus caught by them puts
off his wooden shoes before he begins to drive the horses,
and is careful to lift them again when he comes to them
for the third time. If he does not remember it then, it
can also be done at the sixth time, but if he does not
remember then, or is unfortunate, and does not get into

them quick enough, he must hold out till the cock crows. However, driving the plough with them brings no other misfortune with it than the trouble of running up and down the field all night.   There are many who have had to drive for them, and who have all come well out of it.

The March-stone.

THERE was once a man who was not very particular about shifting the boundary mark between himself and his neighbours, for the purpose of gaining a few furrows, but he had to pay dear for that.   After his death, he had to walk again, and for several generations was heard every evening after sundown, going about dragging the march-stone and shouting "Where shall I set it? where shall I set it?" (Hwo ska æ sæt 'en?)   Finally one summer evening an audacious boy, who was rather late in bringing home the cattle, got annoyed at hearing the ghost's eternal question, "Where shall I set it?" and without further thought, answered rudely, "O, set it where you took it, in the Fiend's name." (Aa sæt'en, som do tow'en, i Fain Nawn.)   The ghost answered, "These words should have been said many years ago, and I would have had rest;" after that time nothing more was heard of him.

The Priest's Double.

A STUDENT was once living with an old priest.   One day he went down into the garden, where he saw the priest sitting, reading a book.   Not wishing to disturb him, he went back to the house, and entered the study, where he found the priest seated, and reading the same book as he had seen him with in the garden. The student was surprised at this and told what he had seen, whereupon the priest begged him to come and tell him the next time he saw this. The student promised to do so, and a few days later he again saw the priest sitting in two different places. When the latter heard this, he immediately took his staff in his hand, and went straight to the figure which sat reading in the garden. When he reached it, however, he at once turned round and walked into the house again. No one knows whether he said anything to it or not, but he looked at it at least. As soon as he had entered the house, he fell dead.

The Keg of Money.

ONE time some men were on a journey, and pitched their tent on a Sunday morning on a beautiful green meadow. The weather was clear and fine, and the travellers lay down to sleep in their tent, all in a row. The one who was lying next the door could not sleep, and kept looking here and there in the tent. He then noticed a tuft of bluish vapour above the man who lay innermost, which in a little came towards the door and went out. The man wished to know what this was, so he rose and followed it. It glided softly across the meadow, and finally came to the skin and skull of a horse that was lying there, and was full of blue flies which made a great humming. The vapour entered the horse-skull, and after a good while came out again. It then went on over the meadow, until it came to a small stream of water, down the side of which it went, apparently looking for a place to cross. The man had his whip in his hand, and laid it across the stream, and the vapour glided along the shaft of it to the other side. Then it went on again for a bit, till it arrived at a mound on the meadow, into which it disappeared. The man stood at a little distance, waiting for it to come back, which it did before long, and then returned in the same way as it had come. It crossed the stream on the man's whip as before, made straight for the tent then, and never stopped until it came above the innermost man in the tent, where it disappeared. The other then lay down again and fell asleep.

On rising to resume their journey, they talked much while loading their horses. Among other things, the one who had been innermost in the tent said, " I wish I had what I dreamed about to-day." " What was it you dreamed ? " asked the one who had seen the vapour. " I dreamed," said the other, " that I went out on the meadow here, and came to a large and beautiful house, where a crowd of people was assembled, singing and playing with the greatest mirth and glee. I stayed a very long time in there, and on coming out again went for a long long time across smooth and lovely meadows. Then I came to a great river, which I tried for a long time to cross, but in vain. I saw then a terribly big giant coming, who had a huge tree in his hand ; this he laid across the river, and I crossed on it. I went on for a long long time, till I came to a great mound. It was open, and I entered it, and found nothing there but a great barrel, filled with money. I stayed there an immensely long time, looking at the money, for such a heap I had never seen before. On leaving it, I went back the same way as I had come, crossed the river on the tree again and so got back to the tent." The one who had followed the vapour began to rejoice, and said to the one who had been dreaming, "Come and we shall search for the money at once." The other laughed, and thought he was out of his wits, but went with him. They followed the same path as the vapour had gone, came to the mound and dug in it, and there they found a keg full of money, which they took back and showed to their comrades, and told them all about the dream.

Soul-wandering.

IT happened once on a farm in Vend-syssel, that some folks had engaged a tailor, who was sitting on the table sewing one evening, while one of the farm-hands was lying on a bench talking to him. During the conversation, the man fell asleep, and soon after this the tailor noticed that something flew out of his mouth, while at the same moment the man ceased to breathe. The tailor thought over this for a little, and finally concluded that this must be the man's soul, taking a little excursion by night. To see the end of this play, he took a rag and laid it over the man's mouth, supposing that in this way he would prevent it from getting in again, when it came back. In a little the soul returned, and sure enough it did try to get in, but being prevented by the rag, it seemed to get lost, and began to flutter about the room. The tailor hopped down off the table, and began to pursue the soul, which he finally succeeded in catching. He wanted very much to get it to tell him something about its excursion, but did not understand the way to do this; however, he had no intention of letting it back to its proper home, when he had got such an unusual catch. He therefore put it into a box, where he kept it for a long time, but finally got tired of keeping it, and sold it to two itinerant Mormon priests.

Two men were once out digging turf, and lay down to take their mid-day nap. A mouse ran out of the mouth of one of them, and when it came back, the other held his hand over his fellow's mouth, so that it could not get in again, and with that the man died.

Fylgja.

THORKELL GEITISSON of Krossavík (E. of Iceland) ordered his thrall Freystein to make away with the child of Ornny, his (Thorkell's) sister. The thrall merely left it in a wood, where it was afterwards found by a man named Krum, who brought it up as his own. The boy was named Thorstein, and throve well. When six or seven years old he began to go to Krossavík, and one day he entered the house, where Geitir, the father of Thorkell, sat muttering into his cloak. The young Thorstein, who was rushing along as children do, fell suddenly on the floor. Geitir set up a loud laugh at this, and the boy went up to him, saying, "Did you think it so very amusing when I fell just now?" "I did," said Geitir, "for I saw what you did not see." "What was that?" asked Thorstein. "I shall tell you," said Geitir; "as you came into the room, there came with you a white bear's cub, and ran along the floor before you. When it saw me it stopped, but you were in a great hurry and so fell over it, and I suspect that you are not the son of Krum, but are of much higher birth." Geitir afterwards told this to his son Thorkell, who, after comparing the stories of Freystein and Krum, was convinced of the boy's real origin, and Thorstein took up his abode at Krossavík.

The Földgie or Vardögl.

THE belief in beings, of which each person has one to attend him, is common over the greater part of Norway, but there are differences both in the name and the idea. In some places they are called Fölgie or Fylgie; in others, Vardögl, Vardygr, Vardivil or Valdöiel, and sometimes Ham, Hug-ham or Hau.

In some districts the Vardögl is imagined as a good spirit, who always accompanies the person, and wards off all dangers and mishaps. For this reason, in many parts of the country, people are still so conscientious as to follow everyone, even the poorest, out of doors, and look after him ; or at least open the door after he has left, in order to give the Vardögl, if it should accidentally have stayed behind, an opportunity to follow its master, who in its absence is exposed to misfortunes and temptations. Among other risks, he runs that of falling into the clutches of the Thus-bet, an evil spirit which similarly attends every person, and is not to jest with. People often show almost incurable wounds of a malignant nature, where this troll has bitten them during the night. Such persons are said to be " Thus-bitten," and the wounds are called " Thus-bites."

In other parts the Fölgie or Vardögl is regarded more as a precursor of the person, which by knocking at the door or window, tapping on the walls, lifting the latch, and so on, gives notice either of the arrival of an acquaint-

ance, or that he is very anxious to come, or that some
accident is about to happen. When the Fölgie shows
itself, it is generally in the shape of an animal, whose
properties stand in a certain relation to the person's disposition ; but each individual always has the same one.
Bold men have, as a rule, a spirited beast, such as a wolf, a
bear, or an eagle. The cunning have a fox or a cat ; the
timid have a hare, a little bird, or the like.

Sometimes, however, the Vardögl shows itself in human
shape, and has then the appearance of its master, but disappears immediately. Such a person is called a "Double-
ganger." Hence it comes that the same person can be
seen in two different places at the same time, the one of
them being the Fölgie. When this appears to the person
himself, many a man is terrified, and believes that he will
soon die.

If any one wishes to know what animal he has for a
Vardögl, he must, with certain ceremonies, wrap up a
knife in a handkerchief, which is held in the air, while he
goes over all the animals he knows ; as soon as the Fölgie is named, the knife falls out of the handkerchief.

The Draug.

THE Draug is variously imagined in different districts of
Norway. In the south it is generally regarded either as
a white ghost, or as a Fölgie foreboding death, which accompanies the dead man wherever he goes, and sometimes shows itself as an insect, which in the evening gives
out a piping sound. In Herjus-dale in Hvide-sö, at the
spot where Herjus Kvalsot was murdered, his "draug"
now walks ; on Christmas Eve it came to his home, and
cried :—

" 'Twere better walking on the floor
Down at Kvalsot as of old,
Than lying here in Herjus-dale
'Neath unconsecrated mould."

In the north, on the other hand, the Draug almost always haunts the sea or its neighbourhood, and to some extent replaces Necken. The northland fishers have much to do with him. They often hear a terrible shriek from the Draug, which sometimes sounds like " H-a-u," and sometimes " So cold," and then they hurry to land, for these cries forebode storm and mishaps at sea.

The fishermen often see him, and describe him as a man of middle height, dressed in ordinary sailor's clothes. Most of the northlanders maintain that he has no head ; but the men of North Möre allow him, in place of a head, a tin-plate on his neck, with burning coals for eyes. Like Necken, he can assume various shapes. He generally haunts the boat-sheds, in which, as well as in their boats, the fishermen find a kind of foam, which they think to be the Draug's vomit, and believe that the sight of it is a death-warning.

Aasgaards-reia.

THIS procession consists of spirits which have not done so much good as to deserve heaven, and not so much evil as to be sent to hell. In it are found drunkards, brawlers, satirists, swindlers, and such like folk, who, for the sake of some advantage or other, have sold themselves to the Devil. Their punishment is to ride about till the end of the world. At the head of the procession rides Guro-Rysse, or Reisa-Rova with her long rump, by which she is distinguished from the others. After her comes a

w

whole multitude of both sexes. If one sees them from the front, both riders and horses are big and beautiful, but from behind one can see nothing but Guro's long rump. The horses are coal-black, and have eyes that gleam in the darkness : they are guided with glowing bits or iron bridles, which, combined with the yells of the riders, create a terrible noise that can be heard a long way off. They ride over water as well as over land, and the horses' hoofs can scarcely be seen to touch the water. Where they throw the saddle on the roof, some one must shortly die ; and where they feel that blows and death will happen at a drinking party, there they come in, and set themselves on the shelf above the door. They keep quiet so long as nothing takes place, but laugh loudly and rattle their iron bits, when blows begin and murder is done. They especially travel about at Christmas, when the big drinkings take place. They are in the habit of resting on the farm of Bakken in Svarte-dal in Upper Thelemark, and usually bake their bread beside Sundsbarm Lake.

When any one hears them coming, he must either try to get out of the way, or at least throw himself flat on the ground, and pretend to be asleep, for there have been instances of living persons being snapped up by the company, and either brought back to the place where they were taken up, or found lying half-conscious far away from it. One Christmas Eve the "Skreia" passed over Nordbö in Nisse-dal, where there was heard a wild cry of "To horse! to horse!" The man went to look out, but before he knew where he was, he was sitting on the ridge of his own house. Still worse did Helge Teitan fare. She was torn out of her own bed, and carried off by the troop. When she came to Holme Lake, a mile from her house, she knew where she was by the many islands. An hour later she was thrown half dead in at the door of her own house. Foam-covered horses, which have been with the troop, are often seen. At Trydal in Gjerre-stad, where screaming children are threatened with "Haaskaal-reia," the farmer was carried off by it one Christmas Eve. In his first astonishment he could not utter a word, but when he had got half a mile north from the farm, he managed to say, " In Jesus' name." With that he was dropped down on the field. Gunhild of Tvedt in Ombli was carried off, along with a black horse from her stable. The horse went as well on water as on land, and galloped at a fearful pace until it came to Ljöse-stad, where Gun-hild was let go. In old days they were so frightened for " Askereia," that no one dared even to sing when it was out ; now they scare children with it. The honest man who is careful to cast himself on his face, or even on his back, and throw out his arms so as to make the sign of the cross, has nothing more to fear than that each one of the company spits upon him. When they have all passed, he spits in turn, otherwise he may take harm by it.

The Gand-reid.

AT Reykir in Skeid (S. of Iceland) lived Rúnólf Thor-steinsson, who had a son named Hildiglúm. On Saturday night, twelve weeks before winter, the latter went outside, and heard so great a crash that he thought both earth and heaven shook. He then looked towards the west, and thought he saw there a fiery ring, and inside it a man on a grey horse. He was riding hard, and soon came past him. In his hand he held a flaming fire-brand, and rode so near that Hildiglúm could see him plainly, and he was black as pitch. In a loud voice he repeated this verse :—

I ride a horse	With ill between ;
With hoary front,	And Flosi's redes
With dewy top	Shall roll to doom,
A doer of hurt :	And Flosi's redes
With ends of fire,	Shall roll to doom.

Then he seemed to hurl the brand before himself east to the fells, and a fire seemed to shoot up to meet it, so great that Hildiglúm could not see the fells for it. The man rode east into the fire, and disappeared there. After this Hildiglúm went in and lay down on his bed, and was long unconscious, but at length recovered. He remembered all that he had seen, and told it to his father, who bade him tell it to Hjalti Skeggjason, which he then did. "You have seen the *gandreid*," said Hjalti, "and that always comes before great tidings."

The Knark-vogn.

THIS spectre moves with a noise like that of a creaking waggon, and derives its name from this. It is believed to consist of spirits of the damned, who are doomed to fly around the earth within twenty-four hours, and always fly in the same direction, namely, to the north-east. Rash persons have called out to it, "Turn about and grease your nave," whereupon it makes for them, and they must escape by getting under a roof, or by their companions throwing themselves above them to protect them from its attacks. In the former case, a "wise" person may turn it back a little, and enable the offenders to escape ; but

even after they have got safely into the house, it has been
heard scraping at the door all night. Where the others
have thrown themselves above the speaker, the knark-
vogn has scraped great holes in the earth round about
them, and pulled at their clothes, but without being able
to injure them. In spite of this protection, it once managed to strike a man in the eyes, which were red to the
end of his days. In the morning they are free from it.

The Night Raven.

THE night-raven is a suicide who has been buried where
three estates meet. Every year he can push to one side
the length of a grain of sand, and so after many years
comes to the surface again. The night-raven then flies
towards the Holy Sepulchre, but is only permitted to go
a certain distance each year, so that it may be centuries
before it gets there. A man was once sitting on the
ground when he heard something beneath him saying,
" Now I turn myself." The man was scared, and the
voice repeated, "Now I turn myself." " What can this
be," thought the man, " I shall say something to it next
time." When the words were repeated for the third time,
he answered, " Well turn yourself, in Jesus' name, and
never do it again." An old priest, however, is said to
have told his communicants that the night-raven was a
ghost who had been laid. The pile driven down at that
spot, makes a hole in its right wing, and if anyone happens to see the sun through that hole, he can thereafter
see things hid from all other eyes. More commonly it is
believed that to see through this hole causes madness or
sudden death.

The night-raven flies about with a cry of " Ba-u, Ba-u," and is ready to attack persons whom it finds outside by night. There is a story of two girls who met it, and escaped from it by fleeing into a house ; in the morning two fiery wings were fixed on the door. It can strike fire with its wings, and is thus visible in the night time.

IX.—WIZARDS AND WITCHES.

Gest and the Witches.

ONE time when King Olaf Tryggvason sat in Thrand-heim, it so happened that a man came to him in the evening, and greeted him becomingly. The King received him well, and asked him his name. He said he was called Gest. "A guest here shall you be, whatever be your name," said the King. "I have told the truth about my name," said the other, "and fain would I have your hospitality if I might." Olaf granted him this, but as the day was spent he talked no further with the stranger, but went immediately to evensong, and then to supper, and after that to sleep.

That same night King Olaf Tryggvason woke up in his bed, and repeated his prayers, while all the rest were asleep. It seemed to him then that an elf or some spirit entered the house, although all the doors were closed. He went before the bed of every one who slept there, and finally came to that of one who lay near the door. There he stopped, and said, "A terribly strong lock is here on an empty house, and the King is not so wise in such matters as others would make him out to be, when he sleeps so sound now." After that he disappeared.

Early in the morning the King sent his page to see who had been in that bed over-night, and it turned out to be the stranger. The King had him summoned, and

asked him if he was a Christian. Gest answered that he
had received the mark of the cross, but had not been
baptised. The King said he was welcome to stay there
at his court, but he must be baptised in that case. What
the elf said about the lock, referred to Gest having crossed
himself like other men in the evening, although he was
really a heathen.

Gest told many tales of far-back days when he had
been with Sigurd Fafnis-bani, and the sons of Lodbrók,
and the King's men were charmed to hear him. Olaf
asked him many questions, all of which he fully answered.
At last he said, "Now I shall tell you why I am called
Norna-Gest," and began the following tale.

"I was brought up by my father at a place called
Græning in Denmark : he was a rich man, and kept a
good house. At that time there went round the country
witches who were called spae-wives, and foretold men's
lives, and for that they were invited and entertained by
people, and received gifts when they went away. My
father did this, and they came to him with a large following, and were to foretell my fate. I was lying in the
cradle, and two candles were burning beside me. They
said that I would be a very lucky man, greater than any
of my ancestors or noblemen's sons in the country ; this
was the future they predicted for me. The youngest
Norn seemed to be held of very little account by the
other two, for they never consulted her in spaedoms that
were of any weight. There was also present a rascal
multitude that pushed her out of her seat, and made her
fall on the ground. At this she became exceeding wroth,
and cried out in a loud and angry voice, bidding the
others cease their good prophecies concerning me, "for I
lay on him that he shall live no longer than until the

candle that is burning beside him is burnt out." At this the elder witch took the candle, and put it out, telling my mother to keep it, and not light it before the last day of my life. After this the spae-wives went away, taking the young one with them in bonds, and my father gave them valuable gifts at parting. After I grew up, my mother gave me that candle to keep, and I have it with me now."

"Will you now receive baptism?" asked the King. "With your advice I will," said Gest, so he was baptized and became one of his followers; he was faithful to him and well liked by the others.

One day the King asked Gest : "How long would you like to live now, if you had the deciding of it ? " "Only a short time," said Gest, "if God so willed it." "What will happen if you take your candle now ? " asked the King. Gest took the candle out of his harp-stock, and the King ordered it to be lighted ; this was done, and the candle burned fast. "How old are you ? " asked he at Gest. "Three hundred winters have I now," said he ; and after that he lay down, and asked to be anointed. The King had this done, and by that time little of the candle remained unburned. They noticed then that Gest was passing away, and just at the same time that the candle burned out, Gest died, and all thought his death remarkable.

The Witch Thorbjörg in Greenland.

THERE was a great famine in Greenland ; those who had been to the fishing had but small takes, and some had not returned at all. There was a woman in the district named Thorbjörg, who was a spae-wife, and was called the Little Witch. She had had nine sisters, all of them witches, but she was the only one alive then. It was her custom in the winter-time to go to entertainments, and men invited her to visit them, especially such as were curious to know their fortunes or how the season would turn out ; and seeing that Thorkell was the leading man there, it was thought to be his business to find out, when this famine that was upon them would cease. Thorkell therefore invited the spae-wife to his house, and a good reception was prepared for her, as was the custom when such women were to be received. A high seat was made ready for her, with a cushion on it, which had to be stuffed with hens' feathers. When she arrived in the evening with the man who had been sent for her, she was so dressed that she had over her a blue cloak with straps, which was set with stones right down to the bottom. On her neck she had glass-beads, on her head a black cap of lambskin lined with white cat-skin. In her hand she carried a staff with a knob on it ; it was mounted with brass, and set with stones about the knob. About her waist she wore a tinder-belt, and on it a great skin-purse, in which she kept the charms that she required in order to get knowledge of anything. She had shaggy calfskin-shoes on her feet, and in these were long and stout thongs with large knobs of brass at the ends. On her hands she wore cat-skin gloves, which were white and hairy inside.

When she entered, it was thought every man's duty to give her honourable greetings, which she received according to the liking she had for each. Thorkell then took the hand of the wise-woman, and led her to the seat that was prepared for her. There he asked her to run her eyes over his cattle, household, and homestead, but she was very reserved about everything. The tables were afterwards laid, and we must tell what food was served up to the spae-wife. For her was made porridge with kid's milk, but for meat to her were prepared the hearts of every kind of animal that could be got there. She had a brass spoon and an ivory handled knife, with two rings of brass on it, and the point of it was broken. When the tables were cleared away, Thorkell came before Thorbjörg, and asked what she thought of his homestead or of his people, or how quickly she could get knowledge of what he had enquired about and all wished to know. She said she would not disclose that before next morning, after she had slept there that night. Next day she was supplied with all that she required to perform her enchantments, and bade them bring her some women, who knew those charms that were necessary to perform the enchantment, and are called Vardlokkur, but no such women could be found. Search was made all over the household whether any one knew them. Then Gudrid answered, " I am neither witch nor wise-woman, and yet my foster-mother in Iceland taught me the charm that she called Vardlokkur." "Then you are learned in season," said Thorbjörg. Gudrid answered, " This is a learning and proceeding of such a kind as I mean to take no part in, for I am a Christian woman." "It might well be," said Thorbjörg, " that you could help folk in this matter, and be no worse a woman than before ; but I leave it to Thorkell to provide all that is necessary here." Thorkell now pressed Gudrid hard, until she consented to do as he wished. The women made a ring round about her, while Thorbjörg sat up on the spell-seat. Then Gudrid sang the song so well and beautifully, that all who were present thought they had never heard it sung more sweetly. The spae-wife thanked her for her

song, and added, "Many spirits have come hither, and
thought it beautiful to hear what was sung, who formerly
would turn away from us and show us no obedience.
Now many things are plain to me that before this were
concealed both from me and from others, and I can tell
you this, that this famine will not last much longer, and
the season will improve with spring."

The Witch Skroppa.

WHILE Hörd and his fellow-outlaws were on Geirsholm
in Hval-firth, he went one summer with twenty-four men
to Saurbæ, because Thorstein Oxnabrodd had boasted
that Skroppa the witch, his foster-mother, could so bring
it about by her magic that the Holm-men could do him
no harm. On reaching the shore, seven of them stayed
to watch the ship, and seventeen went up on land. On
the sand-hills above the boat-sheds they saw a large bull,
which they wished to provoke, but Hörd would not allow
them. Two of his men however turned to meet the bull,
and thrust at him, one aiming at his side and the other
at his head ; but the bull met the thrusts with his horns
in each case, both spears flew back into their own breasts,
and both were killed. Hörd said, "Follow my advice,
for everything here is not as it seems." When they
reached the farm, Skroppa was at home along with the
yeoman's daughters Helga and Sigrid, but Thorstein was
at the shieling in Kúvallar-dal. Skroppa opened up all
the houses, but caused ocular delusions, so that where she
and the other two sat on the bench there seemed to be
only three wooden boxes. Hörd's men spoke of breaking
the boxes, but Hörd forbade them. They then held

north from the farm, to see whether they could find any
cattle. Next they saw a young sow with two little pigs
come running northwards out of the farm, and got in
front of it. Then they seemed to see a great host of men
coming against them with spears and other weapons, and
now the sow with her pigs shook her ears southward
again. Said Geir, "Let us go to the ship : we cannot
deal here with a superior force." Hörd said it was advisable not to run so soon before all was seen into, and with
that he picked up a stone and killed the sow with a blow.
When they came there they found Skroppa lying dead,
and in place of the two young pigs the daughters of the
yeoman were standing over her. As soon as Skroppa
was dead, they saw that it was a herd of cattle that was
coming against them, and not men at all ; these they
drove down to the ship and killed, and took the beef on
board.

The Witch Grima.

THORMOD the skald was wounded in Greenland by the
friends of a man he had killed. Two of his friends found
him and took him to the head of Eiriks-firth, where a
man named Gamli lived up under the glaciers, along
with his wife Grima. The two lived alone, seldom visiting or visited, and Grima was not only a good leech, but
was believed to know something of the old magic. Twelve
months after this, but before Thormod had quite recovered
from his wounds, it happened that Thordis, the mother of
the man he had slain, was restless in her sleep. Her son
Bödvar would not allow her to be wakened, and after she
awoke of her accord, he asked her what she had dreamed.

" I have been far-travelled to-night," said she, "and have learned what I did not know before, that Thormod, who killed my son, is in life and is with Gamli and Grima at the head of Eiriks-firth. I shall go thither and take Thormod, and reward him with an evil death for the great harm he has done us." That very night Thordis and Bödvar with other thirteen men rowed to Eiriks-firth. At the same time Grima was ill at ease in her sleep, and on waking knew that Thordis was coming to them, "for she has now learned by her trolldom that Thormod is staying here with us, and she means to kill him." On the way Thordis got Thorkell, the chief man in Eiriks-firth, to accompany her with twenty men.

Grima had a large chair, on the back of which was carved a large figure of Thor. On this she told Thormod to take his seat when Thordis and her party came, and not to rise off it until they were gone. "Gamli will hang up the pot and boil seal-flesh ; he shall heap sweepings on the fire and make plenty of smoke ; I shall sit at the door and spin yarn, and receive them when they come." When the ship was seen coming to land, Thormod sat down on the chair, and Gamli raised a dense smoke in the house, making it so dark that nothing could be seen. Grima sat on the threshold and span, repeating something to herself that the others did not understand. When the party arrived, Grima denied to Thorkell that they had Thormod there. "It would be strange if you did," said Thorkell, "but we should like to search your house." "You could well do that," said Grima, "though you had fewer with you. I am always pleased to see you in my house, but I have no will to see these folks from Einars-firth doing damage to it." "Thordis and I shall go in by our two selves and search it," said Thorkell. They did so, and took no long time to it, for the rooms were very small, and when they opened up the sitting-room it was full of smoke and nothing to be seen. The whole house indeed was thick with smoke, and on that account they stayed inside less time than they would otherwise have done. When they came out again Thordis said, " I could not see clearly what was in the sitting-room for the smoke. We shall take out the skylight, and let the smoke out, and see what can be seen then." This was done, and the smoke cleared away. Then they could see everything in the room, with Grima's chair standing in the middle of the floor. They saw Thor with his hammer carved on the back of the chair, but could not see Thormod. As they left the room and went out, Thordis said, " Grima has still some of the old faith left when Thor's image is on her chair-back." Grima answered, " I seldom get to church to hear the teachings of learned men, for I have far to go, and few folks at home. Now, when I see the image of Thor made of wood, that I may break and burn whenever I will, it comes into my mind how much greater is He who hath shaped heaven and earth, and all things visible and invisible, and given life to everything." Thordis answered, " It may be you think such things ; but I expect we could make you tell more if Thorkell was not here to protect you, for my heart tells me that you know something of Thormod's whereabouts." Grima answered, " Now the proverb comes to pass, ' He oft goes wrong that has to guess,' and the other one, ' Something saves every man that is not fey.' " With this they parted, and Thordis returned home.

Thordis the Spae-wife.

KORMAK the skald had challenged Thorvard to a holm-gang, and the latter had recourse to a spae-wife named Thordis, whose aid he asked against Kormak, and paid her well for it. Thordis then prepared him for the fight as she thought best. Kormak told his mother, Dalla, of his intention; she asked whether he had good hopes of it. "Why should I not?" said Kormak. Dalla answered, "It will not do, however, to go about it in that way, for Thorvard will not care to fight unless he has some sorcery to aid him. I think it would be wise for you to visit Thordis the spae-wife, for you will have to fight against guile." "I care little for that," said Kormak, but all the same he went and visited Thordis and asked her assistance. "You have come too late," said she; "no weapon can bite him now, but I will not refuse you assistance either. Stay here to-night and enquire into your lot, and I shall be able to bring it about that no iron will bite you either." Kormak stayed there all night, and was wakened by feeling some one handling the covering at his head. He asked who it was, but the person turned away and went out. Kormak followed, and saw that it was Thordis, who by this time had got to the place where the holm-gang was to be fought, and was holding a goose under her. He asked what she meant to do, whereupon she let the goose down, and said, "Why could you not keep quiet?" Kormak then lay down again, but kept awake in order to watch the proceedings of Thordis. She came to him three times, and each time he enquired into what she was doing. The third time when Kormak came out she had killed two geese, and let the blood run together into a bowl, and had already taken the third one and was just about to kill it. "What does this work mean, foster-mother?" said Kormak. Thordis answered, "It will be clearly proved, Kormak, that you are little meant to prosper. I had now intended to destroy the spells that Thorveig had laid on you and Steingerd, and you could have enjoyed each other if I had killed the third goose without anyone knowing it." "I have no faith in such things," said Kormak.

Before the holm-gang Thordis said to Kormak, "I can bring it about that he will not know you." Kormak answered her angrily, said that she would cause nought but mischief, and wanted to drag her out to the door and see her eyes in the sunshine, but his brother Thorgils stopped him.

Thorleif and Earl Hakon.

THORLEIF, a native of Svarfadar-dal in the North of Iceland, being outlawed and forced to leave the country, sailed for Norway, and arrived there in the latter days of Earl Hakon. In the Vik he met with the Earl himself, and refused to trade with him, which so enraged Hakon that next day, while Thorleif was in town pushing his business, he came down to the ship, seized on the cargo, burned the vessel, and ended by hanging all Thorleif's companions. When Thorleif returned in the evening, and found what had taken place, he made close enquiries as to how it had happened, and then in a verse hinted that Hakon might pay dearly for it yet.

Going south to Denmark with some merchants, Thorleif stayed there with King Svein during that winter, and

gained the King's good-will by composing a poem on his
exploits, for which he was also rewarded by the present
of a ring and a sword.   Before long Thorleif grew
gloomy, and showed no desire to share in drinking
with his comrades, or to sit beside them.   The King
soon noticed this, and asked him the reason of it.   " You
must have heard, Sire," said Thorleif, " that he who
enquires into another man's trouble is bound to help
him out of it."   " Tell me what it is first," said
Svein.   " I have made some verses this winter," said
he, " which I call ' Earl's Verses,' because they are about
Earl Hakon.   Now I shall be sorry if I cannot get leave
from you to go to Norway, and recite them to the Earl."
" Certainly you shall have leave," said the King, " but you
must promise to come back to us as quickly as you can,
for we have no wish to lose you."   Thorleif promised this,
and went north to Norway, and made no stay until he
came to Thrandheim, near which Earl Hakon then was.
Thorleif now put on the garb of a beggar and fixed on
his face a goat's beard ; under his beggar's dress he put a
leather bag, so contrived that it should seem as if he ate
whatever food he dropped into it, the mouth of it being
just below the beard.   Then he took a pair of crutches
with a spike at the end of each, and with these went to
the Earl's hall at Hladir.   There he arrived on Yule Eve,
just as the Earl was taking his seat, along with many
other great men whom he had invited to the Yule feast.
The beggar promptly made his way into the hall, stumbled
as he went in and fell on his crutches, and finally took
his seat in the straw near to the door beside the other
beggars.   He soon fell out with these, and began to take
his crutches to them, which they had no liking for, and
cleared away from him.   The noise and uproar of this

were at last heard all over the hall, and the Earl becoming
aware of it, asked the reason of it. On learning that it was
caused by a sturdy beggar, he ordered him to be brought
before him, The carl came, and his greeting was but
short. The Earl asked him his name, family, and home.
" My name is an uncommon one," said he ; " I am called
Nidung Gjallanda-son, and belong to Syrgis-dalir in
Sweden the Cold. I am known as Nidung the Near-
comer, and have travelled widely and visited many a lord.
I am now growing very old, so that I can scarcely tell
my age through failing memory. I have heard a great
deal about your lordliness and enterprise, wisdom and
popularity, legislation and condescension, liberality and
other accomplishments." " Why are you so perverse and
ill to deal with, compared with the other beggars ? " said
the Earl. " What wonder is that," said he, " in one who
goes about destitute of everything but misery and
wretchedness, and has nothing that he needs, and has
long lain out in woods and forests, though he grows
ill-tempered with old-age and all the rest,—he who
formerly was used to having honour and ease with
the proudest lords, and now is hated by every worthless
villager ? " " Are you a man of any accomplishments,"
asked the Earl, " as you say you have been with great
lords ? " The carl answered " Even though there may
have been something of that when I was young, yet now
it may well be come to what the proverb says, that *every
man comes to decrepitude.* There is also a saying that *it
is hard for a hungry man to talk ;* and neither will I talk
with you any longer, unless you give me something to
eat, for old age, hunger, and thirst, so press upon me that
I can stand up no longer. It is very unlordlike to question strangers about everything in the world, and never

take thought of what is fitting for men, for all are so contrived that they require both food and drink." The Earl
gave orders that such food should be given to him as he
required, and this was done. The carl sat down at table,
and promptly began to it, and soon cleared all the dishes
he could reach, so that the attendants had to bring a
fresh supply, which he began to as heartily as the first.
Every one supposed that he ate it, but in reality he
dropped it into the bag already mentioned. Men began
to laugh and make jests on him, but the carle heeded them
not, and did as before.

After the tables were removed, Nidung went before the
Earl, and addressed him : "Take my thanks for that
now," said he, "but they are ill attendants you have, who
do everything worse than you tell them. Now I should
like you to show me your condescension, and listen to a
poem that I have made about you." "Have you made
any poems about great men before ? " asked the Earl.
" I have that," said he. " The old saying may be fulfilled
here," said the Earl, " that *often is the song good that grey
beards make*. Recite your poem, old man, and we shall
listen to it."

Then the carl began his poem and recited on to the
middle of it, and there seemed to the Earl to be praise of
him in every verse of it, and mention made as well of the
great deeds of his son Eirik. As the poem went on, however, a strange thing began to happen to him ; so great
uneasiness and itching spread over all his body and
especially about his thighs, that he could not sit still a
moment. So excessive did this become that he made
them scratch him with combs wherever they could get at
him, and where they could not, he made them take a
coarse cloth and tie three knots on it, and set two men to

draw it backwards and forwards between his thighs.
Then the Earl began to get ill-pleased with the poem,
and said, "Can't you make better poetry, you devil, for it
seems to me this might just as well be called insult as
praise : see and improve it, or I will pay you for it." The
carl promised well, and began to recite the so-called
" Mist-verses," which stand in the middle of the " Earl's
Insult," and of which the beginning is preserved. By the
time he had finished these verses the hall was quite dark,
and then he began again to the " Earl's Insult," and as
he recited the last third of it, every weapon that was in
the hall was in motion without human aid, and that was
the death of many men. The Earl fell into a faint, and
the carl disappeared, although the doors were shut and
locked. After the poem ceased the darkness decreased,
and light was restored in the hall. The Earl recovered
consciousness, and found that the satire had touched him
closely, and left its mark on him, for all his beard was
rotted off, and all his hair on one side of the parting, and
it never grew again. The Earl then made them clear
the hall and carry out the dead. He was sure now that
the carl had been no other than Thorleif, who had thus
paid him back for killing his men and taking his goods.

As for Thorleif, he held south to Denmark, living by
the way on what he had got in the hall, and however
long he was on the road he never stopped till he reached
King Svein. The King welcomed him heartily, and asked
about his journey, and when Thorleif had told him all,
said, " Now I shall lengthen your name, and call you
Thorleif Earls'-skald."

Earl Hakon's Revenge.

AFTER Earl Hakon had recovered for the most part from the injuries caused him by the satire of Thorleif (though it is said that he never was the same man as before), he was eager to revenge himself on Thorleif, if possible. To this end he called upon Thorgerd Hörgabrúd, in whom he put all his faith, and upon her sister Irpa, to send some fiend out to Island who would pay back Thorleif in full. He brought them great offerings and enquired of them, and when he had got an answer that pleased him, he took a log of drift-wood and had a wooden man made out of it. Then by the magic and incantations of the Earl, and the trolldom and sorcery of the sisters, he had a man slain and his heart taken out and put into the wooden one. This he then dressed in clothes and called by the name of Thorgard ; and strengthened him so much by the power of the fiend, that he went about and spoke with men. Thereafter he put him into a ship, and sent him to Iceland for the purpose of killing Thorleif. For a weapon he gave him a bill that he had taken from the temple of the sisters, and which Hörgi had once owned.

Thorgard reached Iceland at the time when men were at the Althing. Thorleif was there with the rest, and one day as he went from his booth, he saw a man coming west over Oxar-á, huge of stature and villainous in looks. Thorleif asked him his name. He said it was Thorgard, and straightway hurled abusive words at Thorleif, who on hearing them began to draw the sword he had received from King Svein. At that moment Thorgard aimed with his bill at Thorleif's middle, and drove it through him ; the latter on receiving the thrust struck at Thorgard, but he plunged down into the earth, so that only his heels were seen as he disappeared.

Thorleif went home to his booth, and told what had befallen him, to the great wonderment of all. Then he threw open his kirtle, which he had been holding tight, and his intestines fell out. Thus died Thorleif with great renown, and all men thought great harm of it. All were sure that this Thorgard had been nothing but sorcery and magic on the part of Earl Hakon. Thorleif was buried there, his grave-mound being to the north of the law-hill, where it may still be seen.

Upwakenings or Sendings.

AT the present day the art of raising a ghost has so much gone out of use, that all are not agreed as to the procedure to be followed in doing so. Some say that a bone of a dead man must be taken and charmed with sorcery, so that it receives human shape, and is then sent against the man whom the wizard wishes to harm. If that person is so wise, that he can hit upon that very bone in the ghost, which was taken from the dead man, or call him by his right name, the ghost can do him no harm, and must leave him in peace.

Some again say that more than this is necessary to wake up a ghost. First of all, it must be done on the night between Friday and Saturday, when this falls between the 18th and 19th, or between the 28th and 29th of a month ; the month or week itself makes no difference. The wizard must on the previous evening reverse the Lord's Prayer, and write it on a piece of paper or skin with a hedge-hog quill, using for this purpose blood

taken from his left arm. He must also cut runes on a
stick, and take both of these articles with him to the
churchyard at midnight.   There he may go to any grave
he pleases, but it is thought safest to keep to the smallest
ones.   He must then lay the stick on the grave, and roll
it back and forward, meanwhile repeating the Lord's
Prayer backwards, together with other incantations, which
few men know.   The grave gradually begins to move,
and various sights appear to the wizard, while the ghost
is being raised ; this goes on but slowly, for ghosts are
very unwilling to move, and say " Let me lie in peace."
The wizard must neither yield to their entreaties, nor be
alarmed at the sights he sees, but repeat his charms and
roll the stick, until the ghost is half up.   At the same
time he must watch that no earth falls outside the grave
when it begins to lift, for such earth cannot be put back
into it again.   When the ghost is half-way out of the
ground, he must be asked two questions (not three, for in
that case he will go down again before the Trinity), and
these usually are (1) what man he was in his life-time,
and (2) how mighty a man he was.   Others say that only
one question should be asked, namely, " How old are
you ? "   If the ghost says that he is of middle age or
above it, it is not advisable to go further, because the
wizard has to try his strength with the ghost, and ghosts
are terribly strong ; it is said that their strength is half
as much again as in their life-time.   This is the reason
why wizards prefer to wake up children of 12 or 14 years
old, or persons who are not above 30 at most, and never
those who are older than themselves.

When the ghosts come up out of the grave, their nostrils and mouth *(vit)* are all running with froth and
slaver, which the wizard must lick off with his tongue ;

some say that this is the origin of the phrase " to lick up a man's wits." Then he must draw blood from under the little toe of his right foot, and wet the tongue of the ghost with this. As soon as this is done, some say that the ghost attacks him, and the wizard must exert all his strength to get him under. If he succeeds in this and the ghost falls, he is bound to be entirely at the service of the wizard ; but if the ghost is stronger than the man, he drags him down into the grave, and no one has ever come back who thus came under the power of the ghosts. Others say that the wizard attacks the ghost, when he is only halfway out of the ground, and throws him on his back, keeping him bound in this position until he has licked his " wits " and wet his tongue with warm blood.

If the wizard does not send the ghost down again, he continues to follow him and his descendants to the ninth generation. Other accounts say that these ghosts continue to grow more powerful during the first 40 years, remain stationary during the next 40, and fall off during the third 40 ; longer life is not granted them, unless some powerful spell is on them.

Skin-coat.

HALL, who lived into this century at Geldinga-holt, in Skaga-firth, was a famous wrestler. Once when on a journey to the south, he encountered another great wrestler, and threw him. The other was angry at this, and threatened to do him a mischief.

At this time there lived at Vatns-skard a farmer who was a wizard. One day in winter as he was watching his sheep he saw a girl dressed in a skin-coat going northward. He called on her and asked her errand ; she replied that she had to kill Hall of Geldinga-holt. The farmer invited her home with him, and she accepted this ; but he led her into the store-room, slammed the door after her, and conjured her to remain there till the room was opened again. With that he went to sleep, strictly forbidding any one to open the room until he awoke. In spite of this, his wife went into it for wool, and then the ghost slipped out. The farmer woke up a little after, and asked who had been in the room. His wife told the truth. "God help me," said he, "Hall is most likely dead by this time ;" and with that he took his stall-horse and rode down to Skaga-firth like a shot, until the horse foundered below him a little way short of Geldinga-holt. Meanwhile on that day Hall had gone to the stable, to comb five foals that he had, and of which he was very proud. As he was about to enter the door one of these was hurled at him with its neck broken. Hall was startled at this, but just at that moment the man from Vatns-skard arrived, and they both encountered the ghost and sent it back to the man who had sent it north.

When the ghost got south again, it was so fierce that there was no managing it, and the man who had wakened it up, finally sent it north again to go wherever it liked. "Skin-coat" drifted north now, and grew so feeble that she did no other harm than scare women and children, keeping out of men's way as much as possible. Finally she settled on a farm out on Skagi, where the good-man was seldom at home, and amused herself with making faces at the children. One time, when she sat on the bed, as she often did, and made grimaces at the little ones, there slipped in Niels the poet, who had a habit of coming in, wherever he thought fit, without giving notice.

He immediately began to recite charms over the ghost, which made its way out through the wall with Niels after it, reciting continuously.   Finally he charmed it down into a mire, and forbade them to cut turf there for so long.   Niels said that he felt very much having to charm down " Skin-coat," for at last she had begun to weep loudly, and had been in white weeds (*i.e.*, after baptism) before she was wakened up.   So powerfully charmed was she, that he was sure he would have recited himself into Hell if he had required to recite another verse.

The Ghost in the King's Treasury.

THE story says that at one time some Icelandic students in Copenhagen had run short of money, as sometimes will happen, and four of them joined with two Danish ones in raising a ghost to get money for them.   Olaf Stephensen, son of Magnus the privy councillor in Videy (Reykjavík), is said to have been " pot and pan " in the whole business ; the others' names are not given.   The ghost they raised had been a Dutchman when alive, and was not quite cold when they charmed him up out of his grave, so they had to feed him like any other man. When the ghost had got his bearings, they sent him to the royal treasury for money.   It unfortunately happened that new money had just been coined, of another fashion than that previously in use, and this had been deposited in the treasury, but not as yet put into circulation.   The ghost took a great quantity of these new coins and brought them to the confederates.   They were rejoiced at this, and spent the money just as if nothing had happened.   Suspicion, however, was awakened when the

new coins came so quickly into circulation, and investiga-
tions were made into how this had come about.   It then
appeared that the money had come only from Olaf and
his fellows ; they were all brought to trial, and the whole
affair came to light.

A Wizard sent to Iceland.

HARALD GORMSSON, King of Denmark, was enraged at
the Icelanders, who had composed a satire upon him.
He proposed to a wizard that he should go in a charmed
shape to Iceland, and see what news he could bring him.
The wizard went in the shape of a whale.   On reaching
the island, he held round the north side of it ; there he
saw that all the fells and knolls were full of land-spirits,
some big and some little.   When he reached Vopna-firth
he entered it, and tried to go up on shore ; then there
came down out of the dale a great dragon, who was
followed by many serpents, toads, and vipers, and these
blew venom upon him.   The wizard sheered off, and held
further west along the shore, as far as Eya-firth.   When
he entered this, there came against him a bird, so large
that its wings touched the fells on both sides, and with it
was a multitude of other birds, both big and little.   Off
he went again, and held round to the west coast, where
he entered Breida-firth.   Here there came against him a
great bull, which waded out into the sea and bellowed
fearfully ; many land-spirits accompanied it.   He set off
again, and held south round Reykja-nes, and tried to
land on Vikars-skeid.   Then there came against him a
hill-giant, carrying in his hand an iron-staff ; his head
was higher than the fells, and many other giants were

with him. Thence he went east along the coast, which
he said was all sands, and rocks, and breakers, and the
sea between the countries so great that it could not be
crossed by ships of war.

The Finns and Ingimund.

INGJALD of Hefn in Hálogaland, who lived in the days
of Harald the Fair-haired, held a great feast, at which,
according to the old custom, they performed magical
rites to enquire into the future.   There was present a
Finnish sorceress, who was set on a high and splendid
seat, and to her each man went in turn to question her as
to his fate.   Grím, however, the son of Ingjald, and his
foster brother Ingimund, sat still and did not go near her,
giving no heed to her prophecies.   The witch then asked,
" Why do these young men not enquire concerning their
fate ? They seem to me the most notable men of all that
are here assembled."   Ingimund answered, " I care not
so much to know my fate as to become renowned, nor do
I think that my destiny lies under the root of your
tongue."   She answered, " Yet will I tell it you unasked.
You will settle in a land called Iceland, as yet largely uninhabited. There you will become a great man and reach
old age, and many of your kinsmen will become famous
in that land."   Ingimund replied, " The answer to that
is, that I have never dreamed of going to that place, and
a bad merchant should I be, if I were to sell the wide and
good lands of my fathers, and go to these deserts."   The
Finn answered, " It will fall out as I say ; and this is the
token of it, that the charm which King Harald gave you
at Hafrsfirth has disappeared out of your purse, and is

now landed in that holt which you shall inhabit, and on that charm Frey is stamped in silver. When you build your farm there, my tale will be found true." Ingimund answered, "If it were not an offence to my foster-father, you would get your reward from me on your head ; but as I am neither a violent nor a peevish man, it may just go past." She said there was no need to get angry over it ; so it would happen, whether he liked it well or ill. And again she said, "The destiny of Grím and his brother Hrómund lies thitherward also, and they will both be yeomen good."

Next morning Ingimund searched for his charm, and could not find it, and this he thought no good omen. Ingjald bade him be cheerful, and let not this spoil his enjoyment or prey upon him, for many famous men now thought it fitting for them to go to Iceland, and he had got nothing but good by inviting the Finnish woman there. Ingimund said he gave him no thanks for that, "but for all that our friendship shall never fail." Then Ingimund went home and stayed with his father that winter. In the spring Grím and Hrómund sailed for Iceland, thinking it of no use to strive against fate. "I will not go thither," said Ingimund, "and we must part here." "That may be," said Grím, "but I shall not be surprised if we meet in Iceland, for it will be hard to flee from destiny."

That summer Ingimund's father died, and by the advice of King Harald he married Vigdis, daughter of Earl Thorir, the King celebrating the wedding with great magnificence. "Now I am well pleased with my lot," said he to the King, "and it is a great honour to me to have your good-will, but there sticks in my mind what the Finnish woman said about the change in my affairs, for I would not have it come true that I should leave my ancestral lands." "I cannot take away from that though," said the King, "if it be done for some end, and if Frey pleases to make his charm land where he wishes to set his seat of honour." Ingimund said he was anxious to know whether he would find the charm or not, when he dug the holes for the pillars of his high seat: "it may be that it is not done for naught, and now I must not conceal the fact that I intend to send for Finns, to show me the nature of the district, and the lie of the land where I shall settle, and I mean to send them to Iceland." The King said he might do so, "but I think that you will go there, and it is doubtful whether you will go with my leave, or steal away, as is now become so common." " That will never happen," said Ingimund, "that I shall go without your consent." With that they parted, and Ingimund went home.

He then sent for Finns, and three of these came south. Ingimund said he would bargain with them, and give them butter and tin, if they would go his errand to Iceland, to search for his charm, and describe to him the lie of the land. They answered, "That is a dangerous mission for messengers to go on, but at your request we shall attempt it. Now, we must be shut up in a house by ourselves, and let no one name us." This was done, and after three nights had passed, Ingimund came to them. They rose up, and breathed heavily, and said, "It is hard for the messengers, and much labour have we had, but we shall give you such tokens that you will know the land by our description if you come to it; but it was difficult for us to look for the charm, and powerful are the witch's spells, for we have put ourselves into great straits. We came to land where three firths enter from the north-east, and there were great lakes at the inner end of one of them. Then we came into a deep valley, in which, under a mountain, there were some holts and a habitable grassy slope. In one of the holts lay the charm, but when we tried to take it, it shot into another one, and leapt away from us always as we made for it, and a kind of veil lay always over it so that we could not take it, and you will have to go yourself." Ingimund said that he would indeed go soon ; there was no use in striving against it. He treated the Finns well, and they departed.

Soon after that Ingimund sailed for Iceland with the King's leave, and landed in the west of the island, where he found Grím, with whom he passed the winter. The second winter he spent in Víðidal on the north coast, and early in the spring they held eastward to Vatnsdal. As they neared it, Ingimund said, " Now the Finns' prophecy will be found true, for I know the lie of the land from their account of it." Ingimund took all Vatnsdal above Helgavatn and Urdarvatn, and chose for his homestead a fair grassy slope. There he raised a great hall a hundred feet in length, and, when digging the holes for his high-seat pillars, found his charm as had been foretold to him. Then said Ingimund, " It is a true saying that no man may kick against his fate, and we shall now take this with a good heart. This homestead shall be called Hof."

The Finn's Travels.

THERE was once a skipper from Vester-vig, who made a voyage to Norway, and was caught by the winter, so that he had to remain there for a time. He stayed with

one of the inhabitants of Finn-mark, and when Christmas
Eve came, his host asked if he would like to know what
they had for their Christmas supper in Vester-vig. Yes,
he would like to know that very much ; he would even
give a pint of brandy to know it. This was agreed on,
and the Finn drank one half of the brandy, and talked a
little ; then he drank the other half-pint, and lay down
on the floor. His wife took a quilt and laid it over him.
He lay there and shook for half-an-hour, after which he
lay still for another half-hour, and then woke up, and told
what they had for supper ; and as a proof that he had
been there, he produced a knife and a fork, which the
skipper recognised as the ones that he himself used when
at home in Vester-vig.

Finnish Magic.

ONE who has lost anything seeks a so-called wise man
or wizard, who promises to strike out the thief's eye.
This is performed in the following way. The troll-man
cuts on a young tree a human figure, mutters some dark
incantations for the devil's aid, and then thrusts a pointed
instrument into the eye of the image. It was also the
custom to shoot with arrow or bullet at some of the limbs
of the figure, by which it was believed wounds and pains
could be created on the corresponding limb of the living
person thus represented. In connection with this might
stand the famous magic art of the Finns, of producing
the image of an absent person in a vessel of water, aiming
a shot at it, and so wounding or killing a hated enemy at
a distance of several hundred miles. Even against the
cattle of others has this sorcery been practised, and

paralytic strokes and other sudden illnesses have from
this received the name of "Shot," or "Troll-shot."

A young Swede had during his travels in Finland
betrothed himself to a beautiful Finnish girl, but on re-
returning to his home he soon forgot his love and his
promise to return to his bride. One day there came to
him a Lapp wizard, and it occurred to the young man to
ask him how things went with his betrothed in Finland.
"That you shall see for yourself," said the Lapp, and
after filling a bucket with water under certain incantations, he bade the young man come and look into the
water. Then the youth, it is said, saw the well-known
beautiful country round the hut of his betrothed. His
heart beat high when he saw her, pale and worn out with
weeping, come out of the door, followed by her father,
who wore a stern look, and carried a rifle in his hand.
The old Finn went to a bucket filled with water, looked
in the direction from which the bridegroom was expected,
shook his head and cocked his rifle, while the daughter
wrung her hands. "Now, he will shoot you," said the
Lapp, "unless you are beforehand and shoot him. Be
quick and aim at him." The old Finn put his gun to his
shoulder, and went up to the pail. "Shoot now," said
the Lapp, "or you are a dead man yourself." The youth
fired, and saw the Finn fall lifeless to the ground. His
conscience thereafter carried him back to his devoted
sweetheart, and he there learned that her father had died
of a stroke on the same day that the Lapp had performed
the magic trick described above. Many such stories are
found even among the Swedish Finns in Wärmland and
Finnmark.

Seeing a Thief in Water.

THERE once lived in Esby, on the peninsula of Helge-næs, a man from whom one thing or another was stolen at different times. On one occasion one of his wife's gowns was stolen, and she gave him no rest or peace, until he promised to go over to Borup, where a wise man lived who had the art of "showing again." The man went over to Borup and had an interview with the wizard, who said to him; "Well, if you have ever stolen anything yourself, you must not come to me; otherwise you may come to me on Thursday, and you shall see the thief."

The man went home, and returned on the Thursday. The wizard then brought forward a pail of water, which he told the man to look down into and he would see the thief. Sure enough he did see him walking off with the gown, and knew who it was; but he was sadly put out to see himself walking along behind him, with four bushels of rye on his back. He let the gown go where it liked, and never again ventured to show his face to the wise man in Borup, who had punished him in this fashion, and shown that he himself was no better than the thief he was trying to catch.

The Stolen Money.

A CERTAIN Sigurd, shepherd at Grund in Svarfadar-dal, came into possession of a considerable sum of money, left by some one who was in his debt. He was afraid to keep the money anywhere but in a sheep-house, which he alone frequented, and there he hid it in a ram's purse. Shortly after he had got the money, an acquaintance of his, also named Sigurd, came to him and asked for the loan of a dollar. Sigurd had no other money but this, so he ran to the sheep-house, whither his namesake quietly followed him and saw where he took it from. Not long after, Sigurd had a look at his purse, but now "the cat was come in the bear's den," for the money was gone and nothing but filth in its place. Sigurd took the loss of the money greatly to heart, but had no idea as to who could have taken it, and least of all did he suspect his friend. At last he decided to go to Klúkur, and ask one Torfi there to help him. This Torfi, who was born about the middle of last century and lived down to 1840, was the son of a priest clever in such matters, and was himself famous in that line. At first Torfi was very unwilling to act, but asked whether he would know the thief if he saw him. Sigurd thought he would, and Torfi then made him look into a vessel of water below the table. There Sigurd saw a man in the act of taking his money. On his head was a hood with the opening turned to the back and holes cut for his eyes ; on his back he wore a grey sack, tied about his neck, and was thus so strangely got up that Sigurd could not recognise him. At this Torfi said that the thief must have suspected he would be searched for, and so tried to disguise himself, but he would not "get a hood out of that cloth" (*i.e.* succeed) for all that. Sigurd might now go home, and the money would be waiting him in the house, except that perhaps one dollar might be missing, and even that he would get later on. Lastly he made Sigurd promise to give him plenty of fish if he got the money, and Sigurd readily promised that. He then held homewards, and arrived there in the evening. Next morning he took a certain Hallgrim with him to the sheep-house, and on arriving there they found the money scattered all over the floor, just as if it had been thrown in at the window. One dollar, however, was wanting. A sprinkling of snow had fallen during the night, and they found tracks leading to the other Sigurd's farm, the person having gone on his stocking-soles.

As for this Sigurd, the same evening that the other one came home he asked for his shoes about bed-time, but would not say where he was going. There was some delay in his getting the shoes, so he went out on his stocking-soles and restored the money, for he had no rest until he got rid of it ; the one dollar was wanting because he had spent it. He confessed this a few days later, and was forgiven by his namesake, while Torfi got his fish.

Showing One's Future Wife.

ONE time two young unmarried men from Svalbards Strand came to Eya-firth, and stayed with Torfi at Klúkur, being acquaintances of his. They gave him some return for the night's hospitality, and old Torfi was quite delighted with them. When they were about to start in the morning, Torfi said to them, " I cannot repay you in any other way, my lads, than by showing you your future wives, if you like." This they readily accepted. One of them was recently engaged, a fact which Torfi did not know, and he thought it would be fun to see whether Torfi would not be wrong. Torfi took them with him into a dark closet, where there stood a vessel apparently filled with water. They were told to look into this, and on doing so saw the liknesses of two girls, and Torfi told them which of the two each of them would marry. The engaged one did not recognize his girl at all ; indeed she was quite another person than his sweetheart. He told Torfi this, but the latter said that all the same it was his destiny to marry the girl he had seen there, and if he liked he would show him the man his present sweetheart would marry, which he then did.

The other one recognized his future wife ; they lived in the same district, but had not at that time thought of each other. All the same, it came about as Torfi had said, and they were married a few years later.

As for the first one, his engagement was afterwards broken off. He moved further north later on, and settled there, and married the woman that Torfi had shown him.

The girl who had been engaged to Torfi's guest became half-silly ; indeed she was of the family of Thorgeir, after whom "Thorgeir's Bull" was named. She asked advice from Torfi, as many did who were assailed by this monster. He gave her a leaf with runes on it, telling her to wear it on her breast, and never part with it, above all not to lose it, for it would cost him great trouble to make one as good again. The girl quite recovered, but one time when she went to church, she lost the leaf. Immediately after this her infirmity came back upon her as before, and Torfi was again appealed to. He was very reluctant to do anything, and said he could not help her completely, but he gave her another leaf, saying it would do her as long as he lived. He was by this time an old man, and had given up using magic ; in fact, it is said he had dropped it all before he died. The girl improved again after getting the leaf, and was married to the man that Torfi had foretold. After Torfi's death, however, she grew ill again, and was confined to her bed. She could never be left alone, and there had always to be a light beside her at night, otherwise she was ready to go out of her wits with fear. She had no other trouble but this uncontrollable terror, which finally killed her about 1860. Everything points to the fact of Thorgeir's Bull having had a hand in her illness.

The Wizard and the Crows.

ONE summer, when the men of King Olaf Kyrri had been round the country gathering his revenues, he asked them where they had been best received. They said that it was in one of the King's shires. "An old farmer lives there," they said, "who knows many things. We asked him many questions, and he could answer them all ; we even believe that he understands the language of birds." "What do you say?" said the King ; "that is great nonsense." Some time later, while the King was sailing along the coast, he asked his men, "What district is this on shore here?" They answered, "We told you about this shire before, that it was here we were best received." Then the King asked, "What house is that that stands beside the sound?" They answered, "That house belongs to the wise man that we told you of." They saw a horse near the house, and the King said, "Go now ; take that horse and kill it." "We have no wish to do him an injury," said they. "I will have my way," said the King ; "strike the head off the horse, and do not let its blood fall on the ground. Bring the carcase out on board the ship, and then go and bring the man, but tell him nothing of this, as you value your lives." They did all this, and gave the old man the King's message. When he came into the King's presence, the latter asked

him, "Who owns the land that you live on?" "You
own it, Sire," said he; "and take rent for it." "Show
us the way along the coast," said the King; "you must
know it well." The old man did so, and as they rowed
along a crow came flying past the ship and croaked
hideously. The farmer looked at it earnestly. "Do you
think it something important?" asked the King. "I do
indeed," said the farmer. Then another crow flew over
the ship and shrieked. The farmer stopped rowing, and
held the oar loose in his hand. "You pay great heed to
the crow, farmer," said the King, "or to what she says."
"I begin to suspect now," said the farmer. A third crow
came flying close to the ship, and croaked worst of all.
Then the farmer rose up, and paid no heed to the rowing.
"You think it something very important now," said the
King; "what does she say?" "Something that it is
unlikely that either I or she should know," said the
farmer. "Tell me it," said the King. The farmer said—

> "Year old yells it,
>   Yet is unknowing:
> Two-year tells it,
>   I trow her no better;
> But three-year threaps it
>   (I think it unlikely),
> Says that my horse's
>   Head is beneath me,
> And you, O ruler,
>   Have reft me my own."

"How, now, farmer!" said the King, "will you call me a
thief?" Then he gave him good gifts, and remitted to
him all his taxes.

A Poet of Might.

ONE time Hallgrím Pètursson was passing Ölvis-haug in
Hafnar-fell, when his guide suggested to him that it
would be interesting to see Ölver rise up, and asked
Hallgrím to use his powers as a poet for this end.   Hallgrím then made this verse :—

> " Cursed Ölver, crawl thou forth from out thy covert ;
>   Loathsome ghost, that lives in pyne,
>   Listen to these words of mine."

The ghost then began to make his appearance, first the
head, which they thought very grim and frowning, and
then he rose slowly up as far as the waist.   The priest's
guide then grew frightened, and bade him for any sake
rhyme the ghost down again.   This he did in three
verses, of which one was,

> " I rhyme thee hence in might of Him
>   That hung upon the tree ;
>   May all the Devil's dwellings grim
>   Their doors unlock for thee ! "

Another story about Sir Hallgrím is that he rhymed a
fox to death.   This fox destroyed many sheep in the
district, and was so destructive that it was believed to be
a "stefnivarg " (an animal sent by a wizard), and could
neither be caught nor killed.   One Sunday as the priest
was performing divine service, and stood in full vestments
before the altar, he happened to look out at the choir-
window, and saw the fox biting at a sheep.   He forgot
for the moment where he was, and said—

> " Thou that killest cottar's fee,
>   Cursèd be the eyes in thee ;
>   Stand thou now like stump of tree,
>   Stiff and dead upon the lea."

This finished Reynard at once, but because Hallgrím had used his poetic gift for such a purpose in the midst of divine service, he lost it altogether, until he repented of his oversight, and vowed to compose something to the praise and glory of God if He gave him back the gift. Time passed until one autumn when the meat was being hung up in the kitchen. Hallgrím's man had this task, and was standing up on one of the rafters, while the priest handed him up the meat from below. "Say something to me now," said Hallgrím, "for I feel as if the gift were coming upon me again." "Up, up," answered the man, meaning that he should hand him up the beef. These words Hallgrím then employed to begin the first verse of his Passion Psalms, which commence,

"Up, up, my soul and all my mind."

The Mice in Akureyar.

THOSE who wish to injure their enemies send against them either the spirits called *sendingar* or animals known as *stefnivargar*. The word *stefni-varg* literally means a wolf *(varg)* that is directed *(stefna)* against something, but in this connection is used of animals which have power given to them by magic, and are then sent to do harm. There was once a rich man in Akureyar, who was a thorough miser, and would never give anything to the poor. To punish him for this, a certain wizard sent him so many "mice-wolves," that they destroyed all he had, and he finally died in the greatest poverty. For a long time after this the mice remained in the island, until the then owner sent for another wizard. He came, and got a whole leg of mutton roasted ; then he sat down on the island, and began to eat this. In a moment the mice surrounded him in crowds to get a bit of it. The wizard rose again, and with the leg of mutton in his hand, went back to the farm, and all through it, until he had gathered round him every mouse on the island. Then he threw the mutton into a deep pit, which he had got dug for the purpose. The mice all sprang into the pit, which was then closed up at once, and the wizard strictly forbade any one to touch it in time coming. For a long time after this there were no mice in Akureyar, but many years later the proprietor of the islands had a foundation dug for some new building, and they were careless enough to open the pit again. In a moment the mice crowded out again, and have ever since been a plague to the islands, which otherwise are so excellent.

Foxes in Iceland.

ONE time an Icelander spent a winter in Finnmark, where an old woman took a liking to him, and wished him to marry her, but he refused, and went home again in the spring. The old woman was greatly displeased, and determined to avenge herself. She took two foxes, a male and a female, and repeated charms over them; then she put them on board a ship that was bound for Iceland, commanding that they should there increase and multiply, and never be cleared out of the country. They should also attack the animal species that they first saw on land there. Now the old woman thought that they would first see men, and meant them to destroy these, but the ship they were on touched first at the east of Iceland, and the foxes landed on the headland now known as Melrakka-nes in Alpta-firth. There they saw a flock of sheep, and these were the first animals that they met with. They have since multiplied and spread over all the land, and attack and kill the sheep.

Gand-reid.

WHOEVER wishes to be able to ride air and water must get the bridle that is known as the "gand-ride bridle." This is made by taking up a newly buried corpse, and cutting strips of skin off the back ; these are used for the reins. The dead man's scalp is next flayed off, and used for the head-piece of the bridle. Two bones of the head are used for the bit, and the hip-bones for the cheeks of the bridle. A charm is then repeated over this, and it is ready for use. Nothing more is required than to put this bridle on a man or animal, stock or stone, and it will immediately rise into the air with its rider and go faster than lightning to wherever is wanted. It then causes a loud noise in the air, which some believe they have heard, as well as the rattling of the bridle.

The Witch's Ride to Tromskirk.

IN Brovst in Vendsyssel there once lived a woman, who was a vile witch. All the ploughmen who served with her became so lean that it was something terrible, although they ate ever so much. One of these, who had come to be mere skin and bone, tried in vain to discover the reason for it. Finally he went to a wise woman, who told him that his mistress was a witch, who rode on him every night to Tromskirk in Norway. "There you have a salve," said she, " and if you anoint your eyes with that, you will waken up outside the Tromskirk in Norway, and find yourself in the shape of a horse ; but as soon as you get the bridle off, you will resume your own form again. When your mistress comes out, see and throw the bridle over her head ; then it is she who must become the horse, and carry you home." The ploughman did as the wise woman directed, and woke up outside Tromskirk in Norway. He managed to get the bridle pulled off, and became a human being again. When the woman came out of the church, he clearly recognised his mistress, who was greatly astounded to see that her horse had become a man, and tried many devices to get the bridle on him again. The ploughman, however, got it put on herself, and she then became a horse. He now rode merrily on her through the air ; on the way he came to a smithy, where he halted and had his horse shod on all four feet, and rode on again. At last they reached home, and the woman went down the chimney into the kitchen. There he took the bridle off her, and she resumed her own shape ; but the horse-shoes she could not get quit of, so it was evident enough that she was a witch, and her husband drove her away.

The Ride to Blaa-kulla.

THE witches blow into the key-hole of the church-door, in order to blow from themselves the Holy Ghost, before they journey to Blaa-kulla to be initiated in the service of the Evil One. The person who does not wish to assist the witches in their preparations for this journey, carefully hides during Easter Week the bread-spade,

oven-broom, rake, and all besoms, for the witches generally go off on some of these on the evening of Maundy
Thursday, and come back next morning before sunrise.
Those witches who have not these implements themselves,
borrow or take them wherever they can get them. Their
own broom-stick is not always sufficient, as some witches
take children with them, to get them initiated in the
black art. The way lies through the witch's chimney up
into the air, while the witch cries, "In the Evil One's
name, up and not down, over all tree-tops, and back again
before daylight." One time it happened that a young
witch, who was going that way for the first time, said in
place of these words, "Up and down till daylight," and
so continued to fly up and down the chimney till daybreak.

At Blaa-kulla the witches are received by the Evil
One in the best fashion. He bears the shape of a man,
but has a horse's foot. The witches give him an account
of all the mischief they have done during the previous
year, and he then teaches the older ones still worse arts,
after which he dances with them all. The festival closes
with a banquet, which to the witches' eyes seems to consist of the rarest dishes. One of the witches, however,
had once taken a little child with her, and this refused to
eat a single bit of all that the Evil One offered, for it
could see that the feast consisted only of snakes, worms,
lizards, and black toads. When the banquet is ended,
the witches ride through the air to their home, but sometimes it has happened that some person has got up so
early as to hear the witches come flying past, making
sticks and straws whirl up high into the air. One time a
boy was standing beside a farmyard on the morning of
Good Friday, when the witches came past ; he threw his

clasp-knife into the whirlwind, where it struck one of the witches on the leg, so that she plumped down into the dung-heap and stuck fast there. The boy would not help her out of it, until she promised him one of her garters, which he kept as a proof that he had really seen a witch.

On Easter Day all the witches must attend divine service in church, but they repeat all their prayers backwards. Any one can see who are witches who has in his pocket three eggs, the first that have been laid by three young hens. With these eggs one can see the witches sitting with milk-pails on their heads, and a cross in their eyes. The milk-pail signifies the power that witches have over other people's cows, so that if a wicked creature of this kind drives a knife into her roof-tree and milks the shaft, she gets as much milk as she pleases from the cows she names, and she sometimes milks them so hard that pure blood comes. If the witch does not want to have the trouble of doing this herself, she has her milk-hares, which suck the cows, and go home to her with the milk. These hares have often been seen in the cows' stalls.

It is told of one witch that she could churn whole pounds of butter in a pail of water. When Maundy Thursday approached, all her neighbours made haste to hide the oven-rake and other baking implements—things that every proper housewife was much more careful about in former days than now. One Easter week, however, it so befell the witch that she had to lie in bed. Her husband noticed that she became the more restless the nearer Thursday came, and asked her the reason. At first she only answered that she had important business which had been neglected ; but when her husband declared himself willing to do it, whatever it might be, she confessed to him her fear of not being able to go with her comrades to Blaa-kulla and hear what was talked about there. The husband asked whether he could not go in her place. She said it could be done if he would only in all respects follow the directions she would give him. He promised to do so. She then put on him her own shape, and gave him a long stick, with which he was to fence with the witches, but every time he struck any of them he was to say "Sore to-day, whole to-morrow." Then she smeared the oven-rake with troll-salve, and instructed her husband that he would fly up through the chimney if he said, "Straight up and straight out, over all beech-tops."

The husband, however, had always had a grudge against his wife's companions, and as he was a soldier, he exchanged the wooden stick for his good sword, and went off to Blaa-kulla. There was dancing and sporting there, but they were no nice sports, and when the witches began to fence with their sticks, the soldier struck with his sword, aiming always at the witches' noses and ears. For every stroke he gave them he said, "Whole to-day, sore to-morrow." This made the faces of the witches anything but beautiful when they came home.

Of course the soldier's wife was looked upon as a traitor by all her companions, and stood in danger of being punished by them and by their master unless she avenged them on her husband. She therefore, while still in bed, took two straws from the mattress, and made with them a pop-gun, loaded it with some charmed material, and aimed it at her husband. He dodged the shot, however, and it was well for him he did so, for it went right through the door-post.

Milk-Hares.

SOME people speak of milk-hares as if these also belonged
to the fallen angels, but this is not at all the case, for
they are made by the witches for the occasion, whenever
they wish to employ them. The milk-hare consists merely
of a few wooden pegs and a stocking-leg. The witches
pour a drop of milk, which they have taken from other
people's cows, into a stocking-leg, and tell it to go and
suck the cows, and then come home and cast up the milk
into the witch's milk-dish. There still lives a peasant in
Slätt-akra, who once shot at a milk-hare when out hunting, under the impression that it was a common puss.
The hare fell by the side of a fence, for no troll-stuff can
stand gunpowder, but when the man came up to lift his
game, he only found some pegs and a stocking leg, of the
same blue colour as those worn by the older women in
the district, while beside this there lay a splash of milk on
the field. He then understood at once what it was that
he had wasted powder and shot on.

Stealing Cream for Butter.

THERE was once a woman in Stödov on Helge-næs who
practised witchcraft. She had the custom, when she was
about to make butter, of saying, " A spoonful of cream
from every one in the county;" and in this way she
always got her churn quite full of cream. One day it
happened that she had an errand to town, just when they
were about to churn, and said to the maid, " You can
churn while I am away, but before you begin you must
say, ' A spoonful of cream from every one in the county;'

I shall take care then that plenty cream will come to you." She then went away, and the maid at once began to pour the cream into the churn, but when she came to say the words that the witch had taught her, she thought that a spoonful from every one was so very little, so she said, "a pint of cream from every one in the county."

Now she got cream, and that in plenty. The churn was filled, and the cream still continued to come, till at last the kitchen was half-full of cream. When the woman returned home, the girl stood bailing the cream out at the kitchen-door, and the witch was very angry that the maid had gone beyond her orders, and asked for a pint instead of a spoonful, for now every one could easily see that cream had been stolen from them. After this the girl never got leave to make the butter by herself.

The Witch's Daughter.

A PRIEST was once out walking with his half-grown daughter. On the way they came past a farm, where a number of ploughs were at work in the fields. "Do you know, father, what I can do?" said the daughter. "I can make all these ploughs stand still." "Let me see you do it then," said the priest. The girl began to repeat her charms, and all the ploughs stopped except one, which she said she had no power over, as it had rowan-tree in it.

When they reached home the priest asked if she knew more than that. She said she could also milk their neighbours' cows. "Let me see that too," said he. The daughter struck two awls into the wall, and began to milk at these. When she had milked for a little she said,

"Now I must milk no longer." "Yes, go on," said the priest. When she had milked for a little again, she said, "Now it is turning red." "Never mind ; go on," said the priest. "But it is nothing but blood now," said the girl. "Go on," said the priest. "The cow is dead now, father," said she. "Then you may stop," said he.

The priest now sent a messenger round to his neighbours, and one of their best milk-cows was found dead in its stall. He saw then that his daughter really could charm, and asked who had taught her. "My mother," said she. The priest's wife was then burned as a witch, but the daughter was spared, being only a child. The priest gave his neighbour another cow for the one that was dead, and the daughter promised never again to make use of what she had learned from her mother.

The Til-beri.

To steal milk or wool from others it is only necessary to procure what is variously called a "til-beri" or a "snakk." This is got by a woman stealing a rib from a dead man in the churchyard on a Whitsunday morning. She then wraps it in grey sheep's wool or yarn stolen from elsewhere, so that it looks like a wisp of wool, and lets it lie for a time between her breasts. With this she goes three times to the sacrament, and on each occasion drops into her breast the wine she takes, so that it falls on the til-beri. The first time she does so it lies quite still, the second time it begins to move, and the third time it becomes so full of life that it is ready to spring out of her bosom. The woman must take care then that it is not seen ; in old days the penalty for having one was either burning or drowning. When it has thus acquired strength, the woman draws blood on the inside of her thigh, and there the creature attaches itself and lives on her blood when it is at home. It is then used to suck other folks' cows or ewes, returning with the milk and dropping it into the woman's churn. The butter made of this looks good enough, but breaks up into small grains or goes into froth, if the mark of the cross is made over it. The til-beri may also be used for the purpose of stealing wool. On one occasion all the wool of a farm was left outside to dry during the night; next morning it was seen all gathered into a ball, which then rolled off so fast that no one could overtake it.

The Tide-Mouse.

IF a person wishes to get money that will never come to an end, one way is to procure a tide-mouse, which is got in this way. The person takes the hair of a chaste maiden, and out of it weaves a net with meshes small enough to catch a mouse. This net must be laid in a place where the person knows that there is treasure at the bottom of the sea, for the tide-mouse will only be found where there is silver or gold. The net need not lie more than one night, if the spot is rightly chosen, and the mouse will be found in it in the morning. The man then takes the mouse home with him, and puts it wherever he wishes to keep it. Some say it should be kept in a wheat-bushel, others say in a small box; it must have wheat to eat and maiden's hair to lie upon. Care must be taken not to let it escape, for it always wants to get back into the sea. Next, some money must be stolen and laid in the hair beneath the mouse, and it then draws money out of the sea, to the same amount every day as the coin that was placed under it; but that one must never be taken, otherwise it will bring no more. One who has such a mouse must be careful to dispose of it to another, or put it back into the sea, before it dies, otherwise he may suffer great harm. If the man dies, the mouse returns to the sea itself, and causes great storms on sea and land ; these are known as " mouse-storms."

The Tale-Spirit.

ONE who wishes to know future events need only procure a tale-sprite, who will tell him all he wishes to know. Whoever wishes to get one must go to some lonely spot, where he knows that no one else will come, for his life is at stake if he is spoken to while he is charming the spirit to himself. He must lie in shadow, looking towards the north, and having a horse's membrane over his mouth and nostrils, and then repeat some magic rhymes. The membrane is taken into the mouth of the person, and the spirit comes and tries to enter there, but the membrane stops him. The man then closes his teeth, thus catching the spirit inside the membrane. He then puts the whole thing into a box, but the spirit does not speak until the man has dropped holy wine on it, which he does secretly when partaking of the sacrament. It may also be given dew that falls in May-month, but this is not necessary. The tale-sprite tells its possessor all that he wishes to know, but talks most freely in sleety weather and east wind. If it escapes from the box, it enters the man and makes him mad. A certain Torfi in Eyafirth had one that had come down from the Sturlunga age, passing from one hand to another, and was hoarse-voiced by reason of old age and neglect. It was kept in a red oaken box, which was given by Torfi to a certain Sigfus in Öxnadal, who shortly before his death buried it in a knoll " in the devil's name."

The Cross-roads.

THE person who wished to perform this rite had to go out on the last night of the old year, taking with him a grey cat, a grey sheep-skin, a walrus hide (or an old bull's hide), and an axe. With all this he betook himself to the meeting of four roads which, in a straight line and without any break, led to four churches. There he lies down and covers himself with the hide, drawing it in under him on all sides, so that none of his body is outside of it. He must then hold the axe between his hands and stare at the edge of it, looking neither to right nor left whatever may happen, and not answering a word although he is spoken to. In this position he must lie perfectly still until day dawns next morning. When the man had thus disposed of himself, he began to repeat certain spells and incantations which could call up the dead. Then if he had any relatives buried at any of the four churches which the cross-roads led to, these came to him and told him all he wished to know of events past and to come for many generations. If he had the firmness to keep looking at the edge of the axe, never turning his head nor saying a word, whatever took place, he not only remembered all that they told him, but could as often as he wished after that consult them with impunity

by " sitting out."   Few, however, escaped successfully
from the ordeal.

Some say that Crossroads are those on hills or moors
from which four churches can be seen.   The oldest belief
is that men should " lie out " on Christmas Eve, because
the new year begins then ; to this day men reckon their
age by Yule nights, and he is said to be *e.g.* fifteen years
old who has lived fifteen Yule nights.   When a man sits
on the cross-roads, the elves come out of every quarter
and crowd around him, inviting him to come with them,
but he must not give them any answer.   Then they bring
to him all kinds of treasures, gold and silver, clothes, food,
and drink, but he must not take any of these.   The elf-
women come in the likenesses of his mother or sister, and
ask him to go with them, and every possible device is
tried.   When day dawns the man must stand up and say,
" God be praised, now it is day over all the sky."   Then
all the elves disappear, leaving all their wealth behind,
and this the man gets to himself ; but if he answers them,
or accepts their gifts, he comes under their spell and loses
his wits for ever after.   There was a man named Fúsi
who sat out on Yule night, and held out for a long time,
until an elf-woman came with a big piece of fat, and
offered him a bite of it.   Then Fúsi looked at it and said,
in words that have since become a proverb, " Seldom
have I refused fat :" he took a bite of it, came under the
spell, and became witless.

Sitting at the Cross-roads.

IF you wish to be rich you must go on Twelfth Night
(old style) and sit where four roads meet, one of which

must point to the church. You must take a grey calf-
skin and a sharp axe, and spread the skin beneath you
on the road, so that the tail is turned to the kirk-road,
but your face must be turned in the opposite direction.
Then you must set yourself to sharpen the axe ; and
whatever may be said to you, you must answer nothing
but, "I am whetting, I am whetting." Whatever on-
goings there may be on both sides of you, you must not
look up, but stare fixedly down at the axe, otherwise it
will go ill with you, and the trolls will take you. When
it draws near midnight, the trolls come swarming from all
directions, dragging gold and costly things, which they
pile up in great heaps round about you, and show you all
this wealth to get you to give a single glance up ; they
also speak to you, make faces, and cut all kinds of capers.
If, however, they have been unable to entice you to turn
your eyes to the gold which they laid beside you, or to
pay heed to themselves out of fear for them, or to get
you to answer them back, then they seize the tail of the
calf-skin to drag it away ; then you must see and be
lucky enough to cut off the tail with the axe behind your
back, but in such a way that the edge of the axe is not
injured. If you succeed in this you are a lucky man, for
then the trolls disappear each in his own direction, and
you get all the gold and precious things that were laid
beside you ; but if you fail in it, the trolls get power
over you, and you will never come back whole from this
expedition.

The Victory-Stone.

THE victory-stone is good to have and carry about on
one's person, for the man who has it always gains the

victory in battle ; wherever he goes no injury can happen
to him either from men or trolls ; fortune always attends
him, everything goes as he wishes, and all people are well-
disposed towards him. No wonder, then, that men are
eager to have such a stone, that brings so much good
with it, but no one knows where this precious stone is to be
found ; the raven knows it, though, and this will tell you
how to get the raven to go for the victory-stone, and how
to get it from him then.

It is a common saying that the raven mates in Feb-
ruary, lays its eggs in March, and hatches in April. Now
when the raven has laid its eggs, the man must climb up
the cliff or ravine where the nest is, and sit there in con-
cealment, remaining perfectly still until the raven flies
away from the nest. Then he must be very quick in slip-
ping to the nest, take the eggs, boil them hard, and get
them laid back in the nest again before the raven returns,
so that it may have no suspicion,—and he must be an
active man who is to accomplish this. The raven comes
back again, and sits on the eggs ; but when it has sat
there till well on in hatching-time, it begins to grow impatient seeing that there is no sign of the eggs chipping
yet, and finally gets tired of sitting any longer. Then it
takes the plan of going to look for the victory-stone, to
lay it in the nest beside the eggs in order to get them
hatched ; and the man must now be on the spot, and
either shoot the raven and take the stone out of its beak,
or let it lay the stone beside the eggs, and then come on
it unawares, before those boiled eggs are fully hatched,
for then it takes back the stone to where it got it.

The Life-Stone.

A CERTAIN man had found a life-stone in an eagle's nest. It was so little, however, that he was afraid he might lose it, so he took the plan of sewing it into his right arm-pit, making sure that it would be quite safe there. After this he went through many perils and adventures, but always escaped unscathed. One time, however, after he was well on in years, he went on a long voyage, the end of which was that the ship was wrecked and all on board perished except himself. He could not drown, having the life-stone on him, and was tossed about in the sea for years on years. It was a sorry life he had, for the sea-monsters caused him various injuries, that would have killed most people. At last he drove on shore somewhere or other, and the first thing he asked was that they should open his right arm-pit and take out the stone. This was done, and the man at the same moment fell into dust.

The Four-Leaved Clover.

THE most wonderful thing my father ever saw was a man who travelled about and bewitched people's sight. He was no outlandish juggler, but a regular Swede, who lived in Helsingborg. He came to one village where a pump-barrel was lying in the street, and through this he crept from the one end to the other. The whole population of the village assembled, and stood round looking on, for the man crept through it several times. Just then a girl came along who had been out in the fields gathering herbs for her mother's pig, and asked why people stood looking at the man creeping along the outside of the

pump. When the stranger heard that she could see cor-
rectly, he insisted on buying the herbs which she was
carrying in her apron, and the girl, who thought that she
could easily pull others again, sold them to him. Scarcely
had she received the money, than she began to lift her
dress, and raised it higher and higher towards the knees,
calling to the others and asking whether they did not see
that they were standing in water. Now that she had sold
the four-leaved clover, the man could bewitch her eyes
as well as those of the others. Many people tell of the
same thing happening at different spots; but I know that
this took place in N., for my father saw it with his own
eyes.

Destroying a Witch's Spells.

IN Passion Week the evil powers play their pranks more
than at other times, so that people have to be on their
guard. Witches, troll-women, and all that kind who try
to do injury to their neighbour by wicked arts, endeavour
during this week to borrow something or other, such as
milk, butter, barm, brandy, etc., but to such requests
every wise good-wife says " No." For if such things are
lent to these people, they charm them, so that the ale
will never brew, the cream never turn to butter ; no
article of the same kind as one has lent out will ever
succeed with any one. Then a wise person must be got
to remove the charm.

It is no more than fifty years ago that our neighbour
had got all his house put under a charm. No calves,
foals, lambs, or chickens were born for a whole year on
the farm. The butter never came, although they put a

pinch of salt in the churn and laid some grains of salt under it, besides making a cross over the lid. They tried setting a fire-steel or a knife beside the churn-stick ; they even shot over it with gunpowder, but nothing helped. It was the same with brewing and baking, nothing succeeded with them. A messenger was sent for a wise man, who travelled about. He promised to give the witch her reward, but made it a condition of his assisting them that for three days they must not lend the least particle, whatever it might be. He then made them procure a black dog without a single white hair on its body. This he buried alive in the fields one morning before sunrise. Then he bored holes in all the thresholds, and laid troll-incense in them. After this he took a knife and cut open the swellings on the backs of the horses and cows. Out of these there came large maggots, and the wise man said that these were all the animals, big and small, that had been intended to be born on the farm during the year ; the witch had turned them all to maggots.

Our neighbour now wanted to see the witch who had done all this to him ; he had his suspicions, of course, but wished to be quite certain in the matter. The wise man was not very willing to raise her shape, but the farmer was determined. They shut themselves up in the still, and strict orders were given that no one was to come in there. The wise man was to raise the witch out of a large mashing-tub which stood empty, but just as her forehead and eyes became visible, they thought that some one opened the door, and he had to stop his exorcism. He declared, however, that if the witch would not show herself, she should at least feel his power. He put some of the cream, barm, brandy, and other articles that had been charmed, upon an iron plate and roasted them on the fire, and whatever the arts may have been that he exercised with the iron plate, it is certain that the witch could not sit down for fourteen days, so scalded was she.

X.—CHURCHES, TREASURES, PLAGUES.

How the First Church in Norway was Built.

IN Norland they tell the following story about the first church that was built in Norway. St. Olaf, King of Norway, went about one day in deep thought, and wondered how he, without laying too heavy burdens upon his people, could erect a church, which he wished to build so large that its equal would be hard to find. As he went and thought over this, he met a man of superhuman size, who asked him what he was puzzling over. "Well may I be puzzled," said the King, "since I have made a vow to build a church, which for size and beauty will not have its equal in the world." The troll offered within a given time to erect such a building, if King Olaf in return, when the work was finished, would give him as payment "the sun and the moon, or St. Olaf himself." The King accepted this offer, but made the plan of the building so large that he thought it would be impossible for the troll to finish it within the appointed time. It was to be so large that seven priests could preach in it at once, without the one hearing or being disturbed by the other. The pillars and ornaments, outside and inside, were to be made of the hardest flint-stone, and several other difficult conditions were imposed; but in far shorter time than was agreed on, King Olaf saw the church finished, all except the spire.   Things being in this condition, King Olaf went in deep distress over hill and dale, and thought of the compact he had made.   Then in the mountain he heard a child crying, and a giantess comforting it with the following ditty :

> "Hush, hush, my little one,
> To-morrow Wind-and-Weather, your father, will come.
> He will bring with him Sun and Moon,
>   Or else St. Olaf himself."

The King became glad then, for trolls lose their power when a Christian man can name them by name.   When he got back, he saw the troll standing on the top of the tower, putting on the spire.   Then St. Olaf cried, "Wind-and-Weather, you have set the spire on crooked."   Where-upon the troll fell down with a terrible crash, and was shivered in pieces, which were all flint stones.   Other ac-counts say that the giant's name was " Slæt," and that St. Olaf cried " Slæt, set the spire straight."

The Building of Lund Cathedral.

THE holy St. Lawrence went about one day over hill and dale, and pondered how he could erect a great and worthy temple to the honour of the Lord.   There came a giant out of a hill, and promised to fulfil his wish, but demanded as payment "Sun and moon, and both St. Lawrence's eyes."   The time allowed him was so short, that it seemed impossible for him to accomplish the work ; but the holy man soon saw that the building was nearing its completion only too rapidly, and that the day was drawing near on which the troll would come and

take his wages. Again he wandered about on hills and
in woods in great distress, but suddenly he heard a child
crying in the inside of a hill, and its mother singing to it—

" Still, still, little one !
To-morrow Finn your father will come,
And you will play with sun and moon,
And both St. Lawrence's eyes."

Then St. Lawrence knew the giant's name and had
power over him.   When the trolls got to know this, they
both went down into the vaults, and each laid hold of a
pillar, with the intention of overthrowing the whole
church ; but St. Lawrence, making the sign of the cross,
cried out, "Stand here in stone till Doomsday."   They
were immediately transformed into stone, and stand there
still, the giant embracing one pillar and the giantess the
other, with the child on her arm.

St. Olaf in Ringerige.

IN old days, when King Olaf went from place to place to
introduce the Christian faith, and to build churches in
place of the heathen temples, he met with much opposi-
tion and many hindrances, not only from his obstinate
heathen subjects but also from the many trolls, giants,
and giantesses, who were then to be found in great numbers in the mountains.   The trolls could not bear St.
Olaf, partly because he caused them hurt by using the
sign of the cross, and partly because he built many
churches, the sound of whose bells disturbed their peace ;
but although they often exerted themselves to the utmost
they could do nothing against the holy king, who
straightway turned them into stone.   Trolls thus transformed by St. Olaf may still be seen all over the country.

One time, when Olaf was going down by the northern Krogklev (the road then kept more to the north than now) a grim giantess suddenly sprang out of the steep cliff. She had a large trough on her back, and cried—

" St. Olaf, broad beard and all,
You ride so near my cellar wall."

But St. Olaf looked at her, and answered—

" As stock and stone shalt thou remain
Until I come this way again."

The giantess may still be seen there turned into stone.

When St. Olaf came to the farm of Sten, where his mother is said to have lived, he resolved to build a church there. A giantess, who at that time lived in the mountain, which has since been called after her, "Gyrihaugen" (the giantess's cairn), was not at all satisfied with this plan. Although she might have learned from the foregoing instance that St. Olaf was not to be played with, she resolved to try her strength, and challenged him to a contest. "Before you are finished with your church," said she, "I shall have built a stone bridge over Stensfirth." Olaf accepted the challenge, and before she was half finished with the bridge, the glorious peal of the bells was heard from St. Olaf's Church. In a rage the troll seized the stones with which she had intended to complete the bridge, and hurled them from Gyrihaugen over the firth at the church, but as none of them struck it, she became so angry that she cut off one of her legs and let that fly at the steeple. Some say that it took the steeple with it, others that she aimed too high. Be that as it may, the leg landed in a bog behind the church, where to this day it causes a bad smell. The bog is still called by the peasants "The Giantess's Pit," and the stones she threw at the church were shown recently on the neigh-

z

bouring farm of Moe. The bridge begun by her is now completed, and on the farm of Sten there long stood the fine ruins of St. Olaf's Church. In old days divine service was held here on St John's Day, but about one hundred and fifty years ago the church was burned down by lightning.

Vattn-aas Church.

IN a narrow dale, shut in by steep mountain walls, in Sigdal, there stands the little old Lovè-Church (Love-kirke), where divine service is held only once a year, on the Sunday after St. John's Day. A crowd of people from the neighbouring districts assemble here on this occasion, and the sick make offerings in an old offertory plate, to regain their health. On the church door the devil is painted with horns and claws. The church is called Vattn-aas (Water-ridge), and according to tradition owes its origin to St. Olaf. As he marched through the land to introduce the Christian faith, he came also to Sigdal, and after he had succeeded in converting the inhabitants, he went out to hunt with some of his followers. During the chase the king and his men lost themselves, so that they neither knew the way back nor forward. Tired and thirsty, he finally came into a narrow dale where he dismounted from his horse, and made the vow that if he found water there, he would have a church built on that spot. Scarcely was this said, when a fountain sprang out of the hard rock. The king and his men, who were nearly fainting with thirst, rejoiced and drank to their hearts' content. King Olaf renewed his vow, and was about to turn his horse to ride away, when he

caught sight of a bull close at hand. He had already
bent his bow, when lo, his eye fell on a little church of
pure gold. After this model the king commanded that
a church should be built on that very spot, and called
Vattn-aas Kirk. In the mountains beside the spring
may still be seen the footprints of King Olaf's horse.

St. Olaf in Vaaler.

ON his journeys about the country to introduce the
Christian faith, St. Olaf came through Solöer-dale to a
farm which lies on the eastern bank of the Glommen, and
which, together with the church and parish, is said to
have got the name of Vaaler after the following fashion.
On this farm St. Olaf held an assembly, and after some
resistance it was decided that the God which the King
worshipped should also be the people's, and that the religion of Odin should give way to that of Christ. It was
also decided, on the King's proposal, that a church should
be built here, as in other places where the new doctrine
had been accepted ; but there arose a great dispute as to
the place where it should be erected. Then, says the
story, St. Olaf bent his bow, shot an arrow, and declared
that the church should be built where it fell. The King
was standing beside the spring which still bears his name,
and the arrow fell in a heap of wood (vaal) lying near the
Glommen, where a wooden church was built, and along
with the farm and parish was called Vaaler by St. Olaf.
This church, to which sick and dying persons used to
offer gifts, stood until 1805, when a new church was built,
in whose ornament chest is found a wrought iron buckle,
which is called St. Olaf's buckle, and is said to have been

deposited in the old church by the King himself. It had formed part of the halter by which the King's horse was tied up.

The King is said to have watered the same horse in the spring, clear as crystal, which bears his name, and never dries up in summer or freezes in winter. A miraculous power was formerly attributed to it—sick persons threw money into it to regain their health ; and it is believed that great misfortune awaits the man who dares to lay hands on these sacred deposits. A few years back it was the custom that the church-goers on all great occasions vied with each other in reaching the spring first, and it was considered something to be proud of to be the first to water one's horse at St. Olaf's Well.

Varnum Church.

A POOR herd-girl, from the farm of Mærsta in Varnum, betook herself one morning to the woods of Vermland with her cattle. As the day was rainy and cold, she took her tinder box with her, as the herds always do, so as to be able to kindle a fire and warm themselves. When she came near Jutebækken in the forest, a giantess happened to come along carrying a box, which she asked the girl to take charge of, while she went to invite some guests to her daughter's marriage, which was to be held in the mountain. The girl took the box and the bergwoman went on. By accident, the girl laid her fire-steel on the box, and when the bergwoman came back for it, she had no power to take it, for the trolls cannot bear steel. So the giantess hurried off, and the box became the girl's property. When she got home and looked to see what was in it, she found a gold crown as well as thick chains and rings of gold. Varnum Church was built with a fourth of the treasure, a fourth fell to the Crown, and the half became the girl's own.

Dover Church.

AT Dover Church there is a "corpse-lamb," which goes about on three legs. When the church was being built, it was necessary to have a living creature buried beneath its foundations. The people there were so poor, that they could not procure anything but a lamb : in other places they had a pig, a horse, or a cow. The old church lay in Illerup, but had become so ruinous that it could hang together no longer, and a new one had to be built. The people wished to place it in Sveistrup, which was nearer the centre of the parish, and contained the manse and school, but what they built there could never hang together, and they could get no church erected at that spot. They were at a loss what to do, till one day a wayfarer came past, while they were struggling away at the building, and said, "What is all this you are about, good people? I think your work looks a little shaky." "Oh," said they, "we want to build a church here, but we can't get it to stand ; it always falls down with us." "Well," said he, "that is not the way to do. You must take two oxen, which have never been in harness, yoke them to a pair of wheels, and let them go after sunset." They did so, and the oxen went so far during the night that they came over to where Dover Church now lies ; there was a large alder-marsh there at that time, in which they landed, and could get no further. So the church was placed in that spot.

The Bergman's Payment.

IN Höjslev there is a farm called Brude-dal (Bride's Dale). Straight west from it lies a great mound, called Stejls-bjærg, in which lived a bergman. The hole he came out at, and the path by which he went down to a dam at the eastern corner of the mound for water, are still pointed out, but the dam is now filled up. His wife also was often seen fetching water; she was a Christian woman from Höjslev. The church was to have been built a little to the north on a brae, called Stötte-bakke, but it was always pulled down again. An old woman went out to see who did this, and met the bergman, who told her that they could not get the church built there, it was too near himself, but they could build it in another place, if they would promise him the first and last maiden bride that came to Höjslev Church. They did so, and now the bergman built as much during the night as the others did during the day. When the church was finished, and the first bride was driving home, the bergman came and carried her off. He could not touch her, however, so long as she wore her bridal ornaments, so he asked an old man to take these off, but he refused. Then he went to a little herd boy and bribed him to do it, after which he disappeared with the bride.

Karup Church Tower.

THE tower of Karup Church was in old days so high that it was famous far and near. It was lowered twice, by eighteen ells the first time, and eleven the second time, but even then it was as high as most church-towers are now-a-days. There was, however, a giant who determined to have it thrown down. He came from abroad, and was so big that the ship he sailed in was right down to the water-line. He required eighty ells of woollen cloth for a pair of trousers, and his wooden-shoes were made of large planks, fastened together by iron rivets. When he came to Torning and Skræ, where there are so many great boulders, he began to throw stones at the tower, but missed it every time owing to the distance. The first stone he threw split in his hands, and one part of it fell in the brook which runs by Karup Mill; in it are still to be seen the marks of his five fingers, and even the lines on these are quite distinct, for at that time the stones were only growing and were somewhat soft. The other piece fell to the south-east of Karup Mill. When he came past Skræ, and there were no more stones, he did not care to go back to fetch some, but preferred to pull down the tower with his hands. In this he succeeded, and pulled it down to a level with the church itself in one day's time. Since then Karup Church has lacked a tower.

The Shifting of Gudum Church.

GUDUM CHURCH near Slagelse lies very low in a meadow beside Gudum River, and its situation is very inconvenient for the congregation, being in a corner of the parish. Originally, it is said, it lay further up and nearer the town, but the Devil, for some reason or other, set to work to shift it. He succeeded in getting it up on his shoulders, but when he had gone a little way, he began to feel it very heavy. Fortunately, at that point he met a peasant, and asked him to give him a lift with it. The peasant

could not make out what kind of person he had to deal
with ; he could see that the stranger had a heavy burden
on his back, but there was like a mist before his eyes, so
that he could not see what it was.   He lent a hand, however, and helped the little that he could, but it soon became too heavy for both of them.   They then came to a
large stone, and the Devil proposed to sit down on this
for a little to rest themselves, with the burden on their
backs.   The peasant began to have suspicions that something was wrong, so he looked under his left arm, and
could then see that it was the Devil with the church he
had beside him.   At this he hurried off as fast as he
could, and the load now pressed so heavily on the Devil
that "his end sank into the stone."   With great difficulty
he managed to rise and drag the church down to the river;
here he had to let it stand, for he could not get it across
the stream.   Between the church and the village they
used to point out a large stone with a seat in it; it was
here that the Devil rested himself with the church.

Hörup Church.

WHEN they were about to build the church of Hörup on
the island of Als, they began at the bottom of the mound
on which it now stands, but during the night the spirits
came and destroyed all that was built during the day.
When the workmen were about to continue their work
next morning, they heard a voice from the mound, which
shouted "Higher up, higher up" (Höger up, höger up).
The command was obeyed, they shifted to a little farther
up, and began a second time; but next morning every
thing was again destroyed, and again the voice shouted,

" Higher up, higher up." Then they began to build on the very top of the knoll, and from that time the voice was silent, and the building was no more disturbed. On this account, the church and the village, which was built there later on, were called " Högerup," afterwards altered to " Hörup." It lies highest of all the villages in the island, so that it can be seen from almost every point.

The Dwarfs' Stone.

THE church and parsonage in Seydis-firth lay in old times on the west (or south) side of the firth, but it is not known what name they bore. Close to them was a huge stone, in which people firmly believed that dwarfs lived, and on that account it was called " The Dwarfs' Stone " (Dverga-steinn). As time went on, it was found inconvenient to have the church and manse on that side of the firth, and both of them were shifted to the other side, where they now stand. The big stone, naturally, was left behind, but when the building of the church was nearly ended, the workmen were astounded to see a house come sailing across from the other side of the firth, and making straight for the church. This continued to approach until it touched the bottom, and took up its position on the beach. They then saw that it was the Dwarfs' Stone which had come there with its inhabitants. They could not content themselves after the church was shifted, and so made their way after it. For a lasting record of the piety of the dwarfs, the church and manse were called the Dwarfs' Stone.

The Church Grim.

WHEN the first churches were built, they were generally consecrated with the observance of various heathen customs which the people would not part with.   One of these was to sacrifice some animal to the old gods beside the foundation-stone or outside the churchyard wall. These animals were buried alive, and it was believed that their spirit or ghost wandered about in the churchyard in the ghostly hours of the night ; they were called " Kirke-grimer."   Many places and churches have, according to tradition, got their names from these spectres, such as "Hestveda" town and church in Skaane, which is said formerly to have been called " Hest-hvita," because a white horse was " Kirkegrim " there.   When such spectres are seen, they are warnings of important events, lucky or unlucky.

It is also related that, under the altar in the first Christian churches, there was buried a lamb to ensure the permanent existence of the church.   This was called the " Church Lamb."   When any one enters a church at a time when there is no service, it sometimes happens (so says the story) that they see a little lamb spring across the choir and disappear.   When it appears to any one in the churchyard, especially to the grave-diggers, it is a warning that a little child is to die.

The Church Lamb.

UP over the eastern arch in Ryslinge Church, lies the church lamb.   In old days the clerk's servant-girl had to give it a bundle of clean straw for its bed on the evening before every church festival. As to the origin of the church lamb, there is a general belief among the people, that when they began to build churches in the country, it often happened that what was built during the day was torn down during the night. Then they buried a living lamb under the building, and after that no one could lay a hand upon their work. The buried lamb then became the " Church Lamb."

An old woman in Ryslinge (Ann Katherine) once saw the church lamb in her young days. She had been sitting up watching a sick woman, and as she was going home, about twelve o'clock at night, she met a solitary lamb on the road, but whether it had only three legs, as a church lamb ought to have, she could not clearly see. When she came home to her parents, she said that she had seen the " Church Lamb," and they thought it was a warning that the sick woman was to die. It was not so, however, for she recovered, but the day after a post fell and killed a little child on the neighbouring farm. So it was the " Church Lamb " she had seen after all.

Thirty years ago, there died a man in Ryslinge Parish. He lived to the north of the village, beside Nörremark Wood. Some days before he died the church lamb was seen going out to his farm. It was in the evening, and when it came to the last house, which lies close up to the wood, the dog there began to bark. When the farmer heard it, he went out to see what it was, and saw the church lamb, which came past the house, and held on its way to the farm, where the man died a few days after.

The Grave-sow.

"WHEN my parents first came to live in Skjensved, it happened one night when my father was from home that my mother heard a little pig squeak outside the window. We had a sow with pigs just at the time, so she got out of bed and ran after it, but it hastily crept out under the gate into the street. My mother followed it, but could not come up with it, till at last it crept under the church-yard gate. At this she felt somewhat strange, and although she was not timid by nature, dared not enter the churchyard, but turned back to the house, where she went to the stye and counted the little pigs. Not one of them was missing. Next day she asked all the neighbours whether they had lost a pig ; they all said " No," but the pig continued to make its appearance every night. The following Sunday my father told this to the old dean, who was far wiser than all other folk on earth. ' Oh,' said he, ' what else is it but a child that has been buried in secret, and now seeks for Christian earth? If you want to get rid of it, you must watch for a night or two and see where it comes from ; dig there then, and if you find a child, take it and bury it in the churchyard. You will be free from it after that.' They did so, and found a little child under an old apple tree. They buried it in the churchyard, and the little pig never came again."

The Buried Bell.

IN Kilde-bjærg in Tömmerup parish there lived berg-folk, who could not bear to hear the great bell ringing in the tower of Tömmerup church. Accordingly they went up into the tower one day, and carried off the bell into the mound. The people of the parish would not stand this, however, and on getting to know that they could quite well dig it up again, if they could only keep silence during the work, they at once began to dig for it. When they had dug for some time, they did find the bell, and got it raised so far that they could fasten a rope to it, to which they then yoked six horses. Just then one of the people unfortunately said, " Now we have it! " and so the bell sank still deeper than before, and only by cutting the rope did they save the horses from going with it.

The Bell of Kværndrup.

MANY years ago the church bells in Kværndrup were to be repaired, as they were not sounding well. A certain Herr Essing was engaged for the purpose, and received a quantity of silver and brass to patch them with. This, however, he put into his own pocket, and mended them with copper and lead. When the bells came to be rung, they were too dull in sound, and the ringers pulled harder and harder at the rope, till at last the motion became so violent that one of the bells broke loose, flew out at the sound-holes, went right over the town, and only came to the ground when it reached a meadow to the west of the village. The strangest thing, however, was that while the bell was on its way above the town, it sang the following verse, which revealed Herr Essing's frauds :—

> " Silver and brass to Essing did pass;
> Copper and lead he used instead."

Three or four men were now sent to search for the bell, and found the hole in which it was lying. They got a rope put round it, and had already pulled it up to the surface, when one of the men declared, with a great oath, that they were sure of it now. Scarcely had he said this, when the bell again sank into the ground, and since that day no one has ever heard or seen anything of it.

The Chest of Gold.

IN the parish of Vatns-fjörd, beside Isa-fjörd, there stands a large mound, in which a chest full of gold is hidden. Many attempts have been made to get hold of this, but have always had to be given up, on account of terrible sights and sounds. One time two young and active fellows decided to dig into the mound, and made their way into it until they came to the chest. It was so heavy that they could not lift it, although they were both strong men. They accordingly dug all round about the chest, and under it as well. It was strongly bound with iron, and had rings in the ends. They fastened a rope to one of these, and the one man went below the chest to lift it up, while the other pulled at the rope. When the chest had been raised a little, the ring broke away from the end, and it fell back upon the man below, killing him at once. The other was scared at this and ran away, taking the ring with him. It was a large copper ring, and he gave it to Vatns-fjörd church, where it may be seen in the church-door to this day.

Others say that several men had united to dig into the mound. They found the chest, iron-bound and fitted with rings. One of them went under the chest and lifted it up, while the others pulled at the rope, which was drawn through both rings. When the chest had all but

reached the brink of the hole, the men above were almost
exhausted, and thought it doubtful whether they would
get it up. One of them said, "It will come up yet, if
God wills." The man below then shouted out: "It shall
up, whether God wills or not." With that one of the
rings gave way ; the chest fell on the man, killing him at
once, and the hole in the mound filled up again. The
others turned away in terror, and gave the ring to the
church, nor did they try the digging again.

Buried Treasure.

IN the parish of Navr, beside Holstebro, lie two large
mounds, one on each side of the village of Alstrup. The
one to the north is called Ringshöi, and that to the south
Möglehöi. In the latter lies a great treasure, which two
men from Alstrup tried to dig for one night. They
worked in silence, until one ear of the copper-pot, in which
the treasure was, was sticking up, but just then one of the
men looked up, and to his amazement, caught sight of
two cocks, which came along the road from Navrtorp,
dragging a huge load of hay. All at once, one of them
became restive, kicked out behind and splintered the
swingletree. The man burst out laughing, and said,
"Well, never in all my days have I seen anything so
funny." With that the pot immediately disappeared, and
all their subsequent digging for it was in vain.

The Smith in Burhöi.

IN the parish of Bur, on the lands of Ny-gaard, lie three
large mounds, in one of which lives a bergman who is a

smith, and has his workshop there. By night one can
often see fire coming out of the top of the mound, and
strangely enough, going in again at its side ; but it is by
this means that he keeps his iron hot. If any one wishes
to have a piece of iron worked by him, he has only to lay
it on the mound, along with a silver coin as payment, at
the same time saying what he has need of. Next morning the coin is taken away, and the piece of work desired
lies there ready and well finished. One time the peasants
of Bur resolved to dig up his treasures, and for that purpose assembled one night beside the mound, with picks
and spades. After they had all been told that they must
carefully avoid saying a single word, however strongly
they were tempted to do so, they set to work ; but
scarcely had they put their spades into the ground, before
all sorts of terrible sights came out of the mound. However, they dug on, undisturbed, and with the greatest
silence, until they got down to a large stone-chamber.
There lay the treasure before them—a large copper pot
full of gold pieces ; but close beside it a big black dog
lay sleeping. One of the men pulled off his jacket, and
quietly laid the dog on this to carry it away, and while
he was doing so, the others stood looking out of the
mound. There came then, out of the mound, a large
load of hay drawn by two cocks, which drew it three
times round the mound ; but all of those present were
careful not to say a word. At the third round, however,
one of the cocks kicked out so violently that it broke the
thick shaft of the cart ; then one of the men exclaimed,
" That was a devilish kick for a cock," but scarcely had
he said this, when all the men were thrown far away out
of the mound, which immediately closed again.

The Treasure in Eriks-volde.

IN the neighbourhood of Maribo is a forest, in the corner
of which is a spot called Eriks-volde. This is a large
mound, surrounded by high ramparts and deep ditches,
and here in olden time there is said to have been a castle
in which lived King Erik, who ruled over a great part of
Laaland. In the heart of the mound a large treasure is
buried. Some men from the neighbouring village of
Erikstrup once tried to dig it up ; they had heard that if
they could work on for six hours without interruption
and without speaking a word, the treasure would be
theirs. They accordingly set to work one evening in
high hopes. When they had worked for a little, the
mound began to shake and tremble beneath them, but
they would not be scared by that. Then they saw a cock
come along, dragging a large bull ; the bull struggled
against it, but to no purpose, the cock dragged it off with
it. Still they kept silence and worked on. In a little
while they saw four mice come past the mound, dragging
a big load of hay ; this looked rather wonderful, but they
did not let it disturb them. They had now got so far
down that the edge of the copper pot in which the
treasure lies began to appear, but just at that moment
one of them happened to look out over the wood towards
the village. "The village is in flames!" he cried, and
they all rushed off to save it, but when they got out
through the wood there was no fire to be seen. They
turned back to get the treasure, but it had disappeared
for ever, and there was no trace of all their work.

Treasure Guarded by a Dog.

A MAN in Lund in Björns-holm parish went out one morning to search for his horse. As he wandered about looking for it, he came upon a black dog, which was lying above a copper pot. The man could see that there was money in this, so he took off his jacket and spread it on the ground, lifted the dog gently in his arms and laid it on the jacket, after which he took the money out of the pot and placed the dog above it as before. Then the dog said, " If you had not lifted me so gently, and laid me so softly, it would not have gone so well with you." There was so much money that he could not take it all home with him, so he laid it in a corner of the wood and went home for a sack. He hung the horse's halter in the tree above the spot, and went off in great delight, thinking he had won all Björnsholm and more. But his joy was short-lived. When he returned with the sack, and looked for the halter, there was one hanging on every tree ! He went about looking under every tree, but when he had done so for some time, there was a noise like a rifle-shot, or worse ; after that he found his halter, but the money was gone, and he had nothing for all his trouble. If he had only taken as much as he could carry when he had the chance !

Gudmund and the Ghost.

SOUTH in Njard-vík there is a mound called Háa-leyti (High's grave), where great treasure-lights have often been seen, and it was commonly said that gold was hidden there. It was long, however, before anyone tried to get it, especially as the mound and its neighbourhood were, and are still, believed to be haunted.

About 1850-60 there lived near the mound a farmer, who was a good smith, and was often at work in his smithy, the doors of which looked right out on the mound. One time he was there working, and along with him one Gudmund, who was a man of sense, and so strong in body that he was considered to be quite equal to any two men. They were talking together in the best spirits, when the farmer happened to look at the mound and saw a blue flame spring up out of it all at once. He proposed to Gudmund that they go to the mound, and try to get at the money, to which Gudmund agreed. They went towards the flame, which sank lower as they approached it, and finally disappeared when they had got close to it. The farmer asked Gudmund whether he would rather deal with the ghost or dig for the treasure, but suggested that he should deal with the ghost, because he was the younger and stronger of the two. Gudmund assented to this, and they agreed that they should share the treasure equally, if they succeeded in getting it. With this the man began to dig in the mound, and Gudmund noticed nothing at first, but before long he felt himself gripped from behind. He turned round at once to offer resistance, but could not get hold of the ghost, who presented nothing substantial to the touch. This went on a long time, and sometimes Gudmund thought he had the ghost under him, but he always slipped from his grasp and attacked him again. Meanwhile the farmer had got down to a large chest full of money, which he dragged off, while Gudmund held his own with the ghost till morning, by which time he was so exhausted that he had enough ado to get home to the farm. He slept till well on in the

day, and on waking went out to the farmer, who was in
the smithy, hard at work. Gudmund asked how much
money there was in the chest, but the farmer said he
would drive the iron spike through him, if he told of their
find. Gudmund thought it is his best plan to give in to
this, and the farmer gave him twenty dollars when they
parted, but Gudmund told the story all the same, not
being afraid of the farmer. Gudmund said that the ghost
most resembled a flock of wool to the touch, and was not
stronger than a stalwart man, nor would he have had
any difficulty in felling him if he had not been so slippery.

The Black Death.

THE pestilence so well known by the name of " The
Black Death," which, with the speed of lightning, spread
from the highlands of Asia on the borders of China, to
the coasts of the Polar Sea, and before whose deadly
breath thousands on thousands perished, was brought to
Bergen by a stranded English ship, and from there spread
with terrible violence from dale to dale, cleared the whole
land of people and cattle, and brought Norway to a state
of weakness which lasted for centuries. The land is said
to have lost two-thirds of its inhabitants. In most of the
mountain districts there are stories of this pestilence,
which, in some places, is called by the peasants "The
Great Plague" (Store-manna-douen), in others "The
Black Death" (Svart-douen), and "The Pest" (Pesta).
Sometimes the pest is imagined as an old sallow woman,
who went round the land with a rake and a besom. Where
she used the rake, some always escaped with their lives,
but where she swept, every mother's son died. For the

most part, she wore a red shirt, and folk were terrified at
seeing her.   Many a dale died out, and only after centuries were the forgotten places discovered, where sometimes the old houses were found, sometimes only the
remains of buildings and other traces of previous occupation.   Such recovered dales were afterwards called
Finddale, Fundarhuse, Findland, etc.   Many of them
were cleared again, but all over the country may still be
found spots which bear traces of former occupation, but
are now used only as summer pastures.

The Black Death in Sætersdal.

BEFORE the pest visited Norway, what is now called
Sætersdal was uninhabited, and used only for summer
pasture ; whereas that called Finddal, now used for the
summer pasture, was then the inhabited district.   Besides the support given to the tradition by the name
Sætersdal itself, there are also found in Finddal traces of
former fields and houses, and in fact on an island in a
mountain lake, which bears the name of Kirkholm, are
found traces of a church and churchyard.

The Black Death wrought fearful desolation in Finddal,
where it only spared a single couple, Knud and Thore
Nuten.   These two continued to live in Finddal, and
although new inhabitants afterwards came into Sætersdal
and settled there, yet Knud and Thore could not bring
themselves to leave their old home.

Thus year after year passed, and the only want, says
the story, that they felt in their loneliness, was that of not
knowing exactly how time went. Especially when the dark
winter came, they were vexed that they did not know when

Christmas was, and so could not keep it at the same time as other people. Now and again a wanderer from the newly-inhabited Sætersdal had brought to them the news of its being repeopled, and so, as it drew near to the shortest winter days, the old couple decided that Thore should go there, and find out how long it was to the great festival. The old woman left her husband completely alone, "took her foot in her hand," and set out on the road. But as she was going past a cliff, and rested there, she heard in clear tones from the mountain.

> " Dainty, dainty Tholè,
> Bake your bread for Yule, O,
> Two days and a single night,
> So long is it till Yule, O."

The old woman hastened back in great joy to her waiting husband, and after this infallible information, they celebrated together the holy festival. No descendants of theirs are mentioned, but by and by the new inhabitants of Sætersdal took possession of Finddal as well.

The Black Death in Denmark.

ABOUT 1350 raged the Black Death, of which history relates that it carried off four-fifths of the population in the Scandinavian countries, which, however, is not quite universally true. Nevertheless, even to this day may be heard faint echoes of the terror which that pestilence caused. It is said that children even avoided burying their parents' bodies, many houses stood empty, and the cattle roamed wild over the fields. A little girl was on one occasion pursued by a bull. While she was running, the pest took hold of her, and she fell dead, so quickly did it kill. The practice of saying "God help you," to one who sneezes, is by some referred to this time ; sneezing was a sign of having caught the pest. The year before it, a vapour was seen to rise out of the ground, and spread itself over the whole country.

In this pestilence all the people in Oster-Lögum parish died out, with the exception of three ploughmen, who shut themselves up above an archway in the farm now owned by Nis Hansen in Havelund. They took with them provisions for six months, but every eighth day they went out and hoisted a piece of fresh beef on the end of a long pole. This hung for the next eight days, and was then taken down. For a long time the meat was always spoiled and black when they took it down, and this was a sign that the plague was still in the air. This went on until the meat was still fresh when they took it down, and they judged that there was no longer any danger. Then they said to each other, " Now we shall go and see our neighbours ;" but they went from house to house and found only the dead, both human beings and animals. In this way they went from village to village over the whole parish. The people lay dead on the fields beside their ploughs, and there was no living thing except eagles and beasts of prey. Houses and farms stood empty for twenty-five or thirty years after that time. A priest was brought out to the church from Aaben-raa, and offered up a prayer of thanksgiving for the cessation of the pestilence.

The Black Death in Iceland.

AT the time when the Black Death began to rage, it was the custom of a certain farmer to hold prayers every morning at all seasons of the year. On one occasion they were busy gathering the hay together, as it looked like rain, when the farmer said they would go home to prayers. Some of the others objected to this, and said it would be more fitting for them to get the hay in, but the farmer insisted, and they all went to the house. During the day there came in sight two tiny tufts of cloud, which came nearer and increased in size till at last they appeared as a man and a woman riding on grey horses. They rode along above the farm, and the woman was heard to say, "Shall we visit here?" "No," said the man, "that was not commanded us." So the Black Death passed over without coming to the farm, and all the people there survived.

NOTES.

PRONUNCIATION.

1. With regard to consonants the following points may be noticed :—

d in Danish, when standing by itself at the end or in the middle of a word, is sounded *th* as in *bathe*. The same rule applies to the Icelandic names in this book, as *d* has been used for ð. After *l*, *n*, *r*, it is not pronounced in Danish, but is sounded in Icelandic (ð after *r*, *d* after *n*, *l*.) Thus Danish *gaard* is = *goar'*, but Icelandic *gard* (garð) = *garth*.

f in Icelandic is always = *v* when not initial, and becomes *b* before *n* (*Hrafn* is pronounced *H-rab'n*).

g is always hard, as in *go*.

j in all the Scandinavian tongues is the consonant *y*, as in German. Occasionally *i* has been printed instead of *j*.

k in Swedish has a soft sound before *ä*, *e*, *i*, *y*, *ö*; thus *kyrka* = *tshirka*.

th in Icelandic names stands for þ, and has the sound heard in English *think*. In Danish, etc., where it occurs initially, it is = *t*.

2. Some of the vowel-sounds in Icelandic and Danish require explanation. In Icelandic :—

á has the sound of German *au*, English *ow*. Thus the name *Hákon* is pronounced *Howkon*. (In Færöese = Danish *aa*.)

au is pronounced *öi* : thus Raud = *röið*, Audun = *öiðun*.

ei and *ey* are sounded as *äi* : *stein* has almost the sound of English *stay in*, pronounced quickly.

æ is pronounced as *eye* : thus *bæ* sounds like *by* in English.

y is equivalent to *i*, and *ý* to *í* (the latter with the sound of English *ee*.)

In Danish :—

aa is a broad *o* sound (*oa*), so that *raa* comes near to English *raw*. The diphthong has also been employed throughout to represent the Swedish circled *a*, which has the same sound.

ö as in German, but *öj* = English *oy*.

y like German *ü*, approaching to an *ee*-sound ; thus *By* comes near to English *be*.

Final *e* is always pronounced in Danish and Swedish, as in German.

AUTHORITIES.

The works from which the greater number of the stories in this volume have been selected are given in the following list, and are referred to in the notes by their abbreviated titles. The list will also serve to indicate the country to which each tale belongs. Where other works than those here named have been used, their titles are given in full, together with the nationality of the story, wherever this is not directly shown by the text.

ICELAND.

Flb. = Flateyjarbók, Vol. I. Christiania, 1860. Part of the great MS. known as the Flatey Book, containing the longer recension of King Olaf Tryggvason's Saga, and numerous legends connected with it.

Hkr. = Heimskringla, the short recension of the Sagas of the Kings of Norway, by Snorri Sturluson ; edited by Unger. Christiania, 1868.

J. Arn. = Jón Árnason's " Íslenzkar þjóðsögur og Æfintýri," 2 vols. Leipzig, 1862-64.

O. Dav. = Ólaf Davidsson's " Íslenzkar þjóðsögur ; " Reykjavík, 1895 (a small volume).

FÆRÖES.

Fær. Anth. = Færösk Anthologi, ved V. U. Hammershaimb. Copenhagen, 1891.

NORWAY.

Faye = Norske Folkesagn, samlede og udgivne af Andreas Faye (2nd Ed.) Christiania, 1844.

SWEDEN.

Afz. = Swenska Folkets Sago-häfder, af Arv. Aug. Afzelius, I., II. Stockholm, 1839-40.

Wig. = Folkdiktning, etc., samlad och upptecknad i Skaane (s. of Sweden) af (Fru) Eva Wigström. Copenhagen, 1880.

DENMARK.

Thiele = Danmarks Folkesagn, samlede af J. M. Thiele. Vol. II. Copenhagen, 1843.

Grundt. = Gamle danske Minder i Folkemunde af Svend Grundt-vig. (2nd. Ed.) Copenhagen, 1861.

Kamp = Danske Folkeminder, samlede af Jens Kamp. Odense, 1877.

Krist. J. F. = Jyske Folkeminder, samlede af Evald Tang Kris-tensen. 12 Vols. 1871-95.

Krist. D. S. = Danske Sagn, samlede af Evald Tang Kristensen. 4 Vols. 1891-96.

GENERAL.

Nord. S. = Nordiske Sagn, samlede og udgivne af C. Berg og Edv. Gædecken. Copenhagen, 1868.

SOURCES AND REMARKS.

I.—THE OLD GODS.

The narratives contained in this section are not part of the old Scandinavian mythology, but give the conceptions of the Old Gods as they were retained in the memories of the people after the introduction of Christianity. Most of them are ancient, but a few traditions have lingered on to recent times.

PAGE.

9. Thorgils and Thor : Flóamanna Saga, c. 20 and 21. The beginning of the third paragraph is condensed. More about Thorgils will be found on p. 276. He lived from 937 to 1022 A.D., and the expedition to Greenland took place in 986.

11. King Olaf and Thor : Odd's Saga of King Olaf Tryggva-
     son. The incident (which is not given in Hkr. but ap-
     pears in a longer form in Flb. I., 397) is assigned to the
     year 998.

12. Raud and Thor: Flb. I., 288-298. The narrative of the
     saga-writer has been greatly condensed in the translation.
     With the living image of Thor compare Earl Hákon's
     wooden man on p. 350.

14. Thor and Urebö Stone-field : Faye, p. 3. The story was
     taken down from a farmer living close to the spot, who
     used the old form *tungum hamri* (the heavy hammer)
     in telling it, " because the old people always say it so
     when they tell the tale."

16. Thor's Hammer : J. Arn., I., 445. A " Thor's hammer "
     was seen by Dr. Konrad Maurer in Iceland in 1858.
     The practice, if not the name, is known elsewhere, in
     Sweden and Denmark (Afz. I., 20 ; Thiele, III., 360.)

17. Thor's Stone-weapons : Afz., I., 10 and 12. With this fear
     of the trolls for Thor, compare the story of the Old Man
     of Hoberg (p. 124). The practice of lifting the small
     stone on top of the big one is observed at " Ossian's
     Grave," in the Sma' Glen, Perthshire.

18. Odin and King Olaf: Flb. I., 375-6. Given also in Hkr.,
     p. 180, with the name Varinn instead of Dixin. King
     Ogvald is thus referred to in Hálfs Saga :—" Finn the
     wealthy, of Akra-ness, lay beside Ogvalds-ness when about
     to sail to Iceland, and asked how long it was since King
     Ogvald fell. Then he heard this verse repeated in the
     mound.

     " Long time backward,   And sailed the sea-trouts'
     When led were to battle   Salt-waved pathway,
     Hundreds of Hækling's   I of this homestead
     Heroes stalwart,   Held the lordship. "

19. The Keel of the Long Serpent : Flb., I., 433-434. This
     was King Olaf's famous ship, the crew of which made so
     brave a fight in the battle of Svöldr (1000 A.D.)

21. The Smith and Odin : Saga Hákonar, Guthorms ok Inga,
     c. 20. Given in Vigfusson and Powell's *Icelandic Reader*,
     p. 216. "Nesjar, the Naze by Laurvík, at the mouth of
     the Christiania Firth : Medaldal, 120 miles away in the

middle of Norway, W. by N. of Nesjar; Jardal, on the Norwegian coast above Stavanger, 70 miles W. of Medaldal." (ib., p. 408.)

22. Odin the Hunter: Krist. D. S., II., C. 23, 57, and 67. The tradition is also given by Thiele (II., 122-123), Grundtvig, and others. The name of the hunter assumes a great variety of forms, the leading types being Wojens, Uns, Jons, Huens (Horns). From the constant appearance of the final *s*, it is possible that "Odin's hunter" was the original conception. There are slight variations as to the reason of his punishment, such as hunting on Easter Day, and the same belief exists about King Valdemar.

24. Odin pursues the Elf-women: Krist., *ib.* 87, 85, and 90. This pursuit is also attributed to King Valdemar. From the length of her breasts, which hang down to her waist, or are thrown back over her shoulders, the female is sometimes called a *slatten-patte* or "flabby-pap" (compare in this respect the giantess on p. 92, and the bergwoman on p. 131).

26. Odin in Sweden : Afz., I. 4.

27. Odin's Cave and Garden: Krist. D. S., II., C. 1. Similar tales of Odin's residence in Möen are given by Grundtvig and Thiele ; the latter says that the peasants leave the last sheaf to him. The phrase, "But Jesus though," is one of surprise or remonstrance : in Möen they say "Men jötten dog" in place of the ordinary "Men jös dog."

28. Frey : Flb. I., 403. The account of Frey's burial is also briefly given in Hkr., p. 11.

29. Gunnar and Frey : Flb. I., 337-339. It is probable that the story preserves some genuine features connected with the Old Northern temple-worship.

32. Thorgerd Hörda-brúd : Fbl. I., 144 and 191. The real cognomen of Thorgerd is uncertain. Hörda-brúd might mean "bride of the Hördar" (the men of Hörda-land), but the name is also written Hörga-brúd (*hörgr* means a sacrificial cairn, but see note to p. 350), and Hölga-brúd (from Hölgi, a mythical king). The great battle with

the Jómsvikings took place in 994 A.D. A temple of Thorgerd and Irpa is mentioned in Njáls Saga, c. 87, 88. "During the night Hrapp went into the temple belonging to the Earl (Hákon) and Gudbrand. He saw Thorgerd sitting there, as big as a full-grown man : she had a large gold ring on her hand, and a *fald* on her head, etc."

35. Freyja and the Kings : Flb. I., 275-283. The second and third paragraphs are only an outline of the original. The story of the battle is briefly told in Snorra Edda (*Skáldskaparmál*, 57), where it is said that it will last till Doomsday. For Ironshield, the former owner of Ivar's sword, see page 42.

39. Loki : Faye, p. 5. In Denmark the same story is told of Christ, and in Iceland of St. Olaf.

II.—TROLLS AND GIANTS.

The stories of trolls, conceived as huge and horrible ogres, are mainly Icelandic ; in the other Scandinavian countries, especially Denmark, the trolls are confounded with the berg-folk, and have little or nothing in common with their older namesakes. Thus the stories on pages 63, 65, and 70, might equally well have gone into the next section, but for the use of the name "troll." In Icelandic other words, such as *flagd* and *skessa* are used for the female troll, and the modern form is *tröll* in place of the older *troll*.

PAGE.
40. The Trolls in Heidar-skog : Flb. I., 257-260. The words of Ironshield on p. 42, "thoughts of great men lie upon me," refer to a belief in soul-wandering ("a person's ill-will or good-will being fancied as wandering abroad and pursuing their object") which is found elsewhere in the sagas.

44. The Trolls and King Olaf : Odd's Saga of Olaf Tryggvason, c. 47. The same story is told in different words in Flb. I., 398-399, and is referred to in Hkr. The expedition to Hálogaland was in 998 A.D.

47. The Hag of Mjóa-firth : J. Arn., I., 152. A farmer in Firth, who died about 1830, declared that he remembered the hag's iron shoe, which was used as a dust-bin.

48. The Giantess's Stone: J. Arn., I., 153. The word rendered "giantess" is *skessa*, a female troll.

50. The Female Troll on Blá-fell : J. Arn., I., 157. The story here given is preceded by a long account of the previous history of the troll. In a second version, Olaf meets the troll in a blinding drift, and seeing blood in her tracks, offers her one of his horses to ride on, if she would "leave it as good as she found it." This refers to the belief that horses are strained by being "troll-ridden."

51. Gissur of Botnar: J. Arn., I., 161, with variant on p. 163. The first version ends with the story of Andra-rímur, for which see p. 57.

52. Jóra in Jóru-kleyf: J. Arn., I., 182. A few topographical details have been omitted. The name Jóru-kleyf occurs in Hardar Saga. According to Landnáma, Oxar-á was so named by Ketilbjörn, one of the early settlers, because of an axe being lost in it.

54. Loppa and Jón : J. Arn., I., 191. Other versions of the tale are given on pp. 187 ff. The one here translated adds that Jón's bones were dug up in the churchyard in the middle of the 18th century ; his thigh-bone reached from the ground to the hip of the tallest man present.

56. Trunt, trunt, and the trolls in the fells : J. Arn., I., 193. The word "trunt" has no more meaning in Icelandic than in English.

57. Andra-rímur and Hallgríms-rímur : J. Arn., I., 196. *Andra-rímur* are a very popular set of ballads. *Hallgríms-rímur* are the Passion Psalms of Hallgrím Peturs-son, which Vigfusson calls "the flower of Icelandic poetry, old as well as modern." See the stories of Hallgrím on p. 369.

58. Hremmu-háls : J. Arn., I., 214. The belief in trolls being turned to stone at daybreak is very common ; compare the "Origin of Drángey" on p. 61.

59. Bergthór in Blá-fell : J. Arn., I., 213. The derivation of Hítardal from the giantess Hít is imaginary, the real form being Hitardal. The cavity in the rock for holding the sour whey still exists, and is used for that purpose.

61. The Origin of Drángey : J. Arn., I., 210. This rocky island was the last refuge of the outlawed Grettir.

62. The Size of Trolls : J. Arn., I., 217.   These later exag-
     gerations may be compared with the giant in the Danish
     tale on p. 399.

63. Trolls in the Færöes : Fær. Anth., I., 356, also given in
     Danish in Nord. S., p. 55 from Antikv. Tidsskrift, 1850
     (not quite so full as in the Færöese).   A number of
     similar tales of elves are told in J. Arn., I., 118 ff; com-
     pare "The Shepherd and the Sea-folk" on p. 228.

65. The Troll and the Bear : Nord. S., 109 (from Grundtvig's
     Gamle Danske Minder).   Variants are given by Faye
     (p. 30) and by Asbjörnsen and Moe (p. 139), the latter
     translated in Dasent's "Popular tales from the Norse."

66. Dyre Vaa, etc. : Faye, p. 19.   With the troll's glove com-
     pare the story of the giant's glove on p. 90.

67. The Trolls in Hedal-skov : Asbjörnsen, Norske Folke-
     Eventyr (Ny Samling) p. 153.   The incident of the
     common eye is familiar in some fairy-tales.

70. The Trolls and the Cross : Krist. D. S., I., 511.   The
     trolls here are the Danish ones = bergfolk.   The virtues
     of the rowan-tree appear in other stories (p. 378).

72. Dofri : Flb. I., 564-6.   The story is very differently told
     in Hkr. (Saga Hálfdanar Svarta, c. 8), and the writers of
     Flb. have also worked that version into their tale of
     Dofri.

74. The Giant on Saudey : Flb. I., 524-530.   The early part
     is slightly condensed, and the last paragraph only an
     abstract of the original narrative.   With the witch's pro-
     phecy compare the story of Ingimund on p. 357.

77. The Giantess's Cave in Sandö : Fær. Anth., I., 332, also
     in Danish in Nord. S., p. 22.   There is a similar story
     about Fjallavatn in Vaagö.

78. Oli the Strong, etc. : Fær. Anth., I., 348-351.

81. Mikines : Fær. Anth., I., 352.   Castoreum was formerly
     used to protect the open boats against whales, who were
     supposed to dislike the scent of. it.   An old story of
     shifting islands in the way here imagined is that of
     Gefjón, and the origin of Sjælland in Denmark (Hkr.,
     p. 6).

83. The Giant on Hestmandö: Faye, p. 10. The Horseman is some 1650 feet high, and the hole in Torgehatten is about 430 ells long, and from 90 to 220 feet high.

84. The Raaman, etc.: Faye, p. 12.

85. The Giant in Dunkeraberg: Faye, p. 13. The value of knowing a troll's name is also shown by the stories on pp. 390, 391.

85. The Giant of Tındfell: Nord. S., p. 47 (from Hammerich's "Skandinaviske Reiseminder"). The incident of the fir-cone is also given by Faye, p. 19.

86. The Giant of Ness: Nord. S., p. 24 (from Afzelius). In this and the following tale the "giant" seems to be more of a bergman, to which the incident of the cow also points; compare the story of the birth on p. 98.

87. The Giant at Lagga Kirk: Nord. S., p. 33 (from Afzelius). For the hatred borne by trolls towards church bells, compare the following tale, and p. 404.

88. The Giant's Flitting: Nord. S., p. 43 (from Grundtvig).

89. The Giant's Dam: Krist. J. F., III., p. 57. The berg-man here is evidently intended for a giant.

90. The Giantess and the·Ploughers: *ib.*, p. 59.

90. The Giant's Glove: *ib.*, IV., p. 50. The' glove worn by the giant was the *lufvante*, which has no divisions for the different fingers.

91. The Giantess and her Sons: *ib.* VI., p. 40. The giantess is called *Giwkuen* (or *Givkonen*), where *Giw* may be the O.N. *gygr*, a giantess. In Wigström (p. 131) a giant's wife is similarly described as throwing her breasts over her shoulders; compare p. 131, and the note to p. 24.

III.—BERG-FOLK AND DWARFS.

Tales of bergfolk are perhaps the commonest type of Danish folk-lore, and nearly all the stories in this section belong to Denmark. They illustrate in themselves almost every feature of the life supposed to go on in the mounds, which are the habitations of the underground people, and require little comment. As already mentioned, the names of "troll" and "bergman" are synonymous in Denmark, and even "nisse" is sometimes employed with the same meaning.

PAGE.

93. The Origin of Bergfolk : Krist. D. S., I., p. 3 and 4, in various forms. The same account is given by Thiele (II., 175) and Faye (p. xxvii), who also mentions the Swedish versions. Compare the Icelandic account of the origin of the elves on p. 142, with corresponding note.

93. The Oldest Man, etc.: Krist. D. S., I., 713.

94. A Meeting with Bergfolk : *ib.*, 36. The idea that bergfolk cannot say "good" appears in other stories ; compare however p. 95.

95. Gillikop : Thiele, II., 243 (Thorpe II., 151).

95. Skalle : Nord. S., p. 72 (from Grundtvig). Stories of shifting the stable or cow-house from above the bergfolk's dwelling are common enough.

97. We others : Krist., D. S., I. 572.

97. The Key of Dagberg Dos. : Krist., J. F., III., p. 12. Dagberg Dos or Daas is a favourite locality for bergfolk tales. In another version the herdboy gets a hat-buckle as a reward, but loses it soon after.

98. A Birth among the Bergfolk : Krist.. D. S., I., 1113, and in many other versions. The toad is a common feature, which may be explained by a confusion of *Tudse* (a toad) and *Tusse* or *Tus* = O.N. *þurs*, a giant. With the use of the salve and its subsequent effects, compare the Icelandic story on p. 144.

100. Life hangs by a thread : Krist., J. F., IV., 33. In other versions a woman allows a toad to escape with its life, is taken down to attend the bergwoman, and sees the millstone hanging above her while doing so. In Thiele (II., 203 = Thorpe, II., 130) it is a serpent that hangs overhead.

102. The Bergman's Christian Wife : Krist., D. S., I., 1126. Compare the previous story on p. 99. The advices given to the midwife in such tales are three in all ; to partake of no food, to choose rubbish instead of gold, and to slip off the horse or waggon as soon as it stops.

103. Working for the Bergfolk: Krist.: D. S., I., 1105. A similar story in Thiele (II., 204 = Thorpe, II., 130).

104. Maid Ellen: Krist., D. S., I., 846 and 848. According to the version in Kamp (p. 149), the brother's name was Sti Pors.

106. The Changeling and Egg-shells: Kamp, p. 19. A very common story. In Krist., J. F., III., 65, the changeling, on being found out, catches hold of its feet and rolls off like a wheel, up hill and down dale as far as the eye can follow it.

107. The Changeling and Sausage: Krist., D. S., I., 1049. This also occurs in many versions; see Keightley, I., 199, and Thorpe, II., 174 (from Thiele, II., 227). In some of these the changeling cannot pronounce the word for sausage, *pölse*, and calls it *ölls* or *höls*.

108. The Troll's Wedding: Nord. S., p. 86 (from Grundtvig). The story appears in many forms. The woman's laughter is caused by a variety of accidents, but the knocking over of a dish is the most frequent.

109. Sten of Fogel-Kärr: Afz., II., 157, translated in Thorpe (II., 86). With Sten's use of the fire-steel compare the tale on p. 396, and that of the knife on p. 169.

110. The Bergman's Daughter, etc.: Nord. S., p. 31, from Hammerich. Versions are also given by Krist. and others. That in Thiele (II., 224) is not translated by Thorpe.

112. Viting is dead: Krist., D. S., I., 313. The names vary considerably in different versions. Sortöje (Black-eye) appears as Solöj, Kolöje, Akeleje, etc., and Viting as Vipping, Vippe, Vibbi, Pippe, etc. Quite different is the "Atis and Vatis" version, which also undergoes many transformations.

112. Tell Finkenæs, etc.: Krist., J. F., IV., 11. Also told in D. S., I., 355, where Finkenæs is said to have been the weakest of three bergmen, and so compelled to leave the mound till Jafet died. In some versions he runs off saying, "Farewell, never want!"

114. Bröndhöj: Thiele, II., 187, translated by Keightley (I., 196) and Thorpe (II., 123). The cat also figures in a Swedish version (Wigstrom, p. 153).

114. Skotte : Thiele, II., 205, translated by Keightley (I., 187)
and Thorpe (II., 132). There are also versions in Krist.,
D. S., I., § 22.

116. Plough-irons made by Bergfolk: Grundt. I., 122.   A
scythe is the favourite implement to order from the
underground smith : it must never be sharpened, or it
becomes quite useless, and generally payment must be
given for it.

116. The borrowed petticoat: Thiele II., 199, translated by
Thorpe (II., 128). The story is not a common one,
apparently.

117. The Bergfolk's ale-barrel : Krist. D. S., I., 468.   Stories
of such borrowings are frequent ; this one occurs in a
Swedish version in Wigström, p. 156.

117. Nisse in the ale-barrel : Krist. D. S., I., 508.   The nisses
in this tale are plainly meant for bergfolk.

119. Bergfolk at the wedding feast : Krist. D. S., I., 517, with
many variants.   Compare Faye, p. 29, translated by
Thorpe (II., 100).

120. Stealing Music : Krist. D. S., I., 693.   The story is a very
curious one, and apparently unique.

121. The Bergwoman's Bread : Nord. S., p. 94 (from Grundtvig).   Similar stories are extremely common.   Sometimes the ploughman gives the bread to his horses, which
grow strong by it.

122 The Old Man of Hoberg : Nord. S., p. 3 (from Bäckström's
"Folksböcker ").   Similar narratives are "The Giant in
Jons-horn " in Faye (p. 16, not given by Thorpe), and
"The Trolls' Fear for Thunder" in Thiele (II., 245=
Keightley I., 193, and Thorpe II., 152).   There is also
a very lively version in Krist. D. S., I., 1408.

126. Bergfolk Militia : Krist. D. S., I., 255.   Some account of
the underground defenders of Bornholm is also given by
Thiele (II., 194,=Thorpe II., 125).

127. The Herd-boy and the Bergman : Krist. D. S., I., 258.
This is perhaps a version of Svend Fælling with his
twelve men's strength, for which see Thiele II., 228
(translated by Keightley I., 203, and Thorpe II., 141),
as well as Krist. D. S., I., 959 ff.

128. The Bergfolk's present : Krist. D. S., I., 484.

129. The Bergman's beetles : *ib.* 634. The gold is also seen in the form of small stones or pieces of coal. Compare the story of Bergthor on p. 59.

130. The Red Stone on Fuur: Nord. S., p. 96 (from Hammer-ich). The latter part is copied from the same source by Thiele (II., 236), and translated by Thorpe (II., 148). A version in Krist. D. S., (I., 651) makes the trolls really fire the man's house in revenge for the theft.

131. The Silver Cup, etc.: Krist. D. S., I., 774. Versions of the story abound in Danish, and present numerous varia-tions from each other. The one in Thiele (II., 232) is given both by Keightley (I., 180) and Thorpe (II., 144). The others collected by Kristensen show the following differences from that translated here. (1) The horseman loses his way, and sees Dagberg Daas blazing with light; the nearer he comes, the smaller the lights grow, until at last they only shine out through little slits. Or the man is sent by the owner of Stubbergaard, with instructions how to act. The mound is standing on four glowing pillars, and a wedding going on inside. (2) The horse-man does not hear about the poison, but either suspects its look, or has been told of it beforehand. (3) Some versions omit the difficulty about the ploughed land. (4) So exhausted is the woman with her running, that she falls down dead, or bursts and gives birth to twins, and is found lying there on Christmas morning by the church-goers. The bergman then comes, lifts a large stone with his five fingers, and lays it above her dead body.

132. One-leg and the stolen Goblet: Krist. D. S., I., 803. Also a very common tale. The cry of "Off the smooth, etc.," is a regular feature in all the versions, though in different forms. In some the pursuing bergman or berg-woman throws a lump of earth after the thief, which re-mains as a mound on the field, or hurls stones, which are pointed out with the marks of fingers on them. In others the trolls shout to the horse, "Stand, gelding," but as the man rides a stallion, they cannot stop him. The cup or horn is either preserved in the district, or was sent to Copenhagen Museum, and many communion

cups are said to have been got in this way. In many
cases the cup is afterwards recovered by the bergfolk.

133. The Bergfolk pass over Limfjord : Nord. S., p. 99. There
are several versions in Krist. D. S., I., § 84, and in
Thiele. Thorhall the prophet saw the mounds opening
and the creatures in them preparing to depart, shortly
before the introduction of Christianity into Iceland (Flb.
I., 421).

135. Reimer's Aerial Voyage : Nord. S., p. 57 (from Grundtvig).
Different versions in Krist. D. S., I., § 81 ; also Swedish
variants in Wigström (pp. 133 and 238). In some of
the Danish ones the return service is to help the bergman in a fight with his neighbour.

137. The Bergman in Mesing Bank : Nord. S., p. 91 (from
Grundtvig). The bergfolk go by sea to Norway in the
story of the " Emigration from Ærö," Thiele (II., 252 =
Thorpe II., 156.)

138. Dwarfs in the Færöes : Fær Anth. I., 326 (also in Danish
in Nord. S., p. 107). The conception of dwarfs here
comes very close to that in the old mythology.

139. Dwarfs in Smithdale : Faye, p. 35.

140. The Last Dwarfs in Iceland : J. Arn. I., 469. For the
significance of the term *krapta-skáld*, see p. 369.

IV.—ELVES OR HULDU-FOLK.

Although the elves (*álfar*) have a place in the old mythology,
and are often mentioned along with the gods, there are few
references to them in the older writings. It is probable that the
Icelandic stories in this section have best preserved the old
conception of the elves. The name *huldu-fólk*, or " hidden
people " is regarded as a milder term than *álfar*, and the elves
are said to prefer to be called by that name. In Denmark the
properties of the elves are largely assigned to the bergfolk ; and
the conception of the former has been greatly influenced by the
chance resemblance of *ellefolk* to *elle-træ*, the name of the alder,
as may be seen from the stories on pp. 180, 181, 184.

PAGE.

142. The Origin of the Elves : J. Arn. I., 5. Another story
(*ib.*) tells how a man received from an elf-girl the story of

their origin. "When the devil raised rebellion in heaven, he and all those who fought on his side were driven into outer darkness. Those who joined neither party were cast down to earth and doomed to live in knolls, fells, and stones, and they are called elves or huldu-folk." According to the same account the elves have no material body.

142. The Elves' House : Huld. I., 38 (Reykjavík, 1890).

143. A Fairy Birth : J. Arn. I., 16. Similar stories on pp. 13 to 23. Some of the variations are : (1) the man goes three times "withershins" round the stone, which then appears as a fine house. The same process turns it into a stone again ; (2) a box of ointment is given to rub the child's eyes with ; (3) the hulduman spits in the woman's eye to destroy its second sight, or wets his finger and draws it round it ; (4) in one version the elf-woman's helper is a small boy. Compare the Danish story on p. 98.

145. Baptising a Fairy-child : J. Arn. I., 54.

146. The Changeling : *ib.* 41. A very similar story of a changeling's pranks is given by Kristensen, D. S., I., 1029.

146. Father of Eighteen Children : *ib.* 42. The elf-woman's reproach is common in the Danish changeling-tales.

148. Making a changeling : *ib.* 44. This perhaps explains why changelings were supposed to increase and diminish their size at pleasure, as in the story on p. 146.

149. The Child and the Fairy : *ib.* 48. A similar story is told of the Icelandic poet Bjarni Thorarensen (*ib.* 45). In another instance the person enticed away bore the marks of the elf-woman's fingers on his cheek all his days.

150. Carried off by the Fairies : *ib.* 56. The story is assigned to a period shortly after the introduction of Christianity.

152. The girl and the Elf-brothers : *ib.* 56.

152. Ima the Elf-girl : *ib.* 100.

155. The Elfin Fisherman : *ib.* 6. The elves in the Færöes also go out fishing ; see the story on p. 164.

156. The Elfin Cow : *ib.* 37, slightly condensed. The method

of securing the fairy cow by drawing blood occurs in another tale. There are also *Huldu-neyt* in the Færöes, and *Hulla-köer* in Norway.

157. The Elf-woman in Múli : *ib.* 36.

158. Fairies' Revenge : Huld. III. 66 (Reykjavík, 1893).

159. The two Sisters and the Elves: J. Arn., I. 124. The story has something in common with the practice of sitting at the cross-roads : see p. 382.

160. The Elves' Removal : *ib.* 126. Compare the note to p. 133 above.

161. Huldufolk in the Færöes : Fær. Anth., I. 327. This view of the elves agrees with the Icelandic.

162. The Dulur Fishing-bank : *ib.* 338. There is a Danish version (somewhat shorter) in Nord. S. p. 167. With the hulduman's advice to the fisher compare that of the merman on p. 222.

164. The man from Gása-dal : *ib.* 339, also in Danish (shorter) in Nord. S. p. 152.

166. The Huldres in Norway : Nord. S. 148 (from Hammerich). Faye's account is given by Thorpe, II., 2.

167. The Huldre's Tail : *ib.* 150 and 151 (from Faye and Hammerich).

168. The Huldre's Husband : Faye, 40 (given by Thorpe, II., 15).

169. The Bride's Crown, etc. : Faye, 25 (also in Thorpe, II., 10).

170. Fairies in the house : Wig. pp. 110, 154, and 155. These house-fairies bear some resemblance to the *vætter*, but are seemingly not identical with them.

171. The Wood-fairy : *ib.* pp. 129-131. The Swedish *skogsnua* corresponds closely to the Danish *elle-kvinde*, as may be seen by comparing the stories about the latter.

173. The Peasant and the Wood-fairy : Djurklou, "Sagor och Äfventyr," p. 135. Compare Chambers, "Popular Rhymes of Scotland," pp. 63 and 66, for similar smart answers.

174. The Wood-man : Wig., p. 158. This kind of being does not seem to be mentioned elsewere.

175. The Danish Ellefolk : compiled from various accounts in Krist. D. S., II., A.

177. The Elf-King : *ib.* II. A., 32-35. The short notice in Thiele (II., 189) is omitted by Thorpe.

178. An Elf-child's Birth : Krist. J. F., III., 57, with a variant in 58.

179. The Changeling and the Stallion : Krist. D. S., I., 1048. Compare, for the age of the child, the Icelandic stories on p. 148. The stallion is similarly employed in the version in Thiele, II., 276 (=Thorpe, II., 175.)

179. The Elf-woman at Fredskov : Nord. S., 121 (from Grundtvig).

181. The Elf-girl and the Ploughman : Krist., D. S., II. A., 81.

182. Elf-charm cured by Lead : *ib.* 83. The process is fully described in Wig., p. 189. " There must be three kinds of lead : church-lead, cloth-lead (from cloth-stamps), and common lead. This is all melted together and poured over a pair of shears, which are opened out in the form of a cross, and laid over a bowl of water. During this time not a word must be spoken. The lead runs together in the water, and forms some figure or other, generally that of a person. In that case, the sick man has met with something, which was laid out on purpose to injure him or some one else. But whatever the lead forms, it must be wrapped up in linen, and laid under the sick person's head, so that he may sleep on it overnight." Compare the following case from the Fraserburgh Kirk Session Records (published by Rev. P. Milne, B.D.,) "Agnes Duff tuik leid and meltit it, and pat on ane sieve on the bairnis heid, and ane coig with watter in the sieve, and ane scheir abein the coig, and the leid was put in through the boull of the scheir amang the watter."

184. Curing an Elf-charm : Krist. D. S., II., A. 104.

185. The Elfin Dance : *ib.* 108.

185. The Lady's Beech : *ib.* 128.

186. Thefts by the Elves : *ib.* 133. With the second paragraph may be compared an Icelandic version in J. Arn., I., 43, where the elf-women are similarly hindered by the crosses

above and below the cradle, and the presence of a two-year old child.

187. The Charcoal Burner, etc.: *ib.* 151, with variants, which also occur elsewhere. In one of these the girl asks the man's name, and he answers "Myself," which leads to the same result as the "Nobody" of Ulysses. The questions asked by the girl and man are in some versions quite meaningless.

V.—NISSES OR BROWNIES.

Stories of the Nisse, a being unknown in older legend, are the especial property of Denmark, though also found in Norway and Sweden. The prevailing gloomy tone of Icelandic folk-lore easily accounts for the absence of this good-natured and helpful creature there. Even the *vættir* in Icelandic writings are most commonly understood as evil spirits (*heidnar* or *illar vættir*). Not a few of the stories in this section have close counterparts in British folk-lore.

PAGE.

189. The Nisse: Nord. S., 80-85. The first part is taken from Faye, and the second from Grundtvig.

191. To catch a Nisse: Krist. D. S., II., B. 11. and 22.

192. The Nisses in Gedsby: Nord. S., 75 (from Grundtvig). Some of the incidents in this recall tales like the "Devil of Glenluce" or the "Drummer of Tedworth," where a more mysterious cause than the nisses is assigned for the disturbances.

195. Father and Son: Krist. D. S., II., B. 34.

195. The Old Bushel: *ib.* 35.

196. The Nisse's Parting Gift: *ib.* 228.

198. Nisse kills a Cow: Grundt. I., 116. There are a good many variants in Krist. D. S., II., B. 180 ff. In some of these the nisse breaks into poetry after bringing home the cow, or cows. Thiele's version (II., 264) is given by Keightley (I., 224) and Thorpe (II., 158).

198. Nisse's New Clothes: Krist. D. S., II., B. 213.

199. The Little Harvesters: *ib.* 38. A similar story of trolls is told in Wigström, p. 134.

200. Nisse's Rest: *ib.* 46. The tale is a very common one. Thiele's version (II., 266) is given by Keightley (I., 227), but omitted by Thorpe.

201. Fights between Nisses: *ib.* 80 and 98. Many other versions are given in the same section. In some of these the victorious nisse says boastfully, "Did you see how I held my own?" In others, one of the nisses comes and asks his master for something to fight with.

203. Nisses fighting as wheels: Krist. J. F., III., 85. This is a very unusual type of nisse-legend.

204. The Nisses' Visits: Grundt. I., 136. The story shows some confusion between nisses and bergfolk.

205. Nisse and the Girl: Grundt. I., 145. Thiele (II., 270) gives the same story of a nisse and a lad, translated by Keightley (I., 233) and Thorpe (II., 164).

206. Nisse as a Calf: Krist. D. S., II., B. 170. A cow or calf is a favourite shape for nisse to assume.

206. The Nisses and their Horses: communicated by E. T. Kristensen.

207. The Nisse and the Ghost: Krist. J. F., III., 102. This combination is a very unique and interesting one.

208. Light high, light low: Krist. D. S., II., B. 128. There are several variants, one of which says that the nisse shouted "Light low!" when he heard anyone coming, and "Light high!" after they had gone past.

209. Nisse's Removal: Krist. J. F., III., 71. Thiele's version (II., 263) is given by Keightley (I., 223) and Thorpe (II., 161). The story is the same as that told by Tennyson in "Walking to the Mail."

210. The last Nisse in Samsö: communicated by E. T. Kristensen. The exact date of the nisse's removal is an amusing feature of the story.

211. The Church-nisse: Krist. D. S., II., B. 15.

211. The Ship-nisses: *ib.*, 18. The second paragraph communicated by E. T. Kristensen.

212. The Swedish Tomte: Afz., II., 169. For the general description of the Tomte which precedes this extract see

Thorpe (II., 91-93); the Swedish conception is not essentially different from the Danish.

213. The Nisse and the Dean : Wig., 138 and 198. The story is an unusual and interesting one.

214. Vättar: *ib.*, 108-110. In Denmark the *vætter* have a worse reputation, as they are believed to suck children's breasts while these are asleep. As in Sweden, they also appear in houses by night, each carrying a light, but the general conception of them approaches more closely to that of the bergfolk or ellefolk. The O.N. *vættir* are supernatural beings, either good or bad according to context. " In the French chronicle of Holger Danske, it says that on the night in which he was born there came in to him six beautiful shining maidens who are called *vetter* (Christiern Pedersen's danske Skrifter, Vol. V., p. 310).

216. Marjun in Orda-vík, etc. : Fær. Anth., I., 327-330.

VI.—WATER-BEINGS.

The merman and mermaid, the river-horse and river-man, are the chief dwellers in water known to popular belief, and are familiar in all the Scandinavian countries, except that the river man (Nök or Neck) does not seem to exist in Iceland in the same form as elsewhere. The *sjóskrímsl* or sea-monster is rather to be compared with the *sjó-dregil* of the Færöes, or the *draug* of Norway.

PAGE.
220. Mermen and Mermaids : J. Arn., I., 131 and 134 (adapted). The belief in sea-cows is also common in the Færöes and in the south of Sweden, where the mermaid's servants are believed to steal fodder from the farms on shore. The sea-bull also visits cows on land, but the calves are born dead, and are full of water (Wig., 136).

221. Then laughed the merman: J. Arn., I., 132. The lines at the end precede a second version on p. 133, and are perhaps part of a poem on the subject. The story of the merman's laugh is found as early as Hálf's Saga, where he laughs at King Hjörleif for striking his dog instead of his wife. The same legend appears in Old Irish in the

tale *Aidedh Fergusa,* where the fairy king, Iubdan, takes the place of the merman. In the description of the fishing tackle, "bitten iron and trodden" means a horse's bit and shoes, while "horse's tire" denotes either foam or sweat. Compare the Færöese tale on p. 163.

223. The merman in the Færöes : Fær. Anth., I., 335-337.

225. The merman in Norway: Faye, 55.

225. The fisher and the merman : Kamp., p. 20. Several variants are given in Krist., D. S., II., D. 4-12.

226. The merman and the calf: Kamp., p. 19. Compare the story of the river-man on p. 245.

227. The dead merman, etc. : Krist., D. S., II., D. 21. In some versions the merman is taken back to the sea on a waggon drawn by two red cows.

227. The Sea-sprite : Fær. Anth., I., 136. Compare the account of the Norwegian *draug* on p. 328.

228. The Shepherd and the Sea-folk : J. Arn., I., 118.

231. The Origin of the Seal : Nord. S., p. 160. The version in Fær. Anth., I., 345, is somewhat fuller in its details.

233. Nykur or the Water-horse : J. Arn., I., 135.

234. Nykur does work, etc. : *ib.,* 136. So the kelpie of the North Esk was compelled to drag stones to build the house of Morphie, and finally escaped by its halter being removed.

235. Nennir : J. Arn., I., 137. Similar stories are told of the kelpie in Scottish tradition.

236. The Long Horse : Nord. S., 221 (from Grundtvig). It is there called the Hell-horse, evidently a mistake. There are many variants in Krist., D. S., II., D. 71-95.

237. Nykur in the Færöes : Fær. Anth., I., 334.

238. The Nök or Neck : Faye, 48-51.

239. The River-horse : Wigström, 110-111 and 153.

241. The River-man : *ib.,* 136 and 172. There is a story of one who had learned music from the Nök in Nord. S., 135, taken from Hammerich.

242. Necken promised Redemption : Afz. II., 154, 155. The *-en* of Neck-*en* is the definite article suffixed. A similar story is told of trolls in Wig., p. 166.

243. The hour is come. : Faye, 51, and Krist., D. S., II., D., 38 and 45.

245. The river-man : Krist., J. F., IV., 72. Compare the story of the merman on p. 226.

246. The Kelpie : Faye, 53. The name in the original is *Kværnknurren.* The kelpie in Scottish tradition is also connected with the mill, as the brownie with the barn.

247. Sea-Serpents : Faye, 58.

247. The Sea-serpent in Mjösen : Nord. S., 171. A slightly different account is given by Faye, p. 59.

VII.—MONSTERS.

The monsters grouped together in this section really fall into two classes,—the dragon, lindorm and viper, which have an independent existence of their own ; and the werewolf and nightmare, which are human beings in monstrous shape. Both conceptions go back to the earliest period, and both are familiar down to the present day.

PAGE.

249. Gold-Thorir and the Drakes : Gull-þóris Saga, c. 3, 4, and 23, 24. The adventures of Thórir in Norway are mythical, but the latter part of the saga is mainly historical.

254. Björn and the Dragon : Bjarnar Saga Hitdœlakappa, p. 12. The date of the incident is about 1012, A.D.

255. Dragons in Norway : Faye, 67. The conception of the dragon here, as in the story of Thorir, recalls the fire-drake of the Beowulf.

255. Dragons in Denmark : Krist., D. S., II., C. 122, 128. This method of despoiling the dragon seems peculiar to Danish folk-lore.

256. The Dragon Disturbed : *ib.*, 137. Compare the stories of treasure-digging on pp. 406-409.

258. The Charcoal-burner, etc. : *ib.* 141.

258. The Lindorm in the Churchyard : Krist., J. F., III., 124. The lindorm is a favourite monster in Swedish as well as Danish tradition, and within the past twenty or thirty years a considerable number of peasants gave sworn testimony that they had seen one. O.N. *lyng-ormr*, a serpent.

259. The Lindorm and the Bull : Kamp. p. 260. The tale is a very common one, and the bull is usually fed up on the same diet.

260. The Lindorm and the Glazier : Thiele, II., 287 (not given by Thorpe.) Somewhat similar is the story in Krist., J. F., III., 122, where the lindorm lies round the church, and is killed by a student.

261. The Lindorm and the Wizard : Krist., D. S., II., E. 89. The story appears in various forms, attached to different localities. In one of these the lindorm is expected, and three fires are made for it, in the third of which it perishes. In others the wise man saves himself in a boat, or on horseback, but sometimes the lindorm destroys him. The death of the man by the hidden bone recalls the story of Orvar-Odd.

263. The Lindorm in Klöv-bakke : Nord. S., p. 179 (from Grundtvig). One may presume that the doctor knew his public.

264. The King of the Vipers : Krist., D. S., II., E. 157, with a number of variants. The story was known in Scotland ; see the "Tale of Sir James Ramsay of Bamff" in Chambers' "Popular Rhymes," p. 77.

265. The Basilisk : Krist., J. F., III., 114. In 115 is a similar story of a lindorm. The ordinary account of the basilisk is given in 113.

265. The Gravso or Ghoul : Nord. S., p. 225 (from Grundtvig). A different kind of Grave-sow will be found on p. 404.

266. Nidagrisur : Fær. Anth., I., 331. *Grisur* is a "grice" or young pig ; the meaning of *nida* and the force of the exclamation "*hasin Loddasin !*" are obscure.

267. The Were-wolf : Krist., D. S., II., F., I. 17, 36 (adapted). The last three paragraphs from Nord. S., p. 185-188

(originally from Grundtvig), Were-wolves occur in the Völsunga Saga, c. 8, but the Danish conception has much that is peculiar in it.

270. The Night-mare: Hkr. Ynglinga Saga, c. 16, and Fær. Anth., I., 330. The passage from Hkr. is the oldest mention of Mara. A very similar account to the Færöese is given by Faye, p. 76, where the verse employed is,

> " Muro, muro, minde.
> Are you herein?
> Out you must go.
> Here is knife, here is spear,
> Simon Svipu's in here."

"Simon Svipu" is the thick growth on old birch trees, and is hung over horses, etc., to prevent Mara from riding them.

272. A Girl as Night-mare: Krist., J. F., III., 103, with variants in D. S., II., F., 78, 79.

273. A Night-mare caught: Nord. S., 191 (from Grundtvig).

274. The Night-mare on horses: Krist. D. S., II., F. 73 and 101.

VIII.—GHOSTS AND WRAITHS.

The most impressive ghosts in this section, it will be seen, are those of Iceland, both ancient and modern. Icelandic literature is so rich in tales of this kind, that those here given must only be regarded as samples. Some of the finest stories from the Sagas, such as that of Glám in Grettis Saga, and the marvels at Fróðá in Eyrbyggja Saga, are omitted here, partly because of their length, and partly because these sagas are accessible in translations. The Danish tales are also a mere handful of what might be brought together, and those of Norway and Sweden are left practically untouched.

PAGE.

276. Thorgils and the Ghosts: Flóamanna Saga, c. 13. The dealings of Thorgils with the god Thor are told on p. 9. The name of Audunn is the same as the O. E. Eadwine, Edwin. The sword given by Audun to Thorgils was called Bladnir, and was afterwards taken back by him in a dream. Somewhat similar to the trouble with

Gyda is the story of Thorstein Svarti and his wife Grím-
hild in Flb. I., 543.

278. Thorolf Bægifót : Eyrbyggja Saga, c. 33, 34, and 63. The
story has considerable resemblance to the more famous
one of Glám in Grettis Saga. With Arnkell's laying out
of Thorolf compare Egil's treatment of his father Skalla-
grím (Egil's Saga, c. 59). Thorodd was afterwards killed
by a bull, whose mother had licked the stones on the
beach where Thorolf was burned.

281. The Ghost of Hrapp : Laxdæla Saga, c. 17 and 24. Olaf
pá was the father of Kjartan, of whose gravestone the
story on p. 289 is told.

283. The Ghost of Klaufi : Svarfdæla Saga, c. 18, 19, 22 and
30. Five ells are equivalent to 6 ft. 3 in., the Old
Northern ell being one of fifteen inches. Cutting off
the ghost's head occurs also in the story of Glám. A
considerable part of the story is omitted after the words
"Why should we further?" in which Klaufi helps largely
to avenge himself, and makes a number of verses. (The
modern pronunciation of the name is Klöivi).

285. Sóti's Grave-mound : Hardar Saga, c. 14 and 15. This is
a very common type of story in the romantic sagas.
Plundering grave-mounds was apparently a common
practice in the Viking Age.

289. Kjartan Olafsson's Gravestone : J. Arn., I., 234. To the
story is added an account of the stone itself. The runes
on it are too much wasted to decide whether it is really
the monument of Gudrun's lover.

290. The Brothers of Reynistad : J. Arn., I., 228-230, slightly
condensed, especially towards the beginning.

292. Parthúsa-Jon ; O. Dav., 37-40. Two other versions are
given in which Jón's fate is connected with the death of
a girl killed by him.

295. The Cloven-headed Ghost : ib., 47-48. Another narrator
says that the ghost was of ordinary size, except his legs,
which were "many fathoms."

296. One of us : ib., 30-33. There is another version in J.
Arn., I., 268, in which the man escapes the ghost's

attack by placing both the money and his iron dress under water, so that the ghost should not feel the smell of earth upon them.

299. Stefán Olafsson and the Ghost : Kvædi eptir Stefán Olafsson, pp. lxxiii.-lxxvi. (Copenhagen, 1886.) Stefán was born c. 1620, and died in 1688. The man who told the story to the old woman could not have been shepherd to Sir Stefán, but may have had it from the real one.

301. Jón Flak : J. Arn., I., 233. In ghost verses the last line is commonly repeated twice, as here.

301. Pleasant is the Darkness : *ib.*, 226. There is a somewhat similar story in Krist. J. F., III., 233.

302. Biting off the thread : *ib.*, 226. The pieces of the needle are stuck into the wizard's feet to prevent his ghost walking.

302. The dead man's rib : *ib.*, 239. The rib was no doubt intended for preparing a *til-beri* ; see p. 379.

304. The Skull in Garth Churchyard : Huld., II., 77. This, and the following tale belong rather to dream-stories than to ghost lore.

305. The Priest Ketill, etc. : J. Arn., I., 237.

306. The Ghost's Cap : *ib.*, 239.

307. The Ghost's Questions : O. Dav. 34. The "evil being" is presumably a ghost, but might be a troll.

308. My Jaw-bones : J. Arn., I., 238.

308. Mother mine in fold : *ib.*, 225. Several other verses are there given as recited by the ghosts of children : one of them is :

" Swift as hawk in air am I,
And underhand as bird on shore ;
My fatherland is Flókadale,
And first I saw the light in Mór."

309. That is mine : Kamp., p. 31.

310. The three Countesses of Trane-kær : *ib.*, p. 155. The Danish ghost-stories are largely connected with exorcism or *nedmaning*, carried out by a priest or clerk. The ghost "looking through" the priests is a curious detail.

312. The Ghost at Silkeborg: Grundt., I., p. 57. The part about driving on "In Jesus' Name" is perhaps an interpolation here, as it has no bearing on the story. Taking off the fourth wheel (generally the left-hand one behind) is a common incident: the substitute is regularly a ghost, or the Devil himself. Ghosts can also be seen by looking through a horse's head-stall, or between the ears of a dog.

314. A Ghost let Loose: Kamp, p. 142. The ghost, when laid, is regularly secured by driving in a stake. When this rots, or is pulled up, the ghost is set free again.

314. Exorcising the living: Kamp, p. 267. The story is common.' In one version it is done intentionally to force a secret from a woman. She offers to disclose it when she has sunk to the breast, but is told that it is too late.

316. The tired Ghost: Kamp, p. 342. The presence of a ghost (even that of a child) on a cart or carriage is always marked by its heavy weight.

316. The long-expected Meeting: Krist., J. F., III., 229. This curious story is certainly not a common one.

318. The dead Mother: Wig., p. 150. In another account (p. 102) it is explained that a woman who dies pregnant will give birth at the same time as though she had been alive. Hence all the necessaries for mother and child are laid in the coffin. If this is neglected, the dead woman appears to claim them, and midwives are bound to attend them if called on. The belief also exists in Denmark.

318. The Service of the Dead: Krist., D. S., II., G., 150. Another version makes one of the dead folk say to the woman, "If you were not my sister, I would bite your nose off." The story is also found in Sweden (Wig., p. 178.)

319. The Perjured Ghost: Krist., J. F., III., 205, with variants. The equivocal oath is known in Highland tradition.

320. Night-ploughing: Nord. S., p. 233-6 (from Grundtvig.) Stories of this practice are very common, and rest on the old Danish system of agriculture, by which the villagers had "rig and rig about."

322. The March-Stone : *ib.*, 240 (from Grundtvig.)   There are similar anecdotes in Krist.   Will-o'-the-wisp (*Lygtemanden*) is explained to be a landmark-shifter (see Thorpe, II., 97, from Afz., II., 172.)

322. The priest's double : Krist., J. F., IX., p. 315.

323. The Keg of Money : J. Arn., I., 356.   The story is also told in Krist., D. S., II., G., 101.

325. Soul-wandering : Krist., D. S., II., G., 105.   The "Mormon priests" form one of the incongruous modern touches that often appear in Danish folk-lore.

326. Fylgja : Flb., I., 253.   The conception of *fylgja* as an animal shape, preceding the person it belongs to, is one still maintained in Iceland.   In the older literature it also means a female guardian spirit, whose appearance foreboded death.

327. The Fölgie or Vardögl : Faye, 68-70.   Both views of the Fölgie here indicated agree with the Icelandic ones.   The derivation of Vardögl is obscure.   Thus—bet is apparently connected with þurs, a giant.

328. The Draug : *ib.*, 72.   *Draugr* is the most general name for a ghost in Iceland.

329. Aasgaards-reia : *ib.*, 62-64.   The common forms of the name seem to be Askereia and Hoskelreia, and it is doubtful whether the word has anything to do with Asgard, the home of the Gods.   Vigfusson derives it from the Swedish *åska*, thunder.

331. The Gand-reid : Njáls Saga, c. 125.   The "great tidings" were the burning of Njál and his sons by Flosi and his followers.   Another usage of *gand-reid* will be found on p. 372.

332. The Knark-vogn : Krist. D. S., II., C. 6 (adapted).   The tradition seems peculiar to Denmark.

333. The Night-raven : *ib.*, II., C. 7 (adapted).

IX.—WIZARDS AND WITCHES.

Norway is described by Adam of Bremen as the favourite home of diviners, wizards, enchanters, and other satellites of anti-Christ, and his words are borne out by the special richness of Scandinavian folk-lore in this department. The sagas abound in the practices of sorcery and magic, most of which are traced back to Odin himself by the author of Heimskringla, and wizards and witches have been familiar conceptions to all the Northern peoples right down to the present day. As in the case of the ghosts, what is here presented to the reader is only offered as a sample of the abundant material to be found in ancient and modern sources.

PAGE.

335. Gest and the Witches : Flb. I., 346, 358-9 (the third and fourth paragraphs are only an abstract). This is one of the many short tales (*þættir*), connected with Olaf's Saga. As to the religion of Gest, it was common for those Norsemen who came much in contact with Christian peoples to receive the *prima signatio,* or mark of the cross. The *prímsignd* man could then hold free intercourse with both Christians and Heathen, and believe in anything that pleased him. See especially Egil's Saga, c. 50.

337. The Witch Thorbjörg : Eiriks Saga rauda, c. 3. This is the fullest account of a witch, and her method of divination, preserved in the sagas. It is in Eiriks Saga that the Norse discovery of America is detailed.

340. The Witch Skroppa : Hardar Saga, c. 26. The time is between 983 and 986. Hörd's dealings with another witch are given in the previous chapter.

341. The Witch Gríma : Fóstbrædra Saga, pp. 95-100. The narrative has been considerably shortened in translating. Thormód was greatly attached to King Olaf the Saint, and fell with him at Stiklastad in 1030.

344. Thordis the Spaewife : Kormaks Saga, c. 22. The hardening of the body against weapons is a common feat of witches in the sagas.

345. Thorleif and Earl Hákon : Flb. I., 207-213. The earlier part is condensed to some extent. The story is given as an early instance of a *krapta-skáld* (see p. 369), and also as a necessary introduction to the tale following it.

350. Earl Hákon's Revenge : Flb. I., 213. The cognomen of Thorgerd is here supposed to be taken from her husband

Hörgi; see the note to p. 32. The belief in such enchanted messengers, or *sendings*, is very common in
modern Icelandic folk-lore; see the tales following this.

351. Upwakenings or Sendings : J. Arn., I., 317-319, with some
minor details omitted. Some thirty pages of illustrative
legends follow on this in Arnason.

353. Skin-coat : O. Dav. 64-66. A representative story of a
sending.

355. The Ghost in the King's Treasury : *ib.* 70. The story is
said to have been a sheer invention of one Gisli Simon-
sen, a Reykjavík merchant, told by him to a credulous
old man, who gave it a wide circulation.

356. A Wizard sent to Iceland : Hkr. Saga Olafs Tryggvasonar,
c. 30. King Harald was in Norway at this time (993).
The animals seen by the wizard are perhaps the *fylgjur*
of great men in each district, who are named by the saga-
writer.

357. The Finns and Ingimund : Vatnsdæla Saga, c. 10-15, with
the unessential parts condensed. The Finns call themselves *sem-sveinar*, a word of doubtful origin. A *hlutr*
or charm of a similar kind (an ivory image of Thor) is
mentioned in Hallfredar Saga.

360. The Finn's Travels : Krist. D. S., II., G. 108.

361. Finnish Magic : Afz. I., 20 and 48. No doubt much of
Scandinavian witchcraft is of Finnish origin.

363. Seeing a thief in water : Kamp, p. 121.

363. The Stolen Money : O. Dav. 78-80.

365. Showing one's future wife : *ib.* 87-89. Of "Thorgeir's
Bull " different accounts are given in J. Arn., I., 348-352.
It was a *sending* in the shape of a half-flayed bull.

367. The Wizard and the Crows : Hkr. Saga Olafs kyrra, c. 10.
Olaf reigned from 1069 to 1093.

369. A poet of might : J. Arn., I., 465-466. An instance of a
krapta-skáld. Hallgrím lived from 1614 to 1674 : for
mention of his Psalms see p. 57, and note. The Irish
poets had similar efficacy in their verses. James Power
(who lived in the first half of last century), by cursing

the memory of Colonel James Roche, split the tomb-
stone above his grave in Churchtown (Gaelic Journal,
III., 6).

370. The mice in Akureyar: J. Arn., I., 439. A similar clear-
ance of mice and rats is found in some Danish stories of
the lindorm, and the Pied Piper of Hamelin is a well-
known instance.

371. Foxes in Iceland : *ib.* 439.

372. Gand-reid : *ib.* 440. The older meaning of *gand-reid* is
illustrated on p. 331. The original force of *gand* is very
obscure.

372. The Witches' ride to Tromskirk : Grundt., I., p. 137.
Tromskirk is the gathering place of the Danish witches,
as Blaakulla of the Swedish.

373. The Ride to Blaakulla : Wig., 113-115. These meetings
of the Swedish witches were notorious during the witch-
persecutions in the 17th century : see "Sadducismus
Triumphatus" and Sinclair's "Satan's Invisible World
Discovered."—Another version of the "up and down"
story is given by Kamp. (p. 263).

377. Milk-hares : Wig., 139. In Scottish tradition it is the
witch herself who assumes the shape of a hare.

377. Stealing cream for butter : Kamp., p. 114.

378. The Witch's Daughter: Kamp., p. 265. The same story,
so far as stopping the ploughs is concerned, appears to
be known in Scotland.

379. The Til-beri : J. Arn., I., 428-432 (adapted). This, along
with the Swedish milk-hare, was probably derived from
Finnish magic, where a similar practice is known.

380. The Tide-mouse : *ib.*, 429. " Flood-mouse " might be a
better rendering, the Icelandic being *flædar-mús.* Vigfusson, however, suggests that the word is simply the
German *fleder-maus* or bat.

381. The Tale-spirit : *ib.*, 435. Stories of the *sagnar-andi* are
not uncommon. By a " horse's membrane " is appa-
rently meant the caul of a foal, as in the Danish belief
about the were-wolf.

382. The Cross-roads : *ib.*, 438 and 125. The practice of
"sitting-out" is very ancient, and is frequently referred
to in the sagas. It was originally only done by women;
the first mention of a man doing it belongs to the 12th
century.

383. Sitting at the Cross-roads : Fær. Anth., I., 342.

384. The Victory-stone : *ib.*, 343. The same procedure is
recommended in Iceland to get possession of the "stone
of darkness," which renders invisible the person who
carries it (J. Arn., I., 650).

386. The Life-stone : Huld., I. 41 ; also told in J. Arn., I. 654.

386. The Four-leaved Clover : Wig., 165. The same properties are attributed to it in Denmark and Iceland.

387. Destroying a Witch's Spells : Wig., 92-95. The employ-
ment of one sorcerer to circumvent another is naturally
common enough. In another case (*ib.*, p. 140) the witch
was actually burned to death by similar means.

X.—CHURCHES, TREASURES, PLAGUES.

The three classes of stories in this section have no necessary
connection with each other, though the buried bell forms a
transition from the church-legends to those of treasure-digging.
They are probably of later growth than many in the preceding
sections, but they are quite as widely diffused, and can hardly
be omitted in any presentation of Northern folk-lore.

PAGE.

390. How the first church, etc. : Nord. S., p. 201 (from Afzelius). This form of the legend is not so common as the
one following. Faye, however, gives a similar version
about Trondhjem Cathedral, which is perhaps meant here.

391. The building of Lund Cathedral : *ib.*, p. 219 (from Afzelius). An Icelandic version is given in J. Arn., I., 58,
and a large number of Danish variants in Krist., D. S.,
III., 938-975. In these the builder of the church shouts
to the troll, "Finn, set that stone further in," or similar
words.

392. St. Olaf in Ringerige : *ib.*, 209 (from Faye). The story
exists in the same form in Sweden.

394. Vatnaas Church: *ib.*, 212 = Faye, 111. The part about the bull and the gold church is not quite clear.

395. St. Olaf in Vaaler : *ib.*, 214 = Faye, 112. *Vaal* denotes a pile of trunks, roots, and branches of trees heaped together for burning.

396. Varnum Church : *ib.*, 204 (from Afzelius).

397. Dover Church : Krist., D. S., III., 870. In other versions two calves are used for the same purpose.

398. The Bergman's Payment : *ib.*, 923, 924. In some versions it is the devil who builds the church and carries off the bride.

398. Karup Church Tower : Krist., J. F., III., 78. In other tales the giants or *kæmper* are credited with building churches, instead of destroying them. The idea of the stones growing at that time is very original.

399. The Shifting of Gudum Church : Kamp., p. 266.

400. Hörup Church : Nord. S., p. 90 (from Müllenhoff, "Sagen aus Schleswig). The derivation of Hörup is of course a piece of popular etymology, the name being one of the many that end in *-rup*, *-drup*, or *-trup*, the English *thorpe*.

401. The Dwarfs' Stone : J. Arn., II., 67. The dwarfs' attachment to the church is a very unusual idea.

402. The Church Grim : Nord. S., 199 (from Afzelius). The belief is general in Sweden and Denmark. Kristensen (D. S., II., H. 5) gives the following account. "When a church was being built, a very big hole was dug in the churchyard, and the first thing that fell into it was buried alive. This was generally a lamb, because it is most often these that run about in such places." With the white horse of Hestveda may be compared the Danish "Hell-horse," which goes on three legs, and is a death-warning ; this is also a church-grim (Thiele, II., 293).

402. The Church Lamb: Nord. S., p. 206 (from Grundtvig). Many stories of meeting the *Kirke-lam* or *Lig-lam* are given by Kristensen (D. S., II., H. 30 ff).

404. The Grave-sow : Krist., D. S., II., H., 87, where there are various other anecdotes concerning it. In one of these

it breaks a man's legs, which connects it more closely
with the *Grav-so* described on p. 265.

404. The Buried Bell : Krist., D. S., I., 1181.

405. The Bell of Kværndrup : *ib.*, III., 529.   Both of these
tales appear in various forms.   The verse in this one is
intended to reproduce the tones of the bell.

406. The Chest of Gold : J. Arn., I., 279.

407. Buried Treasure : Kamp., p. 15.   A very frequent and
widespread story : compare the versions following.

407. The Smith in Burhöj : Thiele, II., 181 (given by Thorpe,
II., 119).   For the incident of the dog, which is very
common, see the second tale after this.

409. The Treasure in Eriksvolde : Kamp., p. 305.   The burning village is also a common deception.

410. Treasure guarded by a dog : Krist., D. S., I., 1261.   A
more unusual type of treasure-tale, but the dog found in
the mound regularly uses the same words.   The multi-
plication of the halter occurs in a different form in a
Highland tale.

410. Gudmund and the Ghost : O. Dav., 60-62.   The belief in
the flame that hovers over buried treasure *(málm-logi* or
vafr-logi) is very ancient : compare p. 249.

412. The Black Death : Faye, p. 127-8.   The pest was so called
from the black spots which accompanied it.   Its date in
Norway is set down as 1350, but the Black Death in
Iceland raged in 1400-1402.

413. The Black Death in Sætersdal : *ib.*, 137-8.   The form
Thole for Thore in the verse is expressive of endear-
ment.

414. The Black Death in Denmark : Krist., D. S., IV., 1711.
In Danish the plague is also called *Mande-gvæl* and
Mærke-död.

416. The Black Death in Iceland : J. Arn., II., 98.   The black
death forms the great break between old and modern
Icelandic literature and history.

INDEX.

FINIS.

www.ingramcontent.com/pod-product-compliance
Lightning Source LLC
Chambersburg PA
CBHW031047110726
47900CB00003B/837